D1496365

The Murder of
Aziz Khan

For THOMAS BERGER

Zulfikar Ghose

The Murder of
Aziz Khan

a novel

1998
Oxford University Press
Karachi   Lahore   Islamabad

Oxford University Press, Great Clarendon Street, Oxford OX2 6DP
Oxford New York
Athens Auckland Bangkok Bagotá Buenos Aires Calcutta
Cape Town Chennai Dar es Salaam Delhi Florence Hong Kong Istanbul
Karachi Kuala Lumpur Madrid Melbourne Mexico City Mumbai
Nairobi Paris São Paulo Singapore Taipei Tokyo Toronto Warsaw
and associated companies in Berlin Ibadan

Oxford is a registered trade mark of Oxford University Press

ISBN 0 19 577988 6

Previously published by
Macmillan London Ltd., 1967
The John Day Company, Inc., 1969
This edition by Oxford University Press, 1998

Printed in Pakistan at
Mas Printers, Karachi.
Published by
Ameena Saiyid, Oxford University Press
5-Bangalore Town, Sharae Faisal
PO Box 13033, Karachi-75350, Pakistan.

Foreword to this Edition

My earliest journeys from my native Sialkot were made during the first years of the fateful decade of the 1940s. There was the slow train to Wazirabad which stumbled and clanked and occasionally pretended it could go fast. It puffed laboriously past farmlands, registering images of agricultural abundance on my childish brain. At Wazirabad, one transferred to the mail train for Lahore or Rawalpindi and on to other destinations. An exceptionally memorable journey I made was to Quetta, with my grandmother, when I was five years old. This and the other journeys—to Jammu, to Lyallpur, to Amritsar—had me staring out in amazement at the changing landscape, from plum orchards near Jammu to the great farms of the Punjab, where the land was green to the horizon and broken only by the silver line of a river, and on to the barren nothingness of the desert as the train made for Baluchistan. By the time I was seven, in 1942, when I went on the longest train journey of my life, from Sialkot to Bombay, I had seen almost all of the Punjab that one can from a railway carriage. In later years I was to see beautiful landscapes in other parts of the world, but those earliest impressions of the world in the Punjab were, if I may use a phrase which sounds a little grand, lodged in my soul.

And once lodged there, the early impression of the land one grows to love becomes a paradigm of physical beauty which then one obsessively envisions either in foreign landscapes, which however are inevitably imperfect, or in one's dreams: one imagines versions of reality which are recollections of a past that is saturated with nostalgia or with a profound sense of loss at having been cast out of the realm of Time; and these emotions, which are an incessant torment deep within the self, comprise a complex anxiety that compels one to transform one's experience into a fiction. The train to Bombay took me to an exile from my native environment to which so far there has been no end. Except for one brief visit to Sialkot because of a death in the family, I did not return to the Punjab for nearly twenty years when, in 1961, the London newspaper *The Observer* assigned me to cover the English cricket team's tour of Pakistan. Once again I found myself arriving at the old stations. Rawalpindi, Lahore, Lyallpur. And again staring at the moving landscape.

But the exhilaration that flared within me from being temporarily restored to the landscape of a childhood paradise was soon extinguished. One consequence (which has been observed universally) of freedom from foreign tyranny is that native adventurers and opportunists instantly leap into the space vacated by the foreign exploiters to aggrandize themselves at the expense of the people; and this seemed conspicuously prevalent in Pakistan. To make things worse, a military dictatorship had established itself in the land. The individual was thus doubly threatened—by the predatory practices of the new industrialists and by the loss of personal liberty. The political hero of my childhood, Mohammad Ali Jinnah, had been given a fancy title which was uttered with hypocritical reverence while his vision of a state in which the individual was free, the very reason for the creation of Pakistan, had been abandoned. The people were poorer than ever; they were ill educated if educated at all; they lived in a condition of unalleviated misery.

It was this perception of a potential paradise lost to the vicious combination of business greed, a military tyranny's lust for power and an increasingly assertive priesthood's repressive imposition upon society, all three of which have been the common forces of exploitation throughout history, that led me to create in Aziz Khan a symbolic monument—a small one perhaps—for the goodness that could have been the foundation of a beautiful country. In my mind, he still stands there, in the middle of a great fertile plain, a gigantic figure as though carved out of granite, staring out with stony resignation and patience at the evil winds howling around his head.

After the cricket tour of Pakistan, which reawakened the imagery of the Punjab in my mind and suggested the material with which to invent a story in which to record that imagery, I returned to London in March 1962. I made some notes for a short story about a farmer who loses his land but it was not for another three years that the awakened imagery demanded that it be incorporated in a longer text. In the meanwhile, I wrote the majority of the poems that went into my first book of poems (*The Loss of India*), began and finished a first novel (*The Contradictions*), and also published an autobiography. Then, during most of 1965, I wrote *The Murder of Aziz Khan*.

The Murder of Aziz Khan is the most objective of my novels. Everything in it—the story, the characters, the plot—is a complete fiction, neither based upon real people nor drawn upon any personal experience. Its literary antecedents are solid old-fashioned writers—George Eliot, Thomas Hardy, John Steinbeck; and during its composition I read Tolstoy's *War and Peace*. But while it is entirely an invention, looking at it three decades later I realize that its climactic metaphor—the image of the dispossessed Aziz Khan staring at his land from behind the barbed-wire fence—is profoundly autobiographical in that it represents my own relationship with my native land. It is a common impulse of the creative imagination to invent a fiction and unconsciously to imbue it with a deep-seated personal anguish.

Zulfikar Ghose
Austin, Texas
March 1998

The Murder of
Aziz Khan

CONTENTS

The Argument

The Argument

When the Shah brothers began to buy land around the small but increasingly flourishing town of Kalapur, where they had established two textile mills, most of the landlords in this part of the Punjab were glad to sell. Cotton was the principal produce of the land here which, though fertile, was not productive enough because of the ancestral methods employed by the cotton farmers. The landlords were aware that in the hands of the Shah brothers, who had the money and the government connections with which to bring in foreign machinery, the land's output and consequently its value would multiply several times; but they also knew that they were in no position to bargain. The price offered by the Shah brothers seemed pitiably small when the landlords thought of the inherent richness of the land whose roots could be said to have been made ultimately of gold; but, taking a measure of their immediate losses and the pressure of present creditors, it was, on balance, still more than tempting to accept the offer which the Shah brothers made, for it would bring in enough money to enable the landlords to pay off their debts and to migrate to some city where they would have sufficient capital with which to start a small business. The offer was to them a chance to rid themselves of subservience to the land and the brutal climate and to escape to cities where air-conditioning and motor-cars would be a purposeful use of wealth which they had hitherto had to expend in canalising water to the land and buying seed and labour, which activities, though they occasionally afforded the vague satisfaction which comes from pursuing an atavistic ritual, had, in the end, always denied them the newer satisfactions which their visits to the cities had shown to be immediately accessible without the fuss which goes with rain, air and earth. So, they, thinking all this independently and sometimes while talking to one another in the bazaar, agreed to sell. Except Aziz Khan who did not think of all this.

Aziz Khan possessed seventy acres in all, which amounted to nothing beside the thousands of acres which the Shah brothers had succeeded in acquiring on all sides of his property. Aziz Khan's seventy acres were in a slight valley, so that he could, in one corner of his land, dam the rain water which flowed down the slopes, and there grow a small quantity of rice. Not to sell, but at least to feed his family and his peasants and, if there was an excess of it, to present to some of his friends. His house was at the top of the slope from where, sitting, as he usually did at twilight, in the veranda or in the front yard, he could survey his entire property and observe the difference of aspect, of improvement or neglect, of blossom or blight, which the day's work had produced on his land.

The cotton plantation came almost to the edge of his house, and when the plants were in bloom, strands of cotton hung in the air as if the air, assuming an aspect of aged dignity, were sporting whiskers. And sometimes, when his household had retired and he was unobserved, Aziz Khan would slip into the plantation under moonlight and feel the cotton-buds by passing a hand gently over them or by putting his mouth to them as if they were balls of candyfloss. As if it was an inspection which had to be carried out: or an instinctive form of imbibing some secret knowledge from the plants: an inspection really of his own soul.

For under moonlight the forms of the earth were liquid and they passed in or out of his body who ventured, in solitude, some gesture of communication with those forms. Especially under moonlight, especially when his own breath was the purest liquid. Thus Aziz Khan. Sometimes almost bewildered as a bird, compelled to let the shy wings of his soul flick from the sides of his body, not knowing what it was he did, never questioning his own actions but performing them without realising that, ardent though his faith was in Islam, the god he was most devoted to was the cosmos.

His large black eyes could be seen at night like a cat's as they caught the moonlight, the warm, intense moonlight of the Punjab; from a distance, one saw two glow-worms floating in the air and then alighting upon the cotton-buds. His white tunic-shirt hung from his broad, muscular shoulders like a drape from a horse, the fan of his turban had the flamboyance of a peacock's tail. If one looked for any sign of affectation in his face, it was to be found in the deliberately groomed moustache which he cultivated to rapier points on either side of his mouth. Authority came naturally to Aziz Khan; his height alone commanded it, if not the creases of his shirt which gave a fair indication of the potential strength of his muscles; yet, if his horses had been his historians, they would have spoken of the softness of his hands to which the world was a cluster of cotton-buds.

Beyond the fields of cotton was a small plantation of sugarcanes. The green, slimly elongated stems sprouted from the tops of the sugarcanes in the curving droop of fountains as if green water flowed from a nozzle at the sugar-canes' ends. Sitting in the veranda at twilight, Aziz Khan found first the white of the cotton and then the green of the sugarcanes restful to his eyes. Leaning back in his chair, he would frequently turn his gaze from one to the other, from one to the other till his eyes shut of themselves and he dozed off and imagined forms, blobs and splashes of pure white and pure green floating in a gyrating motion in front of him as if the earth had exploded and unloosed itself in an anarchy of colour.

To a new visitor to Aziz Khan's land, however, the con-trasting colours might have appeared violent, especially where the brilliantly blue sky curved down over the heads of the sugarcanes. Yet, what seemed most satisfactory to Aziz Khan was that the horizon, the sky touching the sprouting sugarcane stems, was a definite existence on his own land, that it was a dome which enclosed him and all that belonged to him; and he never felt like a man who, coming to a hilltop, discovers that the horizon is not to be found here but that he had been deceived by the limitation of his vision and that the horizon really exists at the crest of the next hill, that the point where it touches the earth is not here, but there, but there, beyond. No; for Aziz Khan, his land was a complete world where only those plants grew of which he had sowed the seeds himself; if not himself, his father; if not his father, his grandfather; which was the same thing, that is, himself, Aziz Khan; for man, sowing his own seed, also created the plant he has desired. And these seventy acres, this piece of earth, this world of Aziz Khan, did not appear to him as land, as a property with a market value. It was a sufficiency of existence. So that nobody could take the land away from him without first taking away his existence.

Sitting in the front yard, in the evening, looking across at the sugarcanes, Aziz Khan would experience a slow, voluptuous relaxation creep into his body and he would accept that as the day's profit, a gift from heaven for what he had done during the day. And he would lean back till his flesh stretched tightly over his bones, so that the bones were touched with the sweetness of rest, too, and sometimes he would look up at the sky, the greying sky with the first bright gleam of some star showing, and breathe deeply the air that hung over his land. Before going into his house for the night, he would sit there, sometimes smoking a *hookah*, and let the land fill his body with its wholeness.

The whitewashed house was rectangular from the front, and the three rooms behind the veranda had high ceilings to keep the cool air in and small windows to keep the hot sun out. At one end of the veranda was the kitchen and at the other the bathroom. The kitchen contained a clay stove in which dung-cakes were burned for fuel, while the bathroom had in it just one tap next to which was a bucket. In front of the veranda was a square plot of hardened earth which served for a front garden though no flowers grew there; a solution of cow-dung and straw was prepared as a thick paste and applied to this plot from time to time so that dust would not rise from it, thus invoking a mixture of earthy odours from the plot.

Behind the house was a similar plot, but wider, and here the household beasts—two buffaloes and three goats—were kept; the back wall of the house, which was the permanent backcloth to the statuesque posing of the animals, was covered with dung-cakes which dried there in the sun and were then scraped off to be collected in a heap in a corner from where they were taken for their various uses. At the kitchen end of the house was a poultry yard where the cockerels waltzed and the hens strutted and the chicks grew to peck querulously at one another's necks. Two horses were tied to the bars of a window at the bathroom end of the house. The back of the house looked on to a narrow stream some thirty or forty yards away where the beasts could freely loiter down and drink. This stream divided Aziz Khan's land from that which the Shah brothers had now acquired.

Aziz Khan had two sons and three daughters, their ages

ranging between eighteen and twenty-seven, the three daughters being married to the sons of the landlords who had now left the country. The elder son, Rafiq, had been engaged to the daughter of another landlord, but, because that landlord had decided to sell his land and to migrate to Karachi, the engagement had been broken off. Javed, the youngest of the five children, was the second son and to Aziz Khan he was still a child.

His wife, Zakia, now in her late forties, gave no thought to any of Aziz Khan's problems, for, indeed, he never mentioned them to her; this was not a peculiarity of his, for Punjabi couples of peasant stock are traditionally uncommunicative to each other on matters concerning the husband's business, their conversation relating itself invariably to the more immediate concerns of the family.

No one in his family, neither the children nor Aziz Khan himself, had ever gone to school, for they had grown up in an atmosphere which may be described as the sufficiency of the earth, an atmosphere in which illiteracy had the advantage of giving one's attentions entirely to the land. They had, however, learned to read and write a little Urdu; and perhaps, in the context of this narrative, it would be more exact to state that by illiteracy is meant an ignorance of English, without a fluent knowledge of which no Pakistani of that time could hope for advancement.

Together with his family, Aziz Khan had forty-six peasants working for him. He had no tenants like the larger landlords and he supervised the work on his land himself. So that he knew the capacity of his land and his own capacity.

The Shah brothers, in striking their deals in the neighbourhood, had been able unobtrusively to survey Aziz Khan's seventy acres. At first, they had considered this property as any other which they were in the process of buying; after the amusement and surprise which they shared as a joke when Aziz Khan rejected their first overture to buy his land, the seventy acres began to appear to them as a desirable complement to the land which they had already purchased in the neighbourhood; a woman, spurning attempts at seduction, would not have been wooed with such determination as with which the Shah brothers began to try to win Aziz Khan's land. When Aziz Khan rejected a further proposal from them, the brothers were considerably annoyed, not to say frustrated; but once the annoyance, the hurt to their own opinion of themselves, to their own sense of power, had subsided, the buying of Aziz Khan's land appeared to them as a necessity, as the last piece to complete the jig-saw puzzle. For three years, as they busied themselves with the construction of the two mills, Aziz Khan's land lay dormant in the minds of the Shah brothers, it lay there like a beast which would one day wake up and perhaps growl at them; and as production began, as the process of the cotton growing, the cotton being harvested, the cotton being loaded, the cotton being transported to the mills, the cotton being fed into the machines, as this cycle of industry began to establish its routine and rhythm in Kalapur and began to bring in the wealth for which the Shah brothers had so assiduously planned, their annoyance with Aziz Khan began to turn into an anger. There were occasions, when, for example, the expert in economics with his degree from London, who was one of their prominent executives and to whom they paid a large salary, pointed out that Aziz Khan's seventy acres made it necessary for the lorries laden with cotton from one of their farms to follow a longer route than would be necessary if that land belonged to them and concluded from this fact that the business had consequently to meet increased transportation costs, something like ten thousand rupees a year in added fuel and maintenance bills, then the brothers would, contemplating the neatly tabulated statistics the economist had put before them, swear at Aziz Khan for his stubbornness at not selling his land. They had made further proposals to him, each time increasing their offer, believing, as all businessmen must believe, since money is the only value with which they interpret human motives, that when a man refuses an offer it is only in the hope of a better offer being made in the future; but Aziz Khan had always replied briefly and politely that he was not interested in selling.

It was not patience which they lost. It was not the blind brutality of power which they possessed which led them to do what they did to obtain the land. It was not a demonstration to the rest of the town of Kalapur that they, since they had brought industry and employment to the town, could act wilfully to achieve their ends. The Shah brothers simply decided, after their last most generous offer had elicited no enthusiasm from Aziz Khan, to take possession of his seventy acres in some other way, and to inflict upon one man the punitive potential of an entire country. Even if this involved murdering Aziz Khan.

Turning events to their advantage, the Shah brothers matched Aziz Khan's simplicity with cunning: they knew how to destroy without letting a speck of dust alight upon the impeccable whiteness of their public name. Often they did not need to mention his name for months; their power was such that even their silence could act as a sanction against recalcitrance.

There were three of the Shah brothers, Akram, Ayub and Afaq—the alliteration might lead one to bemuse oneself with speculations as to the literary preferences of their parents, but that is beside the point. Their beginnings had been obscure, but in 1947, when Pakistan was created, Akram, who had made a few thousand rupees as a money-seller in Bombay, had come to Pakistan and for three years he had looked around Karachi and Lahore, buying something here and selling it there. One could not have said at that time that he would soon become a major industrialist, for his main business was buying goods which someone else had manufactured and selling them to an interested retailer for someone else's subsequent use. Any society with pretensions to the complexities of civilisation swarms with middlemen, narrow-eyed, tight-lipped men who produce nothing and achieve nothing and yet acquire a fortune for themselves. Akram seemed to be fast becoming one of these and if one had predicted his future as a businessman, it would have been as a financier, as one who found no deal too small nor a commission as little as $2\frac{1}{2}$ per cent unworthy of his attentions; and yet he turned to industry, to basic produce.

Akram valued money, for he had had to teach himself how to make it. Pakistan had given him a new opportunity. Bombay had been tough, for there the Hindu money-lenders, who had been at their trade for centuries, controlled finance, gripping the commonest peasant's throat with the claws of compound interest. Now, Muslims, who had always been backward in business in the old India, and who had produced more poets than they had notable businessmen, had a country entirely to themselves. Surely he, Akram, who had learned from hard experience among the mazes of percentages through which the Hindus of Bombay had led him, could slowly create a fortune in Pakistan?

And he was right. Also, he had the talent to shine as brightly as gold in cities where most of the other businessmen were earth-encrusted stones. He was not daunted by the paucity of capital with which he arrived in Karachi. A mixture of bluff, calculated speculation and some judicious mingling with the politicians had brought its own reward. In three years he had made fifty thousand rupees.

It was at the end of this third year that, while travelling by train from Lahore to Rawalpindi, he noticed the wide plains of cotton plantations soon after the train left Kalapur. An idea occurred to him as he pondered the landscape and he decided to spend a few days in Kalapur on his return journey. He knew that nothing would tempt the landlords to sell their cotton to him at a discount of 5 per cent more than the offer of ready cash, for normally the landlords sold their produce by giving three months' credit to the buyers. He decided to take a risk of such a magnitude that his whole body shivered with a frightening thrill at the very thought of it. He made telephone calls to Karachi and Lahore, contacting numerous close friends and a number of important bankers with whom he had made it his business to be well acquainted. He was on the telephone for two whole days, playing the game he enjoyed best, sheer bluff. He found it impossible to sleep during the intervening night as the figure in his mind grew larger than he had imagined would ever be within his grasp. Finally, he raised half a million rupees. It was outrageous, he told himself, his hand shaking as he made some calculations and wrote in a clear, bold hand: Rs. 500,000.

He found little difficulty in persuading the landlords to sell their cotton to him and within the week he had bought half a million rupees' worth of cotton. The two ensuing months, during which he had to wait while the cotton was harvested, were ones of extreme agony and also of keen pleasure. The crop could fail, it occurred to him; he knew nothing of what could happen to cotton. Were there insects which attacked it? Or his stock could catch fire. At times, Akram's anxiety was nearly unbearable; and yet, that was part of the pleasure.

He had gone back to Karachi to follow his normal affairs but returned to Kalapur at harvest time. He stored the cotton he had bought and waited. When the buyers came, he coolly asked for a price which was 10 per cent more than what they normally paid. He left them no choice: either they had to pay the higher price or leave their mills idle.

At one stroke, with one terrifying risk, he had doubled his fortune, the most satisfying aspect of which had been the fact that the money with which he had done so had not been his own in the first place. 'Money makes money,' he was fond of saying, as if it was the highest truth given man to utter, 'that's the beauty of it.'

The fifty thousand rupees profit which he made in this way was not made because he needed the money to feed himself or his family. It was made simply as one pursues an activity for its own end. It gave him a pleasure to appear thus much cleverer than other people. He found, too, that people, rather than being annoyed with his unconventional methods, admired, even applauded him; for he had the gift to make money, a gift which they all desired themselves. It was the one pursuit which their political independence had made possible. Akram, in the eyes of these people, who admired his ruthless methods, was not only a Pakistani enjoying his freedom creatively; he was *the* Pakistani in whose type the successful citizens of the country would need to be moulded.

The brief experience with cotton in Kalapur had given the idea of the textile mills to Akram. Yes, he would become an industrialist, liking the sound of the word, as he credited the money to his bank account under the fawning smile of the cashier. He wrote to his brothers then, who were still in Bombay, that the time had come for them to join him.

To establish the mills, Akram Shah needed land, money and labour. Before his brothers could join him, he worked at these problems, first renting a house in Kalapur and spending a month introducing himself to the town's important people without fully revealing his intentions and hopes of transforming Kalapur from a rural agricultural town to an industrial city. When his presence had been noted by the minor civil servants who administered what items of legislation were imposed by the aberrations of the politicians in Karachi, Akram called on the District Commissioner.

The District Commissioner, Mohammed Karim, was a middle-aged man, large around the stomach, short and oval-shaped, and thin at the top, having a parting on the left side of his head but only half a dozen strands of hair which he placed neatly across his shining dome. His mouth was often seen to remain open in an expression of incredulity at what Karachi might instruct him to do next, so that his chin appeared lost among the folds of flesh that constituted his neck. Mohammed Karim had heard of officers of his own standing in less obscure towns than Kalapur becoming rich overnight; he had heard of officers junior to him being sent abroad to obtain a first-hand knowledge of how other countries solved their administrative problems and being the

23

subject of newspaper articles. Nothing of the sort happened to him and he had often reflected on the plight of being posted in a small town like Kalapur where righteousness was forced upon a man because there was no one around to corrupt him.

When Akram Shah called on him, he received him with a dignified amiability, for Akram had arrived in a car and was wearing a suit; and Mohammed Karim had no way of telling what a man who came to see a District Commissioner might want and when a man wanted something from behind his neatly pressed suit in the Punjab's heat, then there was every hope, considered Mohammed Karim, that the long-neglected District Commissioner might profit from the situation. Mohammed Karim even extended his hand warmly to Akram, and one must admire him for this human touch where many another District Commissioner would have remained imperturbably cold.

The two men talked of the heat and about a cricket match which was being played in Lahore before Akram tossed the golden word *business* in the air and hinted that he was thinking of opening an office in Kalapur and was looking for a business associate. He did not make any definite proposal as yet, but merely talked of generalities and the importance of furthering the country's exports.

It was not necessary, said Akram, that the partner he was looking for should have money, and Mohammed Karim, who was remembering a fog during his student days in London in which he had walked from Westbourne Grove to Elgin Crescent when he had wanted to go to Notting Hill, merely exploded with grunted assents and declared himself to be at Akram's service.

'I'll come to my main point,' Akram said, drawing his chair a little forward with the air of conspiracy, giving the District Commissioner the impression that of all men in Kalapur, he alone had been chosen for this revelation. 'I'm going to open a textile mill,' Akram proceeded to divulge. 'But you know the difficulties, of course. Everyone wants to grab what he can get. One has to be careful. If you . . .' (his voice almost a whisper now) '. . . come in with me, the business will go through smoothly and we'll avoid a lot of trouble.'

The District Commissioner could not tell to what extent, if any, he was being committed, but he vaguely realised that his chance had come at last and was remembering the proverb about Allah rewarding those who are patient. It is not for anyone to ask if Allah, in his divine wisdom, indeed sent his rewards in ready cash, that Allah, in making man in his own image, had also made banks in the image of his own house; enough to state that civil servants in hot climates have a difficult job to do, especially in small towns where little happens, and that in a world where men seek not equality but an inequality in terms of bigger bank accounts than their neighbours, it was just and reasonable for Mohammed Karim, who still had not the slightest notion what Akram Shah was talking about, to give a hint of acquiescence which prompted Akram to state a figure. Nor had Mohammed Karim the slightest notion for what service he was being offered the money, but he accepted it with the greatest show of reluctance while also protesting that the figure should be higher even though it was ten times more than his month's salary. When Akram left, Mohammed Karim realised that he had accepted a bribe, but had not actually received the cash; that he had agreed to help Akram accomplish some deed which must necessarily be crooked to entail a bribe, and yet he did not know what that deed was. But he did not wish to reveal that he was uninitiated in the procedure of corruption, for that would have been a social blunder and a crime against his four children. 'Allah is wise,' he muttered to himself; hopefully.

Akram made further calls on Mohammed Karim, meetings which the District Commissioner found as bewildering as the first, but during the course of which Akram obtained the District Commissioner's signature on certain deeds, giving him possession of some unfertile land which was supposed to belong to the government. This land lay just outside the town on the road to Lahore, a suitable place, Akram had decided, for his mills.

Able now to go ahead unimpeded with his schemes, Akram Shah went next to Karachi where he first lunched with the chairman of a bank. This was no more than a convivial formality, for they had been well acquainted with each other by then and the chairman had always been impressed by Akram's ability to swell his credit at the bank. Akram told him about his scheme and as the two men sat smoking cigars at the end of the meal, the chairman agreed to let Akram have all the credit facilities he needed. Akram then called on another friend, a small round man who was at that time the most influential Minister in the Cabinet. Because of the government's restrictions on the expenditure of foreign exchange, this was a crucial meeting. Akram needed to import machinery from England and instead of sending in applications through the usual channels which have a habit of taking an unusual amount of time, it was best, Akram thought, if the matter was taken straight to the highest level.

The Minister, a charming man of neither education nor ability who had suddenly acquired immense property and influence when the Hindus fled to India in 1947, abandoning their estates, was, of course, a friend; but a friend only of those from whom he received due respect in cash. The political state of the country had been worsening with quarrels among the parties; Karachi swarmed with politicians who snipped the air like locusts with their talk, with men who had no experience of government, who gave no thought to the social amelioration so urgently required in the country, who had neither ideas nor ideals, neither a sense of justice nor a sense of humanity, but who were all aflame with the burning ambition at once to make their fortune, men whose mentality was no different from that of thugs. In this rush for self-aggrandisement, an air of insecurity prevailed in Karachi; so that no Minister was averse to consolidating his position by means of transferring money to banks in Switzerland where personal accounts had hastily been opened, it being tacitly agreed that if you were not in politics to make a personal fortune, however small, then you were a damn' fool. In this atmosphere of patriotic public talk by the Ministers and desperate private greed, when the nation was exhorted to save its foreign exchange by using indigenous products while the Ministers themselves banked millions in their own names in Switzerland, in such an atmosphere, fringe adventurers like Akram Shah prospered.

Akram laid his plans before the Minister, and offered, if the Minister would readily sanction the necessary foreign exchange, to transfer 5 per cent of the total amount sanctioned to the Minister's account in Zürich; the Minister agreed, the machinery was ordered, and Akram Shah's industrial empire had laid its foundations.

Thereupon, Akram returned to Kalapur and proceeded with the buying of more land, the setting up of an office and the enrolling of labour. His brothers now joined him and the work began.

Of the three brothers, Afaq was the only bachelor. Akram was indeed old enough to be his father, being almost twice the age, while Ayub was in his middle thirties. Between Akram and Ayub, there had been two sisters who were married and who still lived in India; and between Ayub and Afaq there had been two more sisters who were also married in India.

Their parents had died and the two elder brothers, for the last twenty years, had had to work and provide for the sisters and for Afaq. Consequently, only Afaq had received any proper education and had been in his second year at the University of Bombay, reading Economics at the Podar College of Commerce, when he left his studies to join Akram in Kalapur. The two wives as well as Zarina, an orphaned cousin of the Shah brothers, were the only other members of the family who came to live in Kalapur.

Zarina's past was obscure. Perhaps the elder brothers

knew something of the relatives who had been her parents; to Afaq, Zarina was a delicate, frail beauty of seventeen, a thin girl who had always been gazing from the shadows of a house. Akram Shah's wife, Faridah, though she had grown a little plump despite having borne no children, was still considered attractive by people who were aware of her husband's wealth. Razia, Ayub's wife, was in her twenties and she had the fullness of figure, the composed air of being a queen about her, which made other men envious of Ayub; and the fact that she had had two daughters lent her authority, especially as Faridah, her nearest rival in public esteem, was childless.

The details of the next three years are not relevant to this record, for it is about Aziz Khan, the landlord who would not sell his seventy acres to the Shah brothers. Enough to say that within the three years their business prospered and that the Shah brothers bought all the land except Aziz Khan's, and that their land produced abundant raw material for their two mills; that the brothers built a mansion for themselves; that Kalapur attracted labourers from remote rural parts of the Punjab and that every labourer was on the payroll of the Shah brothers; that they were respected not only in Kalapur but gradually all over Pakistan, for they contributed handsomely to public charities and, during one year, rewarded twenty of their best workers by sending them on a pilgrimage to Mecca, attracting considerable publicity for this laudable gesture in Allah's service. Their generosity was remarked upon and their textiles were bought in increasing quantities. All these facts, of immense interest in themselves in the social history of a new and a growing country, are unfortunately not relevant here and are best left to the historians of the Shah empire. We need only to bear them in mind in their broad outline.

Afaq

Afaq

It was March and the Shah brothers were contemplating the statistics which their economist and accountant had together produced at a board meeting, showing that though production, following the excellent harvest of the previous autumn, had reached a ceiling, the profits of the business showed no clear increase over the previous year; and, when the monthly figures for the two years were compared, some of the months of the current year showed a decline.

'Gentlemen, we have reached a point of stagnation,' the economist declared, almost as if he was concluding a speech in a debate at the London School of Economics where he had learned an impressive jargon and an ability to confuse people.

'It's an intolerable situation,' the accountant announced. 'This meeting could have taken place a year ago.'

'What makes it so intolerable,' the economist resumed, as if he alone had the right to sum up the affairs of the Shah Industrial Enterprises Ltd, 'is that in principle we have made progress over the last year. We cannot yet be said to have got into full swing, for an industry of this magnitude cannot be said to have established itself until it has been going for, say, twenty years. And from that it follows that each year of the first twenty should show an increase of profits from the previous year. Stagnation is out of the question. Increased production in the farms has not yet begun to show in the output of the mills.'

The economist's exposition was deliberately verbose, and he had a habit of talking rapidly and loudly; he had to show his superiority to the coldly analytical accountant in some way.

'That, of course, is reasonable enough,' the accountant put in ruminatively, 'at this stage. But what is hard to understand is that the mills are already working to full capacity and yet profits have not increased.'

Akram Shah, softly tapping the fingers of his right hand on the teak desk, listened quietly to the two executives' case, but Ayub, who was vigorously nodding his head as each point was made, said, 'We'll have to step up the overtime. Recruit more labourers is the answer. We'll have to start the night shift as soon as we can. The mills can't lie idle at night.'

Afaq, the youngest of the brothers, wondered if the cost of extra labour would justify increased production, but said nothing, having yet to realise that the ratio between necessity and actual business performance was an ever decreasing one.

Akram, however, said with some decision, 'No, we can't start the night shift as yet. It would create an artificial boom. Besides, it would make too heavy a demand on electricity. There's a shortage of power, as you know.'

'Then what about these figures?' Ayub, who detested shelving a problem, asked with some impatience.

'Yes, they do create a difficulty,' Afaq said, for it was time he made some contribution to the meeting.

'How can you explain them?' Akram asked, turning to the economist.

The economist smiled, delighted that the questions should have been directed at him and not at the accountant.

'It seems that there is a wastage somewhere,' he said. 'A leak in the edifice. Wages have remained constant, only executive salaries have gone up. There has definitely been no inflation, no spiralling. Output has been steady without there being a real growth. A growth of one-eighth per cent is neither here nor there. There has been no additional capital expenditure, and this has in fact been a saving in real terms although, of course, we cannot put down as profit something we did not have to spend. And yet, it is clear to me that, making allowances for many such contingencies as I have noted in para two of my report, particularly the sub-para concerning tax relief, that we have fallen slightly behind expectation. Now, I mentioned wastage. Are we sure that instead of what we think is full-capacity production we have only a semblance of it?'

'Why, what can you mean?' the accountant asked, seizing on the economist's nebulous conclusion to expose the essential woolliness of his thinking. 'The reports from the floor managers are perfectly sound.'

'But there are matters beyond our control,' the economist told him sharply.

'Such as what?' the accountant wanted to know.

'Well . . .' the economist shrugged his shoulders.

'Well, what?'

'Well, there's Aziz Khan's property, for example, which I have often . . .'

The economist needed to say no more to silence the accountant, and the Shah brothers returned home that afternoon feeling as though Aziz Khan's land was an aspirin which they needed to swallow to rid themselves of a persistent headache. Afaq, however, did not suffer as much as did his elder brothers, for it seemed plain to him that he was now living in luxury where before he had not always been comfortable and that his own problems were of a much more personal nature than could be resolved by statistical analysis. And yet he did not offer what might have been a common-sensical objection when his brothers said that Aziz Khan had to go.

'What does he want?' asked Ayub with some annoyance when they sat together over tea. Ayub felt more hostility against Aziz Khan than his brothers. Where Akram was content with the accumulation of wealth, Ayub wanted as well the assertion of power to which he felt entitled by the wealth. For him, any problem which could have been em-bodied by a human being could be solved either by the offer of cash or, failing that, some insidious form of destruction. Whenever Aziz Khan was debated, Ayub felt a latent violence within him which he wished he could give vent to. He knew the discipline which could be elicited from rebel-lious men by the brutal use of violence, for he had seen it around him ever since he was a child.

One of his earliest memories of it went back some thirty years when the British ruled India; he was in Lahore then, hardly five, but the memory, perhaps because he was so innocent of human torture then, would vividly return to him. It was a summer month in Lahore, perhaps May, when the midday temperature is well over a hundred. For some reason, perhaps he was with his mother who had come shopping, he was in Mall Road. There was the sound of troops. He was terrified of British soldiers and he held on to the hand which had been clasping his. But he saw. The road was cleared and cordoned off. A number of Indians with nothing on but a loin cloth were taken off a vehicle and were made to stand at attention in their bare feet on the hot, melting tar of the road. He remembered remaining in the shop for a long time, for no one went out while the soldiers were lined along the road. Perhaps the prisoners were made to stand for half an hour, even as little as five minutes. It seemed a long time. Their sweating bodies looked as though they had been dipped in oil as they stood bent under the heat. And then the soldiers made them kneel, from which position they were made to lie prostrate. A little more time passed. The bodies seemed to be melting into the tar. And then the soldiers ordered them to crawl the length of the street on their bellies. All Lahore, and, later, all India was horrified by this atrocity which had been publicly committed with the deliberate intention of dramatising a particular moral for the native political thinkers of the time. Ayub had remembered this incident all his life and had used the lesson he learned when he was a political agitator in Bombay during 1946 and 1947. First agitating against the British for a free India and taking part in attempts to sabotage their military installations, he had changed his politics and begun to demonstrate for the creation of Pakistan once it was beginning to be apparent that the British were no longer an enemy. His enemy was now the Hindus and he organised riots against them. He had never considered it murder, just as war is not considered murder by politicians, but he had killed.

And when he now debated Aziz Khan and asked 'What does he want?' it was an expression not only of his annoyance but also of that violent instinct within him which needed to be nourished continually by the presence of a recognisable enemy.

Akram, silent as a cannon outside a military academy, said nothing but sat doodling on a piece of paper, as if approaches to a solution had to be drilled before they could be effected. His was the inward withdrawal which questions potential strength, weighs up the opportunities and determines whether or not he has the capacity to perform actions he had never before attempted.

Afaq, twenty-two years old and inexperienced in the practice of power, tending to be pragmatic but yet wanting to support his brothers in their designs of aggrandisement, a minor courtier at the table of emperors, said, 'It's only seventy acres. What good will it do us when we get it?'

At last he had said what he had refrained from saying earlier. Akram looked up at him, still doodling, but his face showed little emotion and he said nothing; and if his mouth opened just a little, it was for an involuntary curling of his lower lip.

Ayub, angered by his younger brother's naïveté, experiencing the impatience which he frequently did at Afaq's immaturity, said, 'You don't understand, do you?'

The tone in which he spoke would have been enough to drive away the last bit of common sense from Afaq's mind, such was Ayub's authority; but he was told more.

Akram said, 'There is talk.'

That is all he said, doodling.

Ayub was more emphatic and said, banging the table with his fist, 'Get some economics into your head, man.'

Afaq thought of the daily turnover of thousands of rupees and Ayub went on, 'We've lots of land, yes. Thousands of acres. It's all ours. We've bulldozers and tractors by the dozen. The cotton output has trebled since we began to farm the land. We've taken to growing corn as well. We're planning to enter the soap industry in East Pakistan. We're planning to take over the cosmetics industry in Karachi. We're contributing thousands of rupees to the stadium they're building in Lahore and the hospital they're building in 'Pindi. And all what for? Tell me, little brother, what for?'

Afaq was puzzled; he was being asked too many questions, being told too much in too few words.

'You don't understand, do you?' Ayub said again and Afaq's mouth, which had opened to make some sort of an answer to the earlier question, remained open but only in puzzlement.

Afaq guessed meanings which were never fully expressed to him. He felt vaguely that he was expected to do something, that his brothers were gradually forcing him into a corner and that a time would come when he would have to perform some act of valour in order to emerge, in the eyes of his brothers, a man. But what was the talk which Akram had mentioned so cryptically, who was it who talked and what exactly did he or they say? It would have been so much simpler if they were to tell him: Here is a report, summarise its main points. Or: The rains are expected, go and inspect if the sowing is over. A straightforward directive with a physical end he could understand as he could also grasp an intellectual problem as long as its premises were empirically stated; but this cryptic, obscure way of suggesting ideas to him, as if the brothers were uttering charms at his initiation, did not suit his temperament and succeeded only in confusing him. He knew what the economist had said that afternoon, but what were the economics which Ayub had mentioned, what index finger did they point at which chart of his consciousness? Complexities of thought had been hinted to him and left both unspoken and unexplained. There were motives he could not understand, darknesses to which his pragmatism brought no light. His reasoning was too simple. If the sole purpose of work was to guarantee one's material comfort, then they had already acquired enough; so why did his brothers want to extend their influence over soap and cosmetics? He had his own bank account and his own car; and yet the brothers talked as if they still lived in their former insecurity. He stood up and looked at his brothers. Akram's eyes were lowered as he still doodled, following the random lines with a stern, searching gaze. When he rose, Ayub looked at him with a fierceness which he had noticed in beggars whom he had refused to give a coin.

'I know what you mean,' he said like an ignoramus in an intellectual company who knows that his only defence is a pretence to knowledge, and went out.

Akram turned from his doodling to Ayub.

'He's still a child,' he said.

Ayub pondered the remark, leaning back in his chair, and said, 'I don't think so. We make him out to be a child, but he isn't. He worries, expects reasons for everything. That's perhaps because he didn't have to fight for his life as we did. One day he'll know that for some actions there aren't any reasons. They've just got to be done. For honour, for dignity, for self-respect. Just got to be done. He's got to learn that. Then he'll do something.'

Akram, too, leaned back in his chair, nodding his head slowly in grave acquiescence; whenever Ayub contradicted a statement of his, he always made out a clear case for himself. Akram also knew of Ayub's power of suggestion; he would talk round a subject and tell you something in a circumlocutory way, especially when he wanted you to do something for him.

'What do we do about Aziz Khan?' Akram asked.

Perhaps he was flattering Ayub or delegating to him the responsibility of an unstated action, for he did not mention the pattern his doodles had begun to define in his own mind.

'Nothing for some more time,' Ayub said. 'We must all be in agreement. Therefore, we'll have to wait till Afaq stops worrying.'

Afaq was walking in the garden outside the house. The day had become cooler with the coming of evening. The sun was low, falling full on the house; long shadows seemed pools of water spilled on the lawn. Afaq walked to the end of the garden and paused under a guava tree. He turned and looked at the house. Its pale blue wash looked pleasing in the full light, its several windows shone back at him. One of the lower windows reflected the sun into the swimming pool, which was in the middle of the garden, whence the sun shot up again.

Another window was open and Afaq saw Razia, Ayub's wife, standing there, brushing her hair, her long black hair, her head slightly tilted back; both her arms lifted to the hair had the effect of lifting her bosom and a shadow fell diagonally across her midriff; the tilting of the head, with its consequent drooping of eyelids and the slight pouting of the mouth, almost suggested that she was offering her lips for a kiss to some invisible being at the window. Afaq, seeing her, involuntarily withdrew under the shadow of the guava tree, and observed her thus employed in her idleness. A sudden pressure of heat tapped at his temples as he saw clearly the round-featured face, all concentric circles except for the aquiline nose, of his sister-in-law in the full and mellow spring sunlight of the evening. He remembered the time when, one afternoon two years ago, he had returned from the mill with a headache and had found that she was alone at home, at siesta time when the servants were dozing in their rooms at the back of the house, when she, hearing his footsteps in the hall, had come out of a room and had expressed surprise at his appearance. He had gone to his room and had fallen in his bed and she had followed him, bringing him an aspirin and a glass of water and had stood by his bedside as he swallowed the aspirin; then she had taken the glass from him and, leaning towards him, had put a hand on his forehead, asking, 'You haven't a temperature, have you?' And how he had winced under the softness of her palm, and then, watching her walk across the room to switch on the air-conditioner, her slow walk, the hips swaying, how he had felt a sudden lust to possess her. But she had gone and his headache had worsened.

Odd, he thought, that the memory of that afternoon should persist. He had wondered afterwards what would have happened if he had held her hand when she put her palm to his forehead; or, if he had pulled her down to him. Ayub would have whipped him the way he had whipped a servant once when he discovered that the servant had lied about the price of some article he had been sent out to purchase. For some time he had imagined a clandestine affair with his sister-in-law and he had drilled in his mind the procedure of their love-making; but always, when his fingers still fumbled on the invisible lace, his fantasies had ended with Ayub, the strong and ruthless Ayub, standing with a whip just raised for the first lash.

Zarina, the frail orphaned cousin, was destined for him. He would be married to her as soon as she was another year or two older. This match had never been arranged and it had not been discussed, but Afaq knew sometimes the intentions of his brothers before the brothers themselves made those intentions public; especially when they concerned him. And he knew he could not escape his brothers' intentions. He had thought sometimes of drawing out all his money and going away to Karachi; but he needed much more money to win the independence he longed for. At a time when university graduates were lucky to find clerical employment, it was no use going to Karachi. He continued to tolerate Kalapur and his brothers' arrangements, though sometimes he could have dug his nails into the bark of trees.

He would marry Zarina and empty into her delicate body, her thin thighs, the lust which often hurt his body on hot nights; he would swallow her small breasts, for her beautiful face, the innocent aspect of her eyes, also hurt him when he woke from those nights when he had felt especially tormented by his loneliness and saw her at breakfast.

Afaq watched Razia brush the straight strands of hair that hung down to the small of her back; she will go away, he knew, and sit now in front of her dressing-table and lift the hair into folds and waves high above her neck; she will make up her face and load her lips with lipstick and then change; she will lift her large breasts in her hands and place them gently in the cups of her bra; she will wind a silk sari about her and wear her high heels; and descend slowly down the stairs for the evening with Ayub at the club.

She went away from the window then and he turned to the tree, the smooth-barked guava tree, holding the trunk with both his hands, biting his lips. Afaq turned away and directed his thoughts away from female shapes, the declivities of flesh, and remembered Aziz Khan, the seventy acres. He glanced in a gesture of empty frustration at the garden and noticed that a branch had fallen into the swimming pool. He walked down the drive to the back of the house where three cars and a jeep were parked. He jumped into the jeep and drove away. Driving soothed him, especially in a jeep, especially over a bumpy field.

The sun was almost touching the horizon when he neared

Aziz Khan's seventy acres. He had not thought of coming in this direction or in any particular direction, but here he was on the edge of the strip of land which stuck like a fishbone in the throat of the Shah brothers' vast country. Afaq slowed down as he approached the gate which led to Aziz Khan's house, but accelerated again as there was nothing he had to say to Aziz Khan. Some five hundred yards farther on he turned into a field that edged on to the stream behind Aziz Khan's house. As he was turning into the field, he stopped, noticing a line of peasants, men and women, walking down the road in single file. He turned the jeep round so that it faced the road. He switched off the engine and sat leaning over the steering-wheel. The line of peasants slowly went past him, baskets on their heads, their hands at the baskets. He watched them go past. They turned their eyes towards him, not their heads or voices, only their eyes, and walked on. The sun had set now, there was grey light. One of the peasant women seemed strikingly like Razia in that the gesture of raising her hands to the basket was identical to Razia's raising her hands to brush her hair so that her breasts stood out and her face, though it had never worn any make-up, acquired a femininity which was peculiarly charming in a peasant. Afaq watched her walk away and then, re-starting the engine and switching on the headlamps, he drove slowly up the road, following the peasants whose steps became shuffled and insecure now that they were conscious of an unpredictable machine whining at their heels. Afaq trailed them for a while, amused that he had induced a nervousness among the peasants, and then pressed on the accelerator and speeded away, one hand holding tightly the round knob of the gear lever. Half a mile down the road, the beams of his headlamps caught the eyes of approaching beasts, probably bullock-carts, he thought. But nearing them, he saw two horses being ridden by two young men. He slowed down and stopped, indicating to the men to stop also. Rafiq and Javed, Aziz Khan's two sons, were the horsemen, he recognised.

'Do you always travel on horses?' Afaq asked.

Rafiq, having recognised Afaq, answered, 'Yes, I'm thinking of getting a bicycle sometime but the horse is fine.'

He spoke quite amiably, for although there were differences of opinion between the two families, there was, as yet, no open quarrel. 'But a bicycle would be useless in the fields,' he added. 'You can rely on a horse not to have a puncture.'

In the darkness, Javed stared at Afaq, his horse stamping, almost rearing from the chug-chug-chug of the jeep.

'Have you ever been in a car?' Afaq asked.

'No,' Rafiq replied, becoming a spokesman for the two brothers. 'Actually, I don't even need a bicycle because the only time I need a conveyance is to go to the bazaar, and a horse is as fast and less tiring to ride.'

Javed patted his horse, clicking his tongue.

'What do you do in the bazaar?' Afaq asked; not that he was curious, but he felt like chatting.

'Oh, many things,' Rafiq said. 'Especially on market days. It's difficult to sell our cotton nowadays.' He spoke now without rancour, without suggesting that he had thought up the remark particularly to make Afaq uncomfortable; just matter of fact. 'The buyers who used to come from Lahore don't come any more because you use most of the cotton in this area. In the old days we had definite buyers, but now we don't.'

'How do you sell your cotton, then?'

'Well, we have a broker in town now,' Rafiq explained, not thinking that he was giving away a business secret. 'It means we get a lot less, but at least we still sell it.'

'You wouldn't have any problems if you sold the land, you know,' Afaq said, smiling, as though he were joking.

'That's my father's business,' Rafiq said without sounding pompous. 'All I can say is that he knows what he's doing. Anyway, what would we do once we sold the land?'

'You could live in Lahore. Have you ever been to Lahore?'

'Yes, once. It was very crowded.'

Javed's horse had raised its tail and, stiffening its hind legs, was dropping balls of dung on to the road.

'Didn't you like the women there?' Afaq asked. 'There are none here.'

'Yes,' Rafiq said. 'I saw many. But there's nothing to do in Lahore. Here we have work to do all day.'

'Are you married?'

'No,' Rafiq said, suppressing the notion that had the Shah brothers not driven the other landlords away, he would have been married by now, for he did not want to appear bitter to this youth whose frank manner he was beginning to like. Javed's horse neighed now, prancing away from the heap he had left on the road.

Afaq drove on then, waving good-bye. Rafiq is a simpleton, he thought, a peasant really, and Javed is a child.

He began to question the desirability, so emphatically expressed by his brothers, of buying Aziz Khan's land. One encounter with Aziz Khan's sons did not make Afaq sentimental about the slow efficiency of peasant life, but he did question the larger purpose that moved humanity in one particular direction and not another. The images of Razia and the peasant woman he had just seen on the road passed through his mind simultaneously. Lust, he considered, was nature's means of ensuring procreation and men lived for women no more than trees for rain; yet, there was the hurtful silence of drought. He remembered his student days in Bombay, the two years at Podar College, which had been filled up with so much talk, the endless sitting in restaurants over cups of tea and cigarettes. He had argued then that nature bribed man into procreating by rewarding him with pleasure; but he himself had never experienced that pleasure. There had been picnics to Mud Island and to Vihar Lake to which they had been accompanied by those girls who could convincingly lie to their parents that they were spending the day on a field course or in learning market research techniques at first hand. The picnics tinkled in his memory with the endless giggling of the girls. There were hardly any

43

relationships outside the groups, for it was unthinkable that a boy and a girl should meet alone, perhaps even fall in love with each other and be engaged in those preliminaries of love-making which are considered innocuous. And yet, although he could delude himself that he was not frustrated then, he had enjoyed himself, but now, in Kalapur where he knew no one outside his own family, the frustration was bitter and was made worse by the knowledge that it would not be resolved by his discovering love but by an arranged marriage.

The notion of such a marriage, bringing with it the image of Zarina to his mind, annoyed him; often, he experienced a lust for Zarina but he thought that he would feel cheated if Zarina were thrust upon him as a wife. In his annoyance, he changed down noisily to take a bend where the road led to the mills. He did not look at the mills as he drove past. They were like huge mausoleums whose shapes he knew too well to want to regard them anew with any interest; he valued the mills for the power they gave to his family though he had not as yet essayed to exercise that power himself.

Did one live for work, then? he asked himself, recalling Rafiq's remark that on the land there was work to do all day. His job in the mills was to control personnel: he employed people, gave them work. Was the act of giving others work itself work? A nice question. He recalled the discussions in political economy in the cheap Bombay restaurants. Taxation was the instrument of national progress, he had argued then, excessive profits were the property of the nation which the nation would invest in itself. Would those friends, some of whom were avowed Marxists, seeing him at his desk now, laugh at him? Profit was the power of the individual after all and what was an individual if not a will? His thoughts led him to Aziz Khan again, the one man whose will had stubbornly rejected the logic of geography, economics and the power which the will of the Shah brothers had now determined itself to enforce.

In his conclusions about his own self, his own ideas, Afaq

was wrong in discovering stubbornness as a motive in Aziz Khan's reluctance to sell his land. And neither would his brothers, who were not given to doubts and deliberations like Afaq, have arrived at the meanings which lay behind Aziz Khan's inscrutable refusals. The Shah brothers were up to their necks in money; no aspect of the earth ever appeared to their vision.

Afaq drove past a grove of eucalyptus trees which led to the club. An attendant at the gate, smartly liveried in an embroidered tunic and wearing a turban whose starched fan seemed to grow like a palm-leaf from his head, saluted him as Afaq drove past. Three other attendants greeted him in the car park where long, sleek cars were lined as an exhibition in ostentation. Afaq left his jeep there and walked to the club's entrance. The hall was deserted except for the ubiquitous attendants and bearers; notices on the walls announced the club's activities: dances, bingo sessions, cabarets, the availability of tickets for the forthcoming Test match, a notice inviting interested members to put down their names for the formation of a Polo club, and other items which further the pursuit of pleasure of the rich; there was also a list of names of people who had failed to meet their credit at the club and who were thus publicly scandalised—this particular notice was frequently scrutinised by the members, for they found it entertaining to learn who had fallen on hard times.

Afaq took the door to the right of the hall which led to the bar. A group of people greeted him as he entered, but they were people whom he always greeted in return but with whom he rarely ever talked. He went past them to the dance hall where he knew his brothers and their wives would be.

They were sitting at one of the tables which lined the walls of the long hall at the end of which, on a platform, a band was trying to imitate Xavier Cugat. Razia was saying, '. . . were always coming on Sundays. At least thirty people every Sunday, and poor mummy always cooked even though there were plenty of servants.'

Ayub sat next to her and opposite him, Akram. Faridah, Akram's wife, was also there as Afaq had expected, but he was surprised to see Zarina sitting quietly at a corner of the table. He decided, on joining them, that he would not dare ask Zarina for a dance although his family was considered advanced and modern in outlook. Ayub made room for him as he pulled a chair across.

'Well, little brother,' Ayub said, 'didn't you get time to change?'

Afaq looked at Ayub's white jacket and black bowtie; his hand involuntarily buttoned his own shirt where the chest was showing; he was uncomfortably aware, too, that his hair was dishevelled after driving in the open jeep.

'I would be hot in a tie,' he said. 'Guess what? I ran into Aziz Khan's sons. Have you ever met them?'

'No,' Ayub said, and picked up the glass of whisky so as to hold his surprise.

'I'd met them once before,' Afaq continued. 'Down at the mill when we had a rush of labourers wanting to join and some of Aziz Khan's men had quit his farm and they, the brothers, were pleading with the men to return. You know, what beats me is that they don't hate us.'

'Why should they hate us?' Akram asked, almost ready to laugh to reassure the women that he and Ayub had not become involved in an incipient vendetta.

'Well, I mean we got on well,' Afaq said. 'The younger brother didn't say a word, but Rafiq was at least polite.'

'And don't you expect people to be polite to you?' Ayub asked, for to him more than politeness was guaranteed by their wealth.

Afaq noticed that Zarina was staring at him, as if expecting him to answer Ayub's bullying questions with a firmness which would assert his own independence, but she turned away when he caught her eye. He said softly, looking away from them all and turning his gaze to his lap, 'Sometimes I think we're strangers here.'

Akram was at last able to laugh and the others joined him;

except Zarina who felt as though she had missed the punch line of the joke.

Ayub snapped a finger in the air and two waiters appeared behind him as proof that the rich are most adept at conjuring.

'What will it be?' Ayub asked, turning in his laugh to Afaq.

Afaq was not at all sure whether his littleness was not being demonstrated for public amusement by Ayub's gesture of offering a reward. So that when he replied, 'A fruit juice', it was almost a cynical defiance or perhaps a self-sacrifice which one affects when sulking. Akram cleared his throat and gulped his whisky before ordering another one.

The band now paid tribute to Lawrence Welk. Ayub and Razia rose to dance whereupon Akram shifted his chair a little closer to the table.

'You mustn't mind Ayub,' Akram said to Afaq. 'Have a whisky if you'd like one.'

'No, thanks,' Afaq said, wondering whether he might not again unbutton his shirt.

Now Faridah said, 'Such shah-king pink!' So that a silence may not tinkle among the glasses. And refrained, no doubt with some difficulty, from laughing at the woman in the pink sari, who, Faridah did not care to notice, was waltzing immaculately. Zarina giggled very slightly for Faridah's sake.

'Dyeing is a problem,' said Akram, who, wherever his physical presence might be, always sat in his office.

Zarina looked at the pink sari through slit eyes and it seemed to tear itself into ribbons of clouds at sunset as it floated across the room. She decided that blue was her favourite colour.

'What did Aziz Khan's sons say to you?' Akram asked.

'Nothing much,' Afaq said. 'About the value of horses, I suppose. They were on horseback, returning from the bazaar. They sell their cotton through some broker there and lose on it, they said. At least Rafiq said so, for Javed was silent.'

47

'A broker, eh?' Akram mused. 'I bet you it's that crook Hussain.'

'They didn't say who.'

'I bet you it's Hussain.'

The band now changed to a medley inspired by the General Overseas Service of the BBC, and Akram asked Faridah for a dance. Though her rounded figure was sometimes difficult to manœuvre through a crowded dance floor, Akram, weighing his wife's bulk against the public relations value of a show of connubial faithfulness, thought that five minutes of looking over her shoulder was perhaps a worthwhile investment for the good of his public name.

Zarina thought that her chair would creak if Afaq did not say something now that they were left alone. He talked so little even when in their family, which was not at all like many other old-fashioned, male-dominated Pakistani families, it was not considered improper to be seen talking to a girl of marriageable age, who after all was his cousin. She lowered her head for there were the folds of silk at her lap to admire. Afaq leaned back in his chair, putting his hands behind his head. What was he expected to do? he wondered. The conversations he invented and made to girls when alone in bed at night would have been the envy of an experienced Don Juan. The flatteries he could think up when alone seemed impossible to utter even when the girl was his own cousin to whom he would very likely be married one day. A physical presence made him nervous with its demands on verbal communication. He leaned forward then to hold his glass; if the dance did not end in a minute, he could at least try a sip of fruit juice. Zarina almost raised her head but the pattern of mangoes on the silk, she decided, was smoother than the back of Afaq's hand. The dance did end shortly, and the clapping which followed it could have been the recorded studio applause from a wireless. But his brothers did not return for they now stood with their wives in the middle of the room, talking to some acquaintances.

When the band resumed, to pay homage this time to the

Voice of America, Afaq had already taken two sips and was on the point of swallowing the rest of the fruit juice in one gulp and ordering a whisky.

'Shall we dance?' he said quickly, jerkily, almost as if he had spoken the words before his tongue had in fact uttered them.

It was perhaps too sudden for Zarina, making her almost drive a fingernail through the silk she was stroking. She looked at him for a moment and would have smiled, but noticed that the brothers were now returning and Ayub was already saying, 'Come, you silent lovers, we're going to Mansur's for a game of bridge.'

Zarina blushed a little, not realising that Ayub was again bullying his younger brother.

Behind the coldly indifferent aspect he preserved towards any of Ayub's suggestions, Afaq shuddered at the thought of bridge.

'Count me out,' he said. 'I'm going home. I'm hungry and tired.'

'Yes, but we're eating at Mansur's,' Razia said.

Afaq resisted Razia's invitation and said, 'I know, but it will drag on and on.'

'As you choose,' Akram said as they walked out to the car park.

Afaq walked with them to the door and saw them leave. Razia drew the end of her sari as a veil across her mouth, for dust did dry the coatings of lipstick. She and Ayub were the first to drive away, for Ayub was not one for waiting once a decision had been made. Zarina, as always, joined Akram and his wife. Mansur, who was an executive in an oil company, followed them in his car with his wife. Afaq watched them drive away and returned to the dance hall.

He sat down and ordered a whisky. The band, having exhausted its imitative repertoire, was now playing a nondescript waltz. Afaq sipped at his whisky and looked morosely around the hall. The dancing was too well-mannered and, consequently, lifeless; the dancers were almost all married couples, for if an unmarried girl were to be seen with a man, her matrimonial prospects would be completely annihilated, for no man wanted a woman who had so much as touched another man's hand; and if a married woman danced with someone other than her husband, then she would inevitably be described as *loose* or *free* and her family's honour would be much diminished. The country traditionally guarded its female society with jealousy and suspicion, for women were considered to be property rather than companions. Afaq saw that there was not one person he could talk to, not one woman he could approach from whom he could expect a smile. He gulped his whisky and went to the billiards room. Here there was silence. Four men played at two tables and were too completely absorbed in their game to notice him. The billiard balls clicked, but no voice spoke. He went to the card room where a more mixed crowd was in serious concentration; there were four at each table; the game, which he knew to be rummy, was played for stakes as high as ten rupees per point. No one looked up when he entered. He observed the faces, some harrowed with the accumulating losses, some intensely focused on the fortune they thought was in their hands. The only sounds in the room were those of the shuffling of cards or when a card was thrown down with a sharp flick to win a hand.

Afaq left the club and went to his jeep. He switched on the ignition and let the engine idle for a few minutes. An attenddant watched him from a discreet distance and then shuffled up nervously and began to polish the windscreen with a rag he carried for the purpose. If you're rich enough, you can afford not to give a tip, Afaq thought as he drove away.

He drove slowly round the outskirts of the town, hypnotically following the beams of his headlamps. There was only the darkness to go towards. The darkness which presented ghostly, unreal forms, which beckoned with a strange seduction; as if it led to some reality where the abstractions which puzzled Afaq so much would resolve themselves into some substantial image.

50

2

When Rafiq and Javed reached home after their encounter
with Afaq, they found their father sitting, as usual, in the
yard in front of the veranda. Javed led the horses to the
back of the house in order to feed them and Rafiq walked up
to his father.

'Hussain is being a little difficult,' Rafiq said, whereupon
his father raised an eyebrow not so much in surprise but as
if to ask what difficulties had in fact been presented by the
broker.

'He says he's having to pay double for transporting the
cotton to Lahore,' Rafiq continued, 'because the lorries have
to come empty to Kalapur since the firm which hires them
out can't find any business for them on the way up here. So
Hussain says he now wants a commission of twelve per cent.
To meet all his costs, he says.'

Aziz Khan nodded his head, more in understanding than
in assent, and looked away as if to listen to a cricket chirping
among the plants.

'We don't really have a choice,' Rafiq went on. 'We could
try and produce more to make up for the loss.'

Aziz Khan nodded at this suggestion, too, and would have
touched his son's shoulder in gratitude had not his wife,
Zakia, shouted from the kitchen, 'Rafeeeeq. Come and eeeeat.'

Alone, Aziz Khan breathed a little more easily. He was
fortunate in his sons, he reflected, for neither of them had
expressed a wish to do anything other than work on the land
with him. But he doubted if they could produce more cotton
now that several of his peasants had deserted their toils in
the sun to work in the mills under the more brutal pressure
of clocks. As long as he had his sons, there would be plenty
to do on the land, and he decided that instead of trying to
increase the production of cotton, it would be wiser for him
to use part of his land for growing more vegetables. Aziz
Khan felt too weary to think any more on this subject. There
was little to think anyway, little to plan as long as the land

unfailingly continued its cycle of growth, for he himself was part of the cycle and preferred, for the present, to remain as seemingly insensitive as a plant; and if he did not have any new hopes which he wanted to fulfil, this was because already his life afforded a measure of satisfaction and because the land would always give him work and sustenance, however poor he was.

Darkness was falling on his land. Flights of crows appeared as blobs on the grey of the sky and were soon drawn into the darkness as if a sponge had been wiped across the sky. Aziz Khan took a deep breath, shutting his eyes. He lifted his turban from his head and placed it in his lap; like a pet to stroke. He drowsed. He shifted in his chair. From the front, his legs appeared long in their forward stretch, the heels of his slippers resting on the hard, dry mud of the front yard; his arms were pressed to the sides of his body, the hands at the turban; the head drooped towards his right shoulder. From the back, there was just the tilted head and the broad, square back, firm against the chair. It was difficult to say, however, which aspect indicated his potential strength, for one could also regard him from the sides and remark upon the muscular hardness of his thighs behind the folds of his cotton trousers.

The darkness was increasing about him. Occasionally, he opened his eyes and noticed that one more layer of grey had made the sky blacker; there were also lizards tapping the roofs of their mouths with their tongues. The land breathed out the heat it had inhaled all day.

The oil-lamps being lit within the house cast a general glow upon the front yard where Aziz Khan sat. The land hummed, the plants throbbed; the insect kingdoms were alive; the ants coursed the oceans of mud. Clusters of stars began to appear like gold lettering on the black spine of the sky. Glow-worms hung in the air and these, too, were stars which you could trap in your hand and put into an empty box of matches with a hole in its side and look at the throbbing light within.

In Aziz Khan's mind was the vegetative hopefulness of belief in a fixed order, almost a fatalism which approved only of the sort of routine repetition of which the sun's daily rising and setting were the archetype. But it was night now. The stars had lowered as more and more appeared. So that the land was silhouettes of grey upon black, and the insect sounds were also a necessary animation of the land. Aziz Khan moved, crossed his legs; for even the crystals of earth shifted against one another, for comfort was the gift of darkness.

And he sat there like a lamp in his own land.

Sitting by the clay stove in the kitchen, his wife served dinner to Rafiq and Javed. She did not herself eat as yet. Always, Aziz Khan ate first in that small kitchen, sitting on a mat on the floor, and then the sons. She ate last. She sat there, her black hair knotted in broad plaits, the coarse skin of her face broken at the cheeks and the forehead with pock-marks. She was a heavy woman who gave from the generosities of her flesh, the rolled layers of fat around her stomach.

'There was a letter from Zuleikha today,' she said, passing a *chapati* to Rafiq, although he had not asked for another one. 'She's having her second this summer.'

Rafiq laughed through a mouthful of food. Javed flicked his eyebrows and said, 'They should send their boy here some time. When he grows up.'

'That will be nice,' the mother said, stirring the contents of a pot with a ladle, on the point of scooping out a ladleful for whichever of the two plates appeared wanting.

Rafiq gulped some water and said, 'Yes, Zuleikha would like it, too. At least I should think so. She was the most attached to this house, more than the other sisters.'

'She might have changed,' Javed said. 'Two years in Karachi and who wants to live without a radio?'

The mother said, 'Yes, she might have changed. She's been married five years now. But there's no time to listen to the radio here even if we had electricity one day.'

'Oh, I don't know,' Rafiq said. 'We could have a

loudspeaker outside and listen while we worked in the fields.'

'The sound wouldn't carry,' Javed said. 'Not down to the rice field and I hardly think any farther than the cotton plantation.'

'Depends which way the wind's blowing,' Rafiq said.

'Ah, don't be a duffer, you know the wind doesn't blow here,' Javed said with some irritation in his voice. 'We're lucky to have a whiff of air in the evenings.'

'We could have two loudspeakers, then,' persisted Rafiq, who knew that modern technology was capable of anything. 'Why, even three.'

The ladle came down with a splash into Rafiq's plate and filled it with lamb curry. He broke a piece off a *chapati*, holding it at the edge between his thumb and fingers, and went on eating.

'I wonder what the buffaloes would make of it?' Javed mused.

'About what?' the mother asked.

'Why, the radio, of course,' Javed said.

'Oh, that!'

'They might dry up,' Rafiq suggested, laughing.

'No more for me,' said Javed, anticipating an imminent rapier thrust of the ladle directed, ultimately, at his belly.

The mother looked astonished at this, but did not press.

'We met the youngest of the Shah brothers on our way back,' Rafiq said. 'He was out on a drive. They still want to buy our land.'

'Some people can never have enough,' the mother said with some show of vehemence.

'They're a greedy bunch,' said Javed who had learned to wring the necks of chickens when he was five.

'Oh, we didn't tell you,' Rafiq said, 'we saw their wives go past in a car just when we were getting into town.'

'Yes,' said Javed. 'The two wives, and we found out that the third one is a cousin who might marry the youngest brother. She was looking out of the window. The others had their sari-ends across their faces. But she was looking out. She looked sad.'

'Mother, I think Javed has fallen for her,' Rafiq said.

The mother would have blushed for Javed if she did not know of the propensity of her sons to tease each other with hypothetical marital prospects.

'It's a pity they haven't a grown-up daughter to match with you,' Javed said to Rafiq. 'Listen, Mother, why don't you ask Zuleikha to find Rafiq a wife in Karachi? There's no one left here except the peasants.'

Rafiq cleared his throat since this suggestion seemed to be a plausible one to his mother as was obvious from her contemplative silence. Clearing his throat was the last thing Rafiq did at a meal, as a sort of expression of thanks for the dinner, before he left the kitchen to go to wash his mouth in the bathroom. Javed followed him out.

The mother now rose slowly, pressing a hand against a wall for support. Her cotton tunic shirt came to her knees, and a *shalwar* covered her legs to below the ankles. A piece of gauze material hung over her shoulders and sometimes she covered her head with it or drew it across the face as a veil. She cleared the plates and glasses from the floor and washed them at the end of the kitchen opposite to the stove where a bucket of water lay by a hole at the bottom of the wall through which dirty water drained out. She served herself some curry and, taking the *chapatis* from where they were kept warm in the oven, began to eat. It was perhaps indicative of her character that she did not leave the washing-up until she had herself finished eating.

Like her husband, she was grateful to her sons. They could be so entertaining. She had never quite understood the silent world of her husband. She had accepted him always in the same way as she had done when the match was first announced to her by her parents, with a stoical willingness. And when he first saw her on their wedding-night, she was afraid of the pock-marks. But he had not complained, had hardly said anything to suggest that he had been disappointed. Often, until their last child was born, he had breathed into her all the heat he had imbibed while working on the land; since then, he had chosen to sit outside until his muscles relaxed. And if his breath spoke to her at night, she was never awake enough to hear.

Zakia squatted cross-legged on the floor and ate. There were these new people, the Shah brothers and their family. Someone had told her that they brushed their teeth with a white paste; she hardly thought it possible since *neem* trees were so abundant and a twig off one, with its bitter juice, served so handily for cleaning teeth. But they had money to spend, she supposed, and therefore had to invent ways of spending it, whereas it was clear to her that nature had made man independent by placing him in a chain of interdependence with the vegetable and animal life around him. Zakia had never seen the Shah women and was curious enough to want to be a fly in their drawing-room; just for one evening to hear their talk. They must have many things to talk about since they did no work. She had heard that the wife of the eldest brother was childless, and thought that she must be exceedingly clever, having neither work nor children to take up her time. Her sons knew so little about women, she sighed, sucking at the shreds of lamb in her teeth. Ah, a marriage could be counted upon to provide quite an occasion. Especially a son's marriage.

She had only conducted the marriages of her three daughters from this house, but a son's marriage would be quite something. She must write to Zuleikha about Rafiq; she wondered if a suitable match could be made in Karachi, for there would be few girls wanting to give up their radios and cinemas to come to toil in Kalapur. Yet, Rafiq needed to be married soon, for Javed was no longer a child, and how many years was it since Javed crawled about the front yard while she sat there churning butter? Yes, she would write to Zuleikha at any rate, she determined to herself as she heard her sons go out of the back of the house for their customary after-dinner stroll.

Rafiq and Javed walked towards the stream, past the household beasts.

'Do you know what mother is going to do?' Javed asked.

'What?'

They walked along the stream.

'She's going to write to Zuleikha to find our big brother a wife.'

'Come off it,' Rafiq said, bemused nevertheless.

'I bet you she is.'

'And what if she is? Which decent girl would want to leave Karachi for a peasant's life?'

Rafiq, apparently, had already thought about it.

'Oh, I don't know,' Javed said. 'For people in cities, the country must be a sort of heaven.'

'A place without a cinema is no one's idea of heaven nowadays,' Rafiq said.

'I thought you didn't care for city life yourself.'

'No, I don't. Do you?'

'Not really,' Javed said. 'I suppose we're used to this life.'

'Yes, I suppose so.'

They were some distance from the house now. Javed looked back furtively at the house and the darkness made it appear much farther than it was.

'All right,' he said in a whisper, 'let's light them now.'

Neither of the brothers smoked in front of the parents, it being the habit of the community in which they were born that one did not smoke in the presence of one's parents until one was found out and that one tried not to be found out. They sat on the bank of the stream and Rafiq brought out a packet of cigarettes.

'Damn!' he exclaimed. 'I've left the matches behind.'

'Shit!' Javed said as one who had been let down on an important mission.

After a pause in which they overcame their disappointment, Rafiq said, 'You fancied that cousin of the Shah brothers, didn't you?'

'You're damn right I did. Who wouldn't?'

'Why don't you ask mother to ask for her hand. There won't be this problem of the land then.'

'That'll be great,' Javed said. 'Can you imagine me riding to their house on the wedding day while she zooms out in a car? No, there are only peasants left for us.'

'Some of the peasant women are damn pretty, if you ask me,' Rafiq said.

'I wonder what it's like,' Javed said.

'What?'

'Screwing, what else?' Javed said.

'The riddle goes that it's sweeter than sherbet and bitterer than the *neem* root.'

'Damn the riddle, I'd like to know what it's like.'

'You'll find out,' Rafiq said. 'I don't know myself. You know what I'd like to do? I'd like to find a peasant girl and screw her by this bank.'

'You've got a thing about the peasants, haven't you?'

'They're damn' pretty,' Rafiq said.

They remained silent then. Some years earlier, their talk about sex had led them to experiment with each other, but they were vaguely convinced that it did not approximate to the real thing. Such fraternal homosexuality is not uncommon in Pakistan where women are so strictly guarded that, until they are married, they cannot utter two words to a man without blushing or giggling or going pale; but Rafiq and Javed had abandoned these approaches towards sexual experience on hearing one day in the bazaar that such practices led to blindness.

The brothers remained silent until they returned. The stream gurgled mildly on in its course. Occasionally a crow cawed, thrusting an insomniac beak out of the black blanket of the night. Thin pencil lines of light hung from the stars, but the land was in total darkness. Sounds came quickly, sharply, from the insect world. And there were the ghostly forms of the cotton-plants and the sugarcanes, which, to the brothers, had a distinct reality; even in the darkness, they could have found their way to any one of the plants, for each plant had a clear identity in their minds, and the land a definite substantial image.

3

Zarina detested the bridge party at Mansur's and was glad for Afaq that he had not come to it. The pauses in the game whenever a player contemplated his hand and considered his bid, induced a feeling of suffocation in her and she wished that she had Afaq's stubborn sense of independence. She watched Razia pout her lips and screw up her eyes at her cards, she heard her sigh and click her tongue and occasionally mutter *Hai Allah!* in feigned despair at her hand; she watched Ayub's left foot tapping the carpet impatiently as he waited for his partner to announce her bid; and there was Mansur, praising Akram's each move, carrying courtesy to the point of sycophancy; Faridah sat with Mansur's wife, Azra, not daring to open the volumes of gossip for fear of disturbing the game. And she herself, Zarina thought bitterly, was not even a spectator, but only an item of the Shah brothers' property which they carried with them. She resented her position although she knew that she ought to feel grateful to be in the best Pakistani society. She knew so little of herself, being always alone! She pitied herself for her loneliness. She had no memory of her parents and seemed always to have been wherever Akram and Faridah had taken her. She remembered Bombay with affection, their little two-roomed flat in Mahim where six of them had lived together, for ever getting in one another's way. There, she could stand on the balcony and look at the cars go past in the street and the people who came to the restaurant which was below their flat. Always, there had been something of interest happening, even if it was only a man spitting on the pavement. She had had close friends at the school in Bandra where the nuns had been kind. She had written to some of her friends and had joyously received letters from them, but distance had eventually annihilated the personalities behind the words and she realised that she could not continue to alleviate her loneliness with paper and ink, which were poor substitutes for flesh and blood. The only school in Kalapur had been considered too common for her by the brothers and consequently her education was now neglected, for Ayub had convinced Akram that it would be wrong to send her to a boarding school in Lahore; she did not know that what had clinched his argument was his statement that since she would have one of the largest dowries in Pakistan, whether she married within the family or outside it, she did not need a B.A. to ensure a husband for herself. Often withdrawn into the loneliness of her room, from where the view was of the large garden, she felt uncertain of her place in the family and in the society which the family attracted to itself. She was certain of nothing, having no image in her mind which she could identify as her parents so that she could give her own reality a place in the world. She saw the continuity of generations in other people's families and felt herself to be suspended in spatial emptiness. Having no past other than being in an alien family, she increasingly dreamed of a future which would be creatively her own. Out of this self-absorbed dreaming, she had constructed the one certainty which gave her pleasure and on which she rested her hopes: that she was in love with Afaq. How well they were matched! she would often say to herself with a thrill. They had grown up together and there were pictures in the family album in which he, a boy of ten, was carrying her frail little body on his shoulders. There were times when they had teased each other and quarrelled; but the relationships permitted by childhood were now denied her by his adulthood and by her being almost of marriageable age. Yet, tonight he had asked her to dance, and, although she was glad to have been saved the embarrassment of having to make a decision, she was almost convinced that his silences when he sat near her were a sign that he was secretly in love with her. She wished she could have gone with him in the jeep and been driven fast by him along a straight road with a cool wind blowing through her hair until she was dazed with ecstasy. Oh, if only she could be sure that he loved her! Yes, he did, of course he did; why else did he never speak to her?

'Zarina, you never say anything,' she heard Azra's shrill voice say and she noticed that they were all rising to go to the dining-room.

At last the game of bridge had ended and she blushed a little, smiling weakly in answer to Azra, who went on to state, 'Tariq wrote to say he misses you and Afaq.'

Tariq, who was in Lahore at the university, was her son, and Azra's remark, although she had tried to camouflage it by mentioning Afaq as well, could only be interpreted by the company as meaning that she was tentatively coupling her son's name with Zarina.

Lest the Shah brothers take offence at his wife's presumption, Mansur, giving her a quick glance as if to say, 'Don't spoil our chances with your stupid haste,' said a little too loudly: 'He's doing very vell vith his la.' But his own remark, he realised no sooner than he had uttered it, seemed to be recommending not his son's potential as a future barrister but his suitability as a husband for Zarina. The notion did not escape Zarina, who was trying to recall the last time she saw Tariq without being able to focus on a particular event; now that she thought of him, she found it difficult even to imagine his face. Mansur was disturbed that no one replied and that his visitors only smiled condescendingly.

'Akram Shah sahib, you and Ayub-*ji* must come to shikar vith me next vinter,' Mansur said when they sat down to dinner.

'Shikar, eh,' Ayub said in a tone of voice a little cautious for him.

'Yes,' Mansur went on, his broad-cheeked face bulging with rice. 'Such shikar, such shikar, you von't place any belief in it, I tell you.'

'Up in the north?' Akram asked.

'No, no,' Mansur said just when he was on the point of swallowing a mouthful, so that he choked and coughed out some rice on to his plate. Azra took the opportunity to inquire of Razia if she had seen *Peyton Place*.

'Such a byutifull fillem,' she declared. But Mansur said to Akram, 'No, in East Pakistan, near Chittagong. Such shikar! Deer, not only deer, but the *bara-singha*, the tvelve-hahrned antler, oh, vhat an animal, Allah's own byuty. And there are tigers too, real man-eaterrs, I tell you, vhich terrorise whole villages.'

Mansur paused to thrust a spoonful of rice and chicken into his mouth and Ayub said, 'Interesting, most interesting. But tell me, Mansur-*bhai* . . .' He paused to swallow and Mansur felt flattered that Ayub should address him as a brother even though the suffix *bhai* was commonly used between any two men. 'Tell me, aren't there hurricanes and such things in East Bengal in the winter?'

'True,' Mansur readily agreed. 'Most true. Indeed, the last vun vas most tragic. I sent five thousand rupees to the relief fund. It vas most tragic. But a rare occurrence, only recently become most freqvent. The month of November, however, I can gerr-aunty you is perfectly safe.'

Hearing Ayub use the word *bhai* for her husband, Azra felt prompted to adopt its feminine equivalent when addressing Faridah and Razia, and she quickly rejected Razia's preference for Bette Davis, saying, 'No, no, oh, no, no, no, *baji*-Faridah you vill agree vith me that there is no vun to beat Joan Crafudd in a drummatic role.'

'*Hai Allah!*' Faridah agreed emphatically. 'Those fillems ve used to see in Bombay, vith Joan Crafudd. Gass-light, I remember Gass-light.'

'I'm sure that wasn't Joan Crowforrd,' Razia said, flaunting her superior accent. 'That was Merrle Oberrun.'

'Not Merrle Ob'raan!' the other two cried out simultaneously, and Azra went on, 'It vas deffinutly not Merrle Ob'raan.'

'Oh, I remember,' Razia said, 'it was that Swedish actress.'

'Sveedish?' Azra questioned fiercely.

'Yes,' Razia said, grasping at a name. 'Yes, it was Anita Ekburrg.'

'No, it was Ingrid Bergman and the hero was Joseph Cotten,' Zarina said in a low voice, looking at a pickled chilli and wondering whether she should torment her tongue with it.

When they returned home that evening, Zarina noticed that the jeep was still missing. Afaq had not yet come home. She was both pleased and disturbed, pleased because had he been at home, he would have been asleep by now and she would not have seen him till morning and now there was a chance that when she heard him come, she could perhaps be coming out of the bathroom; and yet she was worried that he should be out so late. She could only think that he was too much in love with her to find peace at home and she wondered where he went and how he consoled himself.

She went to her room and sat in front of her dressing-table mirror, slowly brushing her hair, deferring undressing until after he had returned. She looked at herself and wondered if he found her beautiful. She was so thin! Her face was narrow and there were never any dimples on her cheeks when she smiled. She tried smiling at herself but could produce no dimples. She raised her head and looked at herself through narrow eyes, proudly silent like a model facing a camera. She shook her head so that a lock of hair casually fell across her forehead. She shook her head violently in a theatrical gesture of passionate and excruciating longing, holding her mouth open as though she were letting out an immense sigh. She pressed her arms against her sides and stooped slightly forward, letting her body convulse with imagined sobs at the parting of her lover from whom she had been cruelly separated by fate. She went through the repertoire of an Indian actress.

What would he do if he came in now? she wondered. How would he tell her that he loved her? Would he hold her hand, would he take her in his arms as couples did in American films? Once these questions had exhausted themselves, she looked again at herself.

She decided to cry and to watch herself crying.

She found it difficult to force a tear. She tried sitting with her head in her hands, her fingers riffling her hair. She made low moaning sounds to herself. But the tears would not come. She rose then and stood by the window. The stars shone brightly. Perhaps he had parked his jeep somewhere and was looking at the stars, too, she thought. She felt sad. She pitied herself. And before she realised it, the tears had come of their own; now that she wanted to look at the stars and to speak to them, wish of them an eternity for herself, the tears came. She turned and threw herself at her bed, burying her face in a pillow. She was weeping now, crying bitterly. She was still sobbing when she heard the jeep come up the drive. She drew a sheet to her eyes and heard him jump out of the jeep. She was standing in front of the mirror looking at her own wretchedness when she heard him hastily climbing up the steps; she could tell he was taking three steps at a time, for he was up on the landing in four quick thuds against the carpet on the stairs. She was tormenting herself for making herself look so miserable, for the tears had made her eye make-up run down her cheeks, when she heard him shut his door.

'We'll have to do something about Afaq,' said Akram to his wife, for they, lying in bed, had also heard him come up.

'He's becoming a vild vun,' Faridah said.

'Yes,' Akram said, 'a *junglee*.'

'I donno vhat's come in his head.'

'He needs to get married, that's all.'

'But who's there of our stah-tus?' Faridah asked. 'If the Iqbals in Lahore had a dahter!'

'Them? What could they offer? A Morris perhaps and ten thousand rupees with luck. No, it will have to be some Minister with money in Switzerland.'

64

Her suggestion turned down, Faridah changed the subject. 'Did you hear that Azra voman gassing about her son. Such *imm*pu-dens!'

'Yes, I noticed. She wants Zarina for her Tariq.'

'Such cheek,' Faridah said, making a mock attempt to spit in the darkness.

'Yes,' Akram said. 'I'd rather give Zarina to one of Aziz Khan's sons.'

Faridah was delighted that Akram should use the lowest term of abuse from his vocabulary for putting Azra in her place, and she turned to him with tenderness.

'The will of Allah will be done,' he said in a characteristic Muslim reliance on chance, uttering the phrase which ends many conversations and shelves many problems.

He was soon asleep but she lay awake for some time, regretting that they did not have any children of their own. Her regret was deeper than that produced by their inability to have a child; it was a remorse which was abated only by the reflection of her material comfort. Sometimes she wondered how their marriage had withstood fifteen years of sterility. There had been times when materially they were poor, or at least at that level of lower middle-class strife where poverty is a constant hazard. There had been affection between them, perhaps love; but their relationship had suffered from a crucial lack.

Akram had married her in the hope that a reasonable dowry might enhance his capital and give him a chance to speculate in the stock market. She had not been beautiful and her parents had been anxious for her future, for she was already twenty-eight then. Faridah recalled the wedding, especially the day before when she had to be consoled by her mother, for she had protested that she could not bear the imminent parting; the sorrow had been mingled with an expectant happiness, for there would be a future entirely of her own making. She knew little about men and nothing about love-making, except that certain things happened. The marriage night, when her heart was louder with its throbs than the monosyllables with which she tried to answer her husband, was less eventful than she had expected. Akram had found poetic words with which to thank Allah for her beauty, but had soon said that the wedding celebrations had tired him and had gone to sleep. And then it had been the day of her ritual, symbolic return to her parents' house where her girl-friends had, in the traditional manner of euphemistic talk about sex, teased her about her new experiences. She had blushed and they, not knowing that she blushed for her husband's failure, took it as evidence of experience and teased her all the more till she was driven to tears. Which was traditionally in character, too. Returning finally to her husband's house, she was happy when he kissed her on going to bed the first night. He had essayed into love-play and she felt it her duty to protest when his hand reached for her breast. On the second night, she reluctantly allowed herself to be undressed. The same procedure went on during successive nights until she was emboldened to slip a hand through his pyjama shirt to touch his naked back. They were now familiar enough with each other for her to ask, timidly and obliquely, why he did not also undress. If it was for her to perform that duty, she said, she would willingly attempt it, but she was innocent and awaited his instruction. 'It can wait,' he had said. 'The ecstasy comes in the waiting.' When, some days later, she could bear his procrastination no longer, she had refused him to touch her. She turned away and pretended to be asleep and when he did not approach her, she rose, switched on the light and railed at him for being weak and cowardly. 'Is this marriage? Are ve husband and vife? Are you a man?' she had cried savagely. 'I have to take the man's part in this bed. I have to tell you vhere to put your hand. Don't you know nothing? Haven't you seen dogs? Didn't your boy-friends ever tell you?' He had flinched and bit his lip, and said calmly, 'I have too much experience, Faridah. I'm sorry. The truth is horrible.' She had gone pale at this mysterious statement which, she sensed, had a tragic undertone. Then he told her the horrible truth, that, for her sake, he hoped she never saw his private parts which had been ravaged by venereal disease.

Razia and Ayub had also been awake when Afaq was heard to come up.

'That bastard will be the ruin of this family,' Ayub said. 'What does he think he is, a nawab or something, coming home at this time?'

'He's only a child,' Razia tried to defend her youthful brother-in-law now that her husband was so vehemently abusing him.

'He knows nothing,' Ayub said. 'He has no experience and he tries to be so damn big.'

'But he *is* big,' Razia said. 'He is your brother.'

'My brother!' Ayub exclaimed, almost ready to disown him.

'We should find him a nice wife,' Razia said.

'He can marry Zarina,' Ayub said.

'Did you notice what Azra said?'

'She's bloody mistaken if she thinks we'll give Zarina to her Tariq. She's building castles in the air, I tell you. She thinks she can get a palace for her old age if she can win Zarina for that miserable son of hers. No, we'll keep Zarina in the family, marry her off to Afaq.'

'Why don't we announce their engagement?' Razia asked.

'No, not yet. Let Afaq grow up first. And Zarina. How old is she? Sixteen? Seventeen? No, let her grow up first.'

'In the meanwhile torture the Mansurs?' said Razia, smiling.

'Yes,' said Ayub, laughing aloud, for he relished the notion of torturing his friends. 'Let's make them believe that we find their hints of matching Zarina and Tariq pleasing.'

They were silent for a few minutes. Then he said, 'I wish we had a son.'

'It's Allah's will we had two daughters,' she said. 'Perhaps we'll have a son next.'

'We need sons,' he said as though he was giving a directive at the mills that he needed more labourers. 'Akram will never come up with one.'

Like everyone else, he assumed that either Akram or Faridah was sterile. For Akram had maintained the Islamic pretence that childlessness was no fault of his but was a result of some curse, some devilry; he and Faridah had visited holy shrines where the priests had touched her with sacred emblems to render her fertile and prayed over both of them. Such pilgrimages were no hypocrisy on their part, for who knew but Allah, in his divine wisdom, might not bring about a transformation in Akram's condition? But Ayub was enough of a realist to know that a couple who had not reproduced in fifteen years was not likely to have a child from nowhere. Consequently, he was happy for his own two daughters and hoped that Razia would not only next present him with a son but also continue to produce his progeny so that the Shah empire would ultimately belong primarily to his branch of the family. He turned to her with these thoughts and she, sensing his thoughts, opened herself to his firm grip with the facility of an unlocked door. Though sometimes she found Ayub an ordeal she must suffer for the sake of advancing her own designs of establishing a dynasty. She could love him now but too often could not restrain the annoyance he aroused in her by being too overtly bullying in his attitude; even with her.

In his own room, Afaq lay on his bed, exhausted from his journeys into darkness, dazed now with the hours of hypnotic following of the beam of the jeep's headlamps. And also disgusted with himself. A man had come up to him in a village on the main road outside Kalapur where he had stopped to put water in the radiator. He had wondered if the sahib would like a little something. He had taken him to a deserted, wayside place where there were two huts and introduced him to a man he called *Chacha*, uncle. There were large earthen jars of country liquor and he had been offered the choice of two women, one no more than a girl of fifteen while the other could well have been her mother.

And yet he could not sleep now and lay tossing as though he was still in the jeep, bouncing over rough territory.

4

It was four in the afternoon and Rafiq had just set out on the two-mile walk to the town. The horses were being used on the land, so he had to walk. He could have waited until one horse was free, which would have been in another half an hour, but he would have had to rest the horse before the journey, and even if he walked slowly now, he would reach the town earlier than he would have done on the horse, bearing in mind the duration of the horse's rest. He was in some urgency, for Hussain, the broker through whom Aziz Khan sold his cotton, had neglected to honour a debt of two thousand rupees which had been outstanding for five months. Aziz Khan needed the money, for he had to pay his peasants, some of whom were threatening to leave if their wages were not paid by the end of the month. Hussain had ignored several applications to pay up, and when three of Aziz Khan's labourers had returned late from their lunch and said insolently to his stern admonition of their lateness, 'Vhat do ve verk for, vere's ar vages?' Aziz Khan had turned to Rafiq and said, 'Go to Hussain and ask him to pay up or else we'll do business with someone else.' Rafiq had returned to the house, quickly bathed himself and worn a clean shirt. He had determined, for he liked to calculate the manner of his commitment in the immediate future, that it would take him half an hour to reach Hussain if he walked quickly and forty-five minutes if he walked at his usual pace; a horse, therefore, was quite unnecessary. He knew that he should not walk too hastily, for the exercise in the afternoon's heat would make him out of breath, so that his pace would not be constant throughout the journey and also he would have to stand outside Hussain's office for a few minutes to regain his breath; if he walked normally, however, he would not have to stand outside, nor need to pause at a restaurant for a glass of water, so that the eventual time he would have taken since leaving the house and speaking to Hussain would be the same whether he walked with the urgency his mission required or slowly which his reasoning told him was not any slower. He liked to think in real and not relative terms. So, now he was walking slowly, formulating in his mind an opening sentence with which to confront Hussain.

He considered: 'Mr Hussain, you are a blackguard.'

Was Mr Hussain indeed a blackguard? he wondered. Undoubtedly he was. If he opened with that remark, he would be telling the truth. Therefore, he had better not open with that remark.

He considered next: 'How are you, Mr Hussain? Not too hot, I trust?'

This clearly would not do, for he would have to be smiling in uttering the statement and that would imply a degree of familiarity between him and Mr Hussain which would diminish the severity of his message, for his message was going to be a severe one since he knew that Hussain would not hand him over two thousand rupees in cash immediately and that he would have to leave empty-handed and that, therefore, it would be necessary for him to be stern from the moment he entered his office.

He could try: 'Are you too busy, Mr Hussain, that you can't send what you owe my father?'

No, this was obviously insulting the man, and he must begin amicably.

'Good afternoon, Hussain sahib. I think you can guess what I have come for?'

Perhaps, if he could make a joke of it at the same time, this was a suitable approach? Perhaps he could go on to say, 'Difficult times, eh? Ha, ha, ha.' No. Why was it that you always had to make a joke when demanding money which you were owed?

Rafiq was walking in the middle of the road, for there was no traffic. The road was made of stones, chipped bits of granite. It used to be dirt during his childhood when the only traffic on it consisted of bullock-carts, laden with his father's cotton, making their annual procession to Kalapur. Then, peasants had been recruited at twenty rupees a month for half a year to lay stones on the road. But there had been no steam-roller to press them into place. The road was narrow and there were two grooves on its either side where the passing of the occasional jeep had compressed the stones. The middle of the road was slightly humped as a result and the stones there were loose. He kicked one accidentally and watched it lodge itself in a tyre-track. He walked over, picked it up and placed it again in the middle of the road.

Perhaps he would not need an opening remark, for Hussain might say, 'Ah, Rafiq, come in, come in, my young man. I was just going to send my man with the two thousand rupees. My apologies to your father, my thousand apologies for the delay in making this remittance. How are you, Rafiq? Everything okay?' It would be pleasant if Hussain were to say that but his likelihood of doing so was far less than a sudden rainfall which had never been known to occur here in the month of March. Rafiq frowned. He had already reached the junction where the stone road joined the main, metalled road beside the Shah brothers' mills.

He walked along the high stone wall of the mills and could have, if he raised his left hand, touched the wall. The stone had a roughness which made him want to scrape his thumb-nail along it. It was a long wall, perhaps five hundred yards long, he could not tell, and it would have helped to walk past it more quickly if he could, say, scrape his thumb-nail every third time he put his right foot forward. Would his thumb-nail be bruised? he wondered. Perhaps he could rest his thumb-nail every sixth time by choosing either his index or his little finger for the sensation of nail-scraping, or all his four fingers either randomly or in a set order or together.

He was annoyed that the wall belonged to the Shah brothers; otherwise, surely, he would not have needed to debate whether or not to scrape one or all five of the nails of his left hand. He owed it to his family not to touch anything which belonged to the Shah brothers; why, it was because of them that he was on this walk, worrying about what to say to Hussain; otherwise, he would not have thought about it at all but gone on scraping his nails. Perhaps he would have walked backwards for part of the distance along the wall, for he was sure that the nails on his right hand would not for long have borne the agony of not being scraped along the wall. Suppose he overcame his hesitance, suppose he assumed that the Shah brothers meant his family well; well, he could be absent-minded for a minute, who was to know; suppose he accidentally scraped all the five nails of his left hand in one sweeping arc? No, family honour was family honour. He stopped, looked around that no one was there to observe him, stooped on the edge of the road and hurriedly scraped all his ten nails on the rough road surface, and walked on. Soon he laughed at himself for the things he needed to invent on these tedious journeys.

He went past the gate of the mills, looking determinedly ahead, and when he had gone beyond the gate, he regarded the wall with indifference now that he had overcome the nail-scraping urge. He was more preoccupied with his right index finger which had been slightly cut at the extremity during his hasty scraping. He was just going to suck it when he recalled the propensity of bullocks to urinate as they walk along with their creaking carts. So, he placed his hands at his back, clasping his left wrist with his right hand and occasionally reversing the position.

In all these actions, Rafiq tried to be just to those parts of his body of which he had two members. If he rubbed his left eye for some reason, to expunge a fleck of dust perhaps, he would rub his right eye with exactly the same pressure and in exactly the same manner; if at night he had to insert his right little finger into his right ear-hole after a mosquito had buzzed there, he had to insert his left little finger into his left ear-hole. Such attempts to remain impartial, to show favours to no one member of his body in particular, may perhaps be considered compulsive; but Afaq, when he met him a few days earlier, had been wrong in thinking of him as a simpleton. A man who thought of the nail on his little finger with such serious concern as often to be driven to a state of

anxiety about it can only be described as a highly sophisticated mechanism.

He was once again holding his right wrist in his left hand
when he reached the bazaar and found his way to Hussain's
office. The word *office* is, of course, a misnomer, for no petty
businessman in Pakistan has an office separate from his house
or flat. Often, it is a one-roomed flat with the businessman's
children running about it, a mother, the businessman's or
his wife's, sometimes both, sitting importantly in a corner
and the wife squatting on the floor, picking out the tiny
stones which are added by shopkeepers to rice and lentils
much as wine is adulterated in western countries—for it
must be a universally verifiable truth that petty fraud accom-
panies petty business.

Hussain had a first-floor flat in a small building. Rafiq
went up the dark staircase, under which a peanut vendor
had made his house, and reached Hussain's door in one
breath, for the lavatory on the ground floor, which was used
as a public convenience by the various shopless vendors in
the bazaar, smelt strongly. Hussain's door was open as usual,
and as soon as he entered, Rafiq saw Hussain in bed on the
far end of the room. There was a door by the bed leading to
the balcony which looked over the bazaar, but this door was
shut and consequently it was quite dark in the room. When
Rafiq stepped in, he hit against something and almost
stumbled. A child screamed and Rafiq realised that he had
kicked Hussain's two-year-old son, the fourth of the broker's
children.

'*Yah Allah!*' an elderly voice cried. 'Vhat vizzeterrs are
these? Come hyere, my *balloo*, come hyere, my *batcha*.'

The voice, which went on to make clicking sounds which
are considered to placate children, belonged to Hussain's
mother who was sitting leaning against the wall a yard in
front of the bed. Rafiq saw her now; at least he saw two eyes
nailing a toothless face to the wall; and also saw the child go
bawling to her. He reached in his trouser pocket to see if he
had anything he could offer the child to pacify it. He usually

kept what change he carried in his right pocket, but, in justice to his left hand, he thrust both his hands into his pockets. He had not noticed when he saw Hussain's mother, for his eyes were still adjusting themselves to the light and so far had only distinguished the less nebulous forms, that she sat with her legs stretched full out in front of her so that they were exactly parallel to Hussain's bed. Just when Rafiq put both his hands into his pockets, his left foot struck the obstruction created by the mother's right calf resting comfortably on the floor and Rafiq fell forwards and the mother gave out a short, suppressed scream. Not, however, having his hands immediately available to check his fall, which he would have done by placing his hands as buffers on the edge of the bed, he fell face first upon Hussain's stomach.

'Ah, Rafiq, vhat brings you hyere?' Hussain asked while Rafiq's face was momentarily buried in his stomach.

'*Amma*,' Hussain cried out to his wife who was in the adjoining kitchen. '*Amma*, cha for the vizziterr. And bring a cup for me.'

While Rafiq essayed to take his hands out of his pockets and to stand up, the other three children suddenly appeared in the room and began to shout 'Unkulla 'fiq, unkulla 'fiq, unkulla 'fiq.'

'Vhat is it you all vant?' Hussain shouted at the children. 'Vhat *tamasha* is this? *Allah-ji*, these chillrun!'

'*Yah Allah!*' the mother spoke again. 'Let the chillrun greet their uncle. Allah knows vhat presents he has braht them.'

'Unkulla 'fiq, unkulla 'fiq, unkulla 'fiq,' the chorus resumed itself shrilly with increased vigour now that the grandmother had sanctioned its presence.

'Ah, Rafiq!' Hussain said. 'You come so rarely, *bhai*, vhat's the matter? Ve don't have a plague in this house. Vhat's the matter, *bhai*, vhat's the matter? You don't like your nephews and nieces any more? *Amma*,' he shouted to the next room, 'send Ali to bring some sveetmeats. Allah knows ve do our best for our chillrun's uncle. Vell, Rafiq,

74

say something. Vhy you so silent, *bhai*, vhat do you say? How's Javed? Chillrun, ask how your uncle Javed is.'

'How's unkulla' ved?' cried several voices loudly.

'Vell, tell them, *bhai*. And how's big uncle Khan sahib, Allah prahsperr'ng him all right?'

'How's unkull Ffan sahib?' the children cried.

'You shy, *bhai*? You lost your tongue to some sveetheart? *Amma*, have you sent for those sveetmeats yet? *Vell*, and *begum sahiba*, how's she?'

'May Allah answer her pray-yers,' the grandmother said.

'Come, chillrun, come to your uncle,' Hussain said. 'Sit down, Rafiq, sit down, *bhai*, make it your own bed. Come on.'

Rafiq sat down on the edge of the bed. He had found four annas in his pocket with which he had intended to buy himself a lemonade on his way back, but philosophically distributed these to the children, who ran wildly out, screaming with delight. He was genuinely lost for words for a time; if Hussain had deliberately planned to upset him, he would not have better succeeded.

'Allah forbid, you are not ill I hope?' he managed clumsily to say at last when Hussain's wife, a veil across her face, had come in and served tea and retired.

'Allah knows,' the mother answered for Hussain. 'I keep telling him pour oil on the door hinges, how can you keep coming and going through that door vithout putting oil on the hinges, he's bound to be sick. The devil cursing us aal the damn' time, ve got to put oil.'

'It's the ulsas, *bhai*,' Hussain said. 'The dahcterr says it's the ulsas and Allah knows I paid him three rupees to find that out. Ulsas, he said, drink milk, eat yogurt, avoid bananas and mangoes, do press-ups five times in the mornings and five times in the evenings, eat cahd-liver oil on aal ahd days of the month, have a strong purgative every Sunday, thank you, that vill be three rupees. Vhat a dahcterr, I tell you, a real professional, a smart guy, takes vun look at you and says it's the ulsas. Ah, if I had that education, *bhai*, I'd be rich. Three rupees in vun minute, that's education. He sees maybe a hundred patients a day, that's three hundred bucks gross And aal you got to do is to know vhen a man's got ulsas.'

'Allah knows your father vanted you to be a dahcterr,' Hussain's mother said.

'*Amma-ji*, ve become vhat Allah vants to make us,' Hussain said.

'Allah makes us, my son,' the mother said.

'Father was wondering,' Rafiq began, but Hussain hastily interrupted him, '*Hai*, *Amma-ji*, vhy did I have that cuppa cha, oooooh!'

He pressed a hand to his stomach and groaned.

'Oooooh! Three bucks I paid the dahcterr, and he said, plain he said, drink milk, and hyere I go, so carried off seeing my brother, I go and drink tea. Vhat I doing to myself, *Amma-ji*, throwing good money away like that and not taking advice? Oooooh!'

When he had somewhat recovered from this attack, Hussain said, 'You know, Rafiq, *bhai*, I been meaning to pay a cahl to Khan sahib, but aal the cahls I make are to the dahcterr nowadays. Three bucks every time I go out, *bhai*, vhat a life! You know those la-ry contracterrs I hire from Lahore, those crooks who transportise your ca-tun? Allah vill make them pay for their evil vun day. Vun of them got too heated, the injun boiled over, *bhai*, and caht fire. Vell, vhat do you know, the damn truck vent up in flames and it vasn't insured, *bhai*. Can you believe it, in this day and age, the damn truck loaded vith precious cargo vasn't insured? So the crooks who owned the damn la-ry, Allah damn them too, say it vas an accident, an act of Allah they said, Allah damn them, and von't pay the loss and the mill buying the ca-tun says how can it pay for goods and services it never got. I tell you, *bhai*, the whole vorld is cheating me and on the top of that my own stomach is boiling over vith ulsas.'

As soon as he reasonably could, Rafiq took his leave, holding his nose as he walked down the stairs, sickened by the squalid place and its equally execrable inhabitants. It was already evening outside and he took a deep breath on emerging from the building. He was annoyed that far from obtaining anything from Hussain, he had instead lost the four annas he had possessed when he went into his flat. He began soberly to walk towards his house, keeping both his hands in his pockets. He was vexed that Hussain's pack of lies would cause unnecessary anger in his father and lead to considerable inconvenience, for his father would now have to find a way of obtaining the money from Hussain. He himself had not been able to threaten Hussain in any way and he did not know how anyone else could; it was clear to him that Hussain was taking advantage of Aziz Khan's unpopularity with the Shah brothers whose influence in the town made the police indifferent to the landlord's problems. Lost in these melancholy thoughts, he did not hear the jeep come to a halt beside him as he was walking along the wall in front of the mills and he was somewhat taken aback on seeing Afaq greet him with a cheerful smile.

'Where's the horse?' Afaq asked.

'In the fields,' Rafiq replied.

'You're not walking all the way home, are you?'

'Yes, what else can I do?' Rafiq said.

'It's five miles.'

'No, less than two from here.'

'Still, it's a hell of a way to walk,' Afaq said. 'Jump in, I'll give you a lift.'

'No, I can walk. I'm quite used to it, you see.'

'Come, man, it's nothing to me,' Afaq said.

'It's out of your way,' Rafiq said.

'I tell you it's nothing to me,' Afaq said. 'It'll take me two minutes. Come, don't be so shy. We're not enemies.'

For a moment Afaq pondered his own last remark which he had uttered without thinking; perhaps, he thought, it was true that they were not enemies. Rafiq, too, considered the remark as if examining a coin to make sure it was not counterfeit.

'All right,' Rafiq agreed, 'if it's not too much trouble to you.'

'Friendship's never any trouble,' Afaq said, engaging the gear. 'Well, how are you?' he asked, driving on.

'I'm fine, but things are not so good,' Rafiq said, sitting forward on the seat and holding on to the side of the windscreen.

'Sit back, man, and relax,' Afaq said, ignoring Rafiq's admission that things were not well, for Afaq was sure that the statement reflected on his own family. 'Listen, have you ever been in a jeep before?'

'No,' Rafiq said.

'All right, sit back then, and enjoy yourself.'

Instead of turning right where the stone road led to Aziz Khan's property, Afaq drove straight on along the metalled road, pressing the accelerator pedal to the floor-board.

'Watch her take this bend,' he cried above the sound of the jeep.

Rafiq listened to the desperate tyre-squeal and shut his eyes to the trees which seemed about to burst through the windscreen. The tone of the tyres changed and he opened his eyes again to see the road mercifully straight in front of him.

'Where are we going?' he shouted to Afaq.

'Hell, nowhere, just driving. You enjoying it?'

'Yes, it's terrific, but I've got to be home soon.'

'It would have taken you half an hour walking, so enjoy that time here.'

Rafiq lowered himself in the seat so that he could not see through the windscreen. He enjoyed the sensation of speed as long as he could not see the trees almost swinging right into his face whenever Afaq took a bend.

'Wouldn't you like one?' Afaq asked.

'What?'

'Why, a jeep. Look, how you feel every up and down of the road bang on your backside. That's what I like about a jeep. It makes driving real.'

'Have you ever been on a horse?' Rafiq asked.

'No.'

78

'You should try it, it's great.'

'Listen, I'll do a deal with you,' Afaq said, slowing down now. 'You take me horse-riding and I'll teach you to drive.'

'I don't know if I want to learn,' Rafiq said. 'I mean I'll never have a jeep or a car.'

'Hell, don't be so pessimistic.'

'What's that?'

'Never mind. Don't give up the world before you've seen it. Okay, if you don't want to learn, you don't want to learn. Take me horse-riding and I'll take you on drives round the countryside.'

'Okay,' Rafiq said. 'I'll teach you how to ride a horse.'

Afaq brought the jeep slowly to a halt and turned it round.

'Listen,' Afaq said. 'Would you like to come to Lahore?'

'Why?'

'Hell, for no damn' reason. It just occurred to me.'

'I don't like Lahore,' Rafiq said.

'What the hell do you like?' Afaq asked.

'I like the country here, the way we live here.'

'Sure, it's fine,' Afaq said, and added after a moment, 'All right, we won't go to Lahore. Why don't you come out one evening so that we can see what's happening in this damn' town?'

'I'll have to ask my father,' Rafiq said.

'There's nothing to ask, you're old enough, aren't you?'

'Well, maybe I could slip out. We could arrange a time.'

'That's better,' Afaq said. 'Make your decisions yourself is what I say. Fuck older people and their ideas of right and wrong. You've got to be independent, otherwise what's the use of living?'

Rafiq did not know what to say, for neither was he used to such talk nor did he understand it now that he heard it.

'Do you know any place where one could get a screw?' Afaq asked.

'No,' Rafiq said.

'Well, we'll have to find out, won't we?' Afaq said, laughing because of his secret knowledge, and turning too sharply on to the stone road to Aziz Khan's house, so that Rafiq was thrown on to his side. Afaq decided he would like to take Rafiq to the place he knew.

'Don't you like women?' Afaq asked when Rafiq did not reply.

Again Rafiq did not reply and Afaq said, 'Have you ever had a screw?'

'No,' Rafiq said.

'Tried any liquor?'

'No.'

'You haven't lived,' Afaq said. 'Listen, you probably think what I'm talking of is disgusting. Many people think that. But that's what they wish for themselves, anyway.'

They had reached the gate which led to the house and Afaq brought the jeep to a halt. 'Do you think it's disgusting?' he asked.

'I don't know,' Rafiq said, still sitting in the jeep, and repeated, 'I don't know.'

'Would you like to find out? I bet you, in your secret thoughts you've wanted to have a damn' good screw. I bet you, you'd do it too if you got the chance.'

'I don't know.'

'Hell, you mustn't mind me talking like this. You know, my brothers don't like me. My brothers are bastards, I can tell you, bastards. Sometimes I think I don't have a brother, better to have no brothers than the bastards I've got. Do you mind my talking like this? You mustn't. I've got a lot to say that people don't like hearing. So I keep my mouth shut. Why don't you say something? Listen, you must be frank with me. I'm being frank with you. You don't mind my being frank, do you? What the hell is bothering you?'

'I like you,' Rafiq said. 'I hope my father hasn't seen me come in your jeep.'

'Is that bothering you?'

'No,' Rafiq said slowly. 'I went to Kalapur to get some money from our broker. He's owed it to my father for five months.'

Rafiq proceeded to narrate the whole affair, describing how Hussain pretended he was ill. As he told the story, Afaq remembered that Hussain had been coming to the mills and visiting Akram. He wondered if Akram knew that Hussain owed two thousand rupees to Aziz Khan; very likely he did, Afaq thought, and it was even more likely that Akram and Ayub had asked Hussain to pocket the two thousand rupees simply to test Aziz Khan's capacity to obtain justice for himself. Afaq knew that in any ensuing conflict, Aziz Khan would be the loser, for his brothers would see to it that justice was not done because it did not suit them in this instance.

Acting impulsively in reaction to what he considered were his brothers' plans, he said, 'Listen, you tell your father that Hussain has promised to pay you the day after tomorrow. You come out tomorrow night at ten, I'll have the jeep parked some way up the road from here and I'll give you the two thousand.'

'Why should you pay Hussain's debt?'

'Don't worry, I'll get it from him.'

'It'll be great if you can handle Hussain,' Rafiq said, leaving. 'And thank you for bringing me home.'

'That's all right. See you up there at ten tomorrow night,' Afaq said, indicating a point up the road and, turning round, he drove away.

In accepting Afaq's offer, Rafiq did not doubt that Afaq would get the money from Hussain; in making the offer, Afaq did not care about Hussain, his immediate aim being to spite his brothers in a manner which would hurt most. He did not realise, however, that in this decision he was being as much a political intriguer as Ayub and that his politics did not possess his elder brother's subtlety.

On reaching home, Afaq made straight for his room. When he reached the landing, Zarina's door opened and she appeared, hastily shutting the door behind her and walking hurriedly down the steps. She did not look at him. He turned round and watched her go down, puzzled by her haste, and then turned towards his own room. He had hardly reached it when he heard Ayub's voice shout from the drawing-room: 'Afaaaaq!'

'Afaaaaq!' Ayub roared again.

'Coming,' he shouted back and turned to descend the steps. When he reached the foot of the stairs, there was Zarina again, hurriedly returning from whatever mission had taken her from her room, her head hanging low. Afaq took no notice, for they frequently passed each other in the house in the same manner.

'Yes?' he said, entering the drawing-room.

Ayub was alone in the room.

'Is this a guest house?' Ayub asked before Afaq had shut the door behind him. 'Is this a hotel?'

Afaq looked at him coldly and did not reply.

'I'm sorry there's no register for you to sign,' Ayub went on. 'I'm sorry there are no porters to carry your luggage.'

Afaq pouted his lip and looked through the window at the garden.

'Afaq!' Ayub barked.

'Yes?' Afaq said without looking at his brother.

'I'm talking to you.'

'I can hear. I could hear you if I were in my room.'

Ayub rose from the sofa, Afaq noticed through the corner of his eyes.

'I said I'm talking to you,' Ayub said, now standing in front of Afaq.

He had hardly uttered the last word when Ayub's hand sprang up and was swung across his face. Afaq flinched from the slap and looked his brother daringly in the eye, holding his hands firmly to his sides.

'And when I talk to you, I expect you to look at me, not at flowers.'

Afaq continued to look at him in silent anger.

'I asked you is this a hotel that you think you can go when you like and come when you like?'

Afaq stared at him.

82

'Don't you know your duties? Don't you know what reputation we have? Don't you know anything of family honour?'

Afaq slightly screwed up his eyes but did not turn his gaze away.

'What do you want to do, to wreck us? Do you want us to be poor again and live in a two-roomed flat with no servants? Listen, we are a family and our family is also the business and also the house. What happens to the business and what happens in this house is what happens to the family. And whatever we do and whatever we think, we've got to do it all together. Akram and I have sweated our guts out to bring you up, to give you education. Is this how you reward us? By remaining aloof, by not coming to the parties we, as a family, are invited to, by spending half the night loafing about?'

'Why can't I do what I like?' Afaq said.

'Sure, do what you like once you're married. But you can't run about like this, like some *junglee*.'

'What's marriage got to do with it?'

'Everything,' Ayub said. 'Listen, you know very well that even if you were certified mad, no one would hesitate to give his daughter to you because she will be coming into our family, into our wealth. But we can't have a scandal.'

'What's so scandalous about my spending my time on my own?'

'Little brother, you know nothing. Just do as you're told.'

Afaq looked away: as if the light outside could show him what he needed to know. Just then Razia entered and said to Ayub, 'Munni won't go to sleep unless you read her a story. *Hai Allah!* what's one to do with children!'

She noticed Afaq and said, 'Hello, stranger!' and turned again to Ayub, 'And Dolly won't sleep either because of Munni.'

'Afaq, why don't you go and tell them a story?' Ayub asked him.

Afaq looked at Razia's long hair fallen loosely behind her shoulders and said, 'All right.'

He went up to the children's room with Razia, who said on entering, 'Come on now, sweeties, here's uncle Afaq to tell you a story.'

'Kull 'faq!' the two girls screamed with delight.

Afaq drew a chair to the side of the large bed on which both the girls slept and Razia went and sat on a chair by the window.

'Now, what would you like to hear?'

'A shtory,' the elder girl, Munni, said.

'Would you like to hear what happened to the three monkeys?'

The girls vigorously nodded their heads.

'Well, there were three monkeys,' Afaq began. 'They were not any ordinary monkeys. They were three special monkeys. Now, you'll ask what was so special about these monkeys. What was it that made them so different from other monkeys.'

'What?' cried the girls impatiently.

'Now, don't rush me. You can't rush the story. Yes, these monkeys were certainly *very* different. Well, let me tell you. The first monkey was dumb. The second monkey was deaf and the third monkey was blind. Will you remember that?'

'So sad,' Munni said and Dolly, wide-eyed and open-mouthed, clutched the sheet tightly, holding it under her chin.

'Yes, very sad,' Afaq said. 'So, one was dumb, the second deaf and the other blind. These three monkeys lived on a banyan tree in the jungle. The tree was their house. One day they came down from the tree to go to a banana tree, which was some distance away, to get some bananas for their dinner. They were just walking away from their banyan tree when they heard their friend the owl hoot. Now, the owl was the friend of all the birds and monkeys in the jungle, but he was especially the friend of our three monkeys. Why? Because, as you know, they were special monkeys. And so the owl would hoot in case there was danger whenever they had to go for their food. If he hooted once, it meant that there was a wolf about. If he hooted twice, it meant that there was a wild boar in the jungle. And if he hooted three times, like this, *Whooo, whooo, whooo,* then he was warning the monkeys that there was a tiger near by.

'Well, on this day, just when the monkeys had left their tree, the owl hooted, *Whooo, whooo, whooo,* like that, three times. It was late in the afternoon, and down on the floor of the jungle there were lots of bushes and small trees and the taller trees were so thick that there was very little light. The three monkeys stopped dead with fright as soon as they heard their friend the owl cry *Whooo, whooo, whooo.* The owl's cry was like a blast of cold wind which made them shiver. Wouldn't you be frightened?'

The girls, themselves feeling the shiver, nervously shook their heads in assent.

'But you're asleep,' Afaq protested. 'I said something wrong there and you didn't catch me out.'

The girls looked at each other, wide awake.

'The monkeys were special ones, remember? And one of them was deaf. How could he have heard the owl's cry? In fact, he was walking in front of the others because he had the best eyes and, of course, not hearing the owl's cries, he went merrily along. The dumb one was holding his blind brother by the hand and could not leave him to run after his deaf brother. At the same time, being dumb, he could not tell his blind brother to wait there until he had fetched the deaf one back. Can you imagine what a problem he had? And there was the tiger somewhere near by. If his brother had not been blind, the dumb monkey could have made a sign to him, but he could not speak and his brother could not see. And the one who could speak and see had heard nothing.'

Afaq noticed that the girls had shut their eyes. He remained silent for a moment, but Munni, her eyes still shut, said dreamily, 'What happened then?'

85

Afaq looked at Razia who was watching him from the window and she smiled at him, as much as to say, 'Go on, they may seem asleep but they aren't.'

'Well, the owl heard the deaf monkey trundle merrily along and he knew the trouble the monkeys were in. As you know, he was the monkeys' friend; so he couldn't just sit there on his tree-top house and let something horrible happen to his friends. So, he flew up from his house and dived down into the jungle. He found the deaf monkey and, swooping low in front of him, flapped his wings, balanced himself and flapped his wings once again, balanced himself again and flapped his wings yet once more. The deaf monkey stared amazedly at him and began to laugh, for he thought the owl looked pretty crazy flapping his wings so madly. It did not occur to him that the owl was trying to give him a serious message. In fact, he thought the owl so funny that he sat down to have a good laugh. The owl, satisfied that the monkey would stay there, flew back to where the other two were to direct them to their deaf brother. He was flying low and the dumb monkey saw him coming, but the blind one, of course, only heard the fluttering of wings which might have been anyone's and not his friend the owl's. Maybe, the blind monkey thought, the birds are frightened by the tiger and are trying to fly out of the jungle. He wasn't sure. He was just figuring out the fluttering sound for himself when the owl's wing touched his back; the owl had taken to flapping in front of the dumb monkey just before hooting his message and for a moment he lost his balance and his wing touched the blind monkey. The blind monkey, thinking it was the tiger's paw, let go of his brother's hand and bolted out of sight, knocking himself against many trees and bushes, getting his skin scratched and his head bruised, but determinedly running on.'

Afaq paused again and this time there was no sound from his nieces.

'What happened then?' Razia asked. He rose from his chair and walked to her.

86

'Do you really want to know?'

'I shan't be able to sleep tonight if you don't tell me the rest of the story.'

'It's very long,' Afaq said.

'But I'm dying to know what happened,' Razia said. 'And besides, the girls will want to know first thing tomorrow.'

'Oh, they'll have forgotten it.'

'Children never forget,' she said. 'Tell me, *I* want to know what happened.'

'The blind monkey began to run through the jungle, he kept running, he has kept running, he is still running, blindly bounding along in a crazy kind of determination despite the bruises.'

'That's not true,' she said. 'You're teasing me.'

'It's true,' he said, looking out of the window at the guava tree. 'He's still running.'

'Come, even Dolly won't believe that. That's not how the story went.'

'How did it go, then?'

'How should I know? It's your story.'

'Yes, it's my story,' Afaq said.

'Well, finish it, then.'

He looked at her, followed with his eyes the waving length of her hair.

'The dumb monkey found his deaf brother and explained to him in signs that there was a tiger near by and that their blind brother had run away with fright. The deaf monkey was very sad and rubbed his nose against his brother's shoulder and held his hand. Like this.'

He took her hand and pressed it in his.

'Yes?' she said softly.

'In the meanwhile, the blind monkey's running had dislodged a stone from the side of an incline. The stone fell hard against another. There was a spark. Some dry leaves caught fire. The fire spread to the bushes. Soon the smaller trees were on fire. Within minutes, the jungle was blazing with flames. And then there was the crying of birds, the

87

shrieking of thousands of monkeys, the howling of wolves, the whole jungle was beating madly like a huge drum with thousands of animals stampeding across it, and they were going round and round in circles, unable to find a way out of the fire, and even the tiger was striding with terrifying speed, his tongue hanging out, his eyes ablaze with the flames around him, and soon the trees were crackling with flames, their trunks cracking, bending, whole trees toppling down, adding fuel to the flames, soon there was one huge flame and it seemed that the whole earth had caught fire, and the flame rose higher and higher, it reached the sky, it burned a hole through the sky, and then there was nothing left, nothing left.'

'You've made this up,' Razia said, not taking her hand away from his.

'Of course I've made it up,' he said, speaking softly, almost distractedly. 'It's my story.'

'But it would have had a different ending if you had told it to the children.'

'But you're not a child,' he said. 'I had to change it for you.'

'Afaq, why does the story have such a sad ending?'

'You wouldn't believe me if I said that one of the monkeys went and pulled the tiger's tail and he ran away. Would you? No one can do that to a tiger. Once the tiger comes, he has to show his power. The only power stronger than him is an elemental one. Fire destroyed him, but in doing so, destroyed everyone else.'

'You are destructive,' she said, taking her hand away.

He wanted to hold her face in his hands and say, 'Am I? Are these hands destructive?' But he stood looking at her silently for a moment, afraid that such words would commit him irretrievably to some falsity or to some guilt, from neither of which he could no more have escaped than from self-persecution. He turned away, saying, 'Your children are asleep,' and went to his room. He did not want to revenge himself on Ayub by hurting his wife.

5

He did not change his mind on reflection, but drew two thousand rupees from his bank account the next day and met Rafiq soon after ten o'clock in the evening. He sat hunched over the steering-wheel of his jeep when Rafiq came.

'You got the money?' Rafiq asked.

'Yes, come on in. Let's go for a drive.'

'I had to lie to my brother,' Rafiq said, jumping into his seat.

Afaq laughed, driving away. 'Someone would think you were going to see a sweetheart, the way you talk.'

Rafiq did not say anything, thinking that it was easy for Afaq to talk, being himself independent; but he did not know that the cost of Afaq's independence was Ayub's censure and sometimes his violence and that it was a direct consequence of that that Afaq had come out now with the money.

Afaq drove to the bazaar where they went to a cheap restaurant. The sophisticated coffee houses which had recently opened in Karachi had not yet reached Kalapur and there was nowhere one could go—unless one went to the club—except an ordinary restaurant where tea was one anna a cup. Afaq ordered Coca-Cola.

Rafiq watched with some admiration as Afaq snatched out the straw from the Coca-Cola bottle and, throwing it away, tilted his head and tipped the bottle over his mouth. Rafiq himself shyly sucked at the straw, not wanting to emulate his friend. Afaq put the bottle down and spat on the floor. 'Piss!' he said. 'Can't we get a decent drink somewhere?' He rose and, throwing a coin on the cashier's counter, walked out, Rafiq following. Afaq stood outside the restaurant and cast a gaze around the bazaar.

'Look at the bloody place,' he said. 'What can one do here? Everyone's dead from the soles up.'

Rafiq did not reply; out of politeness.

'Come, let's hit the road. Let me show you the beautiful face of sin.'

They drove off again into the darkness. Rafiq sat holding on to the side of the windscreen, for Afaq was driving fast, cutting into bends, swerving and drifting, so that it seemed to Rafiq that the tyres were constantly protesting and that his own safety was a matter of conjecture.

'There's a place here I found the other day,' Afaq said, slowing down.

'What sort of a place?' Rafiq asked, frightened but ready to be led to hell as long as he did not feel as though he was going to break his skull open against a tree at any moment.

'You'll see.'

Afaq shot off the road on to a clearing on the roadside. Rafiq felt himself being thrown up from his seat only to bounce back, as the jeep bumped across a field, turning sharply this way and that to avoid bushes. Rafiq saw a light in the distance. When they reached it, Rafiq saw that there was a hut there. On stopping, he noticed that there was another hut some fifty yards away. A man had come out on hearing the jeep.

'Ah, *Chacha*,' Afaq greeted him.

'Allah bless you, my son,' the man replied.

'*Chacha*, this is Rafiq. A friend.'

'Welcome, welcome,' the man said, taking them in.

There was a mattress on the floor and a hurricane lamp hung from the ceiling. Two large earthen jars, normally used for storing rice, stood in one corner. There was nothing else, except some glasses.

Afaq tossed a ten-rupee note on to the mattress.

'There you are, *Chacha*,' he said. 'Advance cash.'

'Allah be kind to you, my son,' the man said, stooping to pick up the note.

Afaq flung himself down and snatched the note just before the man could reach it and, lying on his back, Afaq said, 'The goods first, *Chacha*.'

'It's all yours,' the man said and Afaq held the note out to him.

The man pocketed the money and, taking two glasses,

filled them up with some liquid from one of the jars, using a ladle to scoop it out.

Afaq leaped up and took the glasses from him. Rafiq was still standing by the entrance and Afaq said, 'Come and sit down, Rafiq.'

They sat down together while the man stood beside the jars, smiling down at them.

'Here you are,' Afaq said, giving a glass to Rafiq and taking a sip of his own.

Rafiq gingerly smelt at his glass.

'It won't bite, man,' Afaq said. 'It'll kick.' And he laughed.

'It's only sugarcane juice,' the man said, smiling.

'You hear that?' Afaq said, laughing loudly. 'It's *only* sugarcane juice. It will build you up. Go on, don't be a woman.'

Rafiq took a sip. It was foul. He wanted to spit it out. The man noticed Rafiq's reaction and said, 'Rafiq sahib is new to the juice. Take a bigger gulp, sahib, and if you want to spit, go on, do it.'

His religion, the tradition in which he had been brought up, told Rafiq that he must not drink. He had seen peasants take to liquor and ruin their families and, in one wild moment, he saw himself going home drunk, abusing his mother and striking his father.

'Listen, *Chacha-ji* has been to Mecca,' Afaq said. 'He's a holy man and this is his holy water. Have a go.'

Afaq himself had finished his glass and asked the man to refill it.

'If you don't like it, I swear to you I myself will give it up and we'll never come here again.'

Rafiq still hesitated.

Afaq grew impatient and said sternly, 'Listen, Rafiq, if you want that money, you'd better drink up. Otherwise, I'm not giving you an anna and you'll have to invent a new lie to your father.'

Rafiq took a gulp and almost at once spat it out. The taste, however, lingered on his tongue. It was sweet and yet possessed a stinging sharpness. He looked round at Afaq, who was grinning. Rafiq smiled and took a sip and swallowed it.

Rafiq could not tell afterwards at what point he overcame his distaste and began enjoying the drink; nor could he recall when his head began to roll slightly.

'Now, *Chacha*, go and send her in,' Afaq said, throwing another ten-rupee note in the air.

The man picked up the note and, bowing, went out.

'Where's he gone?' Rafiq asked drunkenly.

'Don't you worry,' Afaq said. 'He's just gone into the jungle to meet a fairy who will wave its magic wand over him and he will become a pretty girl of sixteen. Then he'll return. You just see. Go, fill up your glass.'

Rafiq did so and just as he returned to the mattress, a girl entered.

'Hello, my beauty,' Afaq said. 'Look at her, Rafiq. Listen, man, she's prettier than that glass, look at her.'

'Huh,' Rafiq muttered, looking up.

'Come and sit down, my beauty,' Afaq said.

The girl obeyed.

'Hold her hand, Rafiq,' Afaq said.

Rafiq seemed not to understand.

'You show him,' he told the girl.

The girl took Rafiq's hand and held it beside her bosom. Afaq laughed aloud, seeing the frightened look on Rafiq's face.

'Come on, man, do something to her.'

Rafiq just gaped at the girl. The girl smiled as though she was sharing Afaq's joke. Catching her eye when she smiled, Afaq winked and said, '*You* do something to him.'

The girl raised herself a little and, reaching for Rafiq's ear, bit it.

'Oh!' Rafiq uttered a short, sharp cry.

The girl giggled. Afaq laughed louder than ever, rising up from the mattress, almost jumping up in his laughter.

'Go on, bite him, go on, go on.'

The girl took the glass from Rafiq's other hand and gave him a slight push. He fell on to his back on the mattress. The girl opened his shirt and pinched his chest. She bent over and bit his left nipple.

'Oh!' he cried again.

Afaq could hardly contain his laughter. The girl looked round at him as if demanding his approval. 'Go on, go on,' Afaq cried.

She bent over and, holding Rafiq's head down, made as though she was about to kiss him but moved her mouth to his nose and bit the tip. Rafiq uttered a groan. She could smell the liquor coming up in him and quickly sprang up, forcing his face away to the side. Rafiq began to vomit. Afaq stopped laughing. He caught hold of Rafiq's legs and dragged him away from the mattress. Rafiq's vomit trickled along the floor. By the time Afaq had pulled him clear of the mattress, Rafiq had passed out.

'Here, clean it up,' Afaq told the girl, pointing to the area of the mattress where Rafiq had partially vomited.

The girl shrugged her shoulders as if to say that she did not have anything with which to clean up the mess. Afaq went up to her and hugged her. Grabbing her by her hair, he moved her face and kissed her hard. Holding her thus, he untied the loose, long skirt she was wearing. He held her back, got her to step out of the skirt and, picking it up, said, 'Clean it with this.'

She obeyed and when she had done so, he dragged her down to the mattress.

'Come on, my beauty,' he said, undressing her. 'My turn to bite.'

6

The next morning Afaq was still in bed when the brothers were at breakfast with their wives and Zarina.

'It was three in the morning,' Ayub said.

'Yes, I heard him come,' Akram said, sucking loudly at his tea.

'More toast?' Razia asked Faridah, though she need not have inquired, for the silver toast-rack was within less than an arm's length from Faridah.

Zarina lifted a pat of butter with her knife and slowly spread it on her toast, in short concentrated movements as if she were sewing the hem of a petticoat.

Ayub frowned at the women, none of whom had looked up at him. 'What the hell does he think he is?'

His question was spoken a little too loudly and Zarina dropped her knife so that it made a ringing sound against the plate. Faridah munched her toast, loudly crunching it, her lips bursting open with a squelching noise every time her jaw moved. Zarina, trying not to hear her eat, picked up her knife again and scraped some butter off it against the rim of the plate. Razia put another spoonful of sugar into her tea, stirred it, took a sip and softly sighed, 'Aah!' to express her satisfaction with the sweetness.

But Akram said, 'I wonder where he goes.'

'Ali said he saw him in the bazaar with Aziz Khan's elder son.'

'Servants have no business to gossip,' Razia said, at last deciding that someone had to defend her poor brother-in-law.

Faridah looked at her in amazement and Zarina took a discreet sip of her tea.

'Nonsense,' Ayub said. 'Ali was quite right in reporting to me.'

Razia remained silent and thought of the blind monkey running madly through the jungle. Faridah turned again, alligator-fashion, to her toast. Zarina wished she could confide in Razia who was so understanding.

'Well, well, with Aziz Khan's son, eh,' Akram said.

'Yes, isn't it marvellous, the respect he shows to his family,' Ayub said.

Zarina drove an index finger into the side of an eggshell, bursting it, but no one heard.

94

'He needs a vife,' Faridah said. 'That's for sure. He's got everything else.'

Zarina noticed that, in poking her finger at the eggshell, she had broken the nail she had been cultivating for some time.

'I shall have to talk to him about it,' Akram said, rising to go to the mills.

Ayub also rose from the table, but with the intention of going to Afaq's room.

The women were left alone, and Faridah said to Razia, 'Ferozekhan's told me they'd have jhar-jet coming this veek.'

'*Apah*-Faridah, I have so many georgette saris,' Razia protested with a sigh.

'I vaz thinking they might get it in pink,' Faridah said.

'Not *shock*ing pink!'

'Oh no, not shah-king pink,' Faridah assured her. 'A pretty pale pink.'

'I wish Ferozekhan's had some nylon,' Razia said, for the conversation had to be carried on.

'You must go to London for that,' Faridah said. 'They tell me a vunderful store called Jahn Loovis have nylon and shiff-on saris.'

'Ah, London!' Razia said, dismissing the notion as a daydream.

Ayub had slowly walked up the staircase, as if his firm, stern steps were an attempt at admonishing the carpet. He opened the door to Afaq's room. The curtains had not been drawn and bright sunlight fell across the bed where Afaq lay asleep. Ayub walked up to the bed noiselessly. He pulled the sheet off. Afaq did not move, though his body, naked except for a pair of underpants, twitched a little when the sheet was taken away. Ayub bent over him and, holding him by the arms, pulled him up. Afaq fell back heavily when Ayub let go before giving him another pull. Afaq shook his head and made a groaning sound. Ayub pulled him up once more and swung the back of his hand across Afaq's face. No sooner

95

did Afaq's head hit the pillow than Ayub bent ·down and heaved him out of the bed, pushing him to the other side so that Afaq fell on the floor. Ayub went round the bed and, holding him by his wrists, pulled him up on to his feet and delivered a series of blows to his face. Afaq thrashed the air with his hands, swinging his arms wildly. Ayub stepped forward and hit Afaq's chest with his fist. Afaq fell back on to the bed.

Afaq began to cry softly; his teeth seemed to chatter as he sobbed open-mouthed.

'You come home at three in the morning. You still stink of liquor. You are seen in public with Aziz Khan's son. Try it once more, little brother, and you'll know what my whip feels like.'

Ayub uttered his threat coldly, without raising his voice, and walked out to the bathroom to wash his hands before leaving for his office.

Afaq lay in his bed, sobbing, holding the corner of a sheet to his mouth. His temples throbbed with anger; his neck burned as the blood rushed to his head. He thought of Rafiq, the simple-minded Rafiq who had lost his senses no sooner than the girl had touched him. He thought of the girl and the summary manner in which he had made love to her. His discovery of the hut while driving aimlessly about the country had provided him with a channel for the outlet of his frustrations in Kalapur, but the place now appeared in his imagination to be a gutter over which he was holding his sickened body and vomiting out the filth it contained. He thought again of Rafiq and could not help smiling to himself when he remembered how Rafiq had to be revived with cold water and dragged to the jeep. The fresh air in the open jeep had awoken Rafiq at last and, by the time they reached Aziz Khan's property, Rafiq was more or less capable of finding his way to his room, but whether he managed to do so or not, Afaq did not know. He was glad that he had remembered to take the twenty hundred-rupee notes from his own hip-pocket and to stuff them into Rafiq's shirt pocket. He had stopped sobbing now and thought of Ayub. He turned his head, burying his nose in the pillow. If his head had not been so dazed when Ayub pulled him up. If he could have stood firmly on his feet and held his hands fisted in front of his chest. If he could have kept his eyes open. But there was Rafiq, Aziz Khan's son. He was determined to see Rafiq again.

7

Javed woke up when he heard his brother enter that morning. He had slept badly, for this was the first time that Rafiq had given him an excuse for slipping out of the house when the household had retired.

'*Hai Allah!*' Javed said, at once smelling the liquor on Rafiq's breath. 'Where the hell have you been?'

Rafiq glared at him helplessly.

'Bloody hell, man,' Javed said, keeping his voice low. At that moment he saw the edge of a note in Rafiq's shirt pocket. 'What's this?' he asked, taking the notes out. Javed counted the money. 'Two thousand!' he cried in a whisper.

'Hussain's debt,' Rafiq said.

'But where the hell have you been?'

'To hell.'

Rafiq fell on to his bed. Javed let him sleep. He looked at the money in his hands and counted it again. He felt sorry for his brother, pitied him; he looked at Rafiq with love, for it was obvious to him that Rafiq had allowed himself to go through hell to obtain the money; he was certain that Rafiq had done what he had done for the sake of the family. Javed sat by his brother's bed, determined to sit there watching over him until five when he would wake him up, make him scrub his teeth with a *neem* twig until the twig's bitter juice took away the last whiff of liquor from his breath, and make him bathe with cold water; he would himself lather his body with soap, rub him with his own hands at least three times with soap; before the parents rose a little before six. Then Rafiq would go away after breakfast, get some sleep under a tree, and come back and deliver the money to his father.

Javed planned out Rafiq's salvation.

8

The rooms were being vacuumed and Razia, not being able to bear the sound, was walking in the garden. The swimming pool had been emptied. It was rarely used except as an impressive decoration: whenever they had guests for dinner, the swimming pool was cleaned and filled with water so that the guests might be invited to stroll in the garden before dining. Sometimes dinner was served on tables beside the pool. Ayub had used the pool the first summer they were in Kalapur but, finding the exercise odious and not at all exhilarating as it had been in the sea in Bombay, had not continued to do so. It was, of course, out of the question that any of the women should swim in it, for it would have been scandalous if they had appeared in swim-suits. One could not trust the servants, who, although they had learned to remain discreetly out of the way, were always watching and gossiping with other people's servants.

Razia was glad to have the morning to herself and was happy pacing the garden now that Faridah and Zarina had gone in the former's quest for a pink georgette sari. Munni and Dolly had been taken out by their *ayah*: Razia had little to do with her children, except when they went to bed and at children's parties. She was secretly proud to be a mother and yet to have retained her figure; Faridah's childlessness gave her much satisfaction, for she alone had produced the progeny for the great Shah inheritance. There was Afaq, of course, she sighed, picking up a twig. He would marry and perhaps have sons. She broke the twig in two, somewhat annoyed at the notion of Afaq having sons, imagining a diminishing of her own importance in the family. It would not be enough for her to have sons; she must somehow thwart Afaq having sons.

She recalled Afaq's story-telling and how he had stood beside her. She remembered his holding her hand. How could she have permitted that? And yet she had not objected at the time. She had been moved by his speech, she had been carried away by his story. She was certain that Ayub would whip him if he discovered that Afaq had held her hand and stood in close intimacy with her. But what did Afaq feel for her? she wondered. She had sensed that Afaq resented Ayub's dominance; and she herself had sometimes been angry with Ayub for being so rude and violent to his younger brother. Afaq, she knew, was sensitive and possessed a questioning intellect, while Ayub was demanding and dictatorial. But Ayub was her husband and the father of her children, while Afaq was a potential threat to the future power of her own children: and this was her conflict: whether to display a measure of her sympathy to Afaq and thus mock her husband's self-assertiveness or so to compromise Afaq that his brothers would ostracise him, leaving the family's fortunes to her children. If only Ayub did not extend his rudeness to her! Sometimes, she saw him only as an outside agent, almost as an abstraction who existed solely to give her children; at such times, she considered her own reality to be her children. The love which the Hollywood films portrayed had been beyond her comprehension: oh, she had had longings during her youth but those she considered now to be an artificiality to which young girls in Pakistan, unable to have the relations with the opposite sex which were permitted in western societies, were painfully exposed. There was a comfort in belonging to one man and there was happiness in motherhood; her own society considered love as something illicit which happened between foolish couples and the Urdu word for it was embarrassing whenever it was uttered. She did not know what love was and whether it could describe any aspect of her relationship with her husband; she had no enduring memory of his affection. Invariably, it was his voice which dominated their relationship, a loud voice, sharp and frightening sometimes like a dog's sudden bark when you were out at night, so that she herself spoke a little loudly now. And their love-making, undertaken for the utilitarian purpose of procreation, was always abrupt and sometimes brutal, too. She wondered if tenderer relations were possible and again recalled Afaq holding her hand. She recognised the gesture as affection now; she saw his eyes again, looking into hers, she heard his soft voice, desperately conveying some message. Why did the blind monkey never stop running? He is still running, Afaq had said, he is running now. She wished she could understand him, make him happier, and yet she was constantly being reminded of her greater wish to control the fortune of the family.

Engaged in these thoughts, she was a little frightened by the suddenness with which a servant asked her, '*Begum sahiba*, shall we leave Afaq sahib's room?' She must have seen the servant walk up to her but was too lost in her thoughts to have noticed.

'Why, what's the matter with his room?' she asked.

'Sahib is still there,' the servant said.

Razia was surprised to learn this and was on the point of telling the servant to leave his room alone when she decided that here was an opportunity of seeing Afaq alone and yet in a perfectly normal circumstance and said, 'Oh, in that case I'd better go and see if he isn't ill.'

Afaq was lying in bed and when he heard his door being opened, he quickly drew a sheet over his body, which was still naked except for his underpants. Razia walked to his bed and stood looking silently at him for a moment. Then she said, 'Are you all right?'

His eyes flashed briefly and he looked away, saying softly, 'Do I look all right?'

Razia had not failed to notice that his face was bruised but now she also saw a slight red mark beside his lower lip. She sat down on the edge of the bed and slowly advanced a finger to his lip, first gently passing her hand over his cheek.

'What have you done?' she asked.

'I?' he said with some bitterness. 'I have done nothing. This is Ayub's work.'

She bit her lip and lowered her eyes, prepared to be ashamed for her husband.

'Why?' she whispered. 'When?'

'He hates me,' Afaq said without malice.

She looked up at him again.

'I don't know why,' Afaq said. 'I don't know why.'

She saw a tear come to his eye.

'I'm sorry,' she said.

'I don't know why,' Afaq muttered again, and the tear rolled down his cheek, making way for another.

She put a hand to his forehead to soothe whatever pain was threatening to burst from him. But her attempt to comfort him had the opposite effect, for he began to sob.

'Now, don't do that,' she said, herself moved, and beginning to pity his condition.

He turned his head aside and began to cry bitterly. She bent over him, stroking his cheek, saying, 'Don't do that, Afaq, please don't do that.' She was almost whispering into his ear, her face was so close to his. He turned slightly and catching her eye observing him with obvious tenderness and pity, he pressed his head against her shoulder.

'Afaq,' she pleaded, 'don't cry, Afaq, it will be all right.'

But he only cried more loudly, pressing her close to him.

They remained thus for what seemed a long time but was perhaps not more than ten minutes. When his tears had been exhausted, she withdrew and went to fetch a bowl of water and some cotton-wool. She sat beside him and wiped his face. Neither spoke. She saw a gentleness in his face and, since the sympathy which he had evoked from her had emanated spontaneously, she felt for him an empathy, an acute sense of kindred spirit which she had never felt for Ayub. She saw in him something of herself, a reflection perhaps of her own feelings. And he, too, saw her as kind and charitable; as if, in coming to him when he needed affection, in giving that affection and mollifying the hurt from which he suffered, she had given him a part of herself.

Neither spoke. He held her hand and pressed it. She smiled. But there were no words. They rested in a vagueness of emotion.

It is possible that the extremely emotional nature of the situation had exaggerated their regard for each other. For Afaq's emotional condition had been building up during the previous few weeks to a point of collapse; his aimless drives at night, his discovery of the hut where he could buy liquor and sex and the guilt which he experienced from going there, a guilt which he had partly essayed to diminish by sharing the experience with Rafiq and by attempting to make a mockery of it, had all combined to make Afaq want the understanding and affection of another person. Ayub's blows had not hurt him; the bruises had been inflicted within him already.

And when Razia regarded him now, she saw the anti-thesis of Ayub. She did not recognize Afaq's crisis because she was seeing in him a person of her own imagining. She saw those of Afaq's bruises which had been inflicted by her husband and to which she could devote her tenderness. And in giving Afaq her attention, she had discovered in him a person who needed her; observing his gaze of gratitude, she discovered love, recognising it as a capacity for giving.

9

Ferozekhan's was the largest store in Kalapur. The legend on the signboard declared it to be a Fancy Goods Store, but there were other declarations in a variety of lettering, some-times the variety occurring within one phrase:

LADIE'S MATEREALS, EMBROYDERED WORKS,
ENGLISH AND FORRUN PRODUCES, BEST KWALITY
ALLWAYS, CASH TERMS RESPECTED, ALLAH IS KIND,
ALL GUARANTEES GIVEN, FAST COLOURS

The letters had fancifully been worked in gold on the glass of the two shop-windows; there were heavily shadowed slanting letters, the finest of sans serif, letters with seemingly unending flourishes, there were ornate letters with flowers growing around them. In short, Ferozekhan's was no ordinary store, and it was well known in Kalapur that Mr Ferozekhan was a man who had assimilated an eclectic culture.

When Faridah arrived at Ferozekhan's with Zarina, Mr Zaffar Alim-ud-din Ferozekhan, international merchant of Kalapur, importer and exporter of the highest reputation and integrity—for in these terms he styled himself on his note-paper—came shuffling out of the store no sooner than the Shah car drew up along the pavement. He opened a large umbrella of black cotton as soon as Faridah emerged from the car and, keeping himself at a distance and stretching his arm as far as he could, so that he himself would be seen to be taking no advantage of the shade, he escorted Faridah to the store. Zarina walked beside Faridah but did not feel slighted that Mr Ferozekhan should give all his attention to her guardian, for she was accustomed to such neglect.

Mr Ferozekhan's two assistants were utterly dumb-founded in the presence of the richest woman in Kalapur and stood gaping at her in awed silence.

'Ah, *begum sahiba*,' Mr Ferozekhan began, 'Allah be praised you looking so vell. How is Shah sahib? My kindest trust and respects to him. And the second Shah sahib? My truest fidelities to him. May Allah prahsperise you aal.'

'Has the jhar-jet come?' Faridah asked sharply, casting a gaze around the shop.

'*Aré*, Fiaz, and you, Nassim, vhat you staring for?' Mr Ferozekhan said fiercely to his assistants. 'Vhat you staring for, eh? You never seen custom-errs before? Vhere's the jhar-jet of the vhich you opunnd the consignment this very mahrning, having taken deliworry from the Pakistan Government customs at nine-thirty a.m. for the vhich you took two hundred and seventeen rupees net cash from me to pay the customs duty, vhere's the jhar-jet?'

Fiaz and Nassim bolted out of a back door.

'Vas there any pink?' Faridah asked.

'Pink?' Mr Ferozekhan asked. '*Begum sahiba*, I have each and every culler for your sootability, pink, saálmun red, turkwise, emmaruld green, purrpel, midnight blue, dusk grey, baje, pee green, the cumpleet range, *begum sahiba*, the cumpleet range.'

Fiaz and Nassim came hurrying back with rolls of material.

'Hyere you are, *begum sahiba*, each and every culler of the marracullous rainbow to soot your ability.'

Faridah looked sourly at the material as if she despised it. Mr Ferozekhan unrolled the cloth on the counter. Faridah felt the material with her fingers, tentatively at first and then held it in her palm, crumpling it. She was satisfied that it did not seem to crease. She examined the several rolls and asked Zarina if she liked any particular colour, but Zarina only shrugged her shoulders.

'Show me this in naturull light,' Faridah demanded.

Mr Ferozekhan carried the roll to the door and Faridah went after him with Zarina. They had been hearing a noise outside but had paid it no attention, for noise, public argument and the loud exchange of obscene abuse goes on constantly in Pakistani streets. When they came to the door, they saw the cause of the disturbance. A little way down the street, outside a grocery shop, a small, dwarf-like man was being thrown about and kicked by a crowd which seemed highly entertained by the exercise. Punjabi obscenities accompanied each blow.

Faridah did not care to look; nor hear. She decided she liked the colour and returned to the shop, paying no attention to the sufferings of the dwarf called Bakshi.

10

After his morning conference with the floor managers, Ayub went into Akram's office. The latter was glancing at a memorandum he had received from his agent in East Pakistan concerning the desirability of moving into the expanding soap industry in Chittagong.

'It's eleven o'clock,' Ayub said.

'Yes?' Akram said, looking at his watch and wondering if he had forgotten some appointment.

'And where is our little brother?' Ayub demanded. 'Still at home in bed. Unless he's decided to go and have another booze up with Rafiq.'

Akram looked questioningly at Ayub, who went on, 'You didn't see him this morning, did you?'

'No.'

'I did. He stank of liquor. Not whisky, but hard, country liquor, the lethal stuff they make from sugarcane. It's poison, I tell you. Not content with shaming us with such revolting behaviour, he has to add insult to injury by doing his boozing with Aziz Khan's son.'

'Is that so?' Akram asked.

'I told you Ali saw them together in the bazaar last night.'

'Yes, yes,' Akram said as though his words were an attempt to swat a fly which had been irritating him. 'With Aziz Khan's son, eh?' he muttered.

'Yes,' Ayub said, 'he's dragging the family's name into the mud.'

'It's bad, very bad,' Akram said, frowning and looking at a bazaar print of Mohammed Ali Jinnah, the founder of the nation who is spoken of in Pakistan with a similar degree of reverence as is reserved usually for the prophet himself; disdaining idols, Islam accepts verbal idolatry.

'And this problem of Aziz Khan's is nowhere near solution,' Ayub said.

'We've done everything except offer him a blank cheque,' Akram said.

'He has no idea of money,' Ayub said. 'And if Afaq starts becoming chums with his sons, then you can imagine what a head for figures he will have.'

'I wonder if it's time to do anything about Aziz Khan,' Akram said. 'The town respects us now. I wonder if a little pressure through our legal friends might not do the trick.'

'You're thinking of Hussain?'

'Yes, partly, though he's hardly a legal friend.'

'What happened with him?' Ayub asked.

'It remains to be seen. All we know is that he has not yet paid Aziz Khan's debt.'

'Suppose Aziz Khan doesn't press him for the money?' Ayub asked.

'He may not know the value of money,' Akram said, 'but he can't do without it. He has no other source unless he becomes his own broker. Can you imagine him doing that? He can't read or write, except Urdu. His only transport is a horse. All the man-power he has is two sons and a handful of peasants. The peasants won't work for him for ever without pay. He has no idea of running a business when up against modern competition. From where is he going to get the lorries, how's he going to contact his clients? By using pigeons?'

The brothers laughed, and Akram went on, delighting in his own seemingly irrefutable logic, 'No, we don't have to do anything at all except wait. If he goes to law about Hussain, I'd like to know which barrister will defend him. Certainly not one in Kalapur who has any hopes of a bright future here. If he doesn't take Hussain to court, he will gradually kill himself, for he will be driven to a position of isolation where only selling the land will help him. I tell you, he'll come crawling to us yet. We've only got to wait.'

Ayub was satisfied with Akram's logic. 'Yes, that's fine, but what about Afaq?'

'There are two things we can do with him,' Akram said. 'Get him married, let him settle down. He can't go on behaving like a *junglee*.'

'What's the other?'

'Send him to England for higher studies.'

'That would only get him out of the way,' Ayub said. 'It

wouldn't necessarily tame him. For that, we must put him in a cage.'

'Marriage?'

'Yes, the best cage for a wild young man,' Ayub said. 'We were different at his age. We were too busy making a living, but he has too much free time. A wife would soon get him on a tight schedule.'

Again the brothers laughed, though a little mildly this time.

'The question is which family can offer us a daughter,' Akram said.

'Do we have to turn to another family?' Ayub asked. 'I thought the matter was settled and it was just a matter of waiting a year or two.'

'Why, what do you mean?'

'Why, Akram, I'm surprised to realise that you haven't thought of Zarina as Afaq's wife. I thought we'd all taken it for granted.'

Akram looked at the memorandum in front of him and said, 'Taken for granted? I have never suggested it.'

'I know, but you know how something's in the air and one feels it about to happen. Well, you know, that sort of feeling.'

Akram still did not look up, but said, 'I don't think he can marry Zarina.'

'Why, because she's a cousin?' Ayub asked.

'No, it's not that,' Akram said, picking up a paper-knife and tracing an imaginary line vertically along the memorandum.

'There's no harm in their being cousins,' Ayub pressed on. 'There have been marriages between first cousins which have been perfectly normal. Keep it within the family's what I say.'

'They're not cousins,' Akram said at last, looking into his eyes. But he turned away at once to look again at the paper-knife, biting his lip and knowing that he had made a mistake.

'Come, come, what mystery is this?' Ayub asked.

'Well, they're closer relations, that's all I can say. They can't marry.'

'Please don't deepen the mystery,' Ayub said. 'It will only create confusion and unhappiness.'

'I'm sorry, Ayub, the revelation would be more painful to everyone concerned.'

'Listen,' Ayub said in his most demanding manner. 'What you're telling me is that Zarina and Afaq are not cousins, that the relationship is not only different but also closer. What the hell can I conclude? That she is his sister? Or what else am I to conclude? Do you take me for a damn' fool? I know my family, I know how many brothers and sisters I have. So, what is she if not a sister?'

Akram folded a sheet of blotting-paper and began to cut it with the paper-knife.

'She's my daughter,' he said.

Ayub had no words to express his astonishment and Akram was obliged to explain. 'This was two or three years before you came to live with me in Bombay.'

He found it difficult to narrate the whole story.

'Who was the mother?' Ayub asked.

'I wasn't married to her,' Akram said and remained silent, so that Ayub imagined the episode was too painful for his brother to recall. But Akram looked up at him again and said agitatedly, 'You see how important it is for Faridah not to know? I haven't been able to give her a child and if she knows that I had a child before I married her, it would be too painful for her. Do you see? No one must know, do you see? What will happen to Zarina if she finds out I'm her father? How will I tell her, and what will I say to explain that I've called her our cousin all these years? Do you see, Ayub? Do you?'

There was no compassion for him in Ayub's eyes, only a cold hatred; to him it seemed that Akram had upset an important calculation on which their fortune was based. Akram, his head lowered, seemed to have diminished in stature after his confession.

'Do you see?' Akram said softly. 'Do you see why? My brother can't marry my daughter, can he?'

Though that, Akram well knew, was not at all what compelled his head to remain lowered.

11

When they had returned from Ferozekhan's, Faridah declared herself to be too tired to answer the several household problems about which the servants questioned her and announced that she was going to rest until lunch. Razia was nowhere to be found, for by now she had left Afaq's room and retired to her own. Alone, Zarina paced the garden, chewing a sugarcane. She sat down under the shade of the guava tree, propping her chin on her knees which she encircled with her arms in a tight embrace; in this classical pose of lonesome maidens as depicted by Indo-Pakistani films, she gently rocked herself, softly uttering the lovesick lyrics of a film-song. She wished she had a friend to whom she could tell her secret, for she was certain that no one had known the intensity of love which she was experiencing for Afaq. She was certain, too, that her suffering was greater than any other girl had been through; she thought of the legendary heroine Anarkali, who had died for her love, who had gone on singing—according to the film at any rate—about her love while four brick walls were built around her to entomb her alive. But Anarkali had died, Zarina reflected, while she herself had to suffer a living death every time she thought of Afaq. Anarkali was brave in her death, but what greater courage was necessary to continue to live?

She shifted a little, for the tree's shadow was beginning to desert her, and noticed that Razia had appeared and was walking towards her.

'Well, well, what's our heroine up to?' Razia asked, coming and sitting beside her. 'Did you have a pleasant morning?'

'Yes,' she said a little nervously as though Razia had trespassed on her thoughts.

'Did you find any georgette?'

'Oh yes, and pink georgette, too.'

'Well, at least *apah*-Faridah will be happy for a couple of days,' Razia said, smiling.

Zarina smiled back and began to stroke the lawn as though it were a cat.

'What are you thinking about?' Razia asked after a while.

'Nothing.'

'A pretty subject,' Razia mocked. 'I could tell you a great deal about nothing.'

'I was just thinking how pretty it is here,' Zarina said with some effort.

'How pretty is it up there?' Razia asked, prodding Zarina's head with an index finger.

Zarina turned her head away a little, prepared to be teased.

'Let me see now,' Razia said, leaning towards her and holding her head as though it was a crystal ball. 'A *very* pretty subject, nothing. Nothing is slim with dark hair and brown eyes.'

'Don't!' Zarina exclaimed, trying to withdraw.

'Ha, ha,' Razia continued to tease, 'so we're now getting to the truth about our heroine. Let me see what else I can see.'

Just then they heard footsteps by the corner of the house and saw Afaq walk past and enter his jeep. The two watched him silently. Had Razia not experienced the feelings she had in the morning when she sat beside him, she would certainly have called to him and inquired where he was going. Fortunately for her, Zarina did not glance at her, for there was more than concern in her eyes. Nor did Razia glance at Zarina, not until Afaq had driven away. The effect of Razia's teasing and Afaq's appearance had given Zarina's emotions too sudden a jerk and she did not know how to check the tear which had come to her eye. Razia observed it and immediately understood what it signified. Zarina noticed that

Razia had understood her private agony, and, hiding her head in her arms, began to sob. Razia was herself moved, for her own emotions seemed today to be pursuing unfamiliar paths: her morning's discovery of love appeared to be in jeopardy now that the object of her love did not belong to her affections only, for, at least psychologically, Zarina had possessed Afaq before she herself had been drawn to him. Until this morning, she had readily coupled Zarina's name with Afaq in conversations with her husband; but now, despite her own profound sense of loyalty, despite her own ambition for her children, she was annoyed that her own possession of Afaq should be so brief, for here was Zarina, an immature little girl, who had apparently been in love with Afaq for far longer. She hoped that she would be able to dismiss Zarina's feelings as adolescent sentiment.

'I think,' Zarina said, rubbing her eyes, 'a fly has gone into my eye. It's very painful.'

'Go and wash it,' Razia said, whereupon Zarina hastily went away.

Razia tried to reason with herself. She was a married woman. Her husband was a rich and a powerful man. She had two daughters and had every expectation of more children. Could she throw all this away for a passing fancy? She scolded herself for thus belittling the new love which she had discovered and which her imagination was already ennobling into a passion. She was confused. She did not know what would happen next. She did not know how it would all end.

12

There were no more occasions for Afaq and Razia to meet alone, but each was happy in the knowledge of what had happened between them that morning. Afaq spent less time away from the house in the evenings and sometimes, during a sleepless night, wished Razia would slip away from her husband and come to his room. He would have been frightened, however, if she had done so; love was acceptable as a thing in the mind, something with which one could torment oneself, but as a reality it entailed both complications and obligations. Afaq wanted Razia, but in some unobtainable environment of innocence. Razia, too, would lie thinking about him when Ayub had gone to sleep, but, to her, the idea of love was far nobler than any physical commitments; it was more beguiling for her to know that she could smile at Afaq and expect that smile to convey a special significance to him which a third person would not understand than to engineer secret meetings with him.

Some days later, Afaq refused to go to Mansur's for one more tedious bridge party. At first Razia was slightly annoyed that he should want to remain away from her presence, but then told herself that his refusal could only indicate the true intensity of his love, for he could not want to suffer silently in front of her husband, probably preferring to suffer in loneliness. She decided, when they drove away to the Mansurs, that she would try and create an opportunity for their meeting alone—not only to compensate him for this evening's absence but also to reassure herself that the meaning she had discovered of love was indeed true.

Alone, Afaq walked about the house, now in the drawing-room listening to the record-player, impatiently rejecting half-heard songs, now pacing his own room. He was imbued with a sense of futility. He found the work at the mills so trying that he did not know why he did not abandon it, leave his brothers and go and live in Lahore. But he knew he would never go, never himself be able to initiate a move towards independence. He lacked conviction rather than courage, for he followed inclination rather than the dictates of a determined will. Day after day at the mills, illiterate labourers, who could only make a thumb-mark for a signature, queued up outside his office, seeking employment. He interviewed them, receiving nervous grunts in answer. And each day he had to review the labour situation, make an inventory of those who had failed to turn up as though they were items of furniture which had been stolen during the night; for while there was a massive nucleus of labourers who understood the terms of permanent employment, there were many who disappeared on receiving the week's pay-packet as if one handful of notes had provided them with a lifetime's security. It was petty work, finding out how many had gone, and replacing them with new men. He questioned the work's importance and found it trivial.

Once again coming down the stairs from his room, he walked into the garden. He hated his position in the family. Akram and Ayub could well feel complacent, he reflected, for they had achieved what they had most wanted, wealth and influence. He himself felt no urgent passion for these two goals. He thought of Razia and smiled to himself, thinking that it was in his power to wreck Ayub's life by using her; but he soon expelled that thought from his mind, realising that Ayub was too strong, too brutally self-assertive to be effected by his scheming; he knew, too, that when Ayub fell, he would, like Samson, bring down the world with him.

In his impatience with the futility which the house symbolised, Afaq turned to his jeep and drove out. Again without pre-determined destinations to travel towards, again without either material or extra-material purpose, but with a jaw so determinedly set that the sinews below his cheeks tightened into stripes, but with hands tightly gripping the wheel and now fiercely jettisoning the gear lever to change down, but with his soul reaching outwards to an unidentifiable ecstasy, again aimlessly, but passionately, he drove out.

He avoided the road to the hut where he could affect an extravagant personality and purchase liquor and sex, but took the bumpy surface which led to Aziz Khan's property. He drove past it, pressing his foot down. The road led to a settlement of huts where peasants lived, a district known locally as the Kangra Settlement. He drove through the settlement, not caring to slow down although some of the huts were built dangerously near the road and several of the inhabitants, hardly ever seeing traffic on the road, sat on the road's edge because it was cleaner than the mud on which their huts stood. Afaq turned back and again noisily tore through the settlement. A hundred or so yards away from it, in the direction of Aziz Khan's land, was a hillock where the inhabitants of the settlement, having no lavatories, went to excrete. Afaq's headlights caught a peasant girl in the motion of rising laboriously from the ground just as he took the bend which the hillock's presence had made necessary in the road's construction. He braked hard, swerved off the road and accelerated towards the girl. What impulse made him do so, he could not afterwards have explained. The girl stood hypnotised by the headlamps, dropping from her hands the earthen pot in which she had carried water with which to wash her buttocks. Afaq swung the jeep to her side, braked and jumped out. He ordered her into the jeep. She stood there open-mouthed. He gesticulated, thinking that she did not understand his words. There was the smell of shit all around him, too, which was compelling him to act hastily, who, already fired by dangerous speed, needed no further stimulus. Impatient with the girl, he picked her up, bending a little to grab her around the thighs, lifting her with one desperate heave and throwing her into the jeep. He was aware that in doing so, his foot had trod with a revolting squelch into what the girl had only recently risen from dropping, but he was only all the more incensed into hastening away from the place. Before the girl could sit up and attempt to jump out of the jeep, he had leapt into his own seat and begun to drive away. The girl began to whimper. He accelerated. The jeep bounced over the rough surface, throwing her about in her seat. The girl was beginning to utter short screams when he swung the jeep on to the road; the bump was considerable and the girl was thrown from her seat in such a way that her forehead struck the metal frame of the windscreen when the front wheels went over the bump; no sooner than the impact had stung her senses than the rear wheels seemed to kick up so that she was again thrown back. She screamed loudly. Afaq glanced at her contemptuously and drove on, increasing the speed. He did not notice that her forehead had been slightly cut and did not realise that she soon stopped protesting because of her hurt. He slowed down and let the jeep coast along a slight slope, switching off the engine. The girl, noticing that there was no noise from the jeep now and that the rush of the wind had also abated, began to cry anew. Afaq looked at her with increased contempt and, engaging second gear, released the clutch with a jerk to start the engine again, simultaneously pressing down the accelerator pedal. He was near Aziz Khan's land now though he did not know it. It was past ten o'clock, a time by when most country people have gone to sleep and there are few lamps still burning. Annoyed by the girl's crying, he turned the jeep off the road and drove it across a bumpy field. The field sloped down towards the stream which bordered Aziz Khan's land, and Afaq, noticing only the depression in the land and not knowing where he was, again switched off the engine and let the jeep follow its own path until it halted against a slight incline. He got out and, going round the jeep, pulled the girl out. She was crying softly but incessantly, knowing she was too far from anywhere for her crying to attract help.

'Shut up!' he ordered her, but she did not hear him. He repeated his order loudly and, seeing that her only reaction was to try and walk away into the darkness, he grabbed her by the arm and slapped her across the face. She uttered a short scream. Holding her strongly by the shoulders, he pushed her so that she fell backwards but, recovering her balance before she could fall on her back, she again stood erect and tried to shuffle away. Afaq ran to her and, again holding her by the shoulders, pulled her down. She tried to resist, flailing her arms in front of her. He dodged her blows and quickly stepping to her side, gave her a blow on the face. Her senses seemed to be stunned for a minute. But his own blood was hammering fiercer blows at his temples and he did not hear her silence. He tore at her clothes, not looking at her face; had he paused then, he would not only have seen the smear of blood across her forehead but also the fresh trickle from her mouth. But he was mercilessly in the grip of his own lust, his own hatred of all the life around him; they were not his hands which were clawing into the girl's flesh, but those others which had been able to do nothing while Ayub's hands hit him and those others which would have been gentle had a woman appeared to alleviate his loneliness. He did not pause to consider his actions now, having spent night after night contemplating his own inaction.

The girl lay naked in front of him, silent and unresisting. In the same frenzy with which he had driven here and torn off her clothes, with the same relentless throbbing at his temples, he pulled away his trousers and, strongly holding the girl's parted legs, entered her, not noticing that she had gone unconscious in her ordeal. Once in, he flung himself on her, his hands now wringing her breasts, now clutching her neck, now reaching for her buttocks and now again clasping her neck tightly and lifting and banging and lifting and banging her head against the hard earth. He reached his climax when his hands were once again at the girl's neck and, holding his breath just before the final thrust and emission, all his strength seemed to be concentrated in his hands round the girl's throat.

He lay heavily on her, dazed and senseless. She did not move, did not protest. At last he rolled over and lay in his own exhaustion. He noticed that she lay still beside him and saw her face for the first time since coming to the field, saw her in the cold light of the darkness in which he himself lay. He saw the blood, the open mouth. He saw the two nipples which stuck out from her flat chest. He saw her thin, limp legs, her almost skeletal arms. He looked again at her face, the still, open-mouthed, blood-streaked face. He saw that it was almost a child's face, the girl could hardly be thirteen or fourteen. His temples began to throb again, a horror began to choke him. And the girl remained as when he had rolled off her body: still, coldly still, stiffening in the night air like a corpse.

13

Chief Superintendent Fazal Elahi, head of the Kalapur district of the Punjab Police, called at Akram's office at ten o'clock the next morning when Akram and Ayub were drafting their preliminary plans for establishing soap factories in East Pakistan. The men were not unacquainted, for Elahi had helped the brothers in clearing away peasant settlements from some of the land which they had purchased and had received a fair reward for his help.

'There is a stream which backs on to Aziz Khan's land,' he began, taking a chair, 'where the corpse of a young girl who had obviously been raped was discovered this morning.'

He leaned back in his chair, pressing his lips together.

'By Aziz Khan's land, eh?' Ayub muttered, wanting to smile but not daring yet.

Akram looked at Elahi patiently and said, 'Yes?'

'One of Aziz Khan's men discovered it, the corpse,' Elahi resumed his speech and paused to clear his throat. 'And instead of reporting first to his master, he came straight to me. So that there is no question of Aziz Khan's hushing up the scandal on his land.'

Elahi paused to observe the effect of the slight distortion of fact contained in his last statement, for he had decided to interpret the situation in the most advantageous way, and was pleased that Ayub smiled knowingly at him.

'This man will need police protection in case he has betrayed his master's trust. I shall give him that protection and would be grateful if you will make my task easier by employing him here.'

Akram nodded, hooding his eyes. Ayub was rolling his tongue against the inside of his left cheek. Both knew that Elahi would not expect them to be obliging unless they themselves were involved.

'There is one other point,' Elahi said.

Akram glanced up at him apprehensively; Ayub leaned

forward; each expecting a revelation of the extent of their involvement.

'On the other side of the stream to Aziz Khan's land, we have discovered certain tyre-marks. The field there is dry and uncultivated wasteland. The tyre-marks, which are not too conspicuous, are on one or two areas of dust. But an untrained eye will hardly notice them, a fact which is in our favour.'

Again he paused, this time to let his choice of the personal pronoun make its impact.

'A jeep was seen travelling in the direction of Aziz Khan's land last night, but this circumstance need not to be relevant, for although not many people possess jeeps in this area, there is no reason why the possession of a jeep should in any way be considered incriminating. This is all I have to say for the present.'

But he remained in his chair.

'Whom are you arresting?' Ayub asked.

'Why, it's obvious, isn't it?' Elahi said. 'A girl is found next to Aziz Khan's land. She has died of asphyxiation and has been raped. Aziz Khan has two sons, both unmarried. We know from where to obtain our evidence.'

'First-rate,' Ayub said, congratulating Elahi, 'your powers of detection are first-rate.'

Elahi stood up and smiled at the two men.

'Thank you very much for your help,' Akram said, also rising and shaking Elahi's hand.

'At your service,' Elahi said.

'Allah will reward you,' Ayub said.

'Thank you.'

'Come and collect it tomorrow,' Ayub said.

Akram fell back into his chair when Elahi had gone. Ayub turned fiercely to him and said, 'The fucking bastard! Rape and murder!'

Akram was not roused to similar anger, for, despite the shock of realising what Afaq had done, his mind had coldly perceived the tactical advantage over Aziz Khan which his brother's action had brought about—provided that Elahi could successfully prosecute one of Aziz Khan's sons.

'We will have to send him to England,' Akram said.

'I wouldn't care if he hanged,' Ayub said. 'Only it would ruin the family.'

'No, we must be careful. We must send him to England.'

'The bloody fool!'

'No, calm down,' Akram said. 'What had to happen has happened. We wanted him to do something, to become a man. It's not our fault he has to go and do it in a criminal way. It's no use being angry now, think of the business. We'll have to pretend that nothing has happened. Go on normally with our affairs. Then, when all this is over, we'll pack him off to England.'

'The bloody lunatic!'

'No, no, brother, calm down.'

14

Some days later, when he had collected fifty thousand rupees for himself and another fifty thousand to share among his twenty officers, and made sure that he had covered all possible tracks which might lead to Afaq's conviction, the Chief Superintendent drove to Aziz Khan's house with two of his officers. It was evening and Aziz Khan was sitting in the front yard while Rafiq and Javed were at the back of the house, washing the buffaloes. On Aziz Khan's land, the episode of the dead girl was already over; there had been speculation as to the murderer, some of his men naming certain peasants, not because they had any evidence but because of some personal petty feuds with them; conjecture had momentarily abused an innocent person before smearing another; someone mentioned hearing a car at night; another said it was a jeep but a third had emphatically declared that an aeroplane had been flying low; and though the subject was still passingly talked of, its essential matter had been exhausted by now.

Elahi greeted Aziz Khan who turned a silent stare at him and then briefly nodded his head, flicking his eyes also from one to the other of the two officers with Elahi.

'We're making inquiries into the murder of the girl found by that stream last week,' Elahi said, 'and believe that your elder son can assist us.'

Elahi's phraseology did not imply any particular insinuation and Aziz Khan, pointing to the back of the house, said, 'He's there.'

Elahi went round with his men and saw Rafiq in the action of throwing a bucket of water on a buffalo's back and laughing, for he deliberately threw some of the water on Javed who was scrubbing the beast and who protested loudly at the soaking. They saw the police officers then; Javed broke off in the middle of an abusive sentence and Rafiq put down the bucket.

'Are you Rafiq?' Elahi asked.

'Yes.'

'Will you please come with us? We need your assistance in some inquiries we're making into the murder of the girl found near here last week.'

'I know nothing,' Rafiq said.

'I said we need your assistance.'

'But how can I assist?'

'You will soon know.'

'What do you want me to do?'

'Just come to the station with us.'

'What for? Why can't you ask me here? I tell you I know nothing.'

'It's only a formality,' Elahi said, smiling condescendingly.

'Funny formality,' Rafiq said.

Elahi laughed slightly to humour him.

'What do I have to do?'

'Just come with us.'

'Yes, but what do I do when I get there?'

'You'll see. There are some people to identify.'

'Oh, that. All right. I'll go and change my shirt.'

'There's no need to. It'll soon be over.'

Elahi's manner was so disarmingly friendly and charming that Rafiq, believing that he was going for no more than a couple of hours, less if they drove him back, walked with the police officers to the car without even going into the house to say good-bye to his mother and without bothering to disturb his father.

Javed watched the car drive away and for a moment fixed his eyes on the silhouette of his brother's head in the rear window. He was annoyed, for they had not yet finished washing the buffaloes and he would now have to do the work alone.

Javed

Javed

1

Throughout Rafiq's trial, Javed kept remembering their conversation about sex, particularly a remark Rafiq had once made when they were sitting beside the stream after dinner, that he would like to screw a peasant girl on that spot. Javed had not been able to see his brother after the evening when the Chief Superintendent had taken him away on the pretext of wanting his assistance; Javed had not been able to see him to talk to, to comfort, to discover the truth from him. And when he first saw him being led into the court-room, it was a changed Rafiq he saw.

Five weeks of detention, five weeks of the airless dark cell and of the sudden and frequent interrogation had drained the blood from his cheeks; when, spiritless and weary, he would lapse into a semi-conscious stupor, he would be pulled out of his narrow bed and dragged into the Superintendent's office for more questioning. The repetitive process had first confused and then deadened his mind, till he could not tell what the loud, abusive words signified.

And sitting in the strangers' gallery, observing his thinned brother, Javed could not himself concentrate on the dialogue of the court-room although he wanted to hear every word so that he could understand either the truth about Rafiq's conviction or the conscience of men who had chosen him for their accusation. He listened intently whenever a new cross-examination commenced, but often his mind would wander to images of his and Rafiq's past and he would lose the drift of the questioning.

'Your name is Rafiq Khan?'

'Yes.'

'What is your age?'

'Twenty-eight.'

'Are you married?'

'No.'

Out in the hills in the east where they had once camped together for a week, for Aziz Khan had said:

—Here is a riddle: If I have the whole earth for my government, still only one tree can give me shade. What do you make of that, Rafiq? And you, Javed?

And he had asked them to go and live in the hills for a week. Their father could be so inscrutable! Like an old wizard in the stories they had been told in their childhood. Out in the hills in the east, it was a good time the father had chosen, springtime, and miles away the snow was melting on the mountains and here the streams were already swelling and the almond-trees were in blossom.

The electric fan was circling above the judge's head and the voice was circling round the court.

'Have you ever been engaged to be married?'

'Yes.'

'When was that?'

'Three years ago.'

'What happened to the engagement?'

'It was broken off.'

'Suppose it had not been broken off, would it be true to say that by now you would have been married for between two and three years?'

'I suppose so.'

They had left early in the morning, before sunrise. They could walk briskly in the cool of the morning, but Rafiq chose to walk at a slow pace; for Javed was not yet ten and Rafiq knew he would tire too soon if they walked briskly and that way they would not reach the foot of the hills until long after sunrise, whereas if they walked slowly, they had a good chance. He himself would have walked faster but he had measured the distance in his mind and related it to his brother's capacity, which he did not wish to exceed, or make excessive demands upon, too soon. Rafiq preferred to calculate for a future which would soon be the present; therefore, he restrained Javed by starting up a song, a rousing ballad which required so much breath that they had to walk slowly.

'You suppose? Aren't you sure?'

'Yes.'

'Yes, what?'

'Yes, I would have been married by now for two or three years.'

'Time enough for you to have had at least one child?'

'Yes.'

'Where were you on the evening of twenty-seventh March, between nine p.m. and ten p.m.?'

'At home.'

'Can you recall what you did during that time?'

'I went to sleep soon after nine o'clock.'

'Is there anyone apart from members of your family who saw you between nine and ten that evening?'

'No.'

A mile from the hills in the east, and the sun was up. Rafiq had persevered with the ballad in the pink dawn and

Javed, determined not to lag behind in any respect, had continued to sing with him, or chant, or mumble, or whistle. On the dusty paths it had been easy to march to the rhythm of

> Man, man, man is a soldier in the wartime,
> Man, man, man is a peasant during peace:
> Fighting for his country to win his bit of land,
> Man, man, man is just a little beast.

But not now in the bush and the gradual ascent.

'*What is your name?*'

Javed rubbed his eyes to see the words being spoken so that he could hear them.

'*Habib Malik.*'

'*Have you ever seen the accused, Rafiq Khan, before?*'

'*Yes.*'

'*Can you describe the circumstances in which you saw him?*'

The almond trees! Where they rested, the first time away from home. The blossom in that dawn!

'*In my hut.*'

'*Where is that?*'

'*Just off the Lahore road, six miles from Kalapur.*'

'*When did the accused come there?*'

'*About six weeks ago, maybe seven.*'

'*How did he get there?*'

'*On horseback.*'

'*Was he alone or accompanied?*'

'*Alone.*'

'*What did he want?*'

'*Please, sir, I'm a poor man.*'

'*Don't worry, the court will protect you.*'

'*He wanted liquor.*'

'*What else?*'

'*A woman.*'

Where the stream had been whose water at last stopped their singing. That sting of ice-cold water. The plunging of hands, arms. The scoop of water in cupped hands, the splashing of the face. Sitting then on a rock and dipping toes, feet, ankles in water. But it was too cold yet to bathe.

What are they saying, what are they saying?

'*Do you mean a prostitute?*'

'*Please, sir . . .*'

'*Don't worry, the court is not interested in your profession or by what irregular means you earn your money. The court is only interested in the truth about the character of the accused. To return to my question, did you mean a prostitute?*'

'*Yes.*'

'*Did you procure a prostitute for him?*'

'*Yes.*'

The mother had given them six chapatis, cold lamb cutlets and some sweetmeats. The father had insisted that they be given food enough only for one meal; for the rest of the stay they would have to find their own food in the hills. Except for the sweetmeats, they had not hesitated to eat the chapatis and the cutlets the first time they felt hungry, thus exhausting their supply. Nor did they think of looking for wild fowl or any kind of edible vegetable growth until they were high on a hill. The climb had made them tired and hungry. First, on looking down at the valley from which they had come, their eyes brightened at the sight of the distant plain and they searched the direction in which their father's land could be. Then, instinctively, Javed had thrust a hand into the bag, forgetting that it was now empty except for the sweetmeats. He almost began to cry and Rafiq, reprimanding himself for his failure to think ahead, tried to assure him that they had only to find a stream or a lake and they would be sure to find some fowl or beast which they could kill. They sat for a while, nibbling a sweetmeat each and even Javed knew in his brother's silence that they were saving the remaining sweetmeats in case they found nothing to eat. The hill they were on was one of many whose combined summits formed an undulating plateau which was thick with trees. They knew that to move forward was to enter the jungle. But they had no choice. For on this side was only a

beautiful view. They had to go beyond. At least they were
convinced then that they had to go beyond. They listened
for the sound of water and heard only birds. They looked for
the footprints of animals and saw nothing but concentrated
vegetation through which they had to make their own path.
They walked, they walked. Rafiq was determined not to
show his own fear to his younger brother; Javed had made
up his mind not to seem afraid. But they found no water and
the singing birds were too high on the tall trees to be shot
down by a catapult. Even if a stone could cut through all
that foliage. They walked, they walked, in the dark jungle;
although above the trees the sun was bright. At last the sun
must have gone down, for they could walk no longer and
the birds had quietened. They simply collapsed beside a
tree. Again they nibbled a sweetmeat each, catching the
crumbs in the palm so as not to drop any as they slowly and
lovingly ate the ball of butter and sweetened flour. The
jungle's darkness had become a universal night. Javed was
cold when they tried to sleep. So that Rafiq had to lie next
to him, hug him, and not cry himself, till he slept. Rafiq had
not expected to sleep, but the next morning he could not
recall when he had stopped being awake. A bird's cry
had woken him. Not a bird in the trees, but somewhere
lower, somewhere near by. He had risen while Javed still
slept on. And had been surprised to discover that there was
a pool near by. Exhaustion had deadened their senses on the
last night. Here, there was a hollow in the land filled with
water by a spring. He saw it from behind trees, walking
softly, having already learned the indispensability of silence
and stealth in the jungle. A flock of wild fowl had descended
on the water's edge. He took aim with his catapult, knowing
that he must kill one fowl with his first shot, for the birds
would fly away whether he hit or missed. He aimed, his arm
stretched tightly, and steadied his fists. He could feel the
force of the rubber in his extended arm. He hit a bird in its
breast. The flock flew up, squawking like geese. He ran to
the bird he had killed, picked it up, ran back and waited to

see if the birds would return. He heard Javed come up to him. He waved the bird in the air to show him and saw Javed's eyes brighten.

Javed bit his lip, trying to concentrate, for there were words he did not want to miss.

'*What is your name?*'

'*Mohammed Ali.*'

'*Where do you live?*'

'*In the Kangra Settlement.*'

'*Where is that?*'

'*On the road four miles east of Aziz Khan's land.*'

'*What is your position in the Settlement?*'

'*I'm the head-man.*'

'*Have you seen the accused, Rafiq Khan, before?*'

'*Yes, many times.*'

'*Can you recall any one particular time?*'

'*Yes, some weeks ago he came to the Settlement and asked me if I could help in getting more peasants to work on his father's land.*'

'*Who else was there with you at the time?*'

'*My family.*'

'*What does your family consist of?*'

'*My wife and three daughters.*'

'*How old are your daughters?*'

'*Between twelve and fifteen.*'

'*Were they all with you when he visited you?*'

'*Yes.*'

'*Did the accused see your daughters?*'

'*Oh, yes.*'

'*Why are you so sure?*'

'*He was looking at them all the time.*'

'*Is there anything odd about looking at girls?*'

'*We respect Allah . . .*'

'*Yes, yes, but I repeat, is there anything odd about looking at girls?*'

'*No more than a hungry wolf looking at sheep.*'

'*What do you know about the deceased Jumila Bano?*'

'*She lived in the Settlement.*'

'*Did you know her?*'

'*Yes.*'

'*Did she ever visit your family?*'

'*Yes, she was a friend of my girls.*'

'*When did she last visit your family?*'

'*On the same evening that the accused came to see me about the peasants.*'

'*Did he see her?*'

'*Yes.*'

'*Did she stay long at your place?*'

'*Not long, about ten minutes. She had come to ask my girls something.*'

'*When did the accused leave?*'

'*Soon after she did.*'

'*What did you do?*'

'*Soon after he left, I decided to go round the huts to see if I could recruit some peasants for him.*'

'*What did you see on coming out of your place?*'

'*I saw the accused talking to Jumila Bano.*'

Silence and stealth; they had learned the jungle's principal law. Driving their teeth into the fowl's tough meat. They learned, too, to preserve twice as much food as they needed for one meal. Their ability to provide for themselves gave them the freedom to explore. For six days they were content. Among the almond-trees in blossom beside a pool or farther into the thickness and obscurity of growth. They went on.

But he heard and tried to understand.

'*That part of the hillock is used only by women.*'

'*How far was Jumila Bano from where you were sitting?*'

'*Some twenty yards away.*'

'*What did you see when she rose?*'

'*She was just walking away when a man on horseback came up to her. They talked and then she mounted the horse too, and they rode away.*'

'*Which way did they go?*'

'*West.*'

'*That would be in the direction of Kalapur, would it not?*'

'Yes.'

'Which is the first house on the road to Kalapur?'

'Aziz Khan's.'

'Did you recognise the man on horseback?'

'No, it was dark.'

'Is there anyone in the Kangra Settlement who owns a horse?'

'No.'

'Are there any other settlements or villages near Kangra?'

'No. There are only hills in the east and all the other villages and settlements are either to the north or the west of Kalapur.'

'So, if you saw a man on horseback in or around the Kangra Settlement, what would you conclude?'

'I'd know straight away that he came from Aziz Khan's house.'

But then they did not want to go on. They could have. Once or twice they had talked of going on, beyond the beyond they could see. Once or twice, idly. There were the mountains beyond and once or twice they had considered scaling them, but talking idly of course. They could have, they were sure—and why not? they would also ask, biting the fowl's flesh. But then they did not want to go on, not beyond.

—For look, Rafiq said, maybe that's China there. Not there! Beyond there.

And Javed wanted to charge through the jungle like Genghiz Khan, but Rafiq knew that that was only a game.

Speaking more to himself, debating the point, Rafiq said:

—We'll have to stop somewhere. There are limits. We must decide. If we don't decide, we'll go on and on and won't know where we are. We have to decide.

Again Rafiq was calculating, working out, holding the future up like a toddler and coaxing it to walk so that he could observe its steps. He realised that he had to set his own limits. Though Javed would not understand, not yet, but he would, later, understand fully. Rafiq called him back from his game.

The Counsel for the Prosecution made his final speech, but Javed could not understand the English he spoke.

'In my summing-up I would like first of all to thank the witnesses who have appeared to testify to the court. They have all been poor people, humble people, filled with a deep sense of duty, a profound love and fear of Allah, people, in short, of complete honesty and impeccable virtue. Some of them have risked their livelihoods in order to hold the torch of truth in this court. Long may it burn and long may such noble citizens abound in our country.

'A number of basic facts concerning the character of the accused, Rafiq Khan, have clearly been established by the evidence. First of all, the breaking up of his engagement three years ago has led to an emotional disturbance within him, arousing acute feelings of frustration. Secondly, the frustration has engendered a strong reaction: he has been like a man addicted to a drug, for how else can we account for his frequent visits to prostitutes, his unembarrassed staring at girls even in the presence of their parents, and his unashamed approaches in public to a girl? What is more, the girl he was seen talking to was from a poor peasant family and no one can believe that his intentions were honourable. It is clear that he took advantage of her. The final picture which emerges is of a sexual maniac, a person who has not learned the virtue of patience nor understood the wisdom of Allah. In trying to satisfy his evil hunger, he has sought to run his own life and not waited for the gift of life to be given him from above. Not satisfied with dealing with prostitutes, he has sought to defile the innocence of peasant girls. The outcome of such an evil-minded maniac can only be tragic. The tragedy is not his, but ours: we have lost a flower of this earth because this maniac flouted social law, abandoned the customs of his country, and forgot his religion. We have lost a tender girl, a creature of sweet innocence and purity, because this maniac could not control his sexual hunger. She protested, she cried out for her mother while he madly assaulted her, and, himself driven crazy by her screams, he killed her, choked her to death. A death so horrible that no true Muslim would wish it on his enemy. It is a tragic story.

But let me ask you: can we tolerate such a person among our midst, freely entering our houses and threatening our liberty? I ask you: are we to keep our daughters behind locked doors? No, emphatically no. Control, human responsibility, these are the very essence of liberty, and this is why the law must be enforced, this is why society must exterminate the person who lacks that control, who knows no responsibility. There can be no question of mercy in this case: for such a mercy can only mean a lasting cruelty to all the daughters of Pakistan.'

Later, the young Counsel for the Prosecution was congratulated on his brilliant exposition: people who had heard his loud rhetoric, hypnotised by the lilting rhythm of his voice and awed by his astonishing command of English, which they often did not understand, were speechless in their admiration and predicted an outstanding future for him. The Judge praised him, too, having a special word to say about his compassion, and pronounced Rafiq guilty and sentenced him to death by hanging.

Javed had listened whenever the peasants had been questioned in Urdu or in Punjabi. He did not understand any English and he was so carried away by the sound of the Counsel for the Prosecution's speech, that he was prepared to believe in the truth of his statement, whatever it was. But he had not been able to discover for himself any real meaning in the court's proceedings. He was himself confused. He did not remember his brother being away from the house as often as it must have been necessary for him to be if he had committed all the actions the witnesses had attributed to him. Perhaps he had not heard enough. And what about Rafiq, why had he not protested? Javed could only wonder. He was too uninstructed in the ways of the world to realise that the witnesses might be lying, that the whole system of the law was in the hands of a few powerful men; he was too naïve to understand that the awe-inspiring institution of the law was liable to corruption; he was too illiterate and inexperienced to conclude for himself that the secular arbiters of justice were as capricious as a heavenly one; and he did not know the one rule which men obey more readily than any edicts propounded either by religion or by law, that a man must indulge the wishes of the rich. Javed was confused. He never doubted that what he heard was the truth and yet he had an intuitive belief in his brother's innocence. For the first time in his life, he had seen another world than the one to which he had been accustomed: there were complexities; above all, there was a verbal dialogue, which he did not understand. His own despair at losing his brother increased the confusion in his mind.

He found it difficult to speak to his parents; they seemed stone idols he had worshipped too long and now that his soul demanded an answer from them, they were silent. The tragedy had a stunning effect on the family. Javed was drawn less to his father, whose wisdom and authority he had never before questioned. It was an embarrassment for him to approach his mother who sat cross-legged on her bed, staring amazedly in a petrified stance in the manner of one who has suddenly lost vision. Many of the peasants had left during the trial; being gullible people, they accepted the conclusions of the law as truth and considered Rafiq's action to be so immensely evil that for them to continue to work for a house which was now obviously cursed was wilfully to attract the curse, the evil and the consequent tragedy upon themselves. The land was beginning to show neglect. For days, Aziz Khan sat in the front yard, suffering the heat with no more thought than if he had been made of asbestos. Javed did not go to him; nor did Aziz Khan turn to Javed. The mother had ceased to hear her own crying and neither of the parents saw or heard their younger, and now, their only son.

Moving silently about the house, Javed observed his parents. The grief which they now shared had isolated them. His mind was still puzzled. He tried to recall all that he could remember about Rafiq. Little by little, he began to understand his brother's personality, and what he understood was not at all like the Rafiq whose character was now public knowledge. All his deliberations led Javed to begin to suspect the beliefs he had unthinkingly held. For slowly, he was beginning to realise that there were other distinctions than good and bad and right and wrong; there were *values* which did not come from moral rectitude but which society ascribed to certain actions and things. He had known that people often lied, for he had himself had occasions to do so—the earthy primitiveness in which he lived was not free of human injustice; but he had not before experienced the organized mendacity of a whole community. The people he saw in Kalapur were not different from him because they affected a modern sophistication, driving cars and living in air-conditioned houses, but because they maintained a standard of values in which the ability to deceive convincingly had a distinct advantage.

His father, he felt, should have known this, and, in his mind, Javed began to blame his father for Rafiq's death. For Aziz Khan had apparently done nothing to save Rafiq; but Javed did not know that he had not been able to obtain the services of a lawyer in Kalapur and had had to send for one from Lahore, a cheap, nervous barrister who was no match for the young Counsel for the Prosecution with his London education and superior accent. Aziz Khan had prayed during the trial and fasted from sunrise to sunset, but he had not gone to the court. He left the trial in the hands of Allah and saw his own duty to be one of making a direct appeal to Him. He had failed, but he attributed the failure now to his own lack, to his own insufficiency of piety. Or it could be, he reflected, that Allah had a higher purpose for wanting to take away Rafiq. The Muslim adage, *What had to happen has happened*, was constantly on his lips, and he sat in the front yard, a monument to Islam's defeatist fatalism.

But the land in front of him was empty, the plants were withering through neglect. Something had gone out of his world and he was finding it difficult to explain or to understand. He hoped that his son had not committed the crimes for which he had died; but, although he knew the capacity

137

of the peasants to lie, not because they were easily bribed but because they feared anyone with money, he still had no proof of Rafiq's innocence. As yet, he had no firm notion that the Shah brothers might well be the catalysts for the explosion in his own family, though, when he wondered about which moneyed power could have so loaded the case against Rafiq, he sometimes considered the Shah family as having planted the crimes at his own doorstep. Again, it was only a probability and he had no definite proof; he had mentioned the notion to his lawyer, but that stuttering idiot had made nothing of it. It was Allah's will, Aziz Khan frequently sighed to himself as he sat watching the flights of crows over his land.

The few peasants who remained with him, sat idle, gossiping beside the stream where they could keep cool by dangling their legs in the water. The house was strangely inactive, sending out no orders. Javed alone moved there, keeping away from his father and not daring to approach his mother. The house oppressed him; its silences had an unreality which annoyed him. One day he walked into the plantations and spent the whole morning listening to soft insect sounds. He was moved by the sorry condition of the plants. He wanted to console them. He wanted to tend each one himself although he realised no sooner than the feeling surfaced in him that the task would be impossibly immense. Then he came upon a number of peasants lying in the rice field. He scolded them for lying idle when the fields around them were so much in need of attention. They laughed nervously and rose, pretending to turn to work. It was not their fault, Javed thought, for they had done nothing to contribute to the curse which had fallen on the house. He walked back ruefully, trying not to look too closely at the plants.

He saw the house from a distance, his father in front of it. What could they do? he wondered. The land would need peasants, many more of them. Most of all, it would need a master who was driven to work on the land not by mere necessity but by his soul. He doubted if his father could be that master now. He doubted if he himself was capable of such a task. And yet, he was aware of the urgency of doing something. The money had run out. If the present inactivity continued, there would be no cotton to sell and no rice to eat in a few months. He wondered what his father thought, whether he realised his responsibilities. Perhaps if he had been an educated man with a subtler insight into the minds of other people, his father would not have accepted his present situation with such inertia.

The days went by slowly; how many, Javed could not afterwards tell. The inactivity around him oppressed him; until, one day, he felt compelled that something had to be done. The sight of the neglected land and of his seemingly motionless father in front of it made him want to escape from the place, to go elsewhere, to start anew. He looked up at the sky which was white with heat. Miles high, an eagle floated on its wings; there was nothing around it but the glaring sunlight, an emptiness for its surveillance. Javed decided what he should do. He spoke to his father that afternoon.

'I think we should sell the land,' he said.

Aziz Khan looked up at his son; his eyes did not question the presumption of such a suggestion.

'It is yours, son,' is all that he said.

'Shall I go to the Shah brothers and tell them we'll sell?'

'It is all yours.'

'We could go to Karachi. We could live with Zuleikha. Mother needs someone to look after her. The land is going bad with neglect.'

'It is all you have, son.'

'Shall I go and tell them we accept their offer?'

Aziz Khan did not answer but bowed his head so that his chin rested against his chest.

'What else can we do but die?' Javed said bitterly.

'Go, son, do as Allah guides you. It is all you have.' Aziz

Khan spoke softly as though the words were uttered despite his body and that he was not responsible for them.

Javed went at once in reaction to his father's weak statement; he walked away with stiff strides a little ostentatiously as if he were demonstrating a firmness of decision. But Aziz Khan did not see him go.

At the mills, Javed asked to see Akram.

'Well, well,' Akram said, 'why, it's young Khan sahib. Sit down, sit down.' He asked his secretary to call Ayub.

'What brings you here? I was sorry to hear about that business about your brother. Very sorry, believe me.'

Javed stared at him sternly and said, 'We'll accept your offer for our land.'

Just then Ayub entered.

'Come in, Ayub,' Akram said. 'Young Khan sahib here has come to sell his land. It was a terrible business that, terrible.'

'Yes,' Ayub said. 'We were most sorry. Our sincerest condolences to your respected father. It must be a terrible blow to him.'

'You can have the land now,' Javed said as though making an accusation.

'Family respects first, Khan sahib,' Ayub said with no haste in his voice. 'We wish to sympathise with your father.'

'And your mother,' Akram added.

'I wish to sell the land,' Javed persisted.

Akram had drawn out a file from a drawer in his desk and was glancing at some papers.

'We'll accept your offer,' Javed went on.

'Let me see now what it was,' Akram said, turning to the papers.

'It was two thousand an acre,' Javed said.

'Where exactly is your land?' Ayub asked.

'You know very well where it is,' Javed said, looking fiercely at Ayub.

'No, I've never been there,' Ayub said. 'What was it we needed it for?' he asked Akram.

140

'Hm . . . a . . . a small research plantation to try out new fertilisers. Nothing important.'

Akram had taken Ayub's hint and discreetly put away the file.

'Yes, nothing really important.' Ayub nodded his head.

'How much do you want for it?' Akram asked.

'What you offered,' Javed said. 'Two thousand an acre.'

'But, my dear Khan sahib,' Ayub said, 'that was a year ago. And besides, you refused that offer.'

'Yes,' Akram said. 'We needed the land then. But we've been able to make other arrangements since then.'

'Listen,' Ayub said, 'if you're in any difficulty, we'd be glad to help you out. But we don't really need to buy your land now.'

'Please don't mistake us,' Akram said. 'If you're keen to sell, well, we can't really disappoint you. We'd hate to do that, especially now that there is this trouble in your house. But you must realise that when we made our last offer, we desperately wanted the land then. For our research project. But now it will be just an additional burden. We'll make the sacrifice, however. If you really must sell, we'll offer . . . hm . . . let me think, we'll offer . . .'

'Two hundred an acre,' Ayub said.

Javed looked from one to the other and laughed scornfully.

'Your first offer was five hundred,' Javed said, 'and that is what you gave to the other landlords.'

'Yes, precisely,' Ayub said. 'So, you see when we offered two thousand an acre, we were really going out of our way. Now we don't need to do so. We just don't need the land and in paying two hundred an acre, we're simply using up our capital in order to do you a favour.'

'I don't want any favours,' Javed said, rising to go.

'No, no, don't get all heated up,' Ayub said. 'You must realise that everything has a market value. The market value of your land at present is down. In business, you can't afford to lose a good chance. And you had more than a good chance a year ago, you had a super chance.'

'Yes,' Akram said. 'That's the first principle of business.'

'It's two thousand an acre or it's nothing,' Javed said.

Ayub laughed; it was his turn to be scornful; and before Akram could do so as well, Javed said, 'It's nothing, then,' and went out.

Now Akram laughed, too, and Ayub said, 'He'll come crawling back, I tell you, he'll come on his hands and knees. And it *will* be nothing.'

Akram continued to laugh.

Javed went out of the mills looking more serious than when he had come. He was convinced now that he had made a mistake, that the Shah brothers had probably been expecting him to come, as it were, with a begging-bowl. He was convinced, too, that it would have been a mistake to sell the land. There was more than bread and milk involved: his own, his father's and his family's dignity were involved. Humiliated by the Shah brothers, he felt stronger in spirit now, and resolved to himself that he would bring life again to the land even if it meant working single-handed, even if it meant months of deprivation and bitter toil.

When he returned home, he did not go to his father to tell him that his mission had failed. Aziz Khan asked for no explanations. Javed went to bed early that night and made another tour of the fields the next morning in order to determine where he should begin the process of restoration. When the peasants came loitering down the paths among the rows of cotton, he asked them to assemble beside a tree.

'You'd better make up your minds,' he told the peasants, 'whether you want to come here to work or to lie about in the shade telling stories to one another. Whether you want to till the land or to play. But tell me, you Ibrahim, who were recounting many jokes yesterday by the rice field, tell me where are the swings, where are the roundabouts? Do you think this is a playground? Maybe I'm blind and can't see all the amusement around me. Can you give me a hand and lead me to the swings?'

Ibrahim, easily humiliated, bowed his head in shame.

'We're going to start now and you'd better make up your minds at once. If you want amusement, go elsewhere where you can screw the arse-holes of donkeys. I don't want any idlers here. Do you understand? I'll drive the plough through your arses if I find any of you shirking. Now, get the hell out of this shade and start work.'

The peasants, much impressed by Javed's base and earthy language whose vocabulary they fully comprehended, for it almost comprised the entire range of their discourse, scurried off at once. Javed himself took charge of the rice field, inspecting first the water supply.

From a distance, Aziz Khan noticed the activity in the fields. He sat up in his chair, concentrating his gaze so that he could discern the floating brown specks to be the moving bodies of his peasants. He rose to his feet and decided that the white speck must be Javed for he had been wearing a shirt. Javed had not told him the outcome of the meeting with the Shah brothers; but now Aziz Khan realised that Javed had returned empty-handed from them and the activity on the land was his reaction. A slight smile relieved the austerity of his features as Aziz Khan turned his head to the heavens; his lips curled as they instinctively spoke the Arabic words of prayer. He sat down again, grateful that, amidst the tragedy which had struck his house, Allah had once again blessed him in inspiring his younger son to continue the work on the land. And the tears which now came to his eyes could have had their source in some inner life-giving force.

2

Afaq opened a newspaper in the plane from Lahore and, turning the pages with little interest in what they had to say to him, saw his own photograph, taken the day before at the Kalapur railway station. *Mr. Afaq Shah, B. Comm., Merchandising Director of Shah Enterprises Ltd, seen at Kalapur Central station on his departure for the U.K., for higher studies—*

143

the caption declared. Afaq was surprised to see that he had been given a degree by the newspaper. Perhaps Ayub had told the reporter that lie; and also the bit about being the merchandising director: he did not know such a position existed. Garlands of saffron flowers were bunched round his neck, creating an impression in the poorly printed photograph of a thick fur collar. He did not like his own face in the picture. The stern, humourless gaze seemed to betray a fear, a secret anxiety. He put the paper away and looked out of the window. Fourteen thousand feet below, the green of the Punjab was slowly giving way to the Sind desert.

Rafiq was dead. Jumila Bano was dead. And here he was riding the air like a vulture.

He had had no control over the events which followed his rape of Jumila Bano. He had realised the monstrosity of that event soon enough. But no one abused him for his base action, no one accused him of any crime. Instead, his brothers seemed exceptionally pleasant to him and behaved as though nothing had happened; whereas he had seen Chief Superintendent Fazal Elahi come to the mills on a number of occasions and it was obvious to him that his brothers were bribing the officer to save his life. He knew, too, that it was not his life which they were really concerned to save, but the family's name.

At home the women had not even guessed—how could they when they were continually kept amused with superfluous activities? Once, Razia had coyly asked him to come and continue the story of the monkeys to her children, but he had been in no mood to humour her. She seemed hurt that he should turn down her invitation and had not looked at him for two whole days, turning away her face whenever she had occasion to pass him in a corridor. She thought, however, that a scrupulous deference to Ayub's power in the house was the reason for Afaq's refusal, and soon resumed giving him furtive smiles, chastising herself for making tactless suggestions. He wished in his despair that he could still love her, for he thought that Ayub's discovering him with his wife and whipping him would have been far less unbearable an experience than the horror in his own mind with which he had to live now; indeed, Ayub's whip would have been merciful in that it would have expunged the guilt from his mind; or at least diminished it. For physical pain could have been distracting. The less he tried to respond to Razia's glances, the more he felt he loved her; and incapable now of approaching her, however indirectly, he felt all the more remorseful at what he had done. Reacting to the threat of Ayub's power, he had deprived himself of even a temporary happiness with Razia.

In the plane, looking down at the desert now, he remembered Zarina whom he had on occasion caught looking at him from some corner of the house. And remembering her, he recalled the thin, frail body of Jumila Bano. He tried to dismiss Zarina from his mind so that the ghost of Jumila Bano could also be exorcised. What did Zarina want? Perhaps she had a crush on him. She was too young, too impressionable, too much influenced by those immediately near her. Jumila Bano had been young, too. Go away, girl, go away, please. Going over an air depression, the plane suddenly lost a little height, but soon held itself again, firmly breasting the air. Afaq groaned slightly to himself as though he was going to be sick, and shut his eyes.

After spending the night in the hotel at Karachi airport, he boarded a Super Constellation to London. The plane was full. He was surprised to see so many people going to England. What were they all running away from? He soon realised that many of them were peasants who spoke no English. He had read in the papers that England was attracting thousands of immigrants from India, Pakistan and the West Indies because it offered good jobs in factories. He looked around him at the large-eyed Punjabi peasant faces. The men were cheaply dressed in clothes which vaguely resembled suits while the women were still enshrouded in yards of veils. There was a look of fear in their eyes, a fear of the unknown. From their earthy existence on the land under blue skies and a burning sun, they were going to turn themselves to slaves of time and money. But what could they do, since their semi-primitiveness did not give them enough to live on in their simple rural existence? Afaq had read also of the opportunists who were making a fortune by arranging for passports—and faking them when they could not be obtained—and passages for these peasants whose only contact with civilisation was a thumb-mark they made on official documents. He pitied them and felt an empathy with them, for, like him, they too were refugees from the crime of not having fitted into their environment.

He regretted this deliberation, for the word 'crime' brought him back to the particularity of his own offence. He looked out. Far below was the Arabian Sea, on which the ocean liners seemed to be paper-boats in a pond. He was flying towards Persia. The plane coursed the air smoothly, though the engine-noise was clawing at his ears.

The family had gathered around him at Kalapur Central. He remembered how Razia momentarily clasped his shoulder and looked into his eyes when she placed a garland round his neck. He had wanted to stretch his arm to her, to hold her, he had wanted to tell her that he loved her. But she had withdrawn, perhaps suppressing a tear, he did not know. Faridah had joked, 'Don't let the English girrels trap you.' Zarina had stood with her head bowed, and when it was her turn to place a garland, she had quickly, hastily come up to him, her eyes looking past his shoulder, and had almost flung the garland at his head and retreated into her own timidity. The brothers had embraced him, hugging him tightly; for there were photographers about.

And now to England. Rafiq had been hanged, Jumila Bano was dead. And here he was, vermin, running to a hole in the darkness of an alien country.

Razia, Razia! he wanted to cry out to her. He wanted her love. Already he was lonely. She would be a different Razia when he returned. Two years, perhaps more, would pass before he saw her again. She would have had more of

Ayub's children and grown fatter. *Oh, Razia!* Now her image was fixed in his mind: something to give him a hold on Kalapur, something to salvage from the ruin of his youth: the woman who had come to him when he had been injured by her husband's blows, who merely by holding his shoulder for a moment conveyed her love, was beginning to burn up his brain as though it was dry wood so that his mind floated on the dreamy smoke of fantasies. Already; with Persia not yet reached. *Razia!* Already; the westward route was beginning to sicken him.

3

For Zarina it was a time of sadness. The one object which had preoccupied her imagination for so long had been taken away from her. One day, alone with Razia, she could not help bursting into tears when asked, 'What keeps our heroine so quiet nowadays?'

Razia was embarrassed. She had hoped to make Zarina feel livelier by teasing her a little, but the tears were too solemn, too formal a declaration of the depth of Zarina's feelings.

'Come, there's no need to cry,' she said. 'He's only gone for two years.'

It upset Razia to have to say that, for it implied an admission of her sympathy. She wondered whether she ought to feel jealous of Zarina, but decided that the exercise would be totally an abstract one since neither of them had access to Afaq. Seeing Zarina cry uncontrollably, she resolved to keep her own passion to herself.

'You mustn't be so sad,' Razia said. 'You're only in your teens and there are plenty of young men who'd be only too glad to have you. You know *that*.'

'I *love* him,' Zarina said, her mouth dribbling.

Now, it must be stated that the concept of love, which is curiously vague in those countries which have flaunted it for centuries, is still more vague in Pakistan where it is an invention primarily of Hollywood, and when a young girl makes such a statement, she is no more than identifying herself with, say, Natalie Wood.

Razia, however, was impressed by Zarina's impassioned declaration. All she could say in reply was, 'But, Zarina, you're so young. How do you know you're *really* in love?'

'I *know* I am,' Zarina said.

'We all think that at your age,' Razia said. 'And we all need a setback to test us. If you're really in love, two years won't matter.'

Zarina felt slightly consoled and said, 'Two years is a long time.'

'It will pass.'

'And suppose an English girl hooks him in London?'

Razia did not relish that possibility and tried to dismiss it by saying, 'I'm sure Afaq is too sensible for that.'

Faridah entered then and Zarina rose to go and stand by the window so that Faridah might not see her eyes.

'*Hai Allah*, this shahping is tiring,' Faridah declared and collapsed into a sofa. 'And it's so haht.'

'What do you expect, it's May,' Razia said. 'Thank goodness for air-conditioning.'

'Vell, vhat vill you give me for good news?' Faridah asked.

Zarina turned to look at her. Razia thought that Faridah was at last going to announce her pregnancy, but she hoped not.

'I've gaht tickets for *Bhavani Junction*,' Faridah said. 'Oh, there vas such a queue, such a queue, I vent straight to the manager and gaht the tickets from him. It's supposed to be a terrafick fillem. Vith Ah-va Gahdnerr vearing a sari.'

4

Javed wanted to discover some means of directing more water to the rice field. The summer rains were not expected for several weeks yet, but he was not considering the rains; normally, their work on the land followed a routine established by nature but, now that they had neglected the earth for two months, he did not expect nature to be especially bountiful, for nature made no compensations for man's failures. Also, he superstitiously expected a reversal from nature as a reprisal for the two months of inattention. Consequently, he wanted to guarantee success with the crop by creating an artificial supply of water. His thoughts turned to the stream behind the house and he contemplated digging a canal to divert its course to the rice field, wondering why this idea had never occurred to anyone else in the family. This notion was the first attempt at *organisation* on Aziz Khan's land and Aziz Khan did not like it.

'Have you lost your faith in Allah?' Aziz Khan asked him firmly, though there was no trace of vehemence in his voice. 'All my life the land has been rich and unfailing.'

'But we have failed the land,' Javed argued. 'We have to make good our failure.'

'No, my son, Allah will provide.'

Javed was neither foolish nor irreligious enough to contradict his father's unwavering belief. He went away, disconsolate and feeling weary. He had seen some of the Shah brothers' land being farmed. The bright yellow tractors cut through the earth, striping the land with their tyres. He had seen the foremen in their dust-covered shoes, *topees* and sunglasses, directing the labourers. He had seen their land erupt with growth and it had occurred to him that Allah had not penalised them for using chemical fertilisers. What curse was it, then, that insisted that he should go to his land barehanded and employ only the most primitive of tools? He tried to suppress his doubts, convinced that a slackening of faith could have catastrophic repercussions and that he must be content with what was granted him. In the end, Javed had no choice but to remain passively indulgent to whatever fortune or misfortune befell him, for religion, which is conveniently employed by governments to maintain obedient

149

passivity, had for centuries made the Punjabi countryman accept his plight as his *kismet*. And although Javed sometimes fancied himself sitting in an office with an electric fan circling above his head, he could no more depart from the type than expect rivers to flow uphill. It was too early in the history of his family for there to be a psychological accommodation for modern changes: Allah was still the provider.

His mother called from the kitchen when she heard his footsteps in the veranda. He went to her and said impatiently, 'What is it, ma? I'm just going to have a bath.'

She was squatting by the stove, stirring a pot. He observed how much she had thinned during the last two months; sorrow was not only a mental state but afflicted the body also. She sat up from her bent position and passed a hand over the small of her back.

'Ma, why do you have to tire yourself in the kitchen?' he asked. 'Why don't you get a peasant woman to cook for us?'

'If a mother can't cook for her son, what good is she?'

'But you keep complaining about the pain in your back,' Javed said.

'Oh, it's nothing,' she said. 'There was a letter from Karachi this afternoon. From Zuleikha.'

'Is she coming?'

'Well, what do you say?'

'What do you mean, what do I say?' he asked.

'You know what I mean,' she said.

'Ma, I must have my bath. I'm itching all over with sweat.'

'You're working hard, my son.'

'I'm not complaining,' he said.

'Allah be praised,' she said.

'Well, what is it, then?'

'If a mother doesn't cook for her son, who does?' she asked.

'That's an unfair question.'

'Well?'

'Oh no, you're not getting me hooked,' he said.

'Come, what sort of talk is this?' she said, taking some pleasure in assuming a slightly scolding tone. 'If you don't have a wife, who will in this house?'

'Not yet, ma, not yet. There'll be time. There's too much to do at present.'

'Well, I didn't say we'd marry you tomorrow. There'll be an engagement first.'

'Ma, give me time, give me a year, two years. Let me make something of this place.'

'You will, you will. But you need a wife to help you. Zuleikha says she knows a very good family. The daughter's name is Amina. She's eighteen and just finishing school. Zuleikha says she'll inquire and try and get a photo for you to see.'

'We'll see,' he said ambiguously and went to the bath-room.

She turned to the pot then, adding some more chopped green chillies to its contents. Oh, these modern children, she thought, how fussy they were. She felt the pain again in her back and, letting go of the ladle, stooped forward and pressed both her hands to her back. She decided to ask her husband to massage her back with linseed oil before he went to bed. She hoped she could persuade Javed to marry early, for she had remarked how absorbed he was with his own thoughts. She was certain it was not right for him to be companionless. A grandchild would bring so much happiness to her! She sighed, trying to sit up again in order to attend to the cooking. A daughter-in-law would relieve her of so many chores, too, the performance of which was becoming trying for a person in her condition. Also, she would be a companion. And a girl from Karachi was very likely to bring in her dowry one of those battery-operated radios she had heard of. She thought of the dowry being brought to the house from a lorry outside the house by a string of man-servants, ceremoniously carrying in one item at a time. There would be framed mirrors and silver vessels, there would be linen and, of course, a set of clothes for her. Bemused with her reverie, she could forget her pain.

In the bathroom, Javed slowly tilted the bucket of water over his head and let the water pour down his body. He could not have denied that he was a trifle flattered by the thought that his sister was busy finding a wife for him in Karachi. He wondered if he would need to go to Karachi or whether the girl's parents would come and visit them. Perhaps they would invite him and he would have to send them a message saying that pressure of work unfortunately made it impossible for him to leave Kalapur and perhaps they would do him the honour of visiting his parents' house? Oh, that would impress them! He wondered if the girl was of a fair complexion and what sort of figure she had. 'Amina.' He tried out her name on his tongue, letting the water crash down loudly on his shoulders as he pronounced the name to himself. He almost blushed. His mind was filled with female forms. Soon, he could not help remembering his brother and mildly scolded himself for being happy. His thoughts turned to the Shah brothers and his attempt to sell the land to them. He had heard that Afaq had gone to London and he was puzzled, for the brothers were not only masters of themselves but of the whole town and what use could the youngest of them have for higher studies? Could they not have employed someone who already possessed the knowledge which Afaq had now gone to acquire expensively? Javed remembered that Rafiq had once met Afaq in the town and had been driven back by him, but he did not know any more of their relationship. He thought again of the female body and decided to dry himself and dress before he was tempted to waste his energies on the floor of the bathroom.

Although he felt a little self-satisfied and hopeful of a happier future when he walked down to the stream after bathing, he remained apprehensive about the land. Perhaps there was a limit to cultivation; perhaps the land's resourcefulness was not infinite but capable of exhaustion? He thought of fertilisers and mechanisation and regretted his illiteracy. He wanted more from the land than mere sustenance for himself. Life was larger than the dimensions of his own stomach; he knew that much, but had no knowledge of the degree and scope of life's immensity. He had no certainty that his work on the land would be productive. Hitherto, he had taken the processes of growth and decay for granted; but now he questioned with a hurtful self-awareness the purpose and utility of all his tasks. And suppose, he wondered, they had a good crop at the end of the summer, what would they do with it? The conflict with the Shah brothers was ever present in his mind and it acted like a saboteur in his thinking, destroying what notions he had assumed were sacred. He envied their organisation, though not their money, and he wondered why his father should be so adamantly against their methods when it was obvious to him that the divinity which his father so much insisted on placating had not withdrawn its favours from the Shah brothers for their introduction of machinery to the land. In spite of his doubts, Javed remained respectful of his father's wishes and did not neglect his prayers. He did not have the words with which to express the contradiction in his mind and, not understanding the conflict of the ancient and the modern, remained intellectually confused and, consequently, increasingly embittered against both his father and the Shah brothers.

Some days later, the pain in his mother's back worsened. It was morning, past breakfast time, and she had not risen from her bed. Aziz Khan watched her silently, as though the rays from his eyes would burn out her pain. Javed felt helpless, wanting to help, and essayed to relieve the tension in the room by saying, 'It's all the housework you have to do, ma.'

She sighed, thankful for her son's sympathy.

'It's too much for you,' Javed said. 'You haven't been well.'

She smiled at him and Aziz Khan, understanding the

significance of the smile, turned to him and said, 'Get a wife, son. You're right, it's too much for your mother.'

She tried to move in an attempt to communicate her agreement, but her face wrinkled up as she clenched her teeth against the pain.

'What can it be?' Aziz Khan muttered, staring at his wife's stomach as if his gaze could penetrate to her back and discover the source of her pain.

'What should be done?' Javed asked, more intent on searching for a remedy.

'It must be a muscle,' Aziz Khan said. 'Some over-strain.'

'But you've been rubbing it with linseed oil,' Javed said.

'No, there's only one thing to be done,' Aziz Khan said, at last deciding upon a medicament. 'Go, pluck some branches off the *neem* tree. Tear the leaves off and crush them till they're pulped. Add some water and boil them. I'll do the rest.'

Javed went to the *neem* tree at the back of the house and plucked a generous quantity of leaves. He followed his father's instructions, whereupon Aziz Khan immersed some cotton wool in the hot juice. Taking the soaked cotton wool out and letting it cool a minute, he placed it on his wife's back and tied it with a bandage made from a torn shirt kept for such a purpose. Aziz Khan then spread out his prayer-mat beside his wife's bed and said his morning prayers. On finishing, he turned to his wife, repeating the last phrase of the prayer, and, the phrase still on his tongue, he blew his breath on her back.

By the afternoon, however, Zakia's pain had still not abated although Aziz Khan had twice more applied newly soaked cotton wool to her back and said his midday prayer for her. Giving her a glass of hot milk to drink, he sent Javed to fetch Razvi.

Javed, sensing the urgency, for Razvi was never sent for until all home-made cures had failed, rode on his horse to the Kangra Settlement where Razvi lived in a mud hut.

Razvi was the local 'doctor'. Wearing a fez cap, he sat

cross-legged on the floor on a cushion which had once been covered with white linen. His hut occupied a favoured position in the Settlement, for the well from which the villagers drew water for all their needs was just behind his hut: so that he kept an interested eye on the womenfolk who came to the well. Some distance behind the well was the hillock where the villagers went to excrete and the rain which washed away the human dung travelled in the direction of the well: although Razvi did not have the education to inform him of the fact, the quality of the water which the pretty women came to fetch from the well was often the source of his income.

'Ah, young Khan sahib,' Razvi cried on seeing Javed enter, 'Allah bless you vith a thousand prahsperitties. Vhat good fahrchoon brings you hyere?'

In between asking questions and waiting for replies, Razvi had a habit of twirling his moustache and flicking his eyebrows up and down at the same time so that his eyes seemed to be popping in and out.

Javed stared at his eyes and said, 'Mother's got a pain in her back. You must come and see her at once.'

'Yes, yes,' Razvi said, springing up at once so that his fez cap shifted itself to a perilous angle. 'Just let me collect my meddysuns.'

Bottles of gaudy liquids, much like the brightly coloured lotions in barbers' shops, were arrayed on a shelf. He picked one of each colour and put them in a cloth shopping-bag which was lined with earth fallen off vegetables. He opened a drawer and took out a quantity of white tablets. Some of these were quinine and some aspirin. Originally, he had kept them in separate drawers, but during one domestic accident the small chest had been knocked forward and the drawers had emptied themselves on the floor. Never having realised that the quinine tablets were slightly larger than the aspirin tablets, as well as being less flat, Razvi had no way of distinguishing the tablets except the impossible one of licking each tablet to discover the bitterer; he had, therefore, mixed the two lots, convinced that if he prescribed two tablets every three hours for twenty-four hours, then there was statistically a good chance of equal quantities of quinine and aspirin being administered. But some illnesses, he intuitively felt, required only quinine and some only aspirin (and it should be added that he had not bothered to tax his mind with the notion that there were illnesses for which both quinine and aspro were quite useless). Therefore, he now attempted to separate the tablets by a method of which he alone possessed the secret. He took a handful of the mixed tablets and put them in an old biscuit tin he had had the luck once to find in a rubbish heap—the tin had a picture of a rosy English blonde on its side and though the face was pock-marked with rust, Razvi was fond of the tin and had been thrilled when someone deciphered the words on it as *Carlisle, England*. He shook the tin as though accompanying a samba and jerked most of the tablets out on to the top of the chest in the manner of one playing dice. Razvi believed that quinine tablets were heavier than aspirin and the tin-rattling exercise was his method of determining weight, for he was positive that those tablets which now remained in the tin were one hundred per cent quinine. The samba-and-dice-throwing activity sent some of the tablets scattering into obscure corners of the hut; so that after each throw Razvi crawled about on hands and knees to retrieve the tablets. At length, he obtained a dozen tablets from his hoard and, tearing the corner of a newspaper which had been lying on the floor for some days, he crumpled it around the tablets, placed it in his bag and declared himself ready to visit *begum sahiba*.

'The *neem* is untirelee wrong,' he said loudly, admonishing Aziz Khan for his attempts to cure Zakia's backache. '*Begum sahiba* has an antibodyiotic cunndition vhich can't be helped like that. If you must use eintmunt you must fust of aal vash the pashunt vith cold vater. That is the only vay to make the skin sensitised to allow for penetration. No, no, Khan sahib, the *neem* is untirelee wrong. You see the pulsation is rapid. The output of the blood is greater than the input, how can the vains take it? Now vhat happuns is this. Evvry so ahften, the heart is empty. The blood comes rushing back. And vhat is that? Ve cahl that the cardigan cunndition. That is, the heart is in trouble. Now. The pain's in the back, not the chest. This is the centrull pint. Vhat is the back? Heh? Vhat is the back? Aal sahrts of things. There is skin, there is flesh, there are bones. Some pashunts have lengthened lungs vhich curl backvards. There is the spleen, there is the liver, there are the kidneys, there is the stomach, there is the thore-axe reejun, there are the intusstines, oh, so many things, so many things, there are the cells, the eppydermisses, so many things. Some of them are in the front and some at the back. But, Khan sahib, it doesn't take a child to know that a man's body, a voman's body as vell, is a smahl thing, there's not much room in it for aal these so many things, so vhat's at the front is ahlso at the back and wice versah. That is vhy I say, *begum sahiba* has an antibodyiotic cunndition. Her awrgunns are displaced and magnified due to the rapidisation of the blood.'

Razvi prescribed two tablets every three hours and a tablespoonful of his mixture after each meal. Her diet was to be restricted to yogurt, almonds, honey, spinach, boiled carrots, raw radish (grated), curried cauliflower, fried eggs and rice-pudding; she was strictly to avoid milk, peanuts, beef, mango pickle, raw carrots, kidney and liver (lamb's), boiled eggs and *chapatis*. Aziz Khan thanked him and paid him his fee of half a rupee together with two rupees for the goods from his dispensary.

The next morning, Zakia's forehead was burning with fever, she breathed with difficulty, each breath coming from her open mouth like a grunt, and the pain in her back, had it been a knife, could not have driven deeper into her flesh.

Aziz Khan understood this to be the immediate result of the medicine, believing that an illness must grow worse before the medicine can take effect; so, he sat beside his wife, trying to persuade her to chew almonds and patiently giving her the tablets and the mixture.

157

On the following morning, Zakia was delirious with fever and pain. Razvi, the *hakim*, had failed and Aziz Khan realised that in the past, whenever Razvi had been consulted, the illness had been essentially mild and the cure had probably come with the passage of time rather than from the taking of Razvi's concoctions. Now he recognised Razvi's utter uselessness and asked Javed, who had been sitting with him beside the bed for much of the two days, to ride to Kalapur and find a proper doctor. As he rode out, Javed observed that the land was again being neglected.

5

At the end of a conference in their board-room the Shah brothers again discussed Aziz Khan's land.

'I wonder if it was right turning down Javed's offer,' Akram remarked. 'I think he would have come down.'

'I told you,' Ayub said, 'he'll come crawling back.'

'Obviously, two thousand an acre was out of the question.'

'Of course,' Ayub said. 'In our first enthusiasm to be masters of this place, we'd have offered anything if the bastard had been willing to sell. But when I think of it now, two thousand an acre was a hell of a lot to offer.'

'I think Javed would have accepted five hundred the other day,' Akram said.

'I tell you we won't have to pay anything for that land. We'll make Aziz Khan crawl for his pride.'

'I wonder why he's so damn' proud?'

'We'll pull him slowly out like a worm from its hole,' Ayub said, smiling, 'And then crush him under our feet.'

'But the man must be insane not to want the kind of money we offered him. He could have opened a nice shop in Lahore with that. Instead, he's just going to be isolated until he has nothing left to call his own.'

'The miserable worm,' Ayub said, leaving Akram in order to inspect the packaging department.

Ayub walked slowly, as though taking an after-dinner stroll, and watched the machines package the rolls of cloth and was pleased to see the names of cities where the goods were going stamped on the crates. He felt as though the cities were his principalities and remembered the time when the British were leaving India and he was the king of Mohammed Ali Road in Bombay. That was a time of terror in which Hindus and Muslims killed one another and Ayub had seen it as his duty positively to champion his faith. He led a gang which met in a tea-house off Mohammed Ali Road, which was the chief Muslim bazaar in the city, and there they plotted their many acts of arson and murder. Sabotage had been his own speciality. Wearing a Gandhi cap and a red mark on his forehead in order to pass for a Hindu, he once went into a temple and placed fruits and sweetmeats at the feet of an idol; embedded in a water-melon was a time-bomb. His daring and his brutal cunning had given him power over the Muslims in Mohammed Ali Road where he was so respected that no one asked him for money to pay for a meal or an article of clothing, though some of the shopkeepers saw it as their duty to Islam to let him have what he wanted.

Ayub watched the crates being lifted by a mechanical fork-lift truck which carried the crates to one end of the floor where, through a hole in the floor, they were lowered into lorries, which immediately drove away to their destinations—Rawalpindi, Peshawar, Sialkot, Lahore, Lyallpur, Karachi, Hyderabad, Quetta. The whole of Pakistan gaped in at that opening, Ayub was pleased to reflect as he looked over the barrier and saw a lorry being loaded. He applauded mechanisation, not so much for the impression of smooth efficiency which it created in the mills, but for the rapid turnover and profit which it made possible, thus increasing his power. He had been in the habit of seeing the world inhabited by Hindu idols which he had made his business to break up; in the old India, commerce was a Hindu idol, and now, successful himself as an industrialist, he saw Pakistan as the final defeat of Hinduism: the idols were broken, the ideology of power had set in. He walked on, thinking of Aziz Khan, a man of stone, as he kicked a wood-shaving out of his way; his land, Ayub felt, would fall into his hands as surely as rocks from a hillside which had been exploded with dynamite.

At home, his wife fretted over the children. Munni and Dolly were six and four years old and Razia was beginning to worry about their education. Her worry had commenced soon after Afaq left for England, and, having decided that whatever education was available in Pakistan was beneath her contempt, she was at the incipient stage of convincing herself that the only place where her daughters could be educated was Switzerland. She had seen a documentary film about young ladies being given a most sophisticated education in Geneva where the curriculum stressed horse-riding, swimming, the piano (in its dainty, after-dinner form) and a superficial appreciation of the arts. Razia had been impressed. Although her own daughters were far too young for such a finishing school, she was determined that they should be educated in Switzerland.

That evening, when in bed with her husband, she mentioned the notion to him. Ayub was flattered that she should care so much for the children as to suggest a European education for them.

'Perhaps they should first receive primary education in England,' Razia suggested. 'And maybe also secondary. Switzerland is best for finishing.'

'Yes, why not?' agreed Ayub, who would have signed a blank cheque towards any extravagance which drew attention to his power. 'The more varied the background the better.'

Presently, Razia suggested that she pay a preliminary visit to Europe in the summer in order to make the arrangements. 'Think of all the shopping I could do,' she added. 'It would be a real blow to Faridah and her stupid jhar-jet.' She mocked her sister-in-law.

Ayub, enjoying the rivalry between the two women and certain that his own wife was clearly superior, agreed. Elated, Razia shut her eyes and thought of Afaq while Ayub thought of the power he had in the family.

6

Javed rode hard in the mid-morning sun. What would have been a pleasant spring day in a temperate climate was brutally hot in the Punjab's precocious summer. The air had claws. Javed was riding home, his head bowed as if to win some shade from the horse's neck; but the sun was too high for shadows. Some distance behind him, Dr Butt drove sedately in his 1938 Buick.

Dr Butt knew the virtue of maintaining a safe distance. He was likewise cautious in his speech, never hurrying with a diagnosis and always allowing the patient to speak while he himself merely nodded. He watched Javed wearily and was sorry for him that he had had to keep him waiting for well over an hour in his surgery while he attended upon his patients. He drove slowly not because he wanted to be led by Javed, for he knew the way to Aziz Khan's house, but because slow driving was his only form of relaxation from over-work.

Emerging from the car, Dr Butt appeared to be a tall, bony man. His sunken cheeks had the effect of making his eyes seem deeply set and his chin too pointed. Consequently, he gave the impression of possessing both a gravity and a sense of humour, a man who was both stern and kind-hearted.

He entered the room softly, shutting the door behind him. Zakia lay heaving convulsively. Aziz Khan sat beside her on a chair. His shoulders had drooped in this prolonged vigil, his head was bowed and his hands fell limply between his legs. Javed came in and stood in a corner and saw his father rise to make room for Dr Butt.

Aziz Khan rose heavily, greeting the doctor with a nod. His eyes were hooded with fatigue. Dr Butt also nodded. Javed heard the chair scrape the floor when Dr Butt pulled it away a little from the bed and, hearing this sudden sound in the silent room, he became aware of the hens and the cockerels clucking in the poultry-yard. It was almost as though nothing was happening and that it was an ordinary peaceful morning. But his mother's breath came heavily as though the room contained not air but water, as though she were flailing her arms, fighting to keep on the surface.

Gently, as though feeling for a fallen coin in the darkness, Dr Butt first probed her chest with his stethoscope, listening with half-shut eyes. He then took his thermometer from his case, looked at the reading, flicked his wrist, looked at the reading again and placed it in her mouth. He held her wrist and looked at his watch. Outside, a hen seemed to be scolding a cockerel. Withdrawing the thermometer from Zakia's mouth, Dr Butt looked at the reading and made a mental note of it. Next, he softly pressed her midriff, feeling for the stomach and the liver.

'The pain's in the back,' Javed said in his impatience, as though the man of science should also have been a magician and ought to have cured her by now. Dr Butt lifted his eyes and glanced at Javed for a moment, but not reprovingly. Zakia turned over, however, and placing a hand low on her back, said, 'Yes, here, the pain's here.'

Dr Butt prodded the back and pondered the source of the pain. Javed shifted his weight from one foot to the other and Aziz Khan, impatient of the silence, said, 'I applied hot *neem* to the back.' Dr Butt nodded appreciatively, a little indulgently, for there was no harm in the leaves of ancient trees. But Javed was emboldened to say, 'We had *hakim* Razvi to come and see mother. He gave her some tablets.'

'Tablets?' Dr Butt was interested. 'What tablets?'

'These.' Aziz Khan produced a crumpled piece of newspaper from his pocket and showed the remaining four or five tablets to Dr Butt. He took them and put them in his case, saying, 'A *hakim* should know better than to dispense drugs he knows nothing about.'

He proceeded then to take a sterilised needle from a small leather case he carried in his pocket and, pricking one of Zakia's fingers, he obtained a drop of her blood on a glass slide and rubbed her finger with cotton wool which he first soaked with an antiseptic. He put the slide away in its special container and asked Javed for a glass of water. When Javed had gone out to fetch it, Dr Butt took an empty bottle from his case and said to Aziz Khan, 'I shall need a sample of her urine. I'll wait outside.' He walked out with his case as quietly as he had entered a quarter of an hour earlier. He stood in the veranda and looked across the fields. Javed returned with the glass of water.

'Ah! Thank you,' Dr Butt said, taking a sip. 'The cotton doesn't seem to be bearing well under this heat,' he added.

Javed looked at the fields. But he did not need to. He felt bitter, no longer needing his senses to inform him of misfortune. He bit his lip, as though ashamed at the land's being neglected.

'When mother's well again, we'll be able to get the land back to order,' he said. 'What's wrong with her?'

The question came suddenly, sharply; as though on a dark, still night a crow had suddenly cawed.

'What do you think?' Dr Butt asked.

'I don't know. I wish I knew. She's been working so hard. I don't know. It's bending so much. Clean the floors, cook. My brother's tragedy. Who knows, I don't know.'

Aziz Khan came out with the bottle of urine and gave to to Dr Butt who put it into his case.

'Khan sahib,' Dr Butt said, choosing his words slowly, 'we shall have to proceed cautiously. I cannot give you my opinion until I have carried out my tests. I can, however, say with some certainty that the root of the trouble lies in *begum sahiba's* kidneys. What exactly, I cannot say as yet. All I can prescribe at present is that she remains in bed and eats no solids. Only thin vegetable soup which, however, must be well strained and must not contain a single shred of vegetable. Here are some sedative tablets. She can have two at night before going to sleep. No more. Even if the pain is unbearable during the day, try to be patient. Patience and courage. You will be all right.'

The doctor drove away, the wheels of his car raising dust. There was a moan from Zakia's room and Aziz Khan went to his wife. Javed stood in the veranda, the almost full glass of water still in his hand: Dr Butt had returned the glass to him without taking a second sip. Javed tipped the glass and watched the water fall on the hard earth of the front yard where it disappeared instantaneously like spittle on sand. Javed looked up. There was haze in the distance: as though the iron lid of heat was on the point of falling on the earth which had no more in it to Javed's view than has an old rusted cauldron on a rubbish heap. He looked for the horizon, the point where the sugarcanes should have begun to sprout their plumed heads from the canes. There was white heat there. The rice, he knew, would not grow this year, for the sun, continuously moving like a Persian wheel, drew up the water if one turned one's attention away from the sources of its supply. And what could he do? *Mother, mother*, his voice cried within him but the earth he looked at was cracking under the heat and what hardness it possessed beneath its breaking soil, or what generosity, was not yet encompassed by his vision.

That afternoon, Dr Butt sent a messenger on a bicycle to inform Aziz Khan that his wife would have to be admitted into a nursing home. She needed to be X-rayed and her condition required her to be under constant medical supervision. He had succeeded in obtaining a room in the nursing home and would come in his car later in the day, for an ambulance was not available.

Dr Butt arrived shortly before sunset. Aziz Khan was with his wife and, on hearing the car, he came out to the veranda where Javed was sitting.

The doctor shut the door of his car without banging it and greeted Aziz Khan with a nod.

'I hope you agree,' he said, his head lifted so that his chin pointed at Aziz Khan's nose. 'I mean about the nursing home. It's the only course. I've examined the specimens I took this morning and I think that her kidney complaint is complicated by diabetes. We need an X-ray to see what is wrong. And it will be easier in the nursing home to get a second opinion, which might be vital. I've approached Doctor Mirza and he is willing to look at the patient. But most of all, your wife will need the constant care which can only be provided by a nursing home.'

Javed had heard of Dr Mirza, who enjoyed the universal reputation of specialists who command a very high fee, for the fee, rather than their actual achievement, sometimes spreads their fame. Javed knew that he charged seventy-five rupees per consultation whereas the overworked Dr Butt, a man who had never explained his philosophy, was content with three rupees. There was the nursing home, too. What would that cost? Kalapur had no hospital as yet and medical care was the privilege of those who could pay for it.

Aziz Khan had no choice now. He did not think of the cost, but agreed with each of Dr Butt's suggestions. He and Javed carried Zakia to the car and placed her on the rear seat. Aziz Khan accompanied the doctor. Javed saw the car go away slowly, for Dr Butt, mindful of the condition both of his patient and his tyres, took care to avoid bumps and pot-holes. It was some time after the car had disappeared outside his vision that Javed realised that, for the first time in his life, he was alone on his father's land. The sun had just set.

7

Faridah frowned. Akram lay beside her in the bed, smoking. All evening, first at the club and then at dinner, she had been

conspicuously quiet as though suffering a private martyr-
dom. Razia had seemed extravagantly gay in comparison
and even Zarina's usual silence had a charm about it.
Akram's own remarks had seemed solemn beside Ayub's
laughter. She sighed now while he sucked at his cigarette.

'Faridah,' he said softly, not looking at her.

She held her breath for a moment so as to appear more
distant than she had hitherto been.

He leaned to a table next to the bed to stub out his
cigarette and then turned to look at her.

'Faridah,' he said again.

Her self-conscious isolation seemed too dramatic, for his
eyes were too fiercely focused on her now. She allowed herself to look at him but failed to feign the embittered coun-
tenance with which she wanted to face him. Instead, tears
rose to her eyes.

'What is it, Faridah?' he asked, struggling to adopt a
solicitous tone, for he knew well enough the cause of her
bitterness.

'Nothing,' she cried.

'Come, come, it's more than that.' He tried to humour
her. 'Let me think now. You miss Bombay. The sea there.
The picnics we used to have on the beach.'

She did not even shake her head, but, holding her head
against his chest, began to weep in earnest.

'No? I know, you're tired. You need a holiday. I wish we
could afford the time. Just the two of us. Up in Muree
among the mountains, in the cool air.'

It was silly talk, he realised, for she made no response. He
lay back then, holding her head to his chest, stroking her hair.

'You mustn't mind Razia going to London,' he said, and
there was a momentary pause in her sobbing. 'You could go
too, but you know it will be impossible here without you.
We can't have both of you going together. Maybe, you can
go when she returns. You mustn't mind her going first.
After all, she has a good reason to go. She's got to see about
the education of her children.'

The mention of Razia's children induced renewed sobbing from Faridah.

'Oh, please, Faridah,' Akram said with a trace of impatience in his voice, 'please don't start that again.'

'I've started nothing,' she said.

'I know, it's all my fault. I'm the guilty one. I've built up the business, I've built up the fortune simply to make us both unhappy. I get a lot of thanks for the hard work I've done.'

She had not been prepared for his irony, and ceased weeping.

'Vhat can ve do vith the fahrchoon?' she asked in her most unself-conscious manner of speaking English.

'I know, we have no children and can't have any. What can we do?'

She pondered the question a minute and then said tentatively, 'I saw an articull vunce . . .'

'Yes?'

'It said how a voman could get inseminated vith an injection.'

'No, we can't have that.'

'So, Razia and her silly girls get the fahrchoon?'

'There's Afaq, remember. He could have a whole lot of sons.'

'But suppose . . .'

'No, there's nothing to suppose,' he said. 'It's Allah's will, what can we do?'

She turned away to her side of the bed. The conversation was too painful for her, and, besides, they had had it so often with the same negative conclusion.

Akram hoped that she would now go to sleep and, at least for a short while, not torment him with the very ideas which had been causing him considerable anxiety already. While Ayub was indispensable to him, he resented his bullying methods and his air of superiority; and Afaq he had discovered to be absolutely ungifted for business; his own wife was no social asset to him, but, in judging her, Akram

167

did not spare abuse for himself who was incapable of performing his most essential role as a husband. There was Zarina, his bastard child, to whom he could not behave like a father. In these thoughts about his family, Akram felt a keen disappointment when he considered his material achievement: and in this he was like a king, whose crown was all precious metal and gems to the public view but a burdensome headgear to himself.

And yet the only manner in which he could recompense himself was to enlarge his achievement. A projected soap factory in East Pakistan absorbed him more than the textile mills. The latter had established his industrial success, making him famous throughout the country, and there was no more in the business to challenge him. He wanted the intellectual stimulus of new problems. There was the chance, too, of either going himself to East Pakistan or sending Ayub there; it would be easier, he considered, to control Ayub from a distance, for his personality was too dominating when he was in the same office and the same house. Ayub's laughter, so suggestive of mockery, annoyed him. Given a zealous accountant of his own choice and the thousand miles between the two halves of the country, Akram could subdue the laughter, which sounded so malicious to his ears.

In their room, Ayub and Razia had talked about the latter's imminent visit to England. Razia had kept the conversation to schools about which she had been reading in a handbook from the British Information Service. Ayub had gone to sleep, happily reflecting that his daughters would soon be learning to speak English as immaculately as Princess Anne. Razia, however, remained awake and wondered how Afaq would receive her in London. When talking to Ayub about their daughters, she almost believed that Afaq was a fantasy of her idle moments, but when she was alone with her thoughts, he became the reality and all else an excuse for its achievement. She wondered how she could dare to feel so happy, how she could be so pleased with the architecture of her imaginings when its foundation was a lie. She was being reckless, almost wanton with herself, but she did not care. Kalapur had exhausted its pleasures for her; its best society had become monotonous and dull. Her only entertainment recently had been to watch Faridah suffer from jealousy and to observe Zarina's love-sickness follow the conventional course derived from romantic films. It was all too petty for a woman of her taste.

Zarina had spent the evening looking at the calendar in her small diary. She had crossed out the days since Afaq's departure. There was more than half the year to go, and how many more full years she would have to cross out until he returned she did not know. She wished she had been an eagle, floating high in the sky, enjoying its destined solitude. Loneliness which she had not asked for made her as vulnerable as a newly-hatched chick in a yard where cats prowled.

Aziz Khan did not return from the nursing home. The room he had taken for his wife contained two beds and he stayed there with her. Left alone on the farm, Javed wandered listlessly in the fields. His attempts of a few days ago to revive the cultivation of the land had been frustrated and he knew now that even if he could obtain an army of obedient peasants, it was too late for the season's crop. The peasants who still remained had returned to their recalcitrant ways while he had been preoccupied with his mother's illness. He could see them idling in the distance but he did not go to admonish them. He was thankful that they had not disappeared altogether. They would soon need to be paid and he had no money; nor did he know from where his father would find the money to pay for the nursing home.

He went to the nursing home on successive evenings for a whole week. On each occasion, he found Aziz Khan sitting on the edge of his bed, gazing blankly at the polished tile floor of the room. His mother lay breathing heavily, puffing out her cheeks when exhaling, so that the pock-marks on her face seemed to become momentarily enlarged. Javed learned from a nurse that the X-ray had shown that there were stones in her kidneys. He considered this incredible and told the nurse that his mother was not a child to be swallowing stones. The nurse explained that *stones* was a common term given to excess matter in the kidneys, and he ought to ask the doctor for a proper explanation instead of wasting her time with his silly sarcasm. Yes, they were going to operate, she said, clicking her high heels and turning to go away, but they had to wait, for the patient's heart was weak.

Javed watched his father and wondered what magnanimity he possessed which made him endure a ruined family. It moved him to see his father sit out his trials so patiently. He himself had become dispirited and detested the people of Kalapur who had lost their care for the virtues which had once been native to the place. And each time he returned home and wandered aimlessly in the deserted land, he wanted to know why his family, which, for generations, had been respected in Kalapur and had done harm to no one, should now be burdened with tragedy. Even his limited experience and knowledge did not obscure from him the fact that any vicissitude, which was not an organic disease of one's body, was caused by human agents. Having established in his mind what was now a very clear distinction between his family's former prosperity and its present suffering, Javed looked for an equally clear reason for the change. There had been a revolution in Kalapur, altering people's way of living as well as their mentality. It had been caused by the Shah brothers. Javed had long ago realised that his father's refusal to sell his land to the Shah brothers would lead to hardship for his family; he had been able to understand when the hardship had been an economic one, like their inability to sell cotton except through the expensive method of employing a broker; such a situation induced hostility in him against the Shah brothers, but, sharing his father's adamant nature, it had only resolved him not to give in to them. He had, however, been unable to understand the personal hardships. There was obviously no connection between his mother's illness and the Shah brothers; but Rafiq's conviction and death seemed increasingly mysterious to Javed. His mind returned to Rafiq again and again and he began to believe more and more that his brother could not have contemplated, even as an idle speculation, the evil of which he had been considered guilty.

He came across a group of peasants when he wandered to the rice field. They rose to their feet and greeted him nervously. The downcast look in their eyes conveyed the sadness they felt at his mother's illness about which they knew everything, for, although he had told them nothing, a chain of gossip linked Kalapur to the Kangra Settlement. He was touched by their unspoken solicitude and wished he had money to give them. These were the last of the faithful peasants, for he noticed that two more were missing. They, too, had gone to work at the mills. He asked how they could so easily obtain work at the mills and was told that there was a permanent shortage there and all one had to do was to present oneself to an officer and he immediately gave employment.

Walking away, it suddenly occurred to Javed that he might try working at the mills. He could do nothing on the land with so little labour while his parents were in the nursing home. It would be one way of entering into the world of the Shah brothers—and perhaps he might discover if they had had anything to do with Rafiq's conviction. At the very least, he could learn something of their kind of work. Also, he needed what money he could earn.

He was astonished at the ease with which he was given a job when he went to the mills the next day.

'Go-an see the perrsonal offy-sir,' a man said when he inquired at the gate.

The Personnel Officer, who had replaced Afaq, was new to the town and did not know Javed whom he took to be one more of the scores of local peasants he interviewed daily. He offered Javed a choice of a number of unskilled jobs and when Javed seemed to be wavering, he marked him down for the packaging department, took his thumb impression on a card and asked him if he preferred to receive ten rupees a week or fifty rupees a month. Javed accepted the latter arrangement and was directed to the packaging department.

His work had nothing immediately to do with packaging. He was given a stool on an assembly line. There were stacks of cardboard pieces piled on both sides of the stool; he had to take two pieces, one from each side, and staple them together; the stapling was done by a punching machine which came down, as though a fist were being banged, every time he pressed a knob which was conveniently placed beside his right foot as he sat on the stool. All he had to do was to keep his hands clear, which he learned to do automatically, for the cardboard pieces had to be held at the ends so that the two inside edges could be aligned. He stapled each set in three places and then threw the two joined pieces over his shoulder. Every ten minutes, a boy of eight or nine came and replenished his supply of cardboard while his finished work was continuously being carried away automatically from where it fell to a man who joined two sets of them to make a four-sided box. Before Javed took up the pieces, they were already so cut and pressed as to provide the boxes their tops and bottoms, and he was quite impressed with the simple ingenuity of the design which enabled the completed boxes to be stacked flat until they were used. Even at the end of the first day, Javed was pleased with the speed with which he had begun to assemble the two sides. The activity of concentrating on a repetitive and dull task—not at all like working on the land, which could be so exhilarating—had been a sedative to his mind and it was not till he was halfway home that he realised that he could have paid a visit to the nursing home before leaving Kalapur. He hesitated, wondering whether he should return, but decided that he should first go to the house and cook himself a meal after which he could ride to town. He did not want to tell his father yet that he had begun to work for the Shah brothers, for he would neither understand nor accept his motives.

He became accustomed to the routine of working all day and visiting his parents in the evening. On his third day at the mill, he felt as though he had spent many months there. He no longer needed to look at what he was doing; his arms moved of their own volition, his hands picked up and discarded pieces of cardboard without his directing them; he himself seemed not to be there at all. At the nursing home, too, he felt similarly disembodied. His mother remained incommunicative, drugged into restfulness; and his father was inaccessible but for the briefest exchange. Javed felt that although his father's grief was also his, he himself could not surrender the little determination he had found to fight against it by giving himself wholly to that grief. His heart wept when he saw his mother, but his eyes remained fiercely bright; as though he was in a jungle and needed to look beyond the confusion of light and shadow.

When he visited the nursing home some days later, he was told by a nurse in the reception hall that he could not visit his mother, for she had had her operation that afternoon. The news came as a surprise to him, and the nurse explained that Dr Mirza had been to see *begum sahiba* in the morning and had been so satisfied with the condition of her heart that he had ordered the operation on her kidneys without delay.

'Can't I just see her?' Javed asked.

'No, no one's to go in,' the nurse said.

'Where's my father?'

'He's with her,' she said. 'God knows, he shouldn't. The patient must not be disturbed. But he would not budge, he's that stubborn. It's not good, you know.'

'Can I see my father, then?' Javed asked.

'No, you cannot. To see him, you will have to open the door. If you open the door, too much light will go into the room from the corridor. I told you. The patient must not be disturbed.'

'We could switch off the light in the corridor,' Javed suggested.

'No. Somebody might break a leg.'

'How's my mother?'

'How should I know? I'm not the surgeon. Nor her doctor.'

'You know, you're what they call a sporty type. You're so keen to help.'

'I've my orders,' she said sternly. 'Don't be so cheeky.'

But when he had gone from her, she blushed a little and shut her eyes to see more clearly his dark brown pupils which had focused so intensely on hers; and sighed for her prolonged spinsterhood.

He went to see Dr Butt in his surgery. The waiting-room there was so crowded, he had to stand in a corner. He distracted himself by looking at the silent faces around him. He counted the people in the room. There were thirty-three. Five of them were women. Two of the women had children. One of the children was a baby which was crying. The woman rocked the baby in her arms and made sounds with her lips, but the baby cried. No one seemed to hear the crying. No one looked at the baby. Javed looked again at the men. Twelve of them were old, past sixty at least. He looked at each one in turn to see if he could guess at his illness. He could not. There was one, however, whose right arm twitched with rhythmic regularity; the nervous jerk of the arm was followed by a short forward nod of the head which was accompanied by the winking of the right eye. Javed looked at the man for some time, wondering what induced the nervous action in him and whether or not he ever introduced any variety into his action by, say, winking his left eye instead of the right eye. But he did not. The baby cried and Javed looked away from the twitching man. He hoped it would soon be the woman's turn, for the baby's crying disturbed him. He thought again of his mother and wondered how she was. One by one the people around him went to see Dr Butt. More people continued to arrive meanwhile, affording him an increasing variety of diversion. At last the woman with the baby went to the doctor. The muffled cry which he heard from behind the shut door of the doctor's room, disturbed him more than the loud crying when the baby was in the waiting-room. He wondered how the doctor could diagnose a baby's illness when all that a baby communicated to him was an endless wail. It was a good thing we learned to talk so soon; it was a good thing we had words. He tried to imagine himself in the doctor's position, a screaming baby in front of him in its mother's arms. He would look at the baby, feel its body, take its temperature. He would ask questions of the mother. What had the baby been eating and drinking? Could the baby have swallowed a pin? Was the baby constipated? Yes, he concluded, there were possible approaches towards understanding a situation which at first might seem completely impenetrable.

Two hours passed in such observations before it was Javed's turn to see Dr Butt, who admitted him gravely to his room.

'I've come to ask about my mother,' he said. 'I heard she had the operation this morning. I wasn't allowed to see her at the nursing home and no one could tell how she was.'

'Yes,' Dr Butt said, propping his elbows on the desk and resting his head in his hands. 'I'm not a surgeon, of course. So, I cannot tell you anything definite. But I was at the nursing home soon after the operation, and the surgeon seemed satisfied. There is every hope of a recovery. But we must be patient.'

These few words were sufficient reward for the patience which Javed had already exercised. When he had gone, Dr Butt was pleased to reflect that Javed had awaited his turn and not, like many of his visitors who came from good families, assumed precedence over the workers and peasants who constituted the majority of his patients. Such behaviour accorded with his own principles.

Javed was able to see his mother the next evening when he visited the nursing home. He noticed how her cheeks had hollowed and how her shoulders seemed to sag. There had been a diminution of her body: the process of the wearing away of her flesh, he thought, must have been a gradual one over recent weeks. He had noticed it no more than one notices the continual change in a landscape; but now that she had been operated upon, now that something had been removed from her body, he *looked* at her more closely to see changes and saw a smaller, a weaker mother than he had known. The wrinkles which normally came to her forehead when she frowned had now settled there. The flesh below her eyes and beside her mouth was looser and her pock-marks looked like flecks of rust on an old mirror. But she was alive, breathing steadily.

He saw his father sitting on the edge of his bed. And he noticed how he, too, had thinned. Aziz Khan's moustache, which he used to wax to rapier points, drooped as though he had been swimming in a cold river. His eyes seemed to have grown weary with what they had looked at for too long. But, smiling faintly, he greeted Javed with some warmth and this alone was enough indication to Javed that his mother had survived. Nothing was said; only Zakia's breath spoke.

He learned from the house doctor, however, that she would have to remain in the nursing home to allow for her recuperation. Satisfied, Javed returned home to continue his solitary existence. He bathed hastily, for the water was cold in the evenings, walked along the stream, smoked a cigarette and went to bed to rise early for another day at the mill.

On an inspection tour of the mill one day, Ayub was astonished to see Javed working with such facility at the packaging assembly line as to suggest that he had been there for several weeks. He went up to where Javed was and stood behind him. Javed was not aware of his presence, for he was used to people walking in the aisles between the lines and also there was the noise of the machinery.

'That's very good, we ought to give you a bonus,' Ayub said.

Javed turned round to look at him. He was confused for a moment, but recognising Ayub, he stood up and smiled.

'I didn't know you were working for me,' Ayub said. 'When did you get here?'

Javed remarked upon the *me* to himself and said, 'I needed a job and I got one here. Only recently.'

Deciding that affability would serve his purpose better than an assertion of his superiority, Ayub said, 'You should have come to me if you wanted any help.'

'I didn't need help,' Javed said. 'Just a job.'

'But I could have given you something better. This is no job for the son of one of the biggest landlords in Kalapur.'

The irony was not lost on Javed, who knew that the only other landlords in Kalapur were the Shah brothers.

'I quite like this,' Javed said, and added, for he too could be ironical, 'It's very easy. And it's good work. I feel I'm doing something useful.'

'Well, that's very satisfactory,' Ayub said with charm he did not need to feign. 'We'll see how you progress and maybe we can promote you.'

'Please don't treat me as anyone special,' Javed said. 'I'm just an ordinary labourer.'

'Sure, sure,' Ayub said, laughing heartily and going away.

9

Aziz Khan received three bills within two days of his wife being discharged from the nursing home. The largest amount he owed was to the nursing home: the charge for the room and the surgeon's fee amounted to one thousand two hundred rupees. The second was a statement from Dr Mirza, who had examined Zakia on two occasions, each one of no more than ten minutes' duration. The printed statement read:

Dr Mohammed Mirza, M.B.B.S. (Lahore), F.R.C.S. (Edinburgh, U.K.), D.SC. (Chicago, U.S.A.) presents his compliments to *Aziz Khan Sahib* and begs to be allowed to convey to the respected *Aziz Khan Sahib* that his professional fees in regard to specialist consultations amount to Rs. 150 and that this sum is now due and is payable within thirty days of the above date.

The third bill was from Dr Butt. This was in the form of a letter which went:

My dear Khan Sahib,

I am glad that *begum sahiba* has now fully recovered. I hope you will strictly follow the prescribed diet and dissuade her from strenuous activity. My charges for the treatment come to Rs. 30 which you can send at your convenience.

Yours truly,
Anwar Butt.

There was one other letter, from Karachi, awaiting them when Aziz Khan and his wife returned from the nursing home. It was addressed to Javed's mother, and from the handwriting on the envelope, it was obviously from his sister, Zuleikha.

Zakia was well enough to read the letter and it was a sign of her recovery that she exhaustively discussed the probable contents of her daughter's letter before opening it—an old habit of hers. The envelope seemed heavier than usual and, handling it, Zakia declared it to be a long letter, for she was sure it contained more pages than one. She wondered if they had had any rain yet in Karachi; the monsoon was getting later and later every year, she mused. She surveyed all possible events which might have happened in Zuleikha's household: whether Zuleikha's little son had begun to learn the Koran; whether she was expecting another; whether anyone, Allah forbid, had been ill. At last she opened the envelope, first tapping it at the side so that the letter might not tear with the envelope. As her fingers pulled away the edge of the envelope, she muttered a short prayer, the *Bismillah* with which a devout Muslim commences any activity—from eating a meal to dropping a bomb on an enemy.

178

They were all surprised. The letter consisted of one page of neatly written Urdu but it also contained a photograph. Zakia looked at the latter first, holding it away from Aziz Khan and Javed. It was a portrait of a girl. Zakia did not know who she was but could guess. Keeping the photograph in her hand, she proceeded to read the letter, first silently to herself, then muttering its words, and aloud the third time. Javed felt his cheeks burn, for Zuleikha seemed to talk of nothing but the prospect of arranging his marriage to the girl called Amina whose photograph she had enclosed. When Zakia had read the letter aloud, she said, 'Well, let me look at this beauty.'

She studied the photograph with an exaggerated show of attention, tantalising the men with her comments. 'Brown eyes, I should think. The eyebrows are somewhat narrow. I suppose they pluck them till they're like crescents. The mouth's a bit thin. Must be the way she's put lipstick on. Oh, these girls are clever, you know, they leave nothing to chance. But such a perfect nose! It's so straight with such tiny nostrils! And the hair's wavy. Cut short, I bet, like an actress. The cheeks are hollow, though. It must be the impure butter and the weak milk. It will be so much better for her here.'

Satisfied that she had fulfilled her maternal obligation of not perceiving excessive beauty in a prospective daughter-in-law and yet welcoming her to her own house, Zakia passed the photograph on to her husband. Aziz Khan glanced at it, smiled, nodded his head as though he agreed with all that his wife had said, and passed the photograph to Javed. He hesitated a moment, looking in turn at his parents before he took the photograph in his hand. He paused a moment before looking, feeling uncomfortable at the presence of his parents; and knowing, too, that once he saw her, he would not be able to change her from what she was whereas now, not having seen the picture, he could make her take any shape which pleased his fancy. When he looked at the picture, the name *Amina* involuntarily came to his tongue.

Would she look at him like that, he wondered, half-proud of what the camera might record and half-afraid, too?

'Well, my son?' the mother asked.

He did not answer but returned the photograph to her, for it would have shown undue keenness to have looked at it for too long. He smiled, however, when he did so, and his mother needed no verbal assent. He felt embarrassed and, before his mother could begin to make the preliminary teasing remarks common to such a situation, he hastened out of the room. This, too, was in character and both Aziz Khan and Zakia were convinced that Javed would be happy to marry Amina.

'*Hai Allah*,' Zakia sighed, 'I must write soon to Zuleikha and make the arrangements.'

Outside, Javed ran to the stream and walked beside it. He felt light, almost gay. *Amina, Amina*. The name was at his lips. The hot, airless summer evening was cool to his suddenly intoxicated senses.

He would have to give up working at the mill. When he had at last mentioned his job to his father, Aziz Khan had shown neither surprise nor annoyance, but had abstractedly expressed his approval for Javed's desire to make himself useful. Javed considered that he could not work for the Shah brothers when he was married, not with seventy acres of his father's land to look after while his wife managed the house. It would be an entirely new life, a new attempt to come to terms with his existence on the land. He envisaged the busy activity on the land, saw the old peasants returned to the fields and the plants again in blossom. Where would he start and what would he do? The possibilities seemed infinite but the probability of the plantations ever again fulfilling the land's potential had been diminishing with an accelerating momentum which he did not know how to check.

And Aziz Khan had not mentioned how he expected to meet the bills of Zakia's illness. He had expressed no concern at the debt. Javed felt the concern, experienced the problem and was anxious for its solution. It was an anxiety which surged within his breast, making him want to resolve all the difficulties with one determined wave of the arm. He might as well have stood on a seashore and held his hand up like a traffic policeman and expected the waves to obey his command. At least there was diversion, then, a temporary relaxation of stress, now that a proposed marriage held the family's attention. And yet, in spite of the slight depression produced by these cogitations, he thought he saw more life in the land than his recent observations of neglect could encourage him to believe. Certainly, the wheat field was not dead. And, walking slowly back to the house, he realised that, given time, nature will assert itself; that it might not grow with the scrupulous neatness which man's meticulous cultivation bestowed upon it, but it will eventually throw up its abundance, given sun, air and water. Javed learned that the possibility of a renewal could never be precluded, however misused the earth was, however worn one's feelings were. He realised that the essential experiences of life were common to man and the earth on which he walked, whether joyously or wearily.

10

Razia was blatantly happy on the eve of her departure for London. At the dinner party on the lawn beside the swimming pool, Ayub felt especially proud of her. The party was his idea and, although no more than a dozen guests had been invited, he had taken much pleasure in having gold-edged invitation cards printed. Akram had frowned at this extravagance, but to irk the elder brother and his wife had precisely been Ayub's wish. He thought now with satisfaction that Faridah looked decidedly sour.

Certainly, Faridah had little to celebrate. Polite participation was the most she could attempt, and she was thankful for the poor light in the garden. She suffered the party as a monarch suffers criticism—without the chance of making a reply. To be present at the party was a slight to her seniority in the house, for Razia, and not she, was being honoured; and if she had chosen to have a headache and had remained away from it, it would have been too obvious an admission that she felt insulted. She hated the diplomacy she was consequently compelled to employ. Razia noticed a touchiness in her voice and smiled inwardly.

A buffet table was arranged beside that end of the swimming pool which was nearest the house. The curtains had been drawn back in all the rooms in which the lights had been switched on, so that the buffet table was clearly illuminated. There was music coming from the open window of the drawing-room, creating, when the house was seen from the far end of the swimming pool, a mock *son et lumière* effect. Six small circular tables had been set up on this end of the garden; one by one, or in pairs, the guests would walk along the swimming pool, which had been especially filled for the occasion, and, choosing what items of delicacy they fancied at the buffet table, would amble back to where the others sat.

Mansur and his wife, Azra, sat at a table with Faridah.

'Yes, I've heard of Sell-fridges,' Faridah said, for Azra insisted on talking about the shops in London.

'Isn't it vunderful?' Azra went on. 'You come out of Sell-fridges and vahlk straight into Jahn Loovis. And that is not aal. There is Dee Etch Evans, Paali Perr-kins, Neeta-vhere, Dickunce and Jones, Fenn-vicks, Paantings, Jerry and Taam, Barkerrs, Harding and Hahbs, oh, such shahps, such shahps.'

She sighed. Faridah shook her head in a gesture of sympathy as though Azra had been relating a catalogue of misfortunes, and said, 'Aal in Aaxferrd Street.'

'Aal in Aaxferrd Street, *baji* Faridah,' Azra said with emphasis, smacking her lips and sucking at a bit of mango pickle. '*Hai Allah*, vhat is vun to do? I vood go mad, there's no doubting about it.'

'There is Harrudds, too,' Mansur said, not wanting to be left out of the conversation.

'Yes,' Azra said, quickly turning her head for a moment to spit out a chilli which had bit her tongue. 'And Svaan and Ejjer and Gallerry Luffight, it sounds like a *méla*, a prahper fair.'

'And aal in Aaxferrd Street,' Faridah repeated almost mournfully.

At another table, Ayub was glad to have the confidence of Dr Mirza.

'Tell me, doctor sahib,' Ayub was saying, 'and does Aziz Khan have the money to meet your bill?'

'Oh, mine is a small affair, a paltry, petty matter,' the doctor declared, his rubbery cheeks shaking as he spoke. 'Just a couple of brief consultations. But the Khan sahib has trouble on his hands. Oh yes, he has problems. There's the nursing home bill, the surgeon's fee. Oh yes, he has a few headaches. Though I don't think Doctor Butt will be one, he charges so little. That man is a disgrace to the profession, I tell you. He tries to be such a damned do-gooder, slogging away day and night for almost nothing. You will agree, Shah sahib, professional services should not be so cheap that every leprous peasant can command your time. I mean a doctor gives the best part of his life, his youth, to hard study. He merits a decent measure of reward. People like Butt are ruining the profession.'

Ayub listened sympathetically to Dr Mirza's vehemence, but turned the conversation to his own purpose, asking, 'Is the *begum sahiba* quite recovered?'

'I believe so,' Dr Mirza said. 'But can you tell with the peasants? You prescribe them the strictest diet of bread and water and they go home and swallow milk and honey. You tell them to keep away from fatty foods and they put lumps of pure home-made butter on every damned *chapati* they eat. No, the *begum sahiba* has serious heart trouble and she has diabetes. The kidney thing was incidental. Oh yes, that was quite by the way. That's over, but she needs to take more care than I've ever known a peasant take.'

Razia came up to their table, carrying a dish of meat balls.

'*Hai Allah!*' she said. 'What is this, doctor sahib? Not a thing on your plate!'

There were a leg of chicken, a veal cutlet and a salad of chopped radish, cucumber and green chillies on Dr Mirza's plate. Razia placed three meat balls in the plate before the doctor could protest that he was already full.

Chief Superintendent Fazal Elahi sat with Akram and Mohammed Karim, the District Commissioner.

Akram was pleased to hear Fazal Elahi say, 'The crime rate here has been down ever since you opened the mills. Give the people an honest occupation and they learn to live honestly. It works better than religion.'

Mohammed Karim, however, was a little appalled at the hint of heresy; but before he could remonstrate, Akram said, 'Bread in this life rather than butter in the next?'

'Quite,' Fazal Elahi said. 'Paradise in the next world is fine, but a few luxury goods in this aren't unwelcome.'

'The world is changing,' Mohammed Karim said and hoped that the profundity of his statement would not go unnoticed.

At another table, Zarina sat silently with Razia's two daughters, Dolly and Munni, for whose benefit Razia was ostensibly embarking on the trip to London. Zarina wondered if Razia would meet Afaq. Obviously, she would. She was a married woman and could, therefore, talk freely and openly with any male member of the family. She wondered what she herself would feel if she, instead of Razia, had been going tomorrow. She almost blushed to herself. She imagined herself walking down the steps from the plane at London Airport and seeing Afaq in the distance, behind a barrier. He would jump over the barrier and run to meet her. He would stop short of her. They would stand a few feet apart and then, bursting into smiles, would rush towards each other to embrace passionately. But her reverie ended, for a glass crashed at her feet: Dolly and Munni had been tugging at a banana—they knew there were dozens of bananas on the table by the window, but each had decided she wanted this particular banana—and just when Dolly snatched it away, her elbow knocked over a glass of water. Zarina was startled. The reality around her was one of petty bickering, of childishness, when her own dreams possessed brilliance and grandeur.

When dinner was over, the party rose to stroll in the gardens or to stand idly beside the swimming pool. One by one, the guests congratulated Razia on her good fortune to be going abroad and wished her a *bon voyage*. Such well-wishing at least filled up the pauses in the conversation. But Razia did not care to hear any voice around her although she responded readily enough to whoever spoke to her. She was there merely as a smiling face, a moonbeam which shone now on one person and now on another, while the sphere she inhabited was elsewhere.

11

Salim and Riaz were two of the earliest labourers employed at the mills by the Shah brothers. Salim, a gifted organiser, was stockily built; his mouth and teeth were stained red with chewing betel and, although he was not yet forty, he had lost all his hair. He had begun his working life at the age of ten as a *boot-polisher* at the railway station in Lahore where he had had to compete not against other boys of his age but against middle-aged men; once, one such *boot-polisher*, annoyed that little Salim should so successfully evoke pity from waiting passengers as to win jobs which could otherwise have been his, had lifted him up on his shoulders, run out of the station with him and thrown him on the pavement. But little Salim had come back. Rumour of factory work had attracted him to Kalapur where, after only six months as an unskilled labourer at the mills, he had graduated to the position of a foreman, a post which suited his character, for he preferred to see other men work.

Coming from a slightly more stable background, Riaz had matriculated and spent one year at Murray College in

Sialkot; he had, however, failed his first-year exams in Commerce and the inability of his parents to pay for any more of his education had forced him to seek employment. There was nothing he could do in Sialkot except to work in a sports factory, stitching cricket-balls and, not being adept with his hands, he looked for a clerical position which Sialkot did not have to offer. Consequently, he had come to Kalapur where he had been given the task of checking invoices at the Shah mills. Riaz's failure at Murray College had not been one of intelligence; it was simply that instead of keeping his attention on the stolid set-books and grasping the essentials of basic accountancy, he had spent his time in reading such diverse political economists as John Stuart Mill and Karl Marx. By contrast, Salim had no learning; but his early hardships had lent his character both belligerence and ruthlessness. So that, when the two men met, Riaz's cold socialist reasoning, which invariably pointed to the injustices of the capitalist system, had the effect of gradually engendering a militarist mood in Salim. Hitherto, Salim's latent violence and Riaz's revolutionary instinct had been dissipated in talk.

Javed first met them in the canteen where he usually had his lunch. Salim and Riaz knew about the Shah brothers' relations with Aziz Khan and when they discovered that Javed was Aziz Khan's son, they saw in him ideal material for conversion to their ideology. Javed began to be attracted to their ideas, which were expressed in a general form, the target of their attack being the capitalist organisation of society and not the particular establishment for which they worked.

When Razia left for London, Ayub accompanied her to Karachi. He was expected to be away for three days and everyone at the mills knew of his absence, for there was a photograph in the newspapers. To the workers, it was like being unsupervised, for there was a slackness in the air which affected everyone from the floor manager to the most unskilled of the labourers. Ayub had not been omnipresent at the mills when he was in his office, but the very idea of his being near at hand and the likelihood of his suddenly touring the mills had helped to maintain rigid discipline. So that, when Javed met Salim and Riaz at lunch on the first day of his absence, the men felt free to discuss industrial action.

'The power to withdraw labour must remain the workers' indivisible right,' Riaz said.

'And that is what makes the worker stronger than his employer,' declared Salim who had learned a banner headline or two from Riaz. 'In the end, the worker is the arbitrator of the terms on which he may be employed.'

Javed was not altogether convinced, and said, 'But the employer can dismiss the worker and replace him. Then what?'

'All the more reason why the workers must unite,' Riaz said.

'Why we must have unions,' Salim added.

'Do you really think we could strike here and get away with it?' Javed asked.

'Let me put it in simple terms,' Riaz said. 'The power to strike can be and, indeed, is undermined by the high percentage of unemployment we have in Pakistan. For every employed worker there are twenty unemployed workers waiting outside the factory gates. There are problems.'

'We must educate the masses,' Salim said who himself had not learned the alphabet.

'But we could try and test our strength,' Riaz said. 'Look, we have no rights, nothing at all.'

A number of other workers, who had been listening to their conversation, applauded this statement as though it were a hilarious joke and Riaz went on, 'Our wages aren't guaranteed. There's no set scale for each type of work. There's no demarcation of jobs. There's no insurance scheme to pay us a minimum sickness benefit. There's no pension scheme.'

More workers joined those who had already been listening and Riaz, sensing that he had a captive audience, became more impassioned.

'We work six days a week on normal wages and for over-time we get only twenty-five per cent extra. We get no paid holidays except religious festivals. What sort of a social contract is that? On the contrary, the management thinks it's doing us a favour employing us when we all know that without us there would be no production and, therefore, no profit for the capitalists. The worker must be given a share of the wealth produced, for he is a party, an absolutely indispensable party, to the profit. He must share the profit.'

Some of the workers cheered Riaz's speech, not so much out of agreement, for they feared such heresy, but out of good humour. What might have been termed his courage, they considered sheer foolishness, for Ayub would soon come to hear of his speech and no doubt immediately sack him. So that, when Salim turned to the audience and demanded in a voice loud with exhortation, 'Why don't we organise ourselves, why don't we start a union? Hands up those who would like to start a union and be its founder members?' he, too, was loudly cheered. Most of the crowd did not intend the cheering to signify approval of Salim's proposition, for it was the sort of cheering a crowd extends to a horse which, limping, is the last to reach the winning-post.

'That's the spirit,' Riaz said, seeing all the hands go up. 'I hereby declare the Kalapur Textile Workers' Union as constituted.'

'Who'll be its General Secretary?' Salim demanded of the crowd. 'Any nominations?'

'Riaz, Riaz,' cried the crowd, delighted at the length to which the joke was being carried.

'Any seconders?' Salim asked.

Riaz looked down at the floor, overcome with modesty, as though suggesting that he was unworthy of such an honour.

'Yes, yes, Riaz, Riaz,' the crowd cried.

'Hands up those who wish to vote for brother Riaz,' Salim said, more serious than ever.

'Ri-*az*, Ri-*az*,' the crowd shouted and all hands went up.

'I declare,' Salim said solemnly, 'Mister Riaz Mohammed as the duly elected General Secretary of the Kalapur Textile Workers' Union.'

The crowd clapped and cheered.

Riaz lifted his eyes from the floor and addressed the assembly.

'Brothers,' he said, 'I humbly thank you from the bottom of my heart for this honour which you have showered upon my head. I hope I shall prove a worthy servant of all your aspirations. We need two more officers for the committee. Can I please have the nominations?'

'Sa-*lim*, Sa-*lim*!'

Salim was elected.

'And the second nomination?'

'Ja-*ved*, Ja-*ved*!'

And Javed was elected.

So far the crowd had enjoyed the joke. But now, speaking with the gravity and menace of a politician, Riaz said, 'The first rule of the Union will be that all its general meetings will be secret. Any member disclosing any aspect of any of its meetings will be liable to be blacklisted and the Union will do its utmost to see that he is denied work. Secrecy and unity will be essential if we are to achieve our aims. After brother Salim has addressed a few words to the meeting, I shall take the names of those present at this historic meeting so that one day the Union will look back on its records and thank you, its founding members.'

The crowd grew silent at this and before Salim finished making his proclamation, the crowd had begun to be imbued with the fear that what had started as a joke was turning out to be an unpleasant reality; for they knew the capacity of Punjabis to organise their groups with such a militant fervour as to make disobedience dangerous.

12

From Frankfurt to London, the Super Constellation seemed
to ride upon the uneven clouds as though a smoothly travelling car had suddenly hit upon a patch of cobblestones. The
plane strained to maintain its height. The passengers were
advised to fasten their seat-belts. Razia looked out. There
was blue sky and the air seemed in its purest element, but
below were masses of clouds. And then the plane began to
sink with what seemed to her to be desperation. The clouds
came nearer and she thought that there would be a violent
impact when the plane hit the clouds. She shut her eyes. But
nothing happened; only, there was the awful feeling of sinking, sinking. She looked out again and the plane was right
in the middle of the clouds. She held the arm-rests tightly
and, looking round, noticed that the two stewardesses, who
had been gaily going up and down the aisle, had disappeared.
She heard someone being sick and firmly shut her own
mouth. She wished she had not had two heavy suitcases of
excess baggage, for the plane carried a full load, mainly of
peasants emigrating to Britain in search of work. The engines seemed to her to be labouring and she wondered if her
extra luggage was partly responsible. Did I really need all
those clothes? she wondered, holding on tightly to the arm-
rests and finding the giddying sensation begin to induce
nausea in her. When she glanced again at the other passengers, she observed them all to be looking sick and frightened.
She wondered if the captain and his crew were also similarly
afflicted. The notion turned the moisture on her forehead to
a cold sweat, for the plane was still sinking desperately and
perhaps, she thought, the captain had lost control over it.
She was almost on the point of concluding that death in an
air-crash was to be her punishment for her projected sin
when the plane emerged from the clouds and began smoothly
to glide on a steady stream of air. Below her was London, a
mass of bricks, dull in the grey cloud-obstructed light. There
was the capital of what she had known to be western civilisa-

tion. It seemed dead from that height. Afaq would bring it to life for her.

Alighting from the plane, she looked for the airport buildings, for her eyes which had been seeing Afaq now wanted to focus on the reality of his presence. She saw what looked from a distance to be a series of Nissen huts. Surely this could not be *London* airport, she thought, wondering whether the plane had not been diverted to another city; but the captain had announced it to be London. She was struck by the shabbiness of the huts which served as the airport buildings, but, turning around, she saw, far in the distance, new buildings going up as though a set was being constructed for a science fiction film, and decided that the huts must be a temporary structure. As she walked towards the Customs and Immigration entrance, she saw a number of people standing in a gallery; a few of them were waving to some of the passengers who had come with her but she could not see Afaq among them. And when the Customs officer was examining her luggage, she could not remain attentive to his questions, for she kept turning her head to the exit where a crowd of Pakistanis had gathered to welcome their friends. She could not see Afaq among them either. Nor could she find him on coming into the arrivals lounge. She saw a Pakistani woman, who had spent the entire journey from Karachi in full purdah, lifting her head-covering only when she had to eat, look despairingly around for someone, her husband perhaps, and, not finding him, squat upon the floor. Razia decided not to despair and asked the porter to put her luggage on the coach to Victoria.

The coach journey was slow and tedious. No sooner than the traffic would begin to move freely along two lanes, there would be road works necessitating single-file traffic; or they would come suddenly to a halt at traffic lights; or they would be swung in their seats as the coach negotiated a roundabout. She tried to divert herself by looking at what she could see of London. There were the monuments to light industry, factories built in the phony spirit of affected grandeur. When the plane had dived through the clouds, she had managed to suppress a feeling of sickness by thinking of her imminent meeting with Afaq, but now the jerking, stop-go movement of the coach and the annoyance of Afaq not meeting her, made her want to hang her head out of the window and vomit. She pressed a hand to her stomach and tried to breathe steadily.

From Victoria she took a taxi to the Cumberland Hotel. She had Afaq's address and could have gone there first, but decided that if he could not be bothered to come and meet her at the airport, then he could hardly want to condescend to receiving her at his flat. It was two hours since she had landed and she was tired of thinking of him. She had a light dinner at the hotel and went to bed although it was not yet eight o'clock.

She was awakened by voices in the corridor. She looked towards the window and saw the curtains bordered with light. She was not sure for a moment where she was and had to re-enact, in one telescoping image in her mind, the events following her departure from Kalapur until her arrival at the Cumberland Hotel. She switched on the lamp beside her bed and saw that it was six o'clock. She switched off the light and tried to sleep again, for it was pointless to rise. But she could not sleep. She switched on the light again. She picked up the phone and ordered tea and, rising, washed herself. Her mind felt clearer after she had drunk two cups of tea and she decided to expunge from her body what weariness it still contained by having a long hot bath. She lay for half an hour in the bath until she felt faint in the steaming room. Slowly and carefully, she dressed herself. And when she walked down the staircase to go to the dining-room for breakfast, she could have been entering a ballroom. She noticed that it was raining outside, that the morning was grey, and, passing a mirror, saw her own lipsticked mouth and her green silk sari with its gold border as an outrageous contrast to the weather's mood. Arrayed so gorgeously in silk, her gold bracelets clinking at her wrists, where could she go and what could she do on a wet day in London?

'No, not bacon and eggs,' she told the waiter. 'Just eggs. And please remember, no bacon, no ham, no pork.'

And when he had gone, no Afaq, she said to herself. So much for the inspiration of romance! She had begun to chide herself for her foolishness and wondered why she, a respectable married woman of considerable fortune, should be on the point of throwing it all away in an adventure whose only probable outcome would be remorse and unhappiness, why, even tragedy. She wondered if Afaq's not turning up had been a blessing or a sign to her that she could still retreat. No, she said to herself, her heart was already committed, she loved Afaq, and she would much rather suffer whatever humiliation or unhappiness that commitment entailed. The comforts of Kalapur were too confining, especially in that they restricted into the narrow alley of the family the vastness of her emotions which needed the open road. And yet, while dreamily reflecting upon a nebulous glory, she refused to ponder Afaq's absence.

She took her time over the breakfast, having no reason to hurry. She observed through a window that the sun was beginning to appear fitfully. She could at least look at the shops in Oxford Street if the morning provided no other fulfilment. When she had finished breakfast, she went and sat in a lounge where she read the *Daily Express*, a paper which took her mind off her own self-doubts, for she was totally absorbed in what she considered were intimate details about the British aristocracy.

13

Afaq had not joined any educational institute on arriving in England. Instead, he had bought himself a Jaguar XK 140, spent his days idling in his flat, sleeping late, and his evenings in coffee bars and night clubs. He made friends with a number of Pakistani students at the London School of Economics and, through them, with a number of English and Continental girls. One Swedish girl had endearingly and innocently called him 'Ah-fuck' and, though he had proceeded to do just that, he had pointed out that she must call him 'Ah-fahq' when they were with friends. He had been amazed at the facility with which it was possible to have and break off an affair. It suited him, for he did not want a permanent attachment. He enjoyed the availability of variety; but, although he was invariably anxious to discard a girl once he had made love to her, as though she were the peel of a fruit he had eaten, he did not like to consider that the girl he was making love to was promiscuous, for he had not been able to overcome the Muslim male's habit of jealous possessiveness with regard to the female body.

The slender body of Pamela Beresford, however, would not give in to his demands and for two weeks he had been courting her with all the zeal that money could buy. He had taken her to see *The King and I*, which bored her, and when she told him afterwards that she considered musicals too stereotyped in their rigid conventionality and that the theatre was a fit medium only for the drama which explored reality, he did not understand what she meant.

'Let me take you to a real play,' she said.

And Afaq, mistaking this attempt of Pamela's to instruct him in what was important in her culture as a proposition to increase their familiarity, insisted on buying the tickets. She was perhaps too zealous, for when they met for a drink before the play, she told him that it was in German. He laughed.

'No, don't laugh,' Pamela said. 'Please don't take it as a joke. You're going to see the Berliner Ensemble. It's the best thing in Europe at the moment. Doesn't matter if you don't understand a word. Just concentrate on the production, the acting.'

She felt slightly embarrassed, for she had not meant to sound pompous. Speaking with less animation, she went on to tell him about Brecht. He had the right ideals for humanity she said, adding with a shrug of the shoulders, 'Although his interpretation of man's situation usually led him to arrive at a Communist solution.'

'Are you a Communist?' he asked.

'No,' she said emphatically. 'But I think a genius usually has a doctrinaire belief. And yet we love him despite that.'

'Do you love me?' he asked, smiling.

'Afaq, you think of nothing else!'

'Is there anything else?'

'Come.'

And when they were watching the play, she whispered into his ear, 'That's Brecht's wife.'

Afaq was very irritated by the performance of *Mother Courage*. The German was harsh to his ears and, much though Pamela tried to explain the plot to him during the interval, his irritation turned to anger by the time the play ended.

He drove fast to retaliate, foolishly cutting in and out of the traffic and once dangerously overtaking a bus on the inside. He drove to Soho where he took Pamela to a club in Greek Street. He had not said a word since coming out of the theatre, but he felt calmer after the drive which Pamela, however, had found annoying. She disliked disorder, she hated any manifestation of anarchy. And now that they sat down at a table, they stared at each other with a mixture of hatred and determination to influence the other, she to civilise him according to her culture and he to provoke her to let him love her. When the waiter brought them the menu, he was glad to see that the prices were exceptionally expensive. It would impress her when he paid the bill, he thought.

'I enjoyed the play very much,' she said, almost daring him either to participate in her point of view or to abandon her altogether.

But it was useless to talk, for a Negress was entertaining the late-night diners with a voluptuous song, snaking her sinuous, tall figure along the narrow passage between the tables. She smiled as she sang, her white teeth sparkled, matching the single string of pearls at her neck, her honey-coloured skin glistened and when she bent slightly forward, her breasts above the low neckline rippled as though her heart was a stone which had been thrown into the pool of her flesh. It was quite useless to talk.

When they left the club, Pamela was not impressed with the two five-pound notes with which Afaq had paid the bill. She had been maddened by not being able to reach him at an intelligent level, but instead had had to watch him drug himself with what she called a phony atmosphere. She was not impressed by his ostentation and remarked about the club, 'That's not entertainment. That's decadence. That's how Rome went.'

She insisted on being taken to her bedsitter in Linden Gardens when he seemed to be driving towards his flat in Emperor's Gate. When he parked outside the house in Emperor's Gate, she refused to move and said sternly, 'I asked you take me home. Please be polite enough to do so.'

'This is home,' he said, trying to remain good humoured.

'Afaq, please take me home. Otherwise, I shall have no alternative but to walk and find my own way.'

He re-entered the car and shut the door with too loud a slam. She winced: such amateur theatricality was so tiresome. He started the car and let it idle. He turned to her and held her shoulder. He put his mouth at the side of her neck. He rubbed his nose along the neck. She remained stiff, exaggeratedly so. He touched her cheek with his mouth and tried to reach her lips. She turned her head away sharply. He passed a hand across her shoulder, down her arm and to her thigh. She tried to push his hand away. He turned round, held the steering-wheel with his right hand and, engaging the gear with his left hand, accelerated out of Emperor's Gate, not caring to slow down at any of the cross-roads he drove across. They parted hating each other. He was determined not to see her again, while she was indifferent whether he called again or not.

But he could not keep away. And she could not turn him away. They seemed to feel a destructive attraction for each other, although Pamela told herself that her aim was essentially a constructive one. It was only the fact that she repudiated any attempt at seduction which made Afaq want to possess her; she was different from the girls he had hitherto known and made love to. They had all been essentially frivolous, thoroughly content with whatever he gave them and happy wherever he took them. He vaguely recognised the quality of Pamela's intellect. He told himself again and again that he was not interested in her intellect; but it had begun to have a power over him. It was a quality he had never before seen in a woman. It raised her above the commonness of all the other women he had known. And slowly, although he did not consciously believe it, he had first become tolerant of and then interested in what she had to say. He had suggested they go to Stratford for a day since she was so interested in the theatre. Actually, it had occurred to him as a fine compromise: Stratford, along with Madame Tussaud's and the Tower of London, was on the itinerary of every Pakistani tourist in England and, therefore, he did not expect it to be all that dull; at the same time, he knew that Stratford, being an important symbol for Pamela, would win her enthusiasm. At least a whole day's togetherness will mollify her hard feelings, he had thought, while she had accepted the invitation thinking that he had begun to capitulate to her way of thinking.

The day they went to Stratford was the day Razia arrived. In his obsession with Pamela, Afaq had forgotten all about Razia and it was not until he had seen Pamela home and fumbled wearily into his own flat at two in the morning that he realized what he had done. He could already imagine Razia writing home, 'I arrived safely. Afaq unfortunately could not meet me at the airport as he was taking an English dolly to Stratford.' No one would ever understand the most serious of attachments; in Pakistan, European girls were invariably associated with a loose sexuality. He had thought

197

so himself until he met Pamela and, much though he longed to have a sexual relationship with her, he increasingly respected the terms of their friendship which she had gradually been establishing. So, what would he tell Razia? He would have to invent a lie.

He wondered if Razia still had any feelings for him, for she had not, of course, written to him that she was coming to London principally to be with him; all he knew was that she was coming to see about the education of her daughters and had not guessed at Razia's attempted duplicity. He recalled their brief intimacy and the passion they had felt for each other but which they had expressed only by silent glances. But he doubted if she could want anything now apart from a short flirtation during her stay in London. With Ayub always in mind whenever he thought of Razia, he hardly considered himself worthy of her love and the notion that she had come to offer him that love had seemed absurd to him, more a prompting of his own vain opinion of himself than a possibility.

He had to keep Pamela a secret from Razia, not only to explain his absence at the airport but also to guard Razia from a possible hurt. And he had to keep Razia a secret from Pamela, for if she heard of his sister-in-law, she would be anxious to meet her. Oh, it was too confusing, he thought, going to sleep.

He woke up reluctantly at eight and, upsetting the contents of a drawer, found Ayub's letter which gave him Razia's address in London. He could phone her first, but remembered that he had not yet decided what he was to tell her. He hastily dressed and drove to the Cumberland Hotel.

He did not need to ask the porter the number of her room, for he saw her across the hall, sitting reading a newspaper. He gingerly went up to her. She was too absorbed in William Hickey to notice.

'Hello,' he said softly.

His appearance was too sudden for her to assume a pose of offended dignity and she smiled. But immediately frowned, remembering that she ought to look hurt, and determined herself not to express her relief at seeing him.

'I'm sorry, I couldn't meet you,' he said, and was glad that she still held the paper in front of her, for his knees seemed to be knocking against each other. 'I had to go to Stafford to see the General Manager of English Electric. He was going abroad, on a tour of Europe in fact, and it was the only day he could see me until September. So, I simply had to go. Ayub-*bhai* wanted me to find out about some motor generators.'

Since she was resolved not to mention her husband, she was satisfied with the explanation and did not question him further about his visit. The Shah business was the last thing she wished to discuss.

'Well, what can I do for you?' he asked cheerfully, and with some charm, now that the ordeal of lying was over.

'Oh, everything,' she said.

He enjoyed the answer even though he did not know how he should interpret it.

'Come, let's go, then,' he said, wanting to take her hand but restraining himself, for he was not sure yet what she felt for him and nor was he certain what he ought to feel for her. It was an odd sensation walking with her; the sensation that they could do what they liked made him feel exhilarated and he noticed that she, too, seemed to be enlivened by the purer air of freedom.

They walked slowly along Oxford Street, for, coming out of the Cumberland Hotel, it seemed a natural direction. Razia could not decide whether she ought to look at the shops or at Afaq. She had purchases to make and her mood had become so buoyant that the currency of her feelings was pure gold. He had not yet overcome a slight sense of self-recrimination and was depressed on thinking that the pre-condition of his meeting Razia had been the telling of a lie. She was expected to stay in London the whole summer, three months at least, and, not knowing anyone else, she would make an excessive demand on his time. She had not yet told him that her coming to London to see about the education of her daughters had been a stratagem simply to be with him and, since no communication had passed between them, no resolves even when they lay in an embrace on that morning in Kalapur after Ayub had beaten him, it had not occurred to Afaq that Razia had been driven by a romantic fantasy, by some notion of a grand passion—although momentarily he flattered himself into thinking that she had come only to be with him. He had Pamela Beresford to think of. Even if Razia's motives in coming to London had been none other than to inquire into the educational prospects of her daughters, he would have scrupulously wanted to keep Pamela away from her; but now he had strictly to do so in order to protect Razia's feelings. When Razia's visit ought to have been an unencumbered, happy event, it was beset now with anxiety, doubt, and the possibility of suffering.

He already suffered from the conflict, the opposition of attitudes, with Pamela and, as he walked the length of Oxford Street, he thought of the visit to Stratford. He could hardly call it a success. They had driven up in the morning and he had wanted to use the opportunity of a long drive to show Pamela the speed and road-holding qualities of his XK 140 as well as his skill in driving it.

'There's no hurry,' she kept saying, glad that she had remembered to put a scarf in her handbag, for Afaq insisted on having the hood down.

'Look, how pretty that field is,' she said, tightening the knot of the scarf under her chin.

And then later: 'Afaq, don't you like the countryside?'

He had not answered, not even looked at her, but grimly kept his foot down, his leg stiff as though it were in plaster.

'These are the Cotswolds,' she had tried. 'Some of the prettiest villages in England. Millions of tourists come here. From all over the world. And such hills. Beautiful views. The antique shops are becoming a little vulgar, though.'

He changed down to third, approaching a bend, and was satisfied with the note of the engine and the sound of the squealing tyres when he took the bend. She looked for a handkerchief in her bag, for the rush of wind was smarting her eyes. She slid down in the seat and, looking up, watched the tree-tops go past against the sky. She shut her eyes and considered the rootedness of trees. She decided that without silence the exercise of patience would be impossible; and compressed her lips.

On arriving at Stratford, Afaq examined the tyres to see if they had not overheated. He opened the hood and cast a knowing eye at the engine. She stood on the pavement and observed his actions. Having put up the top and locked the car, he joined her, smiling. Believing that anger, often due to trivialities which later reveal their true unimportance, was one emotion mankind could profitably dispense with, she smiled back and held his arm as they walked down the street to find a restaurant.

'You like your car, don't you?' she said, pointing her chin up a little and shaking her head to unloosen her hair now that she had removed the scarf.

'It's a beauty,' he said and turned to the waiter to give his order.

'I was a bit scared,' she said, laughing and thinking that he would be more willing to participate in her lightness of spirit than accept her admonition.

'That's the first time I've done a hundred and ten,' he said, putting the napkin across his thighs.

'Did we go *that* fast?' she asked, suddenly frightened.

'See? You didn't even notice it! The car's that good.'

'I must have been looking at the trees,' she said, suspecting that she must be the antithesis of the commonly displayed advertiser's image of the girl in the sports car, her face turned to the wind and her hair blowing while her shut eyes experienced some inner ecstasy. In seeking out and applauding what was important in her culture, Pamela was concerned about the propagation of falsehood within that culture. For a moment, she wondered whether she ought not to apologise to Afaq for having misled him in his concept of the English. She hoped that he would learn through his experience of what she had to show him, and was prepared to suffer whatever trial she was consequently involved in.

'What's this play all about?' he asked.

'About a king,' she said, 'who's mistakenly jealous of his wife. I think you'll like the story. But don't worry about the story. It's the words I'd like you to listen to.'

'How else can I know the story if I don't listen to the words?' he asked, and she was prepared to laugh with him.

His silence when they emerged from the theatre at the end of the play was all too indicative of the boredom he had suffered. She held his arm tightly and walked close to him as though wanting to make up to him for the commitment of some error. Mercifully, there was rain in the air and, when they reached the car he did not put the top down. He started the engine. She felt sorry for him, almost as if she had deeply wronged him. He did not look at her, but listened to the engine warming up. She turned to him then and, reaching for his cheek, kissed him.

'Is whispering nothing?' she whispered into his ear, her cheek on his. 'Is leaning cheek to cheek?'

She touched his nose with hers and continued to whisper, 'Is meeting noses? Kissing with inside lip?'

And she kissed him, sucking his lower lip into her mouth. Presently remembering another fragment of the quotation, which she had learned four years previously for her A-level exam, she drew away from him, saying, 'Why, then the world and all that's in't is nothing, the covering sky is nothing, nor nothing have these nothings, if this be nothing.'

Perhaps he was touched by the poetry; perhaps the sensuousness of her action had sexually aroused him; she could not tell, but she felt convinced that he had been moved.

He was glad to drive away. He could not understand what had happened in that brief gesture of affection. What was it within him which altered when she had spoken into his ear and touched him so tenderly? His emotions were subtler and more complex than he had been aware. At last he realised that the words which she had spoken were not her own but came from the play. He did not remember who said them or in what context they were spoken. All he could admit to, now that Pamela had made the words her own, was that language had a way of entering the blood-stream and effecting one's heart-beat. He turned to look at her, and smiled.

'Was it too much of a bore?' she asked.

'Well, I think that king must have been mad,' he said. 'First he sees his wife making love to the other king but we know she's quite innocent. So, what are we to believe, that he has hallucinations? And then that business at the end of her being a statue and coming to life is like a fairy tale, isn't it? I mean it's the sort of thing you tell children. It's not a story for adults.'

His complaints, she felt, would not have been considered a naïve attempt at critically appraising the play had he been speaking at an Eng. Lit. seminar, and she almost believed that she had effected the breakthrough in making Afaq see the seriousness of literature.

'True,' she said excitedly, 'there are faults in the plot, but there are psychological insights in the play which are very modern. Of course, the ending is a bit unbelievable. Maybe Shakespeare wanted to write a tragedy and changed his mind half-way. Or maybe something else. The play throws up all sorts of questions and that's half the beauty of it. Leontes thinks his wife is unfaithful but she is not. He thinks that she is dead but she is alive. Truth is not always what we see, and what we think we know perhaps has no reality at all. Maybe that's what the play is trying to say.'

Rain had begun to fall heavily and she stopped her critical dissertation when she noticed that Afaq had screwed up his eyes and was trying hard to find the road in the darkness. He did not answer to any of her points. Perhaps, she thought, he had not heard a word. She would be content, she decided, with what she had so far achieved.

They stopped in Oxford for supper, finding a small Italian

restaurant still open. Afaq let her order, for he was unfamiliar with Continental food.

'No,' he said, 'give me a good musical any day.'

'Afaq, why do you insist on remaining a barbarian?' The argument, she felt, had become repetitive.

'We could live,' she tried once more when they were finishing their supper, 'on bread and water, but we like the rich variety of good food.'

She hardly needed to emphasise her metaphor by stating its correlative, and Afaq said good-humouredly, though ambiguously, 'I'll try anything if you will as well.'

It was well past midnight when they drove through High Wycombe. In spite of the deserted streets and the open road, Afaq, beginning to be overcome by fatigue, was driving at half the pace to what he had maintained during the outward journey. The rain continued and Pamela, a nervous traveller, remained awake with apprehension when she could have slipped lower in the seat and dozed off. Perhaps the journey, undertaken in complete silence since Oxford, had become too trying, she could not tell, but she could not suppress the note of irritation in her voice when, on reaching London, he suggested that she go with him to his flat.

'Oh, what's the use!' he exclaimed and again showed his temper by driving recklessly when taking her home.

'Afaq,' she had said on leaving him, 'I *would* like to see you again.' And added, softly kissing him on the cheek, 'Otherwise there is nothing.'

And now Razia, whom he had thought he loved when he was on the plane from Karachi, walked beside him and he did not know whether he should consider himself fortunate or expect a subtler form of suffering than he had experienced before.

They had reached Oxford Circus and Razia, pleased with her self-restraint in resisting the temptation to go into the shops and buy the many things which had already impressed her fancy, had made a mental note of the programme for her first shopping expedition. But later, later; now, Afaq. She looked up at him and smiled. It warmed him to see her thus and, remembering Pamela's poetry, decided that a look could communicate as profoundly as words. So that he took her hand when they crossed the road. She showed no inclination to withdraw it when they were again on the pavement.

14

Preparations had begun for Javed's marriage to Amina. Formal letters had been exchanged between the parents and Aziz Khan's family had been invited to Karachi for the engagement ceremony, Amina's father, Mohammed Bux, undertaking to meet all the expenses. Aziz Khan had been obliged to decline the invitation for reasons of his wife's health and the work on the land. Consequently, Amina's father had been able to raise the dowry to five thousand rupees together with the linen, crockery and miscellaneous items of furniture which the two parents had already agreed upon.

The coming marriage had imbued Aziz Khan's house with a sense of urgency. Mohammed Bux wrote an elegant prose; his sophisticated Urdu, containing subtle Persian nuances, followed the fashionable style of the former Mogul court; and the arrival of a letter from him was invariably an event. Aziz Khan would read it first silently to himself and then Zakia would read it aloud, often more than once, being carried away by the sonorous rhythm and the graceful phraseology into declaiming it as though she were at a speech contest. A suitable reply would then be considered in general terms before Aziz Khan could make a draft for copious discussion prior to writing the final version. Zakia was happy to be thus active, for arranging a son's marriage is the favourite pastime of Pakistani mothers. It was a better tonic than any of her doctors had prescribed and in her happiness she easily forgot many of the exhortations and admonitions with which she had been released from the nursing home.

Javed was content to be a spectator to his parents' game, for this was his traditional role; and, besides, he valued the happiness which he could see his mother had found. He no longer needed to walk gingerly about the house to which a former cheerfulness seemed to be returning. He thought of Amina in his lonely hours, the thin-lipped and narrow eye-browed Amina, whose postcard-sized photograph was all the knowledge of her which he possessed. He longed to possess the picture, to look at it when he was alone, but custom forbade it. His mother kept the portrait by her bed, but, whenever he entered her room, he made it a point of honour not to look at it. Zuleikha had written several letters, in each one of which she had some new item about Amina to praise; now it was her embroidery and now her surprising facility for a city girl at churning butter; but Javed wanted to know the degree of softness of her hands, the feel of her hair.

The cotton crop had been abandoned but Javed planned to organise new labour after the harvesting season just before the wedding party arrived. He had decided upon a ruthless pruning of the plantation in order to ensure a good crop the next year. Aziz Khan had been able to save a small plot of wheat which would give them enough grain for their own needs till the following spring. The vegetables had been made to flourish again and Javed enjoyed walking among the pumpkins in the evenings. He was glad that the dowry would not only be sufficient to pay off his father's debts but would also meet the cost of labour until they could earn money again from the land. Now that Amina had appeared as an image around which to construct his future, it was possible for him to make calculations for that future. He was paying increasing attention to his family and its property; but he still worked at the mills and intended to do so until just before harvest time. For he had become engaged in a conflict with Ayub and he was determined to resolve it to his own advantage, to win at least one victory against the Shah brothers.

Ayub had come to hear about the Kalapur Textile Workers' Union. He had gone at once to Akram's office and said angrily, 'I suppose you know nothing about it.'

'What?' Akram said, absently pulling out a drawer of his desk.

'The Union,' Ayub said.

'Union?' Akram saw that the drawer contained a report on Pakistan's textile exports to the Middle East. He ought to visit Karachi again, he thought, and renew his acquaintance with the Minister of Commerce who had so obligingly sent him the report.

'They've formed a bloody Union,' Ayub said, too loudly for a man who could exercise power with a whisper. 'I haven't been away three days and the workers have formed a Union. Am I expected to be here all the time to keep order?'

'The floors are your job, the office is mine.' Akram could be coldly severe. 'I've been too busy preparing information for the Minister so that he can land a juicy order for us on his next trade mission. A Union, eh?'

'Yes, a bloody Union. I suppose we'll have a strike the next time I'm at home with a cold.'

'Don't worry,' Akram said, shutting the drawer, 'we could dismiss ten times the men we employ and immediately find new labour to replace them. I don't think anyone who has a stomach to feed would want to strike. Not in this country.'

'But it's an affront, it's a disgrace,' Ayub said. 'We can't allow it. We'll have to prohibit it.'

'Who's behind it?' Akram asked, preferring facts to emotion.

'I don't know. I've only just heard.'

'I think we better find out the complete details. Get your floor managers to produce a report. We'll discuss it more fully then.'

A day later, Ayub had all the evidence before him and he was astonished to discover that Javed was one of the committee members of the Union. His first instinct was to dismiss all of them and this was his intention when he asked a peon to summon them to his office. He changed his mind, however, when the peon had gone. He decided that he could not dismiss Javed, for having him working at the mills was a demonstration to Kalapur that the Shah brothers had succeeded in controlling the one surviving landlord in the area and that their possession of his land would now be only a matter of time. If Javed were to be dismissed, Aziz Khan would again appear to be independent of the Shah authority, he would once again symbolise a form of recalcitrance which Ayub had made it his business to extinguish as though it were no more than a weakly flickering candle-flame. No, he would keep Javed at the mills and think of a way of extorting Aziz Khan's land without paying the smallest coin of the basest metal for it. Impoverished though Aziz Khan had become, the misfortunes of his family had begun to evoke a public sympathy for him, and Ayub was aware of the danger of the landlord being ennobled to the sort of sainthood which the illiterate peasants so readily bestowed upon a suffering man. It was necessary soon for him to act decisively and he saw a way of doing so by having Javed work for him. Since he had decided not to dismiss Javed, he could not very well expel Salim and Riaz. Of course, no one would challenge a decision of his, but he now believed that the political strategist in him could better deal with the threat of the Union than that trait of his character which always reacted violently and destructively. So that when Salim, Riaz and Javed entered his office, he greeted them affably, almost with that exaggerated politeness which cannot fail to appear heavily sarcastic. The smile on his face could have been a sneer.

'Come in, come in,' he said, pointing to the chairs. 'Sit down.'

Salim sat down at once but Riaz hesitated a moment,

searching Ayub's face for the treachery he was certain was ready to ooze from the skin of any capitalist, before finding a chair. Javed remained standing but Ayub insisted that he should take the leather chair opposite his desk.

'Well,' Ayub said, 'I must congratulate you on your popularity at the mills. I believe you were elected unanimously . . .?'

He looked from one to the other, smiling, but the three committee members could have been made of ebony.

'I'll tell you one thing,' Ayub went on, essaying to humour the men. 'All the truly important elections are unanimous. It would be ridiculous to elect people like Khrushchev and General de Gaulle in any other way. What do you say to that Riaz-*bhai*. Aren't they, huh?'

Ayub laughed with the question and Riaz could not tell whether he had been addressed as a brother in the common Urdu usage of the word or whether Ayub was hinting that he knew all about Riaz's Marxism. Riaz shifted uneasily in his chair.

'Anyway, anyway,' Ayub continued, not wanting the interference of silence. 'So we are equals now. We run the mills and you run the men. An excellent arrangement. We could do with more organisation, a greater sense of purpose in this place. I'm all for sharing out responsibility and I don't doubt that you will carry out your part of it satisfactorily. Good. Good. Tell me more about your Union.'

But they had told him nothing yet, Javed thought. Riaz, who had begun to think that Ayub had been genuinely scared by the power of the masses which they had manifested by setting up the Union and that he was not embarking on a game of duplicity, said, 'The Union was established to give the worker his self-respect.'

Ayub nodded his head as though giving his approval to Riaz's statement.

'The worker has no identity,' Riaz continued, 'no individuality. He has simply been a component in the machine. The Union guarantees that he is a human being first.'

Ayub continued to nod at the end of each statement and was trying strenuously to restrain the incipient anger within him.

'Precisely,' Salim interpolated, but Riaz went on as if reciting a charter: 'In concerning itself with the well-being of its members, the Union will lay down a code of conduct for its members. The Union will expect responsibility from the workers, especially with regard to the terms of membership, but also on this important point: that the workers, in expecting the Union to negotiate with the management on their behalf for improved working conditions, will extend their responsibility to the management by concentrating on a high level of productivity.'

'That is very satisfactory,' Ayub said, convinced that Riaz had just improvised this point in the Union's favour out of a fear for him. 'I'm thankful to you for insisting upon productivity. We've had to sack too many workers for slackness.'

'You can rest assured now,' Salim put in, 'there'll be no slackness.'

'Good, good,' Ayub said. 'And you, Javed, what part do you play on the committee?'

'I'm the assistant secretary,' Javed said, but refrained from elaborating on his functions.

Salim felt prompted to announce, 'I'm the treasurer.'

'Indeed,' Ayub said.

'But we haven't,' Riaz quickly explained, 'decided upon a subscription as yet.'

'You've done well,' Ayub said, 'done very well. The men are full of respect for and fear of you. That's the way of authority. You've indeed done well. Thank you for coming to see me. Do let me know if I can help.'

The three rose to go and Ayub said to Javed, 'Wait behind a moment, will you? I'd like to hear about your mother.'

When Salim and Riaz had departed, Ayub asked Javed to take his seat again and said, 'Well, how is she? Recovered by now, I hope . . .?'

'She's back at home now,' Javed muttered. He could not help appearing sullen whenever he talked to Ayub, so that his answers to him always seemed pieces of information reluctantly divulged.

'You know, Javed, the world has progressed. Man knows more about himself now, how to feed himself, how to look after himself, how to produce the things he needs, than he has ever known before. Knowledge is a wonderful thing. It's no use living in ignorance. That's a crime against oneself. Therefore, it's no use living in an old-fashioned way. We must not only accept the changes but also make the effort to go out and embrace the changes. That's how progress is possible.'

'What's this got to do with my mother?' Javed asked, keeping his voice quiet, for he had no cause to want to sound impertinent.

'A great deal,' Ayub said. 'She's been ill, I believe seriously ill. What I'm trying to say to you is that you have to live with the times. Get the best medical help as soon as possible whenever you need it. And that costs money.'

'But you didn't want to buy our land when I came and offered it to you.'

'My dear boy, who said anything about your land?'

'Well, what else did you mean?' Javed asked, his voice rising for the first time. 'Why are you telling me all this?'

'You are young and when one is young it is very easy to fall in with the wrong company. I'm advising you as a friend.'

But Javed, who had learned to guard himself against Ayub's charm and not to accord a literal meaning to any of his statements, did not want his advice.

'I know,' he said, 'you don't like the idea of the Union.'

'No, no,' Ayub said, 'let's keep the Union out of this. But if you want to talk about it, what can you possibly hope to gain by being on its committee?'

'That's my business.'

'But it's part of my business, for the Union affects my workers.'

'I like to do something useful.'

'I see,' Ayub said. 'I was telling you how important it is

to be able to use the progress which technologists have made for us. I was saying how important it is to have money. What I was going to suggest to you was this: what would you say to increased responsibility? You're earning, I believe, fifty rupees a month now. We're satisfied with your work. I would like you to accept the position of foreman of your floor at a salary of two hundred and fifty rupees a month. Think, you could soon save for a radio, and then for a fridge.'

Javed looked at him intently as though he were a geologist and Ayub a new rock specimen the composition of which he needed to identify.

'And if you make a good foreman,' Ayub proceeded with his offer, 'there will be other openings, overseer, floor manager, why, you might even end up as one of our senior executives.'

'And what do I have to do in return?' Javed asked.

'Choose better companions than Riaz and Salim. You must know that Riaz at least is a Communist.'

'In other words, you want to buy me out of the Union.'

'Consider my offer how you will,' Ayub said. 'But remember that I'm the master here.'

'The master of bribery,' Javed said. 'You can arrange anything, can't you, from a job to a hanging?'

The words had come out in a rush and, although Javed had been trying to find the connection between Rafiq's death and the Shah brothers, he had not meant to refer to the injustice until he had some proof on which to base his accusation.

'Thank you for the insult,' Ayub said calmly. 'If you made that sort of statement in public, you'd be gaoled for slander. Go to your work and think over what I've said.'

When Javed had gone, Ayub wondered why he had bothered to exercise his charm and restraint on the three men when he could have dealt with them with his normal ruthlessness which would have made the point more forcibly to the workers than a devious political manœuvre. Believing that no man was without greed, he had wanted to lure

Javed's cupidity; his idea was to give Javed a taste of money by increasing his wages, then to tempt him with a generous loan and then, depriving him suddenly of his source of income by dismissing him at a time when his father's property would be producing no wealth, to ruin him. Ayub still considered the scheme feasible but was now vexed with himself for having thought of it, for it took for granted that Javed would behave according to his own calculations. As for the Union, though he knew that Akram was right in dismissing any possibility of trouble simply because there was an excess of labour in the country, he considered it necessary to demonstrate his power and preferred it that the workers should see the Union as more important and significant than it actually was, so that when he destroyed it, his power would be seen to be proportionately greater. Consequently, now that Salim and Riaz had gone away thinking that they had his approval and confidence, he allowed matters to develop for some days.

But what had Javed's reference to hanging implied? Ayub was glad that he had not betrayed anything; but Javed had obviously been thinking. Ayub was certain that Javed knew nothing positive; otherwise, he would not have been silenced by being called a slanderer. But Javed had been thinking, and that was dangerous. Ayub did not believe that Javed could ever find any proof to establish the crime of which Rafiq had been innocent; but, still, Ayub did not care to spoil his sleep by the reflection that Javed might be gathering evidence and, therefore, he could not afford to take chances.

One day a notice appeared in the workers' canteen stating that the Committee of the Kalapur Textile Workers' Union had decided that each member would pay a subscription of ten rupees a year and that the subscriptions, now due, were payable to Mr Salim Ahmed, Treasurer of the Union. A day later, Salim, while at his duties as a foreman on the weavers' floor, was called by a worker who complained of some defect in his loom. Five minutes later, Salim had lost an index

213

finger in what was later referred to as an industrial accident. Salim was informed in hospital the next day that his services would no longer be required at the mills, for he had been guilty of neglecting safety precautions when inspecting a machine. That same afternoon, Riaz was summoned by his floor manager, who threw a batch of invoices at him as soon as he entered his office, scolded him with an excessive show of bad temper for filling up the forms incorrectly, abused him in no elegant language and demoted him to the position of floor sweeper on the weavers' floor, thus cutting down his salary from one hundred and fifty rupees a month to twenty-five. Riaz stood full of hatred and bitterness, wanting to shout back his defence, but the manager, who had risen from his chair, continued his merciless abuse, taking menacing steps towards him so that Riaz, having to retreat, seemed to be pushed out of the office when the manager finished. Head lowered and tears in his eyes, Riaz did not go to the weavers' floor, but slowly, aimlessly, walked out of the mills.

It was obvious even to the most recently employed workers, who were new to Kalapur and were not familiar with Ayub's methods, that Salim and Riaz had been penalised for their presumption at starting the Union. The story spread through Kalapur, though the only news that concerned the Shah brothers in the local paper the next day was one announcing their donation of ten thousand rupees to a blood centre which was to be opened in Kalapur.

Javed heard the newspaper item being quoted in the canteen and he again began to think of his brother's trial and hanging. Then, there had seemed to be no relation between the facts as he knew them and the facts as they had been established in court; and now, what made scandalous copy for a newspaper had completely been ignored while another fact was being asserted almost as an attempt to distract attention from the scandal. Just as outsiders to his family would never know the real Rafiq, so people outside Kalapur would have a totally different notion of the Shah brothers. Again, Javed was confused. He could not decide where his reasoning led him: there was a parallel but no connection. All he had begun to see was that the world had a way of deceiving itself. He wished he had not referred to the hanging during his interview with Ayub, for it was folly to reveal his suspicions to him. He ought to be careful, he thought, until he discovered the truth.

His thoughts turned to Salim and Riaz. He wanted to be able to help them, to comfort them; for he felt that he had indirectly brought misfortune upon them by turning down Ayub's offer. Perhaps Ayub would have wanted to destroy them in any case, but this notion did not mitigate the guilt he felt. He ought to have been wiser, he ought to have coun- selled caution to them and not let them be carried away by the intoxication of oratory. But he could not make himself visit Salim in the hospital or go and offer solace to Riaz. He did not possess the vocabulary of comfort; verbal ges- tures of sympathy made him feel clumsy.

He hit upon a way of helping Salim and Riaz. He opened a fund for them. He spoke to some workers individually and at once evoked their sympathy, so much so that within two hours, between the lunch and the tea breaks, word had passed from man to man and every worker knew of the fund and was anxious to seek out Javed in order to con- tribute to it.

Ayub would not for long have remained ignorant of the fund but Javed, daring to be openly rebellious, divulged the news himself by deciding to use part of the money he had already collected in placing an advertisement in the local paper announcing the fund and inviting the citizens of Kalapur to contribute. He had reckoned that, if he succeeded, the advertisement would have paid for itself, but, if it brought nothing, then he would reimburse the fund from his own wages. The advertisement became notorious. It was the first public insult which the Shah brothers had suffered— that was the popular interpretation of it and not Javed's intention. People talked about it, discussed it passionately.

People who could not read, had it read to them again and again as though it were a memorable piece of verse. The vendors in the bazaar set up small altars on their stalls, a wooden box or a tin among heaps of flowers, so that people could contribute to the fund. Children soon devised a game which they called 'Da fun'. The richer people, many of whom owed their social position in Kalapur to the Shah brothers, argued about the fund and awaited the outcome, wondering whose turn it was to suffer Ayub's wrath, but some of them secretly sent anonymous donations to the fund.

Ayub saw the dangers and, violent though was his nature, he was experienced enough to know when to be cautious. There was a wave of public feeling against him and he decided that it was best to remain quiet. But only ostensibly. Devising a scheme to win back popularity, he put public relations to work.

He persuaded Akram to fly to Karachi to meet the Minister of Commerce in order to discuss the export of textiles and then to Dacca to further his plans for establishing soap factories in East Pakistan. When Akram left, Ayub personally saw to it that the newspaper carried photographs of the departing Akram Shah and an article describing in the most laudatory terms the reasons for Akram's expedition. He also arranged for a newspaper agency to photograph Akram being welcomed to Karachi by the Minister himself and to send a daily report to the newspaper in Kalapur of Akram's meetings with the Minister. The fund was due to close while Akram was still in Karachi and, by continuing to make a big national issue of Akram's visit after the fund had closed, Ayub succeeded in turning Kalapur's main point of conversation from the fund to the noble work the Shah Industrial Enterprises were doing for the national economy. Satisfied that he could manage public relations with such subtlety that people took for their own the opinions which he had decided they should hold, he could afford to relax, be seen at a polo match or on the dance-floor at the club. His face again radiated with his exuberant charm, but behind the aura of gentle contentment which he managed to exhibit, his mind was trying fiercely to resolve a suitable fate for Javed.

Javed was satisfied that he had performed his duty towards Salim and Riaz. He had been thrilled by the response to the fund but, despite his popularity with the workers at the mills, he was aware of the coldness with which some of the floor managers did not reciprocate his greeting whenever he passed them. He could now have left his job, but lingered on at it in a mood of defiance. It was as though a conqueror had decided to extend his sojourn in his newly-won colony before returning to his capital and was too elated to contemplate that there might be assassins lurking not far from his person.

15

Seeing her husband's photograph, or an article about him, almost every day, helped Faridah to check the vexation which threatened to explode from her. She would not admit that she was bored, not even having her husband's daily return from the mills to look forward to. Now that Akram had gone on his visits to Karachi and Dacca, she felt compelled to remain at home. It would have been an open act of infidelity had she been seen unescorted at the club and while it would have been perfectly in order for her to be at a cinema with Razia and Zarina, she could not have taken that liberty without giving rise to scandalous gossip; in any case, the possibility of her doing so was precluded because of Razia's absence. Her shopping expeditions were strictly utilitarian—visits exclusively to the market to purchase meat and vegetables—for which she wore her plainest clothes. The servants could have done such shopping, but it was necessary for her to be seen to be doing her duty; so that no one could have said that she was in any sense enjoying herself while her husband was away. It was a trial she had to suffer, she told herself repeatedly.

She hardly saw Ayub who worked late and dined at the club, for he paid little regard to his sister-in-law's society. Zarina remained enclosed in her own room or wandered about the garden. Faridah considered that Zarina was coming to the difficult age, for she seemed invariably uninterested in any of her suggestions; although Zarina never refused to do anything, Faridah could sense a sullen resistance in her. She could sense Zarina's desire to be independent, perhaps emotionally if not physically, and felt slightly gratified that Zarina at least possessed a measure of humility and reasonableness; with luck, she was not likely to fall into the silly ways of the teenagers Faridah had seen in Lahore and Karachi.

Zarina was not yet a problem, but Razia's two little daughters were. Faridah left their surveillance to the servants, but not herself checking on the servants, the children were often left unattended. Their shrieks came piercing through the walls, making Faridah clench her teeth each time. They had a way of stamping through the house which rendered useless the sound-proofing quality of the thick carpets. They kicked doors rather than use only the handles and Faridah had noticed how the paint had been chipped at the bottom of several doors. She had scolded them, though not too harshly for fear it might be too permanently damaging to their character—not having children herself, she had read many articles about bringing up children, so that she never knew what was exactly right. She had sent them out to the garden where they had sulked for a few minutes before beginning to tear leaves off trees.

'Oh, chillrun, chillrun,' she sighed to herself. 'If I vas their mudher, I vould not let them tormentize me like this. Such vild vuns!'

But she was not their nor any other child's mother, she told herself ruefully. She thought of the fortune which the family had acquired solely through the efforts of her husband. He deserved better than to have these two inconsiderate girls as his heirs. But what could she do, a virgin at forty-three, what could she do? Anything, even an idiot child of her own would be worthier for the inheritance than these coarse creatures, these over-pampered offspring of Razia's. How she hated Razia's complacent smile whenever she was talking of her children, showing the glint of her white teeth as though it were the steel of a knife! Faridah liked to think that her sufferings had a depth which Razia could never reach with the longest weapon. But she felt so hurt, she wished the inheritance would be left entirely to charity. Just to make Razia feel a fraction of her own hurt. But there was Afaq. If only he would settle down respectably and marry a decent girl, there was a chance, Faridah thought with the sensation of a headache abating, that Razia's hopes would be partially confounded. At least the extent of her influence would be diminished. Although it made no material difference to herself, a more diffuse disbursement of the family wealth than merely to Razia's offspring gave her some satisfaction. She felt slightly relieved at the thought and became charitable towards herself, and considered that, in a sense, it was just that she, to whose family the riches should principally have belonged, should have been deprived of children. It was Allah's justice. For, to have been granted both wealth and children was too much to expect of this life; happiness came from the accretion of complementary satisfactions and since no one could ever be completely happy, it was understandable that she, too, should suffer some lack. But what did Razia lack? she asked herself, suddenly stung by the thought that she was perfectly happy, having all that she desired. No, she felt convinced, retribution would come. Justice, which in Faridah's philosophy could be defined as the occurrence of misfortune to others, would prevail.

She saw Munni fling a branch into the empty swimming-pool but was less annoyed than she might have been an hour earlier. She turned her attention instead to the words of a song which she could faintly hear coming from Zarina's room, an old love-sick song. The record must have been at least twenty years old and, although a popular song at the time, had acquired a classical status. She was touched that Zarina should be playing it to herself, who was younger than the record and who knew nothing of Malika Pukhraj of Jammu except her glorious voice, except the response of her own emotions to the lyrics. Poor Zarina! Faridah thought, she must be in love, but she considered it a vague, a generalised longing which youthful girls traditionally expressed and would have been very shocked indeed if she had been told that Zarina's longings were all too real.

Zarina sat by the record-player, elbows on her knees and her palms clasping her cheeks. She could have wept if the tears might have communicated to *him*. But she had commerce only with the mirror which readily bought her feelings. She wondered what would happen when Afaq returned, how she would first meet him. Like Afaq, she, too, had been erroneously aware that the family intended them to marry and, although that was her dearest wish, she did not want it to happen the way in which it was likely to: which would be Faridah first ponderously telling her about the proposal, so that she would be expected to remain hidden to Afaq, and then the ceremony taking place. Instead, she wanted Afaq's love first. She wanted to be able to tell him that she loved him and she wanted a similar confession from him. She wanted the secrecy of love before the family made it into the public spectacle which a marriage in Pakistan was; she wanted clandestine meetings and the knowing, furtive looks at the dinner table before they sat there as man and wife. She wanted the satisfaction of it being acknowledged as a marriage between lovers and not observed as the philosophic acceptance of a family arrangement. Oh, she wanted so much! And all she had was a room of her own and a family which could trade upon her most private feeling. Why had Afaq not secretly come to her before he went to London? Why had he not declared his love for her and vowed he would remain true to her? She was sometimes angry at the thought of his carelessness, his indifference which she did not doubt he found it necessary to affect in order not to arouse any suspicions in the house. Oh, he was so inconsiderate in his thoughtfulness! Zarina sighed, and would have wept had she not resolved on the day of Afaq's departure that she would cry only once a day and that only at night just before going to sleep.

16

Aziz Khan sat in the evening in the front yard of his house, watching the sun go down on his land. The sun was at the same height as he was from the earth and the two seemed momentarily to be fixed in a silent confrontation. But the sun was setting, slowly slipping away. Its light fell fully on Aziz Khan's face whence it shot back from his unblinking stare. He looked at his impoverished land, falling into a reverie, shutting his eyes, imagining it again to be tall with growth. A fly alighted upon his nose for a moment and he shook his face as if waking up from a dream. What had gone wrong in the order of his existence? he wondered. He had never asked questions, never expected meanings to manifest themselves, for he had never observed the world as a separate existence from himself: his fulfilments had been part of the earth's and his dejections a sort of seasonal regression. Now the withered plants proclaimed the alienation between man and his environment. The latter could be altered by man, but, Aziz Khan decided, finding comfort in his religious primitivism, all decisions were made by a divinity which alone possessed the power of influencing human actions.

But he had begun to ask *Why?* Apart from a benign wisdom, which urban citizens (for what reason, it is not clear) think a peasant possesses, Aziz Khan did not have the intellectual experience to answer such a fundamental question. He had knowledge, however, gained from the elemental sources of human existence, and it might be that his resistance to the question was an emotional and not an intellectual one: perhaps he could have, but had unconsciously decided that he would not.

He thought instead of the actuality before him. There was the debt to pay, over a thousand rupees to the doctors and the nursing home. He was slightly irritated that, after a lifetime of work on so large an estate, he had no money. He had considered himself a wealthy man until the Shah brothers arrived and had been respected in the neighbourhood of Kalapur as a prosperous landlord. But he realised now that then his production, income, and expenditure to continue the production had somehow been equally related and that his wealth had lain in the fact that he could continue the production from one harvest to the next. Once this cycle was broken his real impecunious state was exposed: all he had was the land and what it was potentially worth. And once the crops failed, it was necessary for him to find the capital with which to begin a new cycle of production. Financially, the deterioration had commenced with the pressure put by the Shah brothers on his former buyers to withdraw their business from him. The money he needed immediately to pay for Zakia's illness was little to what would be necessary to begin a comprehensive re-cultivation of the land. He could not expect the peasants to give their labour on a year's credit; he might as well ask them to forego eating for a year. There was some hope of advancement from Javed's marriage, for his prospective father-in-law had promised five thousand rupees. The amount would enable Aziz Khan to make some sort of a start, but he needed two thousand immediately. He could mortgage the land and raise twenty-five thousand at least, but he did not want to do so. He wondered whether he could not borrow two thousand on the security of his son's expected dowry, and went to the one bank in Kalapur to do so.

'No, no, Khan sahib,' the bank manager, wearing glasses with very thick lenses, said. 'Such a loan would be very irregular. I've accepted at a pinch a herd of buffaloes as a security. But that too is very risky. You don't know what disease might not attack a herd overnight. But a son's engagement is a very, very risky matter, very risky indeed. Why, I remember, I was engaged three times before I successfully accomplished a consummated marriage. It's very difficult, very difficult. The first time I had been promised ten thousand rupees. Everything was fine, settled and decided upon with the utmost finality. And then what do you think happened? We found, quite by an accidental chance and to our utterly amazed horror, that they were Syeds. Now, we are Sunnis and no one in our family has ever married a non-Sunni. It's unthinkable and unheard of. It just doesn't bear the weight of thought, Khan sahib. Caste is caste, it's like dye, it's either fast or it runs, why it's like silk and cotton fibres, you can't weave the two together. And do you know, our families came to blows. We'd smeared their daughter's virgin face, they said. Have you ever heard of such an unheard of thing? Oh, it was such a carry on. Now, what would have happened if I had borrowed ten thousand rupees on the security of *that* engagement? It's quite impossible, hopelessly so, hopelessly. Head office will think I've gone mad and taken leave of my senses. Also, times are difficult. Withdrawals are heavy. People are buying and hoarding gold. A year, why six months ago, I could have suggested offering a mortgage on the security of your land. But now we'd be pinched, oh, sorely pinched, to do so. I think your best chance is to go to an old-fashioned money-lender for your present requirements for the time being. I hate to recommend such a person for they are directly the opposite antithesis of true and proper banking. But you are a very good old friend of mine of long acquaintance, and I have to say something to help. My confidential advice is strictly between you and me, however.'

Aziz Khan thanked him and departed without showing any of the bitterness he felt. Later, he asked Javed to go to Hussain to inquire about raising a loan, thinking that Hussain, with an eye always on a quick profit for which he did not need to bestir himself from his bed, would perhaps have a way of finding a money-lender for him.

Javed rode to Hussain's, not hurrying his horse but allowing it to go at the pace it preferred. Once during the journey, he leaned forward to pat it on the side of its neck and to stroke its mane, but for the rest of the time his thoughts did not encompass the existence of the horse. He wondered if he ought now to give up his work at the mills. He was still admired by the workers, but Javed knew that an idol must not walk among his people. He kept his job, hoping that his proximity to the Shah brothers might accidentally reveal the truth about Rafiq. He was surprised that Ayub had not dismissed him or attempted to be rid of him in a manner in which he dispensed with Salim and Riaz. Javed flattered himself into thinking that he was too popular with the workers for Ayub to make any such attempt and it pleased him to be a walking insult to the mills. He took care, however, and was wary of the possibility of accidents. But he must soon give up the job, pleasant though it was to be able to procrastinate giving in his notice. With his wedding less than two months away now, his future was pleasanter in his thoughts. He whispered the name 'Amina' to himself, involuntarily gripping the horse tighter with his knees and leaning forward to rest his cheek against the horse.

He left the horse in charge of a peanut vendor and entered the dark building which had across its doorway so strong a curtain of foul smell that it was sufficient to keep out the occasional intruder.

'Ah, Javed-*bhai*,' Hussain greeted him from the bed in which he lay and on which he made room for Javed to sit. His wife, who was also in the room, hastily withdrew, drawing a veil across her face on the appearance of a man. 'Ve just had our dinna, *bhai*, vhy you not tell us, ve'd've vaited to eat in your distinguishable company. *Amma*,' he shouted to the other room, 'vhat about a quick *baryani* for Javed-*bhai*?'

'No, no,' Javed protested, 'I've just eaten.'

No *baryani* was ever cooked in less than an hour anyway.

'Vhat! I know, I know, Javed Khan sahib, our grub is not much for your likening.'

Hussain managed to look downcast and humble.

'No, please,' Javed said. 'It's just that we were having dinner and father said go and see Mister Hussain about this business. Otherwise I'd gladly have come in time for dinner.'

Hussain groaned, for it was some months since Rafiq had called for the two thousand rupees he owed Aziz Khan and Hussain had first wondered why Aziz Khan had not made more representations and then thought that he had forgotten about the money in the tragic circumstances of his house.

'*Bhai*, you know vhat the dahcter told me? Cansa, he says, indefatigably, cansa strikes at the very boots of man. *Bhai*, you should see my toes, they're purrpel, I've been bedridden like though I vas some damn' harse, Allah knows cansa is that painful. It verks upvard like a river gahn crazy and devellupps into verricose veins. Vunce in the veins, there's nothing to stahp it from getting anyvhere. Aal I do, *bhai*, is lie hyere like one of those damn' Hindu saints by the Ganges and listen to my heartbeat. Anyway, vun is bahrn to live with troubles and Allah be praised ve live at aal. But how's Khan sahib, Allah shahring him vith prahsperitties aal right?'

'He was wondering if you could . . .'

'Oooh! Come, *bhai*, liss'n, liss'n, liss'n.'

Hussain lifted himself and, taking hold of Javed's head as though the ball had been thrown to him in a rugger match, dragged it down to his stomach and lay back again.

'Liss'n, *bhai*, liss'n, vhat you hear there? Tell me the truth, *bhai*, I must know. I can take it, *bhai*, I'm a man. Vhat you hear there? Is it the cansa?'

Javed listened and heard sounds which, in his own stomach, he had understood to be the workings of the digestive system.

'There's a slight rumbling,' Javed said.

'*Rummling?*' Hussain almost screamed out. '*Bhai*, I'm done for. Thassit. Cansa of the stomach. Just vhat the dahcter said, I paid him five bucks for the visit, and he said, Mister Hussain, if you hear rummling in the stomach, then there's no hope for you. And now vhat should I do, *bhai*, I have four chillrun. Allah look after them vhen I'm gahn, but promise me, *bhai*, you'll pay them a visit from time and again, promise that, *bhai*, promise that, and maybe take them to the fair vunce a year.'

Hussain turned his face away, for he had publicly to show that some of his agony was private.

'Father wondered if he could raise a loan of two thousand rupees,' Javed said hastily while Hussain momentarily gave the impression of having departed from this world.

Hussain was struck by the word *loan*, but remained turned away and made a slight moaning sound as though he was still lost in his suffering. Why, he wondered, should Aziz Khan want to borrow two thousand rupees when he owed him precisely that amount? Slowly, he turned round, pressing a hand at his stomach and saying, 'It's slightly less now, the attack's lowered, Allah be praised and gratified. *Amma*,' he shouted, 'Javed-*bhai*'s been hyere two hours and you haven't brought him a cuppa cha yet!'

Perhaps Hussain had heard a cup tinkle, Javed thought, for his wife came in at once, placed a tray beside the bed and retreated to her privacy from where she could hear every word which passed between the two men.

'A loan, eh?' Hussain spoke into the teacup and assumed that Aziz Khan had forgotten about the two thousand he was owed. He must be going mad with troubles, Hussain decided, not being able to think of any other explanation.

'Yes,' Javed said, 'payable back in two months.'

'Vhat security?' Hussain asked.

'My dowry.'

'Vhat! You getting married, *bhai*? Allah's blessings pour on you. *Amma*, bring out the sveetmeats, ve have celebrities to do. Vell, vell, who's the fahrchoonate vun, the lucky bride-to-be?'

226

'She comes from a family in Karachi. The father has an import and export business.'

'*Im*port and *ex*port!' Hussain was amazed.

His wife entered and placed a plate of sweetmeats on the tray, and withdrew again.

'Vell, come on, come on,' Hussain said, 'you first.'

Javed nibbled at a sweet and Hussain thrust three into his own mouth in quick succession.

'Good,' he said. 'So your dowvrey vill be the security, eh?'

'Yes.'

'Vell, *bhai*, I'll have to make enqvyries, I'm just a broker. You know how I got to be called a broker? Vhy, because I'm alvays broke, hah, hah. But I'll find out, *bhai*, I'll drag myself in my cansaruss boots and find some interrusted party. Come back tomorrow and I'll have news for you.'

On the next day, Hussain telephoned Ayub and told him about Javed's visit. Ayub reflected a moment and said, 'All right, I'll lend the two thousand and accept the prospect of a dowry as a security, but on one condition.'

'Yes, Ayub sahib,' Hussain spoke excitedly into the phone.

'That I have Aziz Khan's land as security against the marriage falling through.'

'Aal right, sahib, aal right.'

'Phone me again if he agrees and I'll arrange to send the money to you. But remember, without the double security of the land, there's no money.'

Aziz Khan had been impressed with a packet of gold-edged invitation cards to the wedding sent to him by Mohammed Bux for his own use, a height of sophistication which his family had not before attained. The printed words, in Urdu and in English, seemed to suggest to him an irrevocability and it would be laughably foolish (he considered) of anyone to suggest now that the marriage would not take place. There was a permanence about the printed word. With this assurance in front of him, he did not hesitate to accept the condition which the moneylender, one Ghulam Din of Lahore according to Hussain, had stipulated.

227

So that when Javed gave up his job at the mills, Ayub at least would not have agreed that Javed had succeeded in frustrating the Shah ambitions and that Aziz Khan's family was now about to enter a phase of contentment and happiness.

17

Afaq wrote a note to Pamela saying that he had received a cable from his brothers instructing him to visit a factory in Frankfurt to purchase some motor generators and that he did not know how long he would be away but he would get in touch with her as soon as he returned.

He felt relieved when he had posted it and thought how a lie could liberate the mind from petty oppression. And yet the relief was only momentary, for it occurred to him that he had now precluded the possibility of seeing Pamela secretly and already, after only two days since the Stratford visit, he was anxious to see her again. Perhaps he could ring her in a week's time, for there was no reason why she should expect him to be away for more than that duration of time. But, no. He had already observed Razia's possessiveness and perhaps it was best if he kept away from Pamela while Razia was in London.

For two days they had walked in the West End, eaten in three different restaurants in Soho, and spent one afternoon driving in the country around London. On the second evening, she had insisted on seeing *The King and I* and had enjoyed it immensely while Afaq, with Pamela's cultured voice in his ears, had felt restive on seeing the musical for the second time. 'Hello, young lovers' sounded now like a greeting being broadcast to girl guides all over the world when it had seemed a wonderfully moving cry from the soul when he first heard it.

This was something he would hoard for Pamela, that he had hated *The King and I* the second time. It would please her that he had begun to recognise the counterfeit from the real in her culture, but the notion did not give him as much pleasure as he had anticipated during the performance. For had he not met Pamela, he would not have known of other colours than the gaudy and would have remained permanently deceived by apparent brightness. But Razia was impressed, and when he had taken her to her hotel, she decided that she wanted to see Madame Tussaud's next.

'But that's what *all* Pakistanis do,' he protested, entering the lift.

She was surprised at the note of irritation in his voice and said, when the lift gates had shut, 'Who do you think I am, a Nepalese?'

He was silent until they reached their floor.

'Well, I mean why do you want to see a lot of wax dummies?'

'Because they're supposed to look real,' she said, unlocking the door to her room.

'There's nothing great in that. Look, *I* am real,' Afaq said, shutting the door behind him loudly; for emphasis.

'Oh, Afaq!'

'So?'

'Nothing.'

'Do you want to go there so badly?'

'No.'

'Don't sulk then.'

'I'm not sulking,' she said. 'What have you got to show me instead?'

'I don't know. There's London, there's England.'

'Poor little Afaq. Confused as always. Not knowing what he wants to do.'

'What do you mean *as always*.'

'But you've been a great one for not making up your mind. It's always this and that with you.'

'You're quite wrong,' he said. 'My trouble is I'm far too strong-willed.'

'You're a monkey running blindly through a jungle.'

'Do you still remember that?'

'Yes, and a lot else which you seem to have forgotten.'

'No, I haven't,' he said. 'Perhaps you're right. I am confused.'

She walked up to him and held his hand.

'Poor Afaq,' she said. 'What's troubling you?'

'Nothing. Only the world's much bigger than Kalapur.'

'What can you mean by that? Oh, I know, don't tell me. Our Afaq has found himself a pretty English girl.'

'No, there's more to the world than just building a fortune in some primitive hole.'

'Thanks to the primitive hole, you're rich enough to be here.'

He was silent then and she wondered what else she could say. She had tried sympathy, mockery and reasoning, but had elicited no comprehensible response from him. But this was in his character, she told herself, this is why Ayub, demanding an easily recognisable type of behaviour, had failed to understand him and had reacted violently.

'Our Afaq is a complicated machine,' she said, essaying once more to be sympathetic.

He looked at her and she said, 'Or should I say *my* Afaq?'

His response then led her to believe that she could hold him to her breast like a child or blow him away as though he were a feather, according to her inclination.

18

On giving up his job at the mills, Javed divided his free time between preparations for the wedding and thinking about Rafiq. Suppose, he thought, that Rafiq was framed and suppose that the Shah brothers were behind it, how could this be proved? His experience at the mills and especially his confrontation with Ayub over the fate of Salim and Riaz had taught him the politics of which Ayub was capable. All right, assuming that the Shah brothers conspired against

Rafiq: what then? They would need the assistance of witnesses. That seemed logical. What else? They would need to have control over the police. That also seemed logical. All right; if there was a conspiracy in which everyone who appeared at Rafiq's trial was involved, how could that conspiracy be exposed? Continuing to ask such questions of himself, he concluded that there must be someone who, for some personal motive against the Shah brothers, might be willing to break the silence. He put himself in the position of the peasants who had given evidence against Rafiq: if he had received a hundred rupees, even a thousand rupees, would he remain silent for ever? As a peasant, he might, for a peasant—especially of the sub-human type living in the Kangara Settlement—even if he considered blackmail, would be too afraid to attempt it; and if he could not profit by his revelation, then there was no reason for him to speak. Also, he felt certain that the peasants would know nothing of the Shah brothers' involvement. The police must have handled the whole thing. Therefore, it would be useless for him to try and talk the peasant witnesses into telling him the truth; it would not serve his purpose if all the truth they had to tell was that the police had made them say the things they did.

It occurred to him then that he was on the wrong track. The question he should ask himself, he realised, was: Why had the Shah brothers spent the large amount of money which they must have spent for so big a conspiracy, in order to have Rafiq found guilty?

He was beginning to be confused with too many hypotheses and went to his room, found an old exercise book and a pencil, and wrote his thoughts as follows:

1. A girl is raped and murdered.
2. Rafiq was asleep in the bed next to mine when the crime was supposed to have been committed. (Doubt: unless I was asleep and he went and returned without my knowing it.)
3. If Rafiq was innocent, *who* committed the crime?

4. The Shah brothers bribed the police and several witnesses in order to convict Rafiq.

He was clearer now. The answer, he was convinced, lay in his third and fourth points. He knew that the Shah brothers had a grudge against his father and would take any opportunity to hurt him in some way. But why should they have chosen this indirect and criminal way? Why? They had managed to make his father's business more and more difficult but why did they want indirectly to murder Rafiq? This question gave him one more point, which he wrote down:

5. Was the crime planned by the Shah brothers or did it happen and then they decided to use it against my family?

He decided that it could not have been planned; it was too elaborate, subtle and roundabout a way of hurting a man. If it had happened and *then* they decided to use it for their ends, why should they want to cover up for a peasant ... *was* it a peasant who committed the crime? He had always assumed so, but now that the notion of 'covering up' had occurred to him, his mind leaped several steps of its deductive logic and arrived at the answer: Afaq.

He was astonished now that he had not realised earlier that Afaq had been sent to England soon after the trial was over. Having determined that Afaq was the criminal, he found reasons to support his theory by putting himself in the position of Ayub and Akram. Suppose he had been Ayub and he had suddenly discovered that his younger brother had committed rape and murder: his first instinct would be to think of his family and of his business; he had an important name in the city, why, even in the country; there was too much at stake. To hush up the crime by having a peasant convicted would not be enough; it would be necessary to convict someone from a reasonably good family in order to distract any attention which might fall on his own family. Perhaps not. Perhaps Ayub did not think it this way; it was more likely that he was rushed into the most expedient course. But the connection between paying out the money and covering up for the person who committed the crime was meaningful only when Afaq was named as the criminal.

It was all clear to Javed now, but he knew that his deductions were based on pure reasoning and that he had no evidence to support his conclusion except the circumstantial one of Afaq's being sent to England, which, too, could only be relevant if it was accepted as a fact that the bribes had been paid by the Shah brothers; Javed knew that although no one in Kalapur would doubt that they had done so, there was no proof which he could submit to a court. His next task would be to find that proof.

19

Ayub met the editor of the local newspaper and the Chief Superintendent of Police separately to discuss plans for the day of Akram's return from his successful visits to Karachi and Dacca. Akram was expected to arrive by the afternoon train from Lahore, and Ayub had worked out a scheme which would bring his rewarding excursion into public relations to a resounding climax. He had already arranged that Hussain should deliver the two thousand rupees to Javed on the same afternoon.

'WELCOME HOME!' cried the front-page headline on the morning of Akram's return. The article, composed in an excess of sycophancy, used the imagery of conquest as though Caesar were returning to Rome, and exhorted the people of Kalapur to turn out in their thousands to welcome Akram at the station to show him their appreciation of the work he had done on their behalf.

In promoting the export of our textiles (the article declared), Mr. Akram Shah has carried the banner of Pakistan to the entire Middle East. The crescent and star of the Muslim world will everywhere unfurl itself on fabric woven in Kalapur. Mr. Akram Shah has given a booster to the national economy, for which his gift for earning foreign currency could not have come sooner, and won for us an increased measure of prosperity.

The article continued for the length of two columns. On an inside page, there was a pictorial spread which showed the several stages of Akram's journey to Karachi, and his meetings with Ministers, ending in a photograph of Akram and the Minister of Commerce signing some agreement. 'ALL THIS SO THAT YOU MAY EARN MORE' ran the headline above the photographs.

When the station-master at Kalapur Central saw the newspaper, he felt it his duty to decorate the station with bunting and flowers as though the President of the country was coming on a visit. Shopkeepers in the bazaar, growing excited at the prospect of a richer population, decided to close their shops in the afternoon and put up notices on their walls. The itinerant vendors, who usually spent the day in the bazaar and evenings carrying their goods along residential streets where they chanted aloud their wares, decided to take up position early by the railway station. Just before lunch, Ayub sent a notice round the mills announcing that the mills would close at three p.m., to enable the workers to go and welcome their benefactor.

The train was expected to arrive at four, but soon after lunch crowds had begun to hurry towards the station as though the roads were a wind-tunnel sucking in every passer-by to that direction.

Javed found Hussain in bed when he called on him a little before three o'clock. He had walked all the way from the land, since the horses were being employed by Aziz Khan and a peasant who were surveying the plantations to determine what needed doing when they hired new labour. Javed had not minded walking in the heat, for he was glad that his father had resumed work. Only the sweat made his shirt cling to his back.

'Ah, Javed,' Hussain said, 'you find me in a crittycull time, *bhai*. Just vhen my foot is svollen and I got to lie down. Othervise, I'd have been also at the station. Ah, vhat a bennyfactor our Akram sahib is, he makes the place prahsperise like there was a damn dam in the place.'

'Have you got the money?' Javed asked, wanting to finish with the business.

'Ah, sit down, *bhai*, vhat's the hurry? Sit down, haven't you any comferrtable thing to say to my poor svollen foot?'

'I'm sorry it's so bad,' Javed said, sitting on the edge of the bed.

'*Bhai*, I feel I run the marrathawn. You know vhat the dahcter says? He tells me, Mister Hussain sahib, he says, and I know he got his screwed-up eyes on my five bucks aal the time, Hussain sahib, you gaht to find yourself a sedent-terry position, it's no use this broker's life, running loose like a vild harse. Because you know, *bhai*, valking cahses hammerage of the foot, and me, I can't vear shoes because of the svelling and I go about in slippers like the vorld vas a damn bathroom. It's just asking to aggraviolate the hammerage. But how you keeping, *bhai*, let me not bore through you vith my prahblems, how you keeping, everything okay and settled for the vedding? And how's Khan sahib and *begum sahiba*, foreseeing the great day vith terrafick excitement, eh? You know everyvun's gahn to the station, even the damn servunt. But Akram sahib deserves our fullest fellycities.'

He paused and, noticing that Javed offered no conversation, sighed, raised his head, turned over and took a packet of notes from under his pillow.

'Hyere you are,' he said, giving Javed the money. 'Two thousand, found vith hardship. You know, *bhai*, money's shart in the market. Too many bahrrowers. Hyere, there's this paper to sign. Over the stamp. That cahpy is for you.'

Javed looked at the Urdu and made sure that the terms were as they had agreed upon earlier: the loan was being offered at 5 per cent per month simple interest on the security of his dowry or, failing that, the security of his father's land, and was payable within six months.

He slowly wrote his name over the stamp, handed the paper back to Hussain, examined the copy which he had been given and put it into his pocket. Taking the money from Hussain, he also took his leave.

Outside, the bazaar was deserted. He could see, in the distance, people walking towards the station. He felt curious and thought for a moment that he might go and have a look, but remembered the money in his pocket and decided not to risk having it picked. Crowds of workers were coming out of the mills when he walked past there and he kept his hand in his pocket, firmly clutching the notes. Bodies jostled against him and some of the workers, recognising him, muttered friendly greetings. Finally, he was past the mills and relaxed his pace a little, for his anxiety had diminished. He took out the piece of paper which Hussain had given him and examined it anew in case he had overlooked anything. It seemed in order and, feeling grateful to Ghulam Din, the money-lender mentioned in the document, he put the paper into his empty pocket and again clutched the notes in his other pocket.

When he forked off the main road, he came across two raggedly clothed men squatting on the roadside. They had not been there when he had come to town and they looked like wandering beggars who walk from town to town, living off what coins are thrown to them and what they find among rubbish heaps. When he was some ten or fifteen yards from them, they seemed to have heard his footsteps, for they turned round to look in his direction. He paid them no attention and began to think of the plan he had been formulating to make friends with someone in the police force in order eventually to discover the truth about Rafiq's death; he knew it would be difficult, perhaps impossible; but, on the other hand, perhaps someone, for some reason, would want to talk; and besides, it seemed to him the only approach towards the truth: with caution and subtlety, he might succeed.

As he approached the two beggars, one began to chant, 'Sahib, *roti*, sahib, *baksheesh*.'

'Hungry, sahib,' the other wailed, patting his stomach with one hand and pointing to his mouth with the other.

Javed decided to ignore them and to walk silently past.

But their chanting grew louder and, just when he was going past them, they rose, stooping and making *salaams* as though they they were in front of some idol. He hastened his step. But they begged with a piteous intensity and he could hear them shuffling behind him.

'Sahib, sahib,' they were crying as though to suggest that they would surely die if he gave them nothing.

Javed wondered whether he should keep walking steadily on or break into a run or turn round and scold them for pestering him.

He continued to walk steadily.

'Sahib, two children hungry, sahib,' said one tragic voice and the other, equally desperate, cried: 'Sahib, an anna for *roti*, oh sahib, one anna for *roti*.' And then the two together, 'Sahib, Allah will bless you, sahib *baksheesh*.'

It was too annoying. Javed stopped.

He stopped and, in that moment between his stopping and turning around with the intention of scolding them, he was aware of their sudden silence. When he saw them, they were not bowing in the manner in which beggars continue to do in one's presence. They were standing erect; if the posture of one of them was slightly stooped, it could have been a wrestler's habit of looking for a chance against an opponent. He looked from one to the other. The rags they wore exposed muscles which no beggar could ever have developed. Something shone, caught his eye. He saw that one held a knife in his hand. He looked past them. The road was deserted. He looked to his left and to his right. There were barren fields and the heat rising in the distance. He looked again at the men, their unblinking, murderous eyes. He turned round and began to run. But he had not taken four or five paces when the full weight of the unarmed man fell on his back and he went crashing against the small stones of the road, the man on him.

It was four o'clock. The sun was still high. The temperature was 105°F. Even the stones were hot.

At the station, the train had just arrived. A small area had been cordoned off on the platform in front of the exit. The rest of the platform was packed with people who had cheered when Akram emerged from the train and was greeted with an embrace by his brother and a handshake by his wife. The cameras had clicked, and the other passengers who had alighted or had wanted to take the train were put to considerable discomfort. It was impossible to find a porter, and luggage had to be carried above one's head.

'There are thousands outside,' Ayub told Akram. He had been warned that there would be a reception for him but was amazed at Ayub's ingenuity at organising the whole town to meet him. 'There are loudspeakers, too,' Ayub said. 'You'll have to make a speech.'

A chorus of men especially appointed for the task by Ayub had begun to chant, ' 'krumm*Shah*, 'krumm*Shah*, 'krumm-*Shah*' and the cry had naturally been taken over by the crowd.

'Give them something,' Ayub said. 'Tell them you're donating a sports stadium to Kalapur.'

Ayub had worked it all out.

Akram faced the microphone and looked at it as though it were a shaving mirror which he needed to adjust.

'Friends,' he said, and his face was lathered with sweat. 'I am very touched by your generous welcome.'

He noticed Faridah standing next to Ayub, grave as a monument.

'As you can expect, I am tired after my journey. But not so tired as to ignore my duty to you. My visit to Karachi was a success and the agreement I have reached with the Government will bring more work to Kalapur and each one of you will enjoy the fruit. I want to take this opportunity to an-

238

nounce to you that we are planning new social facilities for the citizens of Kalapur to give them a chance to use their leisure creatively, and as a first step, we will build a sports stadium, which will be a gift to the people of Kalapur from the Shah Industrial Enterprises. I thank you once again for your welcome.'

The cheering, the applause and the chanting was deafening, and it was difficult to get away. Despite the police force lining the way to the car, the crowd had surged forward and wanted to carry him. Ayub had to shout at the men, though not with a show of temper but as though he were asking them to be reasonable. Once they were all in, the car moved slowly, like an ice-breaker through all those people. Akram stood through the open sun-roof, his feet on the seat next to the driver's. He could have been the President of a friendly power on a state visit.

Ayub had settled down in the rear seat with Faridah. He could smile now. He had given Kalapur a king. Faridah's stiff posture, the sharp voice she had of a childless married woman also reassured him. He thought of Razia as of a fellow-conspirator: together, they would produce a usurper for the Shah kingdom. Ayub gently laughed to himself as he watched Akram acknowledge the cheers of the people.

20

He wanted to look at her skin, at a small area of her shoulder, but her hands at his back were pressing him down.

The cultivated nails.

But her breath was hot on his cheek, so that he must give her his mouth.

He pulled away his tongue to put his forehead on her hair which he had earlier loosened, gentle as a Bond Street coiffeur des dames, from its fashionable intricacies.

Her black hair spread upon the pillow.

He touched her shoulder then with his mouth, his tongue

sliding over the collar-bone. There was that square inch of skin and the black birthmark.

The light-brown skin.

His eyes could magnify, find tunnels into the darkness of her body through her pores.

But those nails and the hot breath.

Again those shut eyes of her intensity, her sharp teeth on his tongue. She was moving her chest as though wanting to roll over.

Those scarlet lacquered nails.

And those breasts against his ribs as he rocked. She moved her hand then, held him, guided him. And ran those nails again across his back, finding the fleshiest part of his back to drive into.

He would not, could not take his mouth away then, for her tongue which had flickered snake-like was stiff there now.

Although he wanted to cry her name out for her skin to hear.

For her heels were brackets attaching him to the wall of her body. And he could not, not even as a whisper.

But it was she who took her mouth away and softly cried his name, drawing out the second, longer syllable as a sigh.

Moaning when her heels fell away.

And in the black hair against the pillow he could not open his mouth with a word, nor his eyes, though his mouth opened and shut, opened and shut, struggling for breath in the odour of hair.

Her black hair without the hairpins.

Aziz Khan

Aziz Khan

I

He sat beside her bed, in the glare of her pock-marks, the silent accusation of her heaving flesh. His own breath came heavily, but he hoped she did not hear. There was the cockerel outside at any rate, boisterously self-assertive. And the sweat on her face to which she made no sign of recognition, no more than to the hand he had placed on her arm, absently, in an involuntary gesture of offering the consolation of physical contact when words failed in his throat. Though she had expected no words, for all the poetry she had known had come from his hands. As from her, too, the only tangible expression of love had been a well-cooked meal. Where had he gone wrong? Or she? Error could be committed without an action being performed; as there could be expressions and signs instead of a vocabulary between two people defining the scope of meaning: and more. And there were the body's silences; where were their sources? Hurting neither flesh nor bone, invisibly lodged within, more elusive than a tumour to the surgery of one's will. But painful. Like an absence, like a death, like deaths. The pockets of sorrow in the flesh. The vaults whose iron doors creaked open again and again. The tombs which made man a living monument, a dynasty of sorrow within him. There was the will which would empty out the pockets and spend the loose change of memory on forgetfulness. But the silences returned and the heart continually wove a coarser fabric, making shoddy material of the flesh.

Zakia had not complained of pain though he had observed her rubbing a hand on her chest as though her heart needed cajoling. And she could not have described which pain had returned when Javed's mutilated body was brought to her. The wheat-flour, which she had just begun to knead to make *chapatis* with, still stuck to her hands when the police jeep came up to the house. It had begun to flake off on her palms and she had rubbed her hands together; clapping away the drying flour-paste. She had turned back to look at the fire in the earthen stove, to make sure the spinach would not burn if left unattended for a few minutes, before peering out of the door into the bright sunlight.

The police officers were gentle with the body, instructing each other on how to move it out of the jeep, as though they manœuvred a heavy crate up a narrow spiral staircase. So that the parents' eyes could be avoided and no time would be left for other words. Preferring to be the porters and not the messengers of tragedy, they moved clumsily in the front yard. There was the heat to complain about, to explain away their heavy breathing. They sweated, the corpse heavy in their hands, and looked in bewilderment at the parents as if to ask in which room was the article to be deposited. They had duties to attend to and a duty-book at the station to make an entry in; but, for the moment, covered up their embarrassed inability to make the appropriate verbal gesture with excessive mansuetude. Zakia felt as though she had not been able to light the fire properly and the firewood had begun to smoke and to smart her eyes.

'Attacked by thieves,' one of the police officers had managed to say while the other was already putting the jeep into gear.

But Aziz Khan found that the thieves had not searched all of Javed's pockets, for there was the paper documenting the loan from Ghulam Din of Lahore.

At the inquest, Aziz Khan had to corroborate Hussain's evidence.

'It was a total sum of two thousand rupees net in vun-hundred-rupee notes,' Hussain said, wanting to help with every detail he could recall.

Aziz Khan agreed that he had borrowed the sum from Hussain and that Javed had gone to collect it.

'Rahbry and vilence, prahper thuggism,' Hussain suggested. 'Ve live in an atmahsfeer of vilence.'

'Thank you for your evidence, Mister Hussain,' the Coroner said. 'We're not interested in your opinions.'

Hussain would have expressed his amazement but the Coroner was not looking at him.

The Coroner's report was passed on to the police. After studying the file, Chief Superintendent Fazal Elahi concluded that it was one more case of a man being murdered in order to be robbed, a common occurrence. He had so many similar cases which he had not been able to solve, he told Aziz Khan during his interview. What clues did they have? The murder weapon? No. The serial numbers of the stolen notes? No. Was it one man or a gang? No one could tell. Were they from Kalapur or were they passing through? He did not have a large enough force to scour the country. There would be notices outside his station, of course, and in the villages, offering a reward to anyone who could give information which led to the discovery of the murderer. But had there been any witnesses? If his officers had not been on a routine patrol, the body might not have been discovered for a long time even though the murderer had apparently only flung it off the road and had made no attempt to hide it. He, or they, must have been in a hurry; and this indicated that the murderer must be a good many miles away from Kalapur by now.

'There were witnesses when my first son was murdered.' Aziz Khan was looking into his own lap and spoke the words softly.

'How can you say such a thing, Khan sahib? Your first son was tried in a court of law which found him guilty of rape and murder. If you are not satisfied with the court's findings, you can appeal to the supreme court in Karachi. But you have to have first-class reasons for doing so. You need water-tight evidence. The law is incorruptible.'

'I know, I know,' Aziz Khan muttered, rising to go.

'I will do my best,' Fazal Elahi said. 'I will give priority to this case.'

'I know.'

Zakia had uttered no complaint at all, had not indicated the source of her affliction. She had washed and dressed what remained of her son's body, letting her hands touch what her eyes would not see. And when Javed had been buried, she had fallen into her bed, for the tears had burned her face in the harsh sunlight. Aziz Khan came and sat beside her. He touched her arm where the doctors had wound that rubber tube at the nursing home to test her blood pressure. She could not have said how slowly her blood ran there. He could not leave her; even were she well, he would not have known where to go.

2

Ayub was turning the pages of a newspaper. It crackled like toast at the breakfast table. Zarina found it distracting, for Faridah sat next to her eating a boiled egg with so vigorous a

246

smacking of her lips that it sounded as if she were squelching her way across the muddy bank of a river. Zarina herself opened her mouth fish-like and placed the small silver spoon deep into it, pressed her lips to the bottom end of the handle and sucked the egg on to her tongue; noiselessly; and hoped that Faridah would notice one day. There was Akram, too, drinking tea as if he were gargling, and Zarina wondered if he drank the same way when sitting with a Minister. It was worse at dinner, especially when there was rice, which was almost every day. She had sometimes imagined herself being awarded a prize for being the most correct and silent eater in the world. But Ayub was turning the pages, glancing at the headlines.

'That vas ahful,' Faridah remarked staring at the eggshell, almost as though she were commenting on what it had contained. 'That bijness of Aziz Khan's son. Vhat some people vill do for money. It doesn't stand bearing any thinking about. *Hai Allah*, some people!'

'Ah, stupid people,' Akram said and Ayub peered at him from over the newspaper. 'It's their own fault. Fancy walking about with two thousand rupees in your pocket. People have been butchered for far less.'

Ayub returned to the paper and glanced at the market prices.

'Yes,' Faridah said, sympathising with the egg-cup. 'But still you can't help having pitty for that poor voman. She's lahst two sons for no mistake of her own.'

'She's an ignorant, illiterate peasant,' Akram said sternly. 'If she'd had any sense she'd have made that ox of an husband of hers sell his land years ago and she'd been living in good modern comfort in Lahore or Karachi. Some people are born just to rot away on the land. They don't deserve the consideration Ali gives to the car when he washes it.'

Faridah quickly picked up a toast and began to butter it, not wanting Akram's scolding voice to have all the attention.

'It's his business whether he goes or stays,' Ayub said. 'After all.'

'Yes, we offered him good money,' Akram said. 'But, oh no, he was too proud to move, the ox.'

Faridah munched her toast and Zarina thought of the ear-plugs she had seen advertised in an American movie magazine.

'Sometimes when I think of the stubbornness of peasants,' Akram said, 'I wonder how this country will ever progress.'

'Mules, just stupid mules,' said Ayub, who had driven them as such.

Faridah munched away; for the moment, she had withdrawn from the conversation. No one, she reflected, had her kind nature.

'Any news from Razia?' Akram asked, surprising Ayub with the suddenness of his question.

'There was a letter last week. Why?'

'When's she returning?'

'Oh, in another month, I suppose,' Ayub said. 'She seems to be enjoying herself. I expect you'll be wanting to go next,' he added, looking at Faridah.

She did not like the implication that her sister-in-law set the fashions in the house and scornfully munched her toast before saying, 'England, pooh! I vas thinking of going to Nyu Yahrk. The bullyvahrds in April.'

'You're thinking of Paris, *baji*,' Zarina pointed out.

'Ah, Parris, Nyu Yahrk, Reeyo de Jennaero. But naht England.'

'You have great ambitions to travel,' Ayub remarked, though he spared her his laughter.

'Vhy naht? Health is impahrtant.'

Ayub decided to keep his comment to himself.

'Time to go,' Akram said, rose and walked out abruptly. Ayub sauntered out behind him, having no need to catch up with him, for although the two travelled simultaneously and to the same destination, they went by separate cars.

'He thinks I am jellous,' Faridah turned to Zarina for consolation. 'He thinks he's the big shaht hyere. Pooh! Vithout my husband's hard verk and preparing, he vould still be doing his *gunda*ism in Bombay. A bahrn terrahrist, I tell you. *Hai Allah*, this heat! Ve must go at least to Murree for a veek.'

Zarina could have gone anywhere for consolation; Kalapur reminded her too much of the unhappiness she ought to be suffering.

3

Afaq meditated upon the word *love* while he shaved. Once, a long time ago in his consciousness, Razia had come to him and comforted him. There had been an emotion within him then, a longing. And then he had fled from Pakistan and a voice within him had cried out her name; but then, too, he had been a beaten man, a criminal whose conscience would not stop whipping him and he had cried out to her out of self-pity. On both these occasions he had strongly felt that he loved her. He nodded his head in agreement, having just completed lathering his face. Were commiseration, compassion and the willingness to forgive a wrong the conditions of being in love? This much was true of his relationship with Razia although she did not know what wrongs he had committed. But he was uncertain now. Too often, he had violated where he had wanted to give affection. He had looked for whores before he had found love. And now Razia, perfidious to her husband, had come to him from across two continents. Why? he wondered, drawing the razor along his cheek. A few moments of being with him that morning in Kalapur could not have altered her whole life. And what could she expect from him? What could he offer which Ayub could not give many times over? He tilted his face to shave under the chin. Perhaps there were inadequacies beneath Ayub's surface of belligerent confidence. But where could their involvement with each other lead them? She would soon return to Kalapur and resume her life with Ayub and her children as though nothing had happened for her to doubt her love and attachment to her family. Was it just an escapade then? He lathered his face again. He did not expect her to engineer a divorce. If really pressed, he would have admitted to having been in love with her; but now, with his curious and temporarily suspended relationship with Pamela still unresolved, he could not say he understood the meaning of *love* when its correlative was his love-making with Razia. And yet, if love-making were a measure of love, they had reached depths of feeling which he had never before experienced. Taking up the razor again, he decided to dismiss the questions; at least until Razia went; at least until he could interpret his attachment to Pamela.

He had not seen Pamela for two weeks now. He did not doubt that he would return to her when Razia went. There would be a week or two of duplicity, of lying. Perhaps Razia had altered the future shape of his relationship with Pamela, he could not tell. He rinsed his face and spat into the basin. It occurred to him then that he owed his life to Ayub and his present happiness to Ayub's wife.

He drove her that afternoon to Brighton. There were white clouds in the sky and he had the top down. The road was crowded, though, and he could impress her with the car's speed only in short bursts. She laughed when he overtook a whole stream of traffic behind a lorry, tearing away in second gear which made the engine and the tyres roar. But too often they had to bore slowly through the narrow streets of towns they had to pass; only to couple with a long line of bunched-up traffic when they reached the open road.

But there was the sea, tolerably blue, even though the wind whipped up her sari when they tried to walk to the sea's edge. The pebbles caught at her sandals and scratched her heels. Still, she managed to laugh, holding his arm. The wind came coldly off the sea and she did not care to pursue the impulse she had had of removing her sandals, lifting up the skirt of her sari and going ankle-deep in the water.

'How can people swim here?' she cried into the wind. 'It's so cold.'

'It's not cold for them,' he said, looking at two girls in bikinis.

'I'm freezing,' she said.

'Let's go back, then.'

'Do you like bikinis?' she asked, turning away, for she had noticed how he stared at the girls.

How could he answer that, he wondered, and muttered, 'Well . . .'

'You don't have to pretend,' she said. 'The way you were giving those two the eye, it seems you never saw a woman with her clothes off.'

For their intimacy permitted such teasing, which she enjoyed. He could at least laugh away her question.

The sea appeared more attractive from behind the glass of a restaurant where they sat over tea and cakes.

She continued to tease: 'Don't tell me an English girl hasn't led you astray. You're so experienced.'

Afaq could find refuge only in seeming to pretend, to tell the truth in so exaggerated a tone of affirmation that she would consider it untrue.

'Oh, yes,' he said. 'Let me think now. There was Linda. There was Jane. There was Susan. I forget who came after her. There was Anne. Oh, I don't know. So many, I forget their names.'

'And were they beautiful?' she carried on the game they had played before.

'Oh, ravishing. Figures of curving tension.'

'Who was the most beautiful?'

'One whose name I forget. She had dark hair which she made into a beehive with a thousand pins. She had dark brown eyes which loved me with their gaze. She had light brown skin which was warm to my touch. What else do you want to know? I could describe to you the texture of her skin, the sharpness of her fingernails.'

Razia could now attend to her cake.

'Let's go back,' she said when they emerged from the restaurant. 'This Brighton of yours is too cold.'

The return journey was slower, for they encountered the rush-hour traffic in the towns they had to go through.

'I'm sorry, I should have thought of this,' Afaq said. 'It would have been better if we'd spent another hour in Brighton.'

Their tedious progress made her impatient and the sudden shower which made it necessary for them to stop to put up the top increased her irritation, for her hair had become wet. It had been an aimless journey, salvaged only by their conversation in the restaurant. They drove to her hotel so that she could change and do her hair up again.

'Let's go and see a film,' she suggested.

'Let's eat first. We can decide then what to see.'

He bought an evening paper on the way to the restaurant, which was off Brompton Road. The restaurant was crowded and he glanced at the paper to see what was on before the waiter came to take the order.

'There's nothing worth seeing,' he said, showing her the paper.

She looked down the column and said, 'There's *War and Peace*. Oh, let's see that. I adore Audrey Hepburn.'

'All right,' he said, taking the paper back to see where it was on. 'It's on in the West End and on release in Kensington. The West End will probably be crowded, so let's try Kensington.'

She did not care which four walls enclosed her. Except those of the restaurant which had begun to oppress her. There were too many people, too much food, it was difficult to breathe.

'Why did we come here?' she asked.

'I wanted you to try their trout,' he said.

'They're taking a long time over it.'

'I'm sorry,' he said and realised it was not the first apology he had made to her that day.

Eventually, the trout was served. Razia might have enjoyed it on another day, but she found fault with the sauce which she declared to be tasteless. Afaq, feeling that he was being censured instead of the chef, became silent. The main course had taken so long in being served, that they decided to forego the dessert and Afaq had to placate the waiter's offended look by saying that they were in a hurry. He asked for the bill. That, too, took too long in coming, as though it needed to be seasoned in the kitchen before it could be placed on the table. Afaq did not bother to wait for the change and the waiter, delighted with the tip of twelve shillings when he had expected two, bowed to their backs when they walked out. Irritated that the dinner had been so unsuccessful and that he had paid too much for it, Afaq drove fast to the Kensington Odeon. There was nowhere to park the car, however, and he had to leave Razia at the cinema and find a parking place. He finally locked the car at one end of Edwardes Square and took five minutes reaching the cinema although he ran some of the way. Razia was standing at the entrance.

'Didn't you see the time?' she asked, and the tone of her voice suggested disaster. 'It began at seven-thirty,' she added. 'What's the time now?'

He looked at his watch. It had just gone half past eight.

'In any case, the house is full,' she said.

The difficulty of finding a parking place should have made that obvious to him, and again he apologised to her. They wandered back to the car, walking apart. He drove to his flat and when he drew up to the front of the house, said, 'I'm sorry it's been a wretched evening. Let's hear some music and have a drink.'

She sat down heavily in a sofa as though her own weight was too much for her and the exhaustion of the day's tedium too wearisome for words.

'Put lots of ice in my whisky,' she said, the voice of command coming naturally to her.

'What would you like to hear?' he asked, wanting to follow his own procedure and unwilling to be ordered.

'Oh, anything, but get me a drink first.'

'Oh, all right.'

He went into the kitchen. Razia sighed. She must not be so irritable, she told herself. It wasn't his fault things had gone wrong. Poor boy, he's so helpless and yet how helpful, I do love him for his confused little brain.

But hardly had Razia resolved to restrain expressing her annoyance when she had cause for more irritation. For Afaq returned from the kitchen and said, 'I'm sorry, I've run out of whisky. Will gin do? I've got tonic or vermouth to go with it.'

On another occasion, Razia would have accepted the gin, but now she said sharply, 'Oh, Afaq, go and get some whisky!'

He went out, letting the door bang behind him. He could have walked and taken his time but decided to drive. He had a choice of several off licences in Gloucester Road, but he continued to drive. For the present at any rate, it was more soothing to be in the car than with her, listening to the purr of the engine and not to the screeching tone of her tongue. How anger in a woman made her hateful! He turned into Kensington High Street, thinking that he would drive down Earl's Court Road, buy the whisky there and then return to her. No sooner had he entered the High Street, however, than he discovered that there was a traffic jam there. He could have left the High Street almost immediately and gone down De Vere Gardens or Victoria Road or even, a little later, found an easy passage through Kensington Square. But he remained hypnotically embedded in the jam. Somehow, Earl's Court Road had fixed itself in his mind as a destination, and it was not for another twenty minutes that he reached the turning.

In the meanwhile, Razia sat finding faults with the sofa, shifting her position in it every few minutes. She could have picked up a magazine to read or put a record on the gramophone. But she sat, listening to her own increasing vexation. The springs in the sofa were so tense. If she had known he would be so long, she would have accepted the gin, or even gone without a drink. But one vexation had led to another and though she knew that with a little tolerance the evening could have been fairly successful, the sum of vexations had become irretrievably too large for her management. It was still not too late, however, she hoped, determining herself to help in saving at least a fraction of the day. Too much had already gone wrong, she knew, and when that happened it was best to let the day pass and wait for a more auspicious morning. She rose from the sofa, deciding to confound the mixture of pessimism and fatalism which had been making her so irritable. She chose a long-playing record of soft music and placed it on the player, ready to be played the moment she heard Afaq drive back. She switched off the centre light of the room and switched on a discreetly dim table lamp in a corner of the room. She sat down again and thought how she should look. She let the top end of her sari fall from her shoulder to her waist, so that the tight blouse which left her midriff exposed would reveal something of her bosom, especially if she leaned slightly forward against one of the arm-rests. She thought of letting down her hair, but decided she would leave that ritual to Afaq.

She was pleased with herself now; and her pleasure came from knowing how she could please him. Just then the telephone rang. She did not need to move, for it was on a small table beside the sofa.

'Hello,' she said, picking up the receiver.

There was a short, sharp 'Oh!' at the other end, a surprised female voice.

'Hello,' Razia said again.

'I hope I haven't got the wrong number, but is that Afaq Shah's flat?'

'Yes,' Razia said.

'Oh, I wonder if he's back from Frankfurt.'

'From where?'

'Frankfurt. In Germany.'

'Germany?' Razia asked, keeping her voice soft.

'Yes, he said he was going to Frankfurt to buy some motor generators for his brothers. They have a business in Pakistan.

Textiles, I believe. It was two weeks ago and it just occurred to me I might try and ring to see if he's back. Just in case.'

'No, he's not back,' Razia said. 'Who is it?'

'My name is Pamela Beresford. And you?'

'I . . . I am his sister-in-law, Razia.'

Razia wished she had not admitted to her identity, but the words had come out before she could think.

'How do you do?' Pamela said cheerfully at the other end. 'Could you please tell Afaq when he returns . . .'

But Razia placed the receiver down.

He had taken so long reaching the off licence that he decided to take her a bottle of champagne as well as the whisky. In case she needed to be mollified.

'Allow me to recommend this one, sir,' the man said. 'A 'fifty-two vintage from Roger Doucette, a fine champagne. Extra dry. A wonderful champagne.'

Razia was not in the sitting-room when he returned to the flat and the smile, with which he had entered, faded from his mouth. He noticed, however, that the lights had been dimmed and thought that she must be playing some game with him.

'Razia,' he called softly, placing the whisky bottle on a table and taking the champagne to the kitchen to put it into the fridge. She was not in the kitchen either. The bathroom door was open but there was no light there. Putting the bottle away, he called 'Razia' again, a little louder, adding hopefully, 'Come out, I can see you,' and walked to the bedroom. He paused before he switched on the light, almost expecting to be grabbed by her and thrown on to the bed, but she did not appear and he pulled his finger, trigger-fashion, over the switch. She was not in the room. He noticed, however, a piece of paper lying on the bed. He picked it up. On it she had scrawled words which seemed cryptic and obscure at first but the full meaning of which he realised when he read again: 'I have gone to Frankfurt to buy the motor generators you did not buy in Stafford.'

She had signed herself 'Mrs. Ayub Shah'.

4

Aziz Khan sat beside her bed, his unblinking eyes gazing into her pock-marks; as though there would be an opening there through which he could reach her. He held on to her arm, gripping it like a handkerchief during mourning. He hoped that she would not cede to the world's cruelty. She had so totally surrendered to sorrow. Her absorption was final. As when she would churn the milk for butter. He had few memories of her which did not see her among her utensils. Or milking a buffalo. There was her veil which she had lifted with appropriate timidity on their wedding-night. She had been too overcome with emotion to raise her eyes and he had watched the gold earrings. The oil-lamp burned silently, throwing up a steady flame. Her face was adorned with henna, red dots curving across her forehead just below the line of her hair, large dots at the centre diminishing to a point on either temple. Her eyes remained lowered, absorbed in the heaving of her bosom. The unrelenting satin. He could have looked into her eyes, but when he attempted to raise her chin, touching only an index finger to it, she had turned her face to her right shoulder. The lamp-light caught the pock-marks on her cheek then. They could have been drops of perspiration. Her nose was curved now that he saw her profile, proclaiming her northern lineage. He turned to the brass tray to pick up a sweetmeat to offer her. His left hand at her chin, so that she would turn her face again, and the sweetmeat in his right hand, he made his offering. Something she could see, touch, taste. Her lips moved, made the gesture of acceptance; for the day's feasting had left no appetite for the traditional delicacies of love. How clumsy the procedure of love, he had thought. And yet she exhibited no inhibition a week later when she had settled among the kitchen things and won his approval of her cooking. They held feasts at harvest time, inviting neighbouring landlords and for once permitting a relaxation of the routine by letting the peasants assemble in front of the house.

The peasants would sing and dance. The same songs every year, and yet somehow it was necessary to repeat them. The peasants in their coloured costumes and home-made make-up, so dramatically different from the dust-covered half-naked bodies which had toiled in the sun. There had been the market prices to discuss with the other landlords while the wives were engaged in gigglish gossip. She had been there beside a cauldron of rice, complaining that people did not have the appetite they used to. The noise under the harvest moon. The drums, the songs. And this woman who could not cook enough.

Who breathed weakly now and barely stirred in the airless room. Outside, the land simmered after being on the boil all day. He had brought her cold buttermilk, salted to her taste. He had softly called her name and implored her to take a sip. She had hardly looked, hardly parted her lips when he touched the glass to her mouth, lifting her head to it.

When she wakes, he had told the silence. When the thirst reminds her. He had put the glass down on the floor. When she wakes up thirsty. Whose sleep was entering the Sahara of time.

He wondered whether he should send for a doctor. What ailment would a doctor discover, though, who would not look for grief? He breathed in time with her but, however slowly he did so, she fell behind. He could not hold his breath for long enough to exhale with her and took two, three breaths to her one. There were obstructions within her which he knew no doctor would find. She who had never been ill until this year. Childbirth was the only pain she had known until now. And now disintegration. As though the worn plaster of her flesh must flake off. This blow-lamp of suffering. Where did her breath go after she inhaled, she took so long in breathing out? What emptinesses were there which needed to be filled? A slight puffing of her cheeks, the distended pock-marks; elasticity had gone from her skin. Her face of hammered copper.

He had picked up a fan to give her more air. Though she did not complain of airlessness; nor of any pain. She had said nothing, whose mouth had assumed the texture of burnt firewood. After Javed. She had sought the bed as a tree's shade in the heat. She had looked at the ceiling when he himself could have knocked against walls, blindly, finding his way in the empty house. For vision had turned inwards, had become insubstantial, and the hump-backed earth had vanished. There were the walls to stumble against. Propped on the stick of sorrow. Why should there be words between them? Now? He had tried, if only her name. But she had shut her eyes on the ceiling where the whitewash had begun to appear muddied.

A buffalo moaned outside beside the stream, heavy with milk.

A horse stamped its hoofs, the earth was so still.

The hens scratched the dust.

Was the sun rising or setting, who knew? Which had risen and set, risen and set.

He had cooked some rice and a pot of lentils, thinly slicing the onions. He had put cloves and garlic into the lentils. Though there was no one to eat and his own stomach had refused. He had whisked a jar full of yogurt and made buttermilk. He had washed his hands, giving them at least that much occupation.

And held her arm, clasping it as though his hand were a bracket without whose support she would fall.

He had sat with her like this during the birth of their children. The midwife from Kalapur, sighing ostentatiously like a tragedienne in an amateur drama, had frowned at him but was grateful that he was there like a spotlight on her importance. Her hands were for the assistance of declamations and not births. But she managed with her grotesquely short body to reach the height of usefulness. After the first birth, he knew that Zakia had experienced no more difficulty than if she had forded a stream, stepping on slippery stones. All she had to do was to take care and not hesitate. She had been in the kitchen two or three days later. He knew how much her body could give.

And when a neighbour's wife was taken ill with typhoid. The boy had come to say his mother was so feverish. Hot as a brooding hen's breast, he had said. She had gone to look at Rashidah, he with her. A pool of sweat and agitation, Rashidah, though they could not see the current which surfaced as twitches all over her body. He had paced the veranda with the husband, the ponderous, measured steps of consolation. When she came out, she had gone to inspect the kitchen and then the children's clothes. She heaped the laundry in the bathroom and, a big chunk of yellow bar soap in hand, began to wash the clothes. He was still in the veranda, sitting now, listening to the gurgling of the *hookah* as he smoked, when she walked across the front yard with a basket of washed clothes, taking them to the back of the house to spread them out on the grass. He waited until the doctor arrived before leaving the husband, but she stayed on to cook. They had not asked her to, for there were the servants, but she knew what had to be given.

Who was giving nothing, not even a sign now. He fanned her face as though there were flies there. Her breath had pauses, varying like the pauses of punctuation in a syntactically complex sentence which jerkingly gropes towards a full-stop.

5

Again the long flight, the Super Constellation's throbbing, the constant vibrations within the cabin, and against the darkness of the sky outside the flames of the engines. But the plane was half empty and Razia did not suffer any guilt because of her excess baggage when once the plane unexpectedly lost height. She held on to her arm-rests and shut her eyes; but her stomach could have been a pebble thrown into a pond. It was three days since she had shut her ears to Pamela Beresford's voice.

The morning after the evening of vexations and the night of despair she had gone to the airline to book her flight. There was shopping to keep her busy. Oxford Street was like a grab-handle in a bouncing bus now that her mind was all ditches. She bought lengths of mohair for Ayub, silk pyjamas in Bond Street, silk shirts, silk ties, monogrammed handkerchiefs. As though it would be a luxury to touch him again. She bought him a set of miniature vintage cars, a pair of opera glasses (there was neither opera nor theatre in Kalapur, but the glasses had such attractive gold rims), a Shakespeare jug, Coronation ashtrays, golden cufflinks: anything, anything with which she could surround him, alter him. For the Ayub she had left was the one she had set out to be unfaithful to; the one she was returning to she would need to worship. She bought frocks for her daughters, picturebooks, toys, puzzles. She bought printed Swiss cotton for Zarina and quantities of voile, georgette, nylon and chiffon for Faridah, including six yards of the most shocking pink georgette she could find. For Akram, she bought a pen, ballpoint and pencil set, expensively made of gold. She ordered a hi fi, a refrigerator, an electric cooker and an electric sewing machine to be sent by sea.

So that when she arrived, no one would notice any changes in her face, any sign of recent tears; there would be the presents to take everyone's eyesight and breath away.

She spent one afternoon visiting a girls' school in Surrey, to accomplish the one task which all Kalapur knew to be her reason for going to England. Miss Priscilla Blackwell (known to the school as The Spool, for her speeches on Speech Day, announcements in assembly, admonitions in her study and explanations in divinity lessons had the habit of unwinding interminably) showed her the new science lab., in the senior part of the school, while declaiming an inventory of all that it contained right down to the quantity of test-tubes in stock.

'Unless any were broken on the last day of term,' Miss Blackwell added.

She was narrow-shouldered and her bosom had gone the way of a silent volcano. Only her nose erupted, giving a fiery glow to her face.

'Your daughters will be most welcome,' Miss Blackwell said, entering the art room of the empty school. 'When they are of the right age. But you can never enrol soon enough. I wonder if we shall ever catch up with the bulge.'

Razia, unfamiliar with contemporary native terminology, wondered at Miss Blackwell's last sentence, looked down her sari to see if her physique presented a false impression of pregnancy, and said, for she had to say something, 'We're hoping for a boy next.'

'Oh yes?' said Miss Blackwell in the voice she used when a pupil was telling an obvious lie. 'We don't encourage freedom,' she added, and it took Razia a moment to realise that she was referring to Art.

'Artistic expression has to be strictly disciplined," Miss Blackwell went on. 'There's geometrical drawing, still life, nature representation, portraiture, the exact delineation of buildings and monuments, a measure of romantic fantasy is allowed in landscapes, but otherwise we adhere to the exact. In water *and* in oil. You will agree, Mrs Shah, that young ladies have to be taught to come to grips with the world in which they live. They must learn to look at truth, don't you think? We all know that there is no dearth of young men who are very willing to deceive them.'

Young men were an evil Miss Blackwell could well do without.

'One of our rules is to keep the twentieth century out,' she declared in the library. 'That is not to say we are old-fashioned. But we admit only the tried, the proven. A writer has to be dead a long time for him to begin to live. That is, if he has any life in him at all.'

Miss Blackwell was proud of her aphoristic turn of speech. She stood for a moment enraptured by a portrait of Alfred, Lord Tennyson which graced the wall: long-haired, unshaven, if Tennyson had looked exactly like that a hundred years later, he would have passed for a loathsome beatnik. Though Miss Blackwell had not thought of Tennyson when she had felt almost stifled to death on coming across a group of similarly long-haired and unshaven men when she had had the misfortune to encounter some of the Aldermaston marchers outside the Albert Hall one Easter.

At last they had come out of the building and walked across the school grounds. Miss Blackwell seemed to hop like a blackbird looking for worms. 'There's the gymnasium, of course, and riding and swimming. It's best to be prepared for everything, don't you think?'

As though by everything Miss Blackwell meant even being starred as Tarzan's mate.

Razia agreed, signing the papers, and telling herself that she must remember to cable Ayub of her arrival.

Ayub met her at Karachi, touched her on the shoulder. She was glad of all the small items of luggage she carried; and if there was any remorse betrayed by her face, it could be attributed to fatigue. They had to wait an hour before the connection to Lahore. She could ask about the children. Fortunately, on the plane to Lahore, they served lunch and there was only the final train journey to go through which might involve a prolonged verbal engagement. In their separate compartment he felt safe enough to tell the story of how he had managed to manipulate the local press to swing public feeling in his own favour.

'Akram's now set on soap,' he said. 'A factory's under construction in Chittagong.'

She smiled, which required less effort than speech.

'Did you see Afaq at all?' he asked suddenly, and she remembered the letters she had written in which she had talked of the weather and the sights of London.

'A couple of times,' she said, looking out of the window at the green land.

'But I'll tell you about him later.'

'Why, what's the mystery?'

'Nothing. I'm very tired now.'

He stared at her as though seeking an explanation; but she closed her eyes, slowly drawing down her eyelids.

The family and the press photographer welcomed her at the station. She embraced her daughters. Zarina looked at her tearfully, for Razia knew her secret, when they hugged each other. Faridah was so serious, Razia had to smile to reassure her that their relationship could still be amicable. They embraced, Faridah kissing the air when their cheeks touched. Akram stood starched in white and offered a limp, bony hand.

She allowed them to persuade her to go to bed. It was late in the afternoon and she slept till dinner. She had a cold shower on rising and spent a long time making up her face. She had given so much of it to Afaq.

At last they could see the presents she had brought. Soon the sitting-room took on the atmosphere of a jumble sale.

'There are three more suitcases,' she said, 'which are coming separately. And things like the fridge had to be shipped.'

She won the approval of everyone. They were seeing themselves with their new possessions and less of her, she noticed with satisfaction.

Ayub was the happiest and wore the silk pyjamas that night.

'I'm still very tired,' she said, dissuading him from any anticipations he might have of making love.

But he was too exultant to notice and talked of the power he now had.

'I told Akram to go to Karachi to meet the Minister. I rehearsed all his moves. Told him what to say, how to appear when there were photographers around. He's the goat now and the string is in my hand.'

She did not hear what else he had to say about himself. She had gone five thousand miles away from that voice.

'What?' she had to ask when she suddenly heard him mention Afaq.

'I said what was it you were going to tell me about Afaq?'

She put on the wounded look she had practised; paused sufficiently, and then said softly, 'He assaulted me.'

'What?' Ayub barked.

'He took me to see a musical one day. Afterwards, he said let's go and have dinner. He took me to a night club when he had made it out to be just an ordinary restaurant. We had a meal there and he proposed that we should dance. I said, no, thank you, you might be my brother-in-law, but you're not my husband.'

Ayub nodded his head in approval of this sentiment, and she went on, 'Then he said, come to my flat, I have some new Indian records you'll like. You know how I used to like Indian songs which you can't get in Pakistan any more, and so like a fool, not thinking twice about it, I went. How should I have known? He's only Afaq, goodness, he's been like a little brother for ten years, I remember saying to myself. Well, I sat down in a sofa and he put on some records. He asked if I would like some whisky. Of course not, I said, what do you take me for, a *sharabi*? So, he poured some for himself. You should see him drink, you won't recognise him. And then. I was listening and he came from behind me and put a hand on my shoulder. Afaq! I said. What are you doing? But instead of answering or being shamefaced, he came round and fell on me and began to bite my neck. Oooof! The smell of whisky! I could have screamed. I tried to push him away, but he seemed to have gone mad. He was half on me and half on the floor, kneeling against the sofa. I realised what I should do. I kicked my leg, hitting him between his thighs with my knee. Where it hurts. He drew back for a moment and I slapped him and went mad at him, abusing him for his madness. He did not try again. And I left him. It was late and I had trouble finding a taxi.'

Razia had begun to cry as she spoke. It could be that she heard her own words as an obituary of her love, but Ayub thought that the experience was too much for her to relate.

He was overcome with rage.

'Do you know why that bloody idiot is in London?' he said, his voice angry. 'You wouldn't believe it.'

Razia waited not to believe, knowing that she would have to.

'He committed rape and murder.'

Razia shut her eyes and found it difficult to swallow. She had taken too big a mouthful of Afaq.

'Who saved him from the rope? Who paid out a hundred thousand rupees in bribes to save his skin? I did. And now the fucking idiot is thanking me for it, is he?'

But Razia's crying had turned to a hysterical weeping.

For there was louder abuse in her ears than any Ayub could utter, directed at herself. And the voice which spoke it was her own.

6

He had stopped fanning her, though his hand had not tired. It was dark, the sun had set and he had not left her to light the lamp. A stranger entering the room might have seen nothing, but Aziz Khan, who had sat there while the light gradually diminished until it was dark, could see the unmoving mass of his wife's body. His hand was a bracelet on her arm. He had dropped the fan next to the glass of buttermilk. His eyes were open and wide; as in amazement or stupefaction.

Now he rose to fetch the lamp; stood for a moment in the veranda. Blessed land which had known neither hurricanes nor floods, so why this storm within him?

He filled the lamp with kerosene, lit the wick. And sat again beside her. The little movement had made him breathe so hard. His eyes would not see while the breath rose like a tempest within his breast.

He saw Javed's funeral again, remembering how he had hitched up a horse to a cart to take the coffin to the cemetery next to the mosque in Kalapur. His actions had not been his, but hypnotically pursued by a man who walked in his body. Two peasants had helped him to place the coffin in the cart. Dust and sweat grained his own face like the timber he carried. They had driven slowly, Zakia beside him, her eyes already narrowed.

Right through Kalapur where the bazaar had not been too busy to notice. A few walked some distance with the cart, offering the consolation of silent accompaniment. But he had not looked to see who. Men, some men. The vendors' cries had been stifled for a moment, muffled, choked. There had been no friends to come to the cemetery. The horses' hooves had gone all the way.

The hard earth, the naked sun.

A matter of letting a timber box lie beneath that earth under that sun, what else could life come to?

Words were spoken.

Listened.

And lost in the haze which made a distorted illusion of the horizon.

What else, what else?

This bowed head and, in the still, mid-summer heat and the silence of the skies, this tempest.

No, no, no, no, no.

Leaving the cemetery; walking out with bowed head, eyes on the dusty path, hating the hard earth. And then looking up, seeing Bakshi by the gate. Bakshi the grave-digger. Bakshi the idiot, humped little bow-legged man who could not speak but only mutter 'Huh-huh-huh', whether he was spoken to or not; who had no words. Aziz Khan had caught his eyes when he walked out of the gate, the brightness and the almost morbidly joyous sparkle of his eyes. Bakshi was grinning, or appeared to; for his mouth was always open, his thick lower lip dangling as if about to fall away from his face, his tongue hanging out. Dog more than man. He was scratching his groin. The idea that the world could conceivably have been populated with Bakshi's kind crossed Aziz Khan's mind. God had made man too well for him to be happy. But he had passed out of the gate, leaving Bakshi to gape at him.

The slow, meaningless drive back to the empty house.

A desert to drive through.

And he sat here beside her bed, exchanging the charity of silence, and it seemed this was how they had always been.

He continued to look at what he had not yet seen.

There were insect sounds outside and the crows noisily racing into the night. The ants were at their business. A mosquito had life enough to attract a whole room's attention. There were the worms.

But so little air.

And then he noticed what his own heavy breathing had obscured, and held his breath, his hand tightening on her arm.

She was dead.

He remained there, his hand on her arm; silent, unmoving; his unblinking stare on the earthen-pot texture of her cheeks, her disintegrating flesh; in the dark, still night.

7

Ayub walked into Akram's office. His breath was exploding from his body. There was agitation even in his hands. Akram gazed up from a file, a report on the availability of ground-nuts in East Pakistan. He had been thinking of soap; in his mind, he had begun to wash the nation's hands. He picked up a ballpoint and a clean sheet of paper, placing the latter across the file. To make lines on, circles and squares and what geometry occurred to his hand. For it was obvious that Ayub had a lot to say.

'Afaq,' he said, sitting down, 'tried to assault my wife.'

Akram's hand shook, a nervous twitch as though his wrist had been pricked, but he tightened his grip over the ballpoint.

'Oh God!' Akram said, looking down into his lap. 'What's our family coming to?'

'You can't imagine how it has affected Razia,' Ayub said. 'She was shocked, of course. And then miserable that it was my brother who should have attempted the assault. A passer-by, a stranger could be understandable, but a brother!'

'Poor Razia!'

'What will he do next? What, I ask you?'

'He's a born criminal.'

Akram, too, could be severe.

'He's a disaster to the family. Give him half a chance and he's prepared to ruin us all.'

'He's done nothing right all his life,' Akram said. 'And he's had the best chances. He had the education we never had. He never went without food. We've been too good to him.'

'In Bombay his friends were communists. Here he knew where to find whores and liquor. But not content with that, he had to commit rape and murder. We save him from the rope, send him to England, but his criminality doesn't end there. He sends us a sample by air mail. Razia has been crying all night.'

'This is serious,' Akram said.

'Of course, it's bloody serious,' Ayub shouted but, catching Akram's cold eyes, went on less loudly, 'As far as I'm concerned, it's the end. He's not my brother any more.'

Akram could not deny Ayub the right to disown Afaq, but realised at once that its consequence would be to make Ayub's children the sole inheritors of the vast Shah business.

As if to emphasise the point, Ayub added, 'And I don't see how any member of our family can now want to have any dealings with him.'

So that Akram had to affirm that he disowned Afaq, too. Or else lose Ayub's support. And he knew that without Ayub his knees would give way.

'If it weren't for the business,' Akram attempted to test an approach, 'we could have done without him.'

'But what good is he to the business? He's nothing but a hindrance.'

'He might change. You might need him. One day.' Akram was aware that, not finding reasons for Afaq's retention, he was turning to excuses.

'He's a born criminal. You said so yourself.'

Ayub, however, was being painfully explicit.

'But think of it,' Akram said, pausing a moment to stare at a very straight line he had drawn in his doodling. 'We have textiles here and soon we'll have soap in Chittagong. There are plans for cosmetics in Karachi. We need our own people to look after all these enterprises. One's own kith and kin, even if they're criminal or plainly stupid, are preferable to outsiders.'

It was a remote hope and Akram knew of its vulnerability as soon as Ayub answered.

'How can you be so prejudiced?' Ayub disagreed. 'Sometimes I can't understand you. You're a first-class businessman with a wonderful sense of organisation. And then you fall for the old Pakistani sentiment of keeping it all in the family. Look at the really big businesses. Shell. I.C.I. No, I don't see the advantage of keeping a criminal brother in the business. Cut him out as you would an idle mill-hand. We're too big now. We don't own ourselves any more, but the country does. There's too much at stake. You should know that.'

Akram could not deny the force of Ayub's argument. He tried another approach.

'I know,' he said. 'I know that.'

The straight line had become a triangle on the sheet of paper in front of him.

'But the public confidence in our business rests on us,' he went on. 'The market would tremble if it were made public that there has been a split in the family. To outsiders, it would seem that this was the first stage of our family's disintegration. We couldn't afford that. We symbolise the success of family endeavour. That matters in Pakistan.'

'All right, the market will tremble. There may even be a damned earthquake. But even devastated cities recover and rebuild with a fresh vigour. The confidence in the business comes from its resources, its accumulated capital, its investments, its production, its plans for expansion and its ability to do so, confidence comes from maintaining a rising level of sales. We do all that. The whole country knows it. And I don't see why anyone should find out what's happening within the family. It's a private matter, anyway. It will be an arrangement between us two. That's all.'

Akram wondered if indeed it were only that much. He thought of a possible objection and said, 'But it will have to be done legally and that could lead to undesirable publicity. You know how keen journalists are to find dirt.'

Ayub, however, would see no objection, the logic which ruled him was so rooted in selfish interest.

'No,' he said. 'I repeat that the arrangement has to be between us two only. All we need to do is to tell Afaq that from now on he's on his own. He can live and work in England if he likes. But he's not receiving a penny more from us. If he comes back, if he dares to come back, he'll have to reckon with me. That's all.'

Akram did not ask 'Or else?' He knew that there could be no compromises with Ayub for whom elimination was the only solution to a problem. If a fly appeared in the room, Ayub would not open the window to give it a chance to escape, but kill it with one thwacking blow. Akram felt a little sympathy for Afaq, who was someone he had protected for too long and now had instinctively tried to do against Ayub's venom. But Ayub was right in comparing him to an idle mill-hand; in fact, he was worse. Akram's hesitation was the stuttering of an incipient fear that once Afaq had been eliminated, Ayub would have only Akram in the way of total power. It had been the way of the Moguls, fratricide. But Ayub's grievance was a real one; his wife had been assaulted (unless, of course, it was a plot), and it takes far less than a misplaced handkerchief to imbue the Pakistani male with the passion of Othello. Akram had to agree, however he interpreted Ayub's motives.

He turned to his file on soap again on Ayub's departure, wondering which perfume ought to be added to give their product its uniqueness.

8

Razia felt freer now that the Afaq episode was over, ending in what she thought was her victory. There had been a stage when she had considered herself to be genuinely in love with Afaq, but now that she thought of it, it had been only an escapade which she had explored fully. There could only have been repetitions. She would have had to return to Ayub and her children. The alternative was disintegration. She congratulated herself that she had fulfilled all her expectations from her love and at the same time not only maintained her marital dignity but also turned the episode to the advantage of her own family. Afaq himself had given her both a way of retreat and a reason for her destroying him. She could not have achieved her purpose better if she had planned it all in advance. And who would believe him if he protested that she had lied? That a Pakistani mother should go all the way to London in order to seduce a young brother-in-law was unthinkable; laughably so.

She realised one day that she was pregnant again, a happening which she might not have relished earlier but was proud now and hoped that it would be a son. Going away from Ayub had at least made him more acceptable on her return; at least for the time being. It gave her pleasure to contemplate the power she now had over the family. But a disturbing thought occurred to her. The dates of the month flicked through her mind and she realised that the child she carried was very probably Afaq's and not Ayub's. She tried to repress the notion; as though it were a hole in a wall which could be covered up by hanging a picture. She was momentarily afraid, for it seemed to her that they were all in some way cursed; in seeking to establish happiness, each one of them had taken the short cut of immorality. She did not care to compute those of Ayub's crimes of which she had some knowledge; Afaq had committed rape and murder; Akram, though he gave the impression of being scrupulously correct, could never have achieved his ambitions without Ayub's destructive connivance. While Faridah was cursed by childlessness, she herself probably carried a bastard within her. Only Zarina, Razia concluded, had escaped from a moral corruption, but she was too young to have any perceptions beyond the self-deceiving vision of infatuation.

Zarina did not know how to console herself. Nothing had been explained to her, no reasons given why Afaq had been dismissed from the family. It was too cruel, almost as if the family had discovered that they loved each other and was determined to maintain their separation. She imagined Afaq taking to drink in London and thinking of her with the desperation of a drug-addict. Or perhaps he lay forlorn in his bed, unable to do anything but sing sadly to himself. Unshaven, unwashed, he would be pining away for her. She wished she could overcome the tyranny of the elders, win her independence by winning Afaq. How he must be missing her! She wished he could see her cry. Instead, she sat in front of the mirror, trying to show herself what it looked like being unhappy, really unhappy. She hoped, however, that her face was paler than it appeared to be in the mirror.

In London, Afaq had given a simple explanation to Pamela after Razia's departure. For Pamela was, of course, curious to know why his sister-in-law, of whose presence in London he had told her nothing, should answer his telephone. Afaq had told her the truth as Kalapur knew it. 'She was here to see about her daughters' education and since I was in Frankfurt, she used my flat.'

Pamela found him humbler and less demanding. She was convinced that he was beginning to accept her point of view. One day he told her without any dramatic preface that his brothers had decided to disown him.

'But why?' she asked.

'Because I'm no good,' he said.

'Afaq, I can't believe that.'

'You've seen me. You yourself have criticised the way I live.'

'But not so bad as to go to the extreme of disowning you.'

'They've stopped my allowance,' he said.

'It must be that sister-in-law of yours,' she said.

'Oh, I don't care,' Afaq said, wanting to deflect her from pursuing her insight. 'I'll get a job.'

'You'll have to live a lot less extravagantly.'

'I don't care.' Abnegation came easy now in a mood of self-martyrdom. 'I'll sell the car. I'll give up the flat and move into a smaller room.'

She remarked to herself that the fewer possessions he had the more she would be able to give to him. He was resigning from his past, abandoning those flourishes of his behaviour which he had ostentatiously exhibited to her during their first meeting. As she saw it, the playboy had matured into a man. There was hope for him, she thought, and for her.

9

He turned over, for it could have been a dream, and pressed an ear against the pillow. As though a wasp had come into the room. The noise was not continuous and did not seem to come from a stationary object. Nor did it maintain one level of intensity. Its pitch altered, vibrating suddenly from what sounded like a distant, monotonous humming. Aziz Khan lifted himself on his elbows, stared at the wall in front of him and listened. There was silence, not even insect sounds. He fell back on to his pillow and watched the ceiling before shutting his eyes again. He preferred to sleep, for it was the one physical condition which tolerated loneliness. He slept best in these early morning hours after his mind had tired of its restless cawing; his eyes, too, had acquired the crow's suspicious glance, that sideways look which indicated a doubtful evaluation of what it saw. It was no effort to let the morning pass while he lay entombed in his cool room from which he could keep the sun out. Even when a shaft of sunlight pierced through the small window. There was nothing he wanted to see of the bright world outside. Whose colours had failed him. On some days, after he had lain all night attempting to stop his tongue from its involuntary mutterings, he would sleep on throughout the day; rising when darkness had set in and obscured the land's harshness, he would sit in the veranda or in the front yard, prepared to deceive himself. Darkness was a balm. He could dare to touch his own skin in the darkness; for the heart needed the sympathy of fingers pressing at the bosom. But how his tongue conspired with his mind, the babblers!

Accusations despite his insistence that Allah. . . . And blasphemy, that easiest of verbal oaths. But in the darkness he could grip his mouth, sitting beside the plants as though he lay in ambush.

Where was there an end to it?

He who bore the name of a dead family could be stiff as a corpse in the darkness.

Though he could not bear the silent withering of the vegetation who had not wept when he placed his own wife into the earth.

The earth which had become all too fragile.

He was aware of the noise again. Something was going and coming not too far away, a machine was throbbing, jerking, chugging, grinding. He concentrated and decided it must be an engine of some sort. He tried to determine where the noise could be coming from. It was too near to be on the road and it did not seem to come from behind the house, from the other side of the stream.

It could be only on his land.

He remained in bed, listening to the sound. He could also hear voices though he could not distinguish any words. Finally, he rose.

He stood in the doorway and saw a bulldozer being driven

on his land. A man wearing a white hat and carrying some papers in his hand was directing a labourer who was driving the bulldozer. They were driving a path along the edge of the cotton plantation. His eyes narrowed, interrogated by the light. The bright yellow bulldozer was going back and forth, like a guard on patrol, flattening the land. Aziz Khan held himself by the door, feeling giddy. He saw his chair in the veranda and, walking slowly to it, sat down. From there he observed the bulldozer go back and forth, slowly increasing its distance away from the house. An hour passed. Aziz Khan watched the bulldozer come in his direction and recede, repetitively. He was too dazed by the action to ask yet who the men were and by whose authority they had come with their machine on his land. But presently, the man in the white hat came up to him. He saw him coming from a long way off, the white spectre in the burned green and brown of the land. He had a white bush-shirt hanging over the waist of his white trousers. His black shoes were covered with dust. The clerk sahib; even Aziz Khan, who had preferred to have little to do with such men, could place him at the centre of petty officialdom. He walked with a stiff, purposeful stride as if to reassure himself of his efficiency. And his importance, for all things he did were important, indeed, urgent. He could not fret enough, looking repeatedly at his wrist-watch as he walked.

He had no word of greeting for Aziz Khan when he reached the veranda but, taking the papers from under his arm and holding one out, said, 'I have this court order to serve on you.'

He handed the paper to Aziz Khan who looked at it and returned it at once with a slight shrug of the shoulders. From which the man understood what he already knew, that Aziz Khan could not read English.

'It's a court order,' he said, keeping his eyes on the paper.

'What for?' Aziz Khan politely inquired rather than demanded.

'You borrowed two thousand rupees from a broker named Hussain some time ago.'

Aziz Khan remained silent, for his tongue had on its tip another speech and not one which would have been meaningful to the man in his silly white hat. What was the use since Javed was dead?

'You gave as security the prospective dowry of your son,' the man resumed and again waited.

Aziz Khan turned his eyes to the ground, like an accused hearing judgement.

'Failing the dowry, you offered your land as security.'

The hard earth, burdened with too much sun. He had walked as far as the sugarcanes after Zakia had been buried. The gritty earth.

'The court has settled the land on your creditors,' the man said, relieved that he had come to the end of his summary of the situation.

Aziz Khan nodded his head. Not to agree, but as a gesture that he understood. The man looked at his watch.

'Who are my creditors?' Aziz Khan asked.

The man showed him the paper and pointed a finger to some words, saying, 'Why, look, the Shah Industrial Enterprises.'

Aziz Khan took the paper from him.

'Get out of my land,' Aziz Khan said quietly but with an authority which was so much part of the voice that the man involuntarily took a step back.

'You can't do this, you know,' the man said nervously. 'You can't do this.'

'Get out of my land.'

The man was retreating.

'You won't get away this this, you know. The land isn't yours any more. Just you wait. They'll come to evict you if you don't move out soon.'

Aziz Khan stared at him.

'Get out. And take that machine away before I get my horses to drag it into the stream.'

The man was already going though he continued to say, 'You won't get away with this, you won't.'

Aziz Khan did not hear him any more, having his own voices to listen to. He looked up at the sky, at the late summer heat, at the fists of his God.

He bowed his head.

Whom else must I bury?

He rose at last and went to his room. He searched among his things and found the paper which Javed's murderers as well as the police had neglected to remove from his pocket. He looked at it, read through the Urdu statement. His creditor was Ghulam Din of Lahore and not the Shah Industrial Enterprises. Lies, lies, he muttered, deceit and fraud. He went to the bathroom and bathed himself in preparation to visit the Chief Superintendent of Police. It had been a trick. If they had lent money, then they must have murdered Javed. It was a trick to get his land.

He had to wait a long time before Chief Superintendent Fazal Elahi could be free to see him. In the meantime Fazal Elahi had telephoned Ayub, just in case there were any facts he ought to know.

'Please read this,' Aziz Khan said when he sat in front of Fazal Elahi, giving him the court order.

Fazal Elahi glanced at it.

'Who are my creditors?' Aziz Khan asked when Fazal Elahi looked up from the paper.

'The Shah Industrial Enterprises.'

'Now read this.'

Aziz Khan gave him the Urdu statement.

Fazal Elahi looked at it vaguely.

'And who are my creditors according to that?'

'Ghulam Din of Lahore,' Fazal Elahi said.

'Well?'

'Well what?'

'You are a police officer. What do you make of that?'

'What should I make of it?'

'It's obvious, isn't it? If I borrowed the money from

Ghulam Din of Lahore, then the Shah brothers have no right to touch my land. How can the court give them my land?'

'Don't you know?'

'What?'

'Ghulam Din of Lahore is a subsidiary company of Shah Industrial Enterprises.'

'A trick.'

'Come, come, Khan sahib.'

'A lie.'

'But, Khan sahib, you've only got to check . . .'

'Fraud and murder.'

'Khan sahib!'

'You call yourself a police officer? They lend me money under a false name. They kill my son. They come to take away my land. You must know a lot about corruption. Can't you see the truth?'

'Khan sahib, I sympathise with all your troubles. I am sorry. Fate has been cruel to you. You have had too much tragedy. I am sorry it is affecting your judgement. You are under stress. Your mind is strained. You must really see a doctor. You ought to go away to Karachi or Lahore. Where you can be with someone of your family, one of your daughters, perhaps, someone who can look after you. All this has been too much. It is not unusual for the mind to break under such stress. You really must take care. And advice.'

Aziz Khan did not care to hear more. He walked out, thinking he ought not to have come; thinking, too, that he ought not to have said so much. But his hands had been idle for so long now and his tongue had begun to talk. It was a mistake, a mistake. He had become too accustomed to living in a desert; he ought not to have expected an oasis.

10

The construction of the soap factory in Chittagong had reached a stage where it was necessary for either Akram or

Ayub to go and supervise the work. Akram knew that whoever went would have to stay there when production began. He would have gone himself if the only alternative had been to live in Kalapur. But he had Karachi in mind for himself, for, once the soap was successfully marketed, he hoped to enter the cosmetics industry in Karachi and make his own home there. Kalapur no longer interested him intellectually, for the business was progressing successfully and there were no problems for his inventive mind; Chittagong, on the other hand, offered the stimulus of a new organisation, but its society was even less attractive than Kalapur's. Ayub's personality had been too dominating in the family and it would be better to have him at a distance; also, Akram believed, Ayub would be well advised to begin his life anew in a community in which there was less scope for the exercise of his destructiveness, though on this point Akram could not be sure, for he was aware that Ayub's character was such that he was likely to find victims among the meekest people. Nevertheless, Akram was resolved that Ayub should go to Chittagong and, placing a model of the factory on his desk together with three files, he sent for Ayub.

'Well, you can say that Shah soap is ready to be launched,' Akram said pleasantly when Ayub had taken a seat.

Akram caressed the model with the tips of his fingers. Ayub leaned back in his chair, smiling.

'We'll have to think of a good name for it,' Ayub said.

'Yes, of course,' Akram said. 'We can't call it Shah soap. Have you any ideas?'

Ayub shrugged his shoulders and said, 'The publicity boys will do the thinking. That's what we pay them for.'

'Precisely.' Akram was glad to have some statements from Ayub with which he could agree. 'I think it's going to be a winner,' Akram added.

'Quite right,' Ayub said. 'Our name will sell anything.'

'But we can't take the sale for granted. We will need a much more aggressive approach than we've needed with textiles. Textiles had a ready market. But there's soap and soap. The market is flooded. The competition is tough. We'll need a forceful personality behind the product.'

Ayub understood Akram's implication, but chose to misinterpret it, saying, 'I shall be glad to give my ideas to the publicity boys. I'd willingly drive them until the soap oozes out of their eyeballs.'

'Would you like to take charge of them, then?' Akram asked.

'Sure. I'll go and give them a lecture right now if you like.'

'No, the publicity office here is concerned only with textiles. We'll keep the two separate. You'll need to recruit new staff for Chittagong and run it on the spot.'

'Are you telling me to go to Chittagong?'

'I'm not telling you to go,' Akram said, carefully picking up the model and placing it on the edge of the desk. 'I thought we agreed that the soap will need your dynamic personality behind it. It follows, therefore, that you take charge of it, and that of course will demand your presence in Chittagong.'

'You put it pleasantly,' Ayub said, 'but it amounts to the same thing. You are just telling me to go to Chittagong.'

'I don't know why you should interpret it that way. There is exciting new work to be done in Chittagong, work which will need a creative mind. It will be an honour to go there.'

'Why don't you go, then?'

'Look at all this,' Akram said, opening the files and pushing them towards Ayub. 'You will find here the organisation I've created. Planning has been my work, execution is yours.'

There was literal truth in that, Akram reflected; not that he wished to censure any of Ayub's barbaric acts, for they had been committed for their common benefit.

'You've planned it, you go and carry it out,' Ayub said.

'No, I can't go to Chittagong.'

'Why?'

'We'll keep Kalapur our headquarters. And besides, I need to be within easy reach of Karachi.'

'It's only a few hours by air from Chittagong. It takes

longer from here because you have to take the train to Lahore first.'

'That's not what I meant.'

'What did you mean, then?'

'Oh, never mind.'

Akram felt that somewhere in the conversation he had made a tactical mistake; he had not intended to alienate Ayub. While he reflected a moment, Ayub said, 'Why do you want to get me out of the way?'

'I'm sorry,' Akram said, speaking softly. 'I don't know why you are persisting in finding a sinister motive in all my decisions.'

'So, it's a decision, is it?'

'There you are. Make everything I say sound sinister. Listen, let's approach this calmly, shall we?'

Ayub chuckled as if to suggest that Akram ought to speak for himself.

'Let's approach it rationally,' Akram went on. 'We are building a factory in Chittagong. The time has come for one of us to go there and to run it. For one of us. I suggested that you go because I think you are better suited for the job. But you seem to have taken my suggestion to imply some evil motive on my part. I suppose if I had said that I was going, you would have asked whether I wanted to get away from you.'

'Not at all, brother,' Ayub said, smiling, 'you're welcome to go. I'm quite happy here. Besides there are one or two things I haven't finished here.'

'Personal matters must not enter into business,' Akram said. 'As far as the business is concerned, you have finished your work here.'

'Have you forgotten?'

'What?'

'It was here, in this very room, three years ago was it, that we decided, no, we pledged ourselves to be masters of Kalapur. Remember the occasion? Ali had brought the message that Aziz Khan had turned down our offer to buy his land although we offered two thousand an acre. And remember what we decided? That we'd get his land if we died doing so.'

Akram remembered, and Ayub went on, 'At first we had economic reasons for wanting his land. And then, gradually, we realised we were fighting against the pride of one man. And our own pride, our own honour were in question.'

'Are the economic reasons still valid?' Akram asked.

'I don't care a damn if the economic reasons are still valid or not. He is a living insult to me, my family and my business. I've almost got him now. And I'm not leaving until I have.'

'But he's ruined already. He has lost his family. We have legal possession of his land and can drive him out and put a fence round it when we want. I don't see how he can exist any more as a problem. The moral is clear to everyone in Kalapur. No one can oppose us and hope to get away with it.'

'But the man lives and is a danger to us.'

'Ayub, this is a small matter. There is nothing he can do that will harm us. No one will dispute our power in Kalapur.'

'I'm sorry, you don't understand my way of life. I can't leave things half done.'

'All right. Suppose we can deal with him. Will you go to Chittagong then?'

'No. I like the Punjab. I'm a Punjabi. I don't want to go and live among the Bengalis.'

'Ayub, this is childish. For I could say the same. And may I point out that a businessman cannot allow such considerations to come in his way. And may I also point out that we are Pakistanis and they, in Bengal, are also Pakistanis. I don't know what provincialism has got to do with business.'

'You are pointing out too many things, brother.'

'I think you're being very foolish.'

'And I think you're being very bossy.'

'Well, who's the boss here? Who began the mills? Who raised the money? Who organised the manufacture, promotion and distribution of textiles?'

'I suppose I've been sitting on my backside doing nothing.'

'No, no, Ayub, I'm not saying that you haven't been indispensable. I'm fully aware that without your support and assistance, and especially with your management of the workers, this business would have been nothing. But I am the managing director as well as the majority shareholder. And it has been my business ability which brought the organisation into being in the first place.'

'Are you threatening me?'

'No, no, why should I? I'm pointing out our mutual responsibilities. And I'm saying that your responsibility now is to go and look after the soap factory.'

'And I refuse.'

'Why?'

'I told you. I like it here.'

'No, Ayub. I suggest you seriously think this over.'

'There's nothing to think. I just don't want to go.'

'I'm not sure whether I appreciate your attitude.'

'My attitude is quite simple. You claim to be an able businessman, but you're so dependent on the family. I've told you many times, we ought to create a higher management so that we don't have to be patrolling the factory floors all the time.'

'That will come,' Akram said. 'Obviously, it will come. But at this stage the business needs our personal attention at every level.'

'There are only two of us, Akram, what nonsense are you talking. Suppose we had factories in Lahore, 'Pindi, Sialkot and so on. Would we be expected to fly to each one every day?'

'We don't have factories there, there's no supposing. By the time we have factories there, we'd have built a greater organisation.'

'I suppose Faridah will have had a couple of dozen sons by then.'

'Ayub, there's no need to be nasty and there's no need to bring my wife into this.'

'I don't like your ways. You run a huge industrial empire as though it were a little shop.'

'Are you teaching me my business?'

'I'm pointing out the obvious.'

'Listen, Ayub, you're going too far. I'll remind you again. I am the boss here.'

'Try sacking me.'

'I have the power.'

'Don't deceive yourself.'

'I repeat I have the power.'

'You ought to see the documents I keep in my safe deposit. There's enough there to hang Afaq and have you behind bars for a long time.'

'And I suppose your own hands are white as milk.'

'You produce one piece of evidence against me,' Ayub said, laughing.

'I don't have to sack you to be rid of you if I want to. I've only got to sell my shares and that'll be your end. No, I could make it worse for you. I could invite the government to nationalise the firm.'

For once Ayub had no reply to make, and Akram could look him daringly in the eye and say, 'I have nothing to lose. I have no children and I shall lose the business anyway when I die. Why not make a great gesture to the country, give the nation the business and win myself a place in history? They might even give me a government post as a reward. What will they give you? What will they give your children? You've got high hopes! So you see, either we're dependent on each other or I turn to the government. You have to decide now whether you're going to let me make the decisions, or you and your children are going to suffer. So, what is it going to be? Chittagong, or the collapse of your dreams?'

Ayub looked at him with suppressed anger and made no reply. Akram continued to stare at him. Ayub rose, picked up the three files from the desk, looked for a moment at the model of the soap factory, and walked out.

They did not see each other again that day until the evening when they sat down to dinner with their wives and Zarina. Ayub seemed jovial and self-assured as usual. Akram had not expected him to be transformed into the image of humility, but he found Ayub's conviviality a little disturbing. From past experience, he knew that he could expect irony from Ayub and, in anticipation of it, he said to Razia, 'Well, Razia-*bhain*, you can start packing your bags again. I think you will be going on your travels again soon.'

'Are you taking up fortune-telling?' Razia remarked. 'You haven't even looked at my palm!' She could mock, too.

'Not a question of prediction at all,' Akram said.

'But a business decision,' Ayub interpolated.

'What do you mean?' Razia was a little perplexed.

'We're going to Chittagong,' Ayub said, and there was nothing in his tone to suggest whether or not he enjoyed the prospect. 'To take charge of the soap,' he added.

'Oh!' was all the comment that Razia could make.

'I suppose you can call it a clean start,' Akram dared to say.

Ayub allowed himself to laugh, and even Faridah, who had been surprised by the suggestion, giggled a little. Zarina was relieved that the sharer of her dreadful secret would soon not be constantly near her.

'They make beautiful muslin in Dacca,' Razia said, having searched her mind for a recommendation of East Pakistan.

'I've heard a lot about Cox's Bazaar,' Ayub said.

'Yes, and you must see Mansur and find out about the shikar he was talking about,' Akram said.

Zarina was sorry that there was a pause in the conversation, for she preferred their noisy chatter to the sound of Faridah eating. She always managed to sit next to Faridah so that she would not need to look at her, opening and shutting her thick lips. It was too hypnotic, all that gravy smearing the red lipstick and the food rolling over the tongue whenever the mouth smacked open; whereas, sitting next to her, she could try not to hear. She could concentrate on her own unhappiness and let the little explosions of misery in her mind distract her.

'You're very quiet nowadays,' Zarina heard Ayub speak to her.

Surprised, she looked up from her plate, for she was rarely addressed so directly during dinner, and immediately turned her attention to the fried aubergines.

'Quiet as a love-bird,' Razia said. 'Though love-birds do sing a lot.'

Zarina could not look up. It was too cruel. And she felt certain that Razia had given away her secret. She stuck the fork into an aubergine, but could not lift it. They will mention *him* now, she thought, they will spill it all out. She could hardly see the aubergine any more.

'Do you miss your parents that much?' Ayub asked, speaking slowly, staring at Zarina's bowed head.

Akram paused in his chewing and looked across the table at Ayub. Zarina, however, felt a little relieved and lifted the aubergine from the plate and opened her mouth towards it.

Just then Ayub asked again, 'Do you remember them that much?' And the aubergine fell back on to the plate, for her hand shook.

At least she could look up and meet Ayub's stare and say, 'No.'

'Vhy manshun them?' Faridah asked. 'Poor girl doesn't even know who they vere.'

Razia did not know Ayub's intentions, but, spontaneously malicious, she said, 'It must be sad to be an orphan at so young an age.'

'I don't know. I wish I knew.' Zarina could only mumble the confusion in her mind.

'Have you ever asked?' Ayub said.

Zarina looked at him for a moment, despairingly, not knowing what he meant. She saw Akram also staring at her, but did not know what that signified either.

'Vhat are you saying!' Faridah admonished rather than questioned.

'Have *you* ever asked?' Ayub said to Faridah. He could be so impolite, even contemptuous, Faridah thought.

'Enough, Ayub,' Akram said, trying to remain coldly severe. 'There's no need to cause unhappiness.'

'Truth hurts, brother.'

'Vhat are you trying to say?' Faridah asked loudly as though she were knocking on a door and knew that when it opened it would reveal something disastrous.

'I am asking Zarina if she remembers her parents, but apparently Akram has some reason for stopping the conversation,' Ayub said.

Razia understood now and said, 'It would be comforting to have their photograph, don't you think, Zarina?'

Zarina stared at Razia and then at Ayub, who said, 'Yes, some record, some relic, some souvenir helps.'

'It helps to know your mother had the same colour of eyes,' Razia said.

'Vhat is aal this?' Faridah asked, turning to Akram. 'Vhat truth?'

Akram looked at Ayub and said, 'If you know anything, tell it. What's all this mystery?'

'There's no mystery. I just asked Zarina why she was quiet, whether she remembered her parents, but you people seem to make a lot of fuss over a simple question. There's no mystery at all.'

Ayub was content to leave it at that. But Akram knew that it was only an overture, a preliminary statement of a theme which would be repeated presently: Ayub would wait for a decisive moment to win full advantage of the ultimate revelation.

They ate silently for a few minutes, each chewing his own thoughts. But Ayub had not been subtle enough and his tone had been too pointedly vicious when he had questioned Zarina. Faridah was not convinced that there was no mystery; nor was Zarina. Faridah, who was accustomed to Ayub's method of suggesting meanings, understood sooner than Ayub had calculated that she would. She put down her knife and fork and looked up at Akram. Her mouth shut and opened with a loud smack as she swallowed.

'Akram!' she said. 'Akram!' And looked at Zarina, but could not assemble in her mind the words she must utter. She rose, pushing her chair away so that it fell on its back, and walked out. They watched her go out, all except Zarina who was looking at Akram and finding her own jaw sag and her mouth begin to quiver.

Although it was not half a minute since Faridah had left, Razia thought that the silence would burn a hole through the room. But now Zarina rose, her mouth already uttering sobs, and walked away.

A servant entered, thinking dinner was over, but Ayub said, 'We haven't finished yet.' And he went away.

'You will never finish,' Akram said, 'until you've destroyed the whole world.'

Ayub chuckled.

'What have I done to deserve this?' Akram asked. 'Made you richer than you'd ever have been by your own efforts. Given you more power than you've ever had. Isn't there enough for us all to share? It was bad enough having Afaq whose crimes were against other people, and now must you commit crimes against your own family? Just because I insisted that you go to Chittagong you waste no time to dig a hole for me to fall into!'

Ayub did not care to answer.

'I can see it now,' Akram said, turning to look at Razia. 'You suffer from the old Mogul disease, can't wait for the king to die but must plot against him. Despite all their wealth, sons imprisoned their fathers and brother killed brother. I don't think now that Afaq assaulted you. You made it all up to have him out of the way. Very clever! Maybe you even enticed Afaq, tempted him to assault you. How very clever!'

'Ridiculous!' Razia exclaimed. 'Why should I lie? I have children.'

'Motherhood doesn't prevent you from having affairs,'

Akram said and waited to see if Ayub was incensed against his wife. Ayub looked at Razia, but she knew how to maintain the face of innocence. 'How you did it is besides the point,' Akram went on, 'but you've worked it all very well. It's clear to me now. Knowing that my wife was childless, you plotted to have Afaq out of the way because he was a threat to what you would inherit. But why? Why can't you be content with what you have? We could have had so much more. Together, with trust, with affection, we could have built up more and more. But now? How can we work together? How can Faridah look at me? And Zarina? And how can any one of us look at you? What are you suggesting, that we dissolve the business right now, part company and never see one another again? What else can you expect now?'

'You have nothing,' Ayub said. 'You have lost the love of your wife, your illegitimate daughter knows the fraud you've practised on her all these years, you have nothing.'

'And you want everything.'

'Yes, everything.'

'Why couldn't you have waited?'

'Waited? While you planned to invite the government to nationalise the firm? Or, if Faridah won't give you a child, what's to stop you from marrying again? I'm surprised that hasn't occurred to you who've been such a careful planner.'

Akram at least had the satisfaction that there was something Ayub did not know.

'Because you're so full of evil scheming yourself, you expect me to be so, too,' Akram said. 'You're wrong, so wrong. I had hoped we could work together, that we could build a great industry together. It was a shame that Afaq committed the wrongs he did. Now we have lost it all.'

'I don't think you'll want to ask the government to nationalise the firm,' Ayub said.

'Why not? What do you expect me to do, to hand over everything to you, to hug you in public and tell the world, look what a wonderful brother I have?'

'No, I don't expect a public spectacle. But I told you there's enough in my safe deposit to make your blood go cold.'

'No,' Akram said, 'there's nothing which can possibly incriminate me which will not also incriminate you. Our sins are interlocked, they are two lips sealed over the same deed.'

'That's what you think. But try and recall one cheque which you haven't signed to pay bribes with.'

'We always paid cash.'

'Not always. But the cheques are nothing.'

'What have you got against me, then?'

'Why should I show you my hand?'

'You have found it too easy to kill,' Akram said. 'I wonder how long you can hope to escape your conscience.'

'Who is completely innocent?' Ayub demanded.

'Who indeed! Your wife, perhaps.'

'I don't enjoy being insulted,' Razia protested.

'I didn't accuse you of anything,' Akram said. 'Why do you start as though some ugly deception were being revealed?'

'Cut out the slander, Akram,' Ayub said.

'Cut out my tongue, then!' Akram shouted. 'A scheming, murderous pair, you have less right to belong to my family than Afaq. Go on, make it all public. Tell the world what Afaq did. Tell the world what I did. Why don't you, if your only pleasure in life is destruction? And let the world know something of your own evil, too. We have a wonderful, loving family!'

'There's no need to be bitter,' Ayub said. 'You do as I tell you and nothing need be public.'

'Do as I tell you,' Akram mocked. 'That's all you wanted, *that's all*. It's too late now, don't you see? Hatred and blackmail never formed an association.'

11

But on this morning his body was a minion to the heat, turning this way and that. Even during its dew-time the morning was excessively hot and he could not remain long in bed once the sun, casting a beam through the window on to his bed, had woken him up from his wearied sleeplessness. On other mornings he had pulled a sheet over his head when the beam had entered but now his body was fragmented into drops of sweat so that the ray of light momentarily flickered there and through the sweat on his eyelids he saw himself cradled in a rainbow.

It could be that he no longer saw things in their true shape.

He had slept without a shirt and drawn no sheet over his body. Waking, he noticed, as he lay with his hands behind his head on the pillow, the sweat running down his chest towards the concavity of his stomach.

How he had thinned!

He rose and went to the bathroom and bathed himself, pouring the water over his head not with the usual jug from the bucket but by lifting the bucket above his head and tilting it, letting the water bounce down like a cataract across the rock-face of his chest, letting the cold tongues in the water lick his body of its heat.

Thankful that he had the strength for at least that much.

On this morning.

He went to the room and put on a clean white shirt and massaged oil into his head.

He sat on the edge of the bed and, getting his shoes from under the bed, polished them and put them on.

The oil on his head, he decided, had now settled into his scalp; so, he rose and combed it and then wound his turban round his head.

He went to the kitchen to make tea.

He took the pot of tea to the veranda and sat there, drinking from his cup. Swallowing with solemn sips as though he had been asked a question and needed to cogitate.

In front of him was his ravaged land that had never asked any questions. The plantations of sugarcane and cotton, destroyed now, held in their torn flesh the ghosts of his family. The bulldozer had left its tracks; like scars after an operation on a human body.

He understood it all now, the machine which had worked in the mind of man. And yet the larger purpose of its working was beyond his understanding and the understanding of his ancestors who had been thus coldly murdered.

There had been exhumations in his mind, reincarnations. His tongue had talked. This silent man.

But he saw less. His gaze had turned more and more inward lately. This bowed head.

He had thinned, hardly eating anything, but sitting in the veranda when he was not in bed. Even when the sun was at an angle and turned its nozzle at him to flood him with heat.

His burning eyes.

The flies settled on the back of his neck even though he was continually slapping them away.

Yet, what did he see within himself?

Not an emptiness, surely, this man whose external world had methodically been razed to the earth, and only the earth remained, in its exposed, crumbly form, for him to call his own, the earth to which he had held on so stubbornly.

Whose mind was more than the gritty sediment of vanished rivers.

Inside Aziz Khan was that iota of wholeness which had been his life, and though his life had been reduced to an embryo of what it had once been, the embryo was still complete, still possessed the capacity, though not the will, to strive towards a new wholeness.

Whose flesh was drops of sweat.

But this man, who had never in his life uttered more words than were necessary, who had toiled all day with his hands, was unaccustomed to the vocabulary of introspection. Though there were the accusations now, the voices which had fingers to point to the desolation in front of him.

Why, why, why, why, why.

He sat in the veranda with a vacant gaze, occasionally

lifting his head, looking at the emptied land in the heat which coiled about his body like little stinging worms.

This manacled minion on this morning of heat, the thorns in the air.

The utter finality of his slow breath.

This bowed head, listening to the voices within him. There was nowhere to go from where he was. Most people would want to go beyond. That horizon, and that. Why? he had asked so often sitting there in the veranda. If you are there why go to be somewhere else? Because you can only be where you are and wherever you go you are getting nowhere except farther away from where you want to be, from where you are.

This man who had been to the hills in the east and sat under the almond trees waiting for the wild fowl to come to the pool's edge. Who had tired of pretty views and returned to the flat, sloping land.

Now a monument himself though no one had come to look; an inscription in a dead language; a hieroglyph the new literacy did not care to interpret.

This ox among the tractors.

Though he would have maintained that productivity, profit and progress did not necessarily improve a man's moral worth: had his tongue been as competent as his hands.

He shifted uncomfortably in his chair, knowing he must rise, knowing that although justice was ultimately unobtainable, he must nevertheless pursue it. He rose then, thinking he must go, he must go. To Lahore, to Karachi, for no one would believe him in Kalapur. For how long could he wait for divine justice to manifest itself? He had waited after Rafiq only to see Javed murdered. He walked into his room and began to tie clothes into a bundle; and the few belongings which were necessary. He took what money he possessed and walked out hurriedly, impatiently. No one saw him leave his land. A horse, tied to the side of the house, neighed. They saw him walking through the bazaar but did not speak to him. They saw him walking towards the railway station. One heard him buy a return ticket to Lahore. For he must come back to his land when the money ran out, when he had done what he must do.

He sat on a bench on the platform, looking at the signals and at the gleaming tracks. He had two hours to wait. He remembered the first time he went to Lahore, a boy of fifteen or sixteen then, to visit his uncle Zia Ullah. There was no railway connection with Kalapur in those days and he went in a cart to Wazirabad. That alone took two days. He spent the time watching the bullocks flick their tails at the flies which kept buzzing around their hindquarters, and gazing at the countryside. It was all farmlands on the way to Wazirabad. Wide, open country. During the second day it seemed that he had been travelling in the cart for months. The land was unending and he had felt that the Punjab in which he had been born was an infinity in which he was no more than a speck of dust. And even then he had thought, suppose he were Akbar and had conquered the whole of Hindustan, would he be better in any way?

Suddenly there was noise about him. The train had arrived. Platform vendors moved busily from window to window, selling tea and savouries, getting in the way of passengers. He pushed himself through a crowded doorway of a third-class compartment. The wooden benches in it were packed with people. The floor was crowded with luggage and people. He found a spot on the floor, a small area which, with a little pushing, he could make large enough to sit upon. When the train moved on, he had no view of the country outside and could not tell in which direction the train was moving unless he remembered that the engine was to his right. But shutting his eyes, dozing off, and then waking again, he could not tell which way he was going.

When he had first visited uncle Zia Ullah in Lahore, he had been shown the city by a cousin. Zia Ullah was his father's brother, but had chosen to leave the land in Kalapur and had become a knacker. The young Aziz Khan had gone

295

to his shop and seen the raw, stinking hide and the yard at the back where the horses were slaughtered. His eyes had burned. 'There's money in anything,' uncle Zia Ullah would repeatedly say, but when he died, the family had quarrelled over the inheritance.

The heat was like a lid over that yard, boxing in the smell of blood. Shahid, the cousin, had shown him the wider streets of Lahore, the shops, the banks, the court of justice, the cantonment where the English soldiers lived. But each time when he had returned from Lahore, he had felt freer, clearer in mind.

But on this morning when he had woken the air had been thick around him and on leaving his land he had not looked upon it.

In Lahore now, where could he go? It was evening, the bazaars were tracks for the hounds of sensuality. It was years since he had been here but still he did not need to look to find his way.

His cousin Shahid had not yet returned from his shop but his wife, Abida, was there to greet him; and her two boys who looked at him with awe. She made him tea and offered him some savouries.

'Lie down till he comes,' Abida said. 'These train journeys are more tiring than a week's work. Would you like to bathe first?'

He let her suggest distractions. For she could see what he needed to do.

Shahid greeted him warmly when he arrived, removing his Jinnah cap and hugging him.

'This is a wonderful surprise,' he said when they sat on the floor around the plates and dishes Abida had already placed there. She waited upon them while they ate.

'You don't have to tell me, I know,' Shahid said. 'News travels. Especially bad news. I'm glad you came. We were beginning to be worried how you could manage alone. We heard from Zuleikha. She said she was thinking of going to Kalapur with her little boy. To look after you. That would

296

be a good idea. At least for some time. A grandson can be very good company.'

'No, she must not come,' Aziz Khan said. 'No one else must suffer.'

'What had to happen has happened.'

'No one else must be murdered.'

'What are you saying, Aziz-*bhai*?'

Aziz Khan told him about the Shah brothers and how he thought they must be implicated in the deaths of his sons.

'But you must go to the police,' Shahid said.

'I tried in Kalapur,' Aziz Khan said. 'They won't believe me. That's why I've come here.'

'Have you any proof?' Shahid asked.

'Don't you believe me?'

'I believe you. But I'm not a court. You don't have to prove it to me. For a court you'll need evidence. What evidence have you got?'

'I've got nothing,' Aziz Khan said as though he might be answering some other question.

'If you need any money . . .'

'No, no.'

After dinner, they went out to the bazaar and strolled for half an hour. It was Shahid's habit, to stroll after dinner before retiring for the night. There were no parks, no open spaces in this part of Lahore; only the bazaar. There were the lights and the bright eyes of people, Aziz Khan observed. The sellers and the buyers. Shahid did not talk now. There were the cries of the vendors, the simultaneous noise of so many people talking that few words were meaningfully audible.

The next day Aziz Khan went to the police station. Shahid directed him to it, accompanying him for part of the way before going on to his shop. It was a large, square building with a flag on it. Aziz Khan did not know what he should do or say when he entered it. He found himself in a hall with a bench in it and he decided to sit down and reflect what he should do. Now that he questioned himself, he did not know why he had come to Lahore. He was not known here. His anonymity ought to have been his advantage, but he doubted it now. He decided to ask to see an inspector. He rose from the bench and walked into a room; the door was open and he could see uniformed policemen sitting at desks. He walked a little past the entrance and stood in the room. He saw now that there were three policemen. They had all noticed him entering but each had begun to make out that he was busier than the others. An electric fan slowly circled above the one who sat in the centre of the room and Aziz Khan concluded that he must be the most important. He approached him slowly, not knowing whether he was doing the right thing. The man banged a rubber-stamp on a paper a little too loudly. At last he looked up, narrowing his eyes and called to the one on his left, saying, 'Aré, Choudari, vill you see vhat this person reqvires?' Aziz Khan looked at the other man who was now regarding him with feelings of suspicion, irritation and distaste.

'I want to see the inspector,' Aziz Khan said, still standing near the man in the centre but looking at Choudari.

'Vhat?' Choudari said with a show of alarm.

'There are inspectors and inspectors. Superintendents, deputy superintendents, chief superintendents, urban inspectors, district inspectors.' The man sitting under the electric fan would have given a more detailed analysis of the Punjab's police structure, but he had said enough, for his two colleagues were laughing already.

'I want to see the chief,' Aziz Khan said.

'Liss'n, *bhai*,' Choudari said and Aziz Khan took a step towards him. 'Vhat's your prahblem? Ve're under-staffed and over-verrked, vhat's your prahblem?'

'I've been cheated,' Aziz Khan said.

'That! It's aalvays happ'ning in life, *bhai*, vhich you got to take as it arrives.'

'My sons have been murdered.'

'By whom?'

'By the Shah brothers.'

'There are millions of Shah brothers, this is fertile country, *bhai*.'

'The Shah brothers of Kalapur. The ones who own the textile mills.'

'Them,' the man in the centre said. 'They are respectable people. Anyvay, if they are in Kalapur, then this is a matter for the Kalapur police.'

'The Kalapur police are in their pockets,' Aziz Khan said.

The accusation that their brother officers in another city were corrupt did not meet either with their belief or their approval; the statement was too offensive to their ears for them to take any more serious interest in Aziz Khan.

'Liss'n, *bhai*, there's no inspector here,' Choudari said in a voice he would have used if he had been scolding a child. 'If you got any prahblems, go to a lahyer. This is the wrahng place.'

'But you need money for that. What does a man do who needs justice?'

'Listen, mister, you heard Choudari give you good advice. Take it.'

Aziz Khan withdrew and walked out slowly. He spat in the dust of the street. Men in suits and ties walked past him to their urgent appointments. He stood still a moment, this turbanned man, wondering which way to go, this cumbersome sundial in a society which had taken to wearing wristwatches. He remembered the way to the high court, another building with a flag and noble words inscribed upon its face of stone. He was stopped from entering it. He went and sat under a palm tree. He noticed another, smaller entrance through which people seemed to be going freely. He walked to it and went in, eventually finding himself in the visitors' gallery. He looked down upon the court, heard the English words. The judge, weary and bored, sat with shut eyes, his face in his palms. The people around him listened quietly, intently, Aziz Khan noticed, and, like them, he was a spectator at a court of justice. A woman was being cross-examined. She wore a bright green silk sari and resplendent jewels hung from her neck and her ears. Her face was heavily made-up. Sometimes she gave one word answers, sometimes she spoke at length. The language and the procedure were both alien to Aziz Khan. He did not know who was being tried for what offence. It was all theoretical and general to him. He wondered if the offender would be punished, whether the punishment would be reasonable, whether justice would be done. He looked at the judge and wondered if he had a headache. He imagined himself in the judge's position, coming to the court day after day and listening to other people's quarrels. He must receive a good salary for sitting there. But he must see the judge, ask for his help.

When the case was adjourned, the judge rose and walked out solemnly. Aziz Khan hurried down in order to wait by the main entrance for the judge. People were already coming out of the court. Some stood by the door, discussing the case excitedly, waiting for their cars. Soon there was a line of cars and the crowd in the entrance grew bigger. A large car stood in front of the entrance, but its owner was still inside the court, and he seemed to be holding up everyone else. Aziz Khan had stood in a corner so that he would not be in anyone's way and now he was crowded in. He saw the judge emerge and tried to move towards him. But the other people in the entrance were trying to make way for the judge, pushing Aziz Khan to the wall. In a moment the judge had driven away, and soon the crowd dispersed, leaving Aziz Khan alone in the entrance. The sentry still stood there, like a chained dog, staring at him as if daring him to enter the court. Aziz Khan walked away. He knew there was a park near by where he could lie down in the shade of a tree. A feeling of futility, of the inevitable uselessness of action, filled him. There were procedures and protocols, the appropriate channels and the machine. He knew nothing. He found a tree, a tall eucalyptus. He touched its bark. He sat down. He, who had given verbal allegiance to his god, did not understand the ways of men who trusted only words on paper. To him, existence had been meaningful only as a cycle of growth. What was existence to them who glanced at their watches a thousand times a day? He did not know, who was a spectator merely. They turned their assurances into documents, their money into numbers on paper; they made rules which many of them were continually breaking. They needed judges to settle their quarrels, bankers to look after their money; they needed legislators to give them direction and to guard their frontiers; they needed a thousand devices to entertain them; the clerks had taken over. He must return to his land, which was all he had, all he needed. No one could help him. He was incapable of entering into their complexities and he had no evidence, Shahid had said, he had no bits of paper. The clerks would not read his face or understand what his tongue spoke. He must return to his land. There was nothing else.

He walked towards the station. The morning had passed. It must be late afternoon. He could not tell. He could have gone to Shahid's shop on the way to the station. Shahid would want explanations for his failure; he would give advice, suggest ways, go to this man and that, he would say, see this clerk in order to see another of slightly higher importance, go on ascending the hierarchy of clerks; keep busy and you won't realise the essential futility of what you're doing.

No.

Aziz Khan decided not to see Shahid again. He walked on slowly. The intense heat attacked him from every side; it was worse than on the land, he reflected, for the brick buildings boxed in the heat, making the treeless street a river of haze. He did not know how far the station was, only the direction.

He was exhausted on arriving at the station. He had not eaten anything since breakfast and he made his way to a refreshment room. He sat for half an hour, eating a plate of rice and curry and drinking tea. He noticed that it was after four o'clock. He asked a porter which platform he should go to for the Kalapur train. The porter told him that he could go to platform three if he liked, but there was no train till seven the following morning. Aziz Khan went to platform three and lay down on a bench. He fell asleep.

12

There had been tears during the night after the quarrel between Akram and Ayub. Zarina would have been inconsolable had anyone come to her room and pleaded with her not to cry. She wished she would die, life was so cruel. Everything seemed to her to be calculated to make her unhappy. First they had taken Afaq away from her and now this revelation. Who had been her mother? she wondered. Was she still alive? To what eternal misery was she condemned? It was all too overwhelming for her raw emotions.

When Akram tried to enter his bedroom, he found that Faridah had locked it from the inside. He knocked on the door and said softly, 'Faridah . . . Faridah.'

'Don't come to me,' he heard her scream at him and burst into a loud crying.

'Let me in, Faridah,' he implored, but she was crying too loudly to hear.

Ayub and Razia, in their room, heard him go down.

'Why did this happen?' Razia asked.

'He was plotting, I tell you,' Ayub said. 'He's burned up inside with jealousy. He wanted us to go to Chittagong. Why? He could have gone there himself for a month, organised the factory and left it in charge of a manager. No, he was plotting something. Jealousy has been killing him.'

Razia was prepared to accept the explanation, and said, 'What will happen now?'

'We shall see. It's his move next.'

'But what will happen to the business if you two are parted?'

'The business will be mine,' Ayub said. 'He has nothing to work for. You just heard. His wife has rejected him. In another room, his daughter is probably cursing his name.

If he does anything mad like asking the government to nationalise the firm, I'll have him proved unsound of mind, incapable of judgement. He can't win.'

Razia was not convinced. Hitherto, she had enjoyed family politics. To cause petty irritation to Faridah, knowing that no real harm would be done, had been entertaining. But now, much though she wanted to share the power Ayub wanted, she was disturbed by the grief which had been caused to Faridah.

'Couldn't we have waited?' she asked.

'No,' Ayub said, annoyed that she should find the slightest objection to what he had done.

She was silent then, and thought of the child within her and of Afaq. Why wasn't life simpler? she wondered.

The next day, Ayub went to the mills as usual. He and Razia had breakfasted in their own room and he asked her to meet him in the club in the evening. They would dine out. He did not see Akram in the house. Perhaps he was still asleep in the guest room; he did not pause to inquire. At the mills, however, a foreman told him that Akram had arrived earlier and was in his office. Ayub wondered what move he was contemplating, but decided to work as usual in his own office and to await developments.

Later in the morning, Hussain telephoned him.

'I have some interrusting inferrmation,' he said.

'What is it?' Ayub demanded.

'Shah sahib, it's verth quite a laht, a very intelligunt piece of looking on my part on your behalf.'

'I'll tell you what it's worth. What is it?'

'Aziz Khan, sahib, I just saw vith my very own eyes going through the bazaar. Vahking like he vas fast asleep vith his eyes open. I fahllowed him. He vent to the station. I vaited in a cahrner and saw him buy a ticket. Vhen he had gahn into the station, I asked the ticket-vallah to vhich destination the aforegoing customer had purchased a ticket and he told me Lahore. Sahib, he is right now vaiting on the platform for the arrival of the train on vhich he can depart to Lahore.'

'All right. Thank you.'

Ayub put the receiver down and began to think how he could finish this nonsense about Aziz Khan once and for all. If only to show Akram how he could act. Presently, he sent for the supplies and construction managers.

Since arriving early at his office, Akram had sat at his desk with a sheet of paper in front of him, a ballpoint pen in his hand. From time to time, he had lit a cigarette, looked at his watch; he had shifted a glass paperweight from one place to another on the desk; he had adjusted a tray containing papers so that its outside edge was parallel to the side of the desk; he had opened his drawers one by one and pushed them back again; there was the pile of unopened letters to his right; he had looked at the envelopes and then stacked them neatly like a pack of cards, regretting that the neatness was marred by the envelopes being of unequal length. He had looked at the blank sheet of paper and shifted it so that its bottom edge was parallel to the edge of the desk. When he had not been able to write with the ballpoint, he had taken out a fountain pen and held that poised for a long time. He shook his hand over the paper. A drop of ink fell out. He rolled the sheet of paper into a ball and threw it into the wastepaper basket. He placed a new sheet of paper on the desk. Lighting another cigarette, he noticed that there were flecks of ash on the desk. He placed the cigarette in the ashtray, cleared the area of his desk where there seemed to be bits of ash and pushed them away with the side of his hand. He put back the items he had removed and leaned back in his chair to see if the symmetry which he had achieved earlier had not been disturbed. He noticed that there was a faint fingerprint on the clean sheet of paper. He looked at his hands. Some of the ash he had wiped away stuck to the side of his right hand. He rose and went to a small room adjoining his office where there was a basin with running water. He washed his hands with soap, working up a lot of lather before rinsing them. He soaped his hands twice and held them under the tap for a long time. He dried his hands on a clean towel, meticulously passing the towel in between his fingers. He returned to his desk and took out one more clean sheet of paper to replace the one which had been slightly marked. He held the pen again in his hand and shut his eyes in concentration. He opened his eyes to look at his watch. Time was passing. He shut his eyes again and thought. Faridah, Zarina. Faridah, Zarina. His brain was ticking monotonously. No, no, it was the air-conditioner, humming in the background, asserting its power. He had never heard it before. He had become used to its noise. He put away his fountain pen and took out the ballpoint again. He could hear the telephone ringing in his secretary's office. He had told him not to transfer any calls to him, to tell the callers that he was in conference and would not be available all morning. The secretary was male, a middle-aged man named Pareira. Akram thought of him, his bony hands and his sunken cheeks. He had never before thought of Pareira as he was thinking of him now. Often he had called over the intercom, 'Come in, Pareira, will you?' or 'Pareira, fetch me the export file', but he had never thought of Pareira as Pareira. Once Pareira had said that his wife had given birth again and had joked about the 'again' because how else could he be serious and Akram had given him a ten rupees a month rise but he had not, he thought now, asked how many children he had. Perhaps he had come from Goa or Bombay or Karachi or Calcutta, one of those Christians who pursue one clerkship after another across the sub-continent. He remembered that the Christians during the British rule had felt themselves especially privileged, for, sharing the rulers' religion, they could easily believe that they also shared their superiority. And then independence came and they had to befriend either the Hindus or the Muslims; they had to debase themselves, too, into lying that they had much in common with their culture, the Hindus' or the Muslims', whichever of the two happened to predominate in the community in which they found themselves. Who was Pareira, why was Pareira in Kalapur? These questions bemused him for some time.

What am I doing, what am I doing? Akram said to himself, thinking that he should not be thinking of Pareira, but his hands were sweating and he could not touch the paper with sweaty hands. Even the ballpoint pen was slipping now that he tried to hold it firmly in order to write. He put the pen down and rose again to go and wash his hands. He looked at the bubbles of lather, the little explosions of soap-suds. He returned to his chair and faced again the blank sheet of paper. There were flowers in the fat bubble of the glass paperweight. He picked it up. How did they get the flowers in, how did they manage to make the glass so heavy? He noticed that the tiny flower-heads were made of paper. There must be an industry in that, in tiny paper flower-heads. He put the paperweight down in a different place than from where he had picked it. He noticed the grain of the wood, the table's surface. What was it? Ebony, mahogany, teak, walnut, pine? He did not know. He had not learned to identify the texture of wood. None of ebony, mahogany, teak or walnut had the shape of a tree in his mind. He could imagine a tree. A trunk with branches and leaves, but he could not imagine a particular tree which would be one of ebony, mahogany, teak or walnut. There were other trees the names of which he knew. Some, like pine, he could imagine and some he could not. But the grain of the wood of his desk was pleasant to look at. Was that why he had chosen the desk? No, he had not chosen the desk. The interior decoration firm from Lahore had chosen it for him. He had merely signed the cheque. Why had they chosen this particular desk? Did they think he would work better on it, contemplating the fine grain? What am I thinking, what am I thinking? Faridah, Zarina. Faridah, Zarina. The time, the time. This pen, this paper. Dear Prime Minister, No modern nation can hope to have a place in the world without healthy industries. Commerce has created empires, commerce has discovered new worlds. Industry is our strength at home and abroad, giving employment to our people and bringing in money for our country. He picked up the paper, tore it into bits and threw it into the wastepaper basket. He took out a new sheet and placed it in front of him. If his sins were catching up with him in this world, what hope had he in the next? Did he believe in the next world? Islam, the ritual turning towards Mecca five times a day, the stoical tolerance of poverty and disease in the expectation of a paradise, the endless ablutions and prayers, the fasting and the sacrifice, Islam, the tyrant of Pakistan which compelled a people's slavery. He had had nothing to do with it except superficially. He did not have the time for it, the washing of the hands and of the arms up to the elbows, the washing of the mouth and the washing of the feet, and the imbecilic gestures of piety, bending, bowing and falling prostrate in front of the whitewashed blank wall of the mosque. He did not have the time for all that. People prayed, asked for wealth and health. He knew how to make money and he had good doctors. What was the difference? How long would Pakistanis continue to deceive themselves that Allah was a substitute for learning? What am I thinking? Faridah, Zarina. One hundred thousand rupees could buy five thousand pounds on the black market or about seven thousand if he could persuade the Minister that he needed to buy more machinery to keep up with the export orders. He could send Zarina to school and university in England. Or Faridah and Zarina could go on a six-month tour of the world. No, no, not distintegration, not liquidation. It will never be the same integrated family and business. A moral weakness has been exposed, it will never be the same again. But contain, hold, strain mind and body, do not break. What have I done to deserve this?

Akram crumpled the sheet of paper into a ball, rolled it in his hands and threw it into the wastepaper basket. He put the ballpoint pen away. He flicked the intercom switch and said, 'Pareira, I can now take calls again. And send me a cup of tea, will you?' He rose and went to wash his hands.

13

He ought not to have slept, for he was awake now and it was only eight o'clock in the evening. He had to wait another eleven hours for the train, and knew that he would not be able to sleep now for much of the night. He went to the refreshment room and had a meal. It seemed the same plate of rice and curry which he had eaten some four hours earlier. After eating, he wandered back to the platform. An express had arrived, from Karachi or from Peshawar, from one end or the other of the country, he did not know. The whole station, and not just the platform on which it stood, was crowded. The train stopped at Lahore for a whole hour. People who were catching it at Lahore had already settled in. The first-class passengers had rolled out their bedding on their berths and, wearing pyjamas, were standing outside their compartments, smoking and chatting with friends who had come to see them off. For the third-class passengers, there was no hope of a seat for anyone who had not been at the platform the moment the train arrived at the station. Those who had managed to enter the large compartments had locked the doors from the inside and hung out of windows in order to block any entrance to the dozens of passengers who were fighting to get in. Those who could not enter the train were shouting at those who had done so, abuse was being exchanged along the entire length of the platform, except at those places where the pyjama-clad passengers were smoking and chatting. Threats mingled with the abuse, threats to call the police, to report to the stationmaster. Several policemen, however, were walking about the platform and listening to the people who were threatening to call the police. At one point, two passengers had come to blows, for a man who was denied entrance to a compartment had dragged down a man who was hanging from a window. Porters, who, with special commissions in mind, had managed to find seats for the inter-class passengers were finding it difficult to get the luggage of the passengers in and were abusing the passengers for expecting too much of them. In the six-berth second-class compartments, the passengers who had reserved their berths had rolled out their bedding, but more passengers had turned up with second-class tickets but without a reservation for a berth. Those who had reserved the berth, claimed full right to it while those who had not made a reservation demanded their right to sit at one end of the seat. No one was prepared to make compromises, however, and obscene language was exchanged when appeals to the spirit of Islam and democracy had failed. Finally, the train slowly moved out of the platform with many people hanging on to the doors, and the station seemed suddenly silent. It reminded Aziz Khan of the silence on his own land; but the arrivals and departures of people, whose destinations were unfamiliar to him, continued to distract him.

It was a long night. He should have gone to Shahid's, or even to a hotel, and rested properly. But he had not been able to leave the station although the thought of finding a bed for the night had occurred to him. He was afraid of over-sleeping and missing his train, afraid that Shahid might talk him into staying on in Lahore. He wanted to return to his land. It was a long night on the platform, now sitting upright and now lying down on the bench. Occasionally he had walked up and down the platform. On one or two benches, men lay asleep, curled against the hard wood. Sometimes a group of railway workers would walk silently, sleepily past, one carrying a lantern, walk to the end of the platform where the platform sloped down to the level of the tracks and gradually disappear into the night; until he could see only the lantern, its little spot of light becoming tiny as a speck of dust. He sat again on his bench, dozed off and shook himself awake to lie down before dozing off again. He was woken by the sound of a locomotive, steaming, puffing in spasmodic bursts and then easing off. He saw it through half-open eyes. There was no train attached to it. As it went past him, he saw two faces in the driver's cabin, black and glistening in the glow of burning coal. Images and fantasies, reality and unreality kept him awake and asleep, there and not there. Afterwards, he could not tell what he had seen and not seen. Red lights turned to green and green to red and when he looked in the distance, the platform seemed to have become longer in the darkness, he could not tell whether the light he looked at was red or green. Once, he must have slept for a long time, though he could not tell for how long; it could be that he had just fallen off asleep and woken a minute or two later and the duration of being asleep had seemed a long time; or it could be that he had slept for much longer, an hour, two hours, or even longer; how could he tell? He had not observed the time when he had fallen asleep and now there was no way of ascertaining the time unless he walked down the platform to the point from where he could see the station clock. But if he did go to see the clock to see the time, it would mean nothing, for he had not seen the time when he had fallen asleep. He heard crows cawing somewhere far in the distance, distinctly cawing somewhere in the open air. And then they stopped. He wondered whether it had been crows cawing. Nobody else cawed, it must have been crows. Perhaps the men he had seen disappear down the line were making some noise which for a moment had reached him and had seemed to be like crows cawing. No, he was certain it was crows. If it was important and if it mattered to his destiny, he would affirm that he had heard crows cawing soon after he had woken up after a long or a short sleep, the duration of which was not as important as its soundness, its dreamlessness. Where was he? Yes, Lahore, there was the sign in front of him saying Lahore in Urdu and in English. He looked at the English letters and tried to work out how they could mean Lahore. The English word was longer than the Urdu word, though the word was the same. He looked hard at the English letters, tried to give a sound to each letter which would add up to the word Lahore. But no, the word was not the same, for in Punjabi you pronounced it as

Lowr and in Urdu as La-whore. How did the English pronounce it? They must pronounce it either as Lowr or as La-whore, very probably as La-whore, for Urdu had always been the fashionable language, its accents had always been imitated. But whichever way the English pronounce Lahore, their word for it was longer physically. He realised he had been making a mistake, for, following the Urdu habit of reading from right to left, he had been looking at the English word from the right to left. The sign was some distance away from him, far enough for him to see the whole signboard as a complete unit, but he had been looking only at the English word and although he had been seeing it as a whole, he had been looking at it from a certain point of view, that of seeing the constituents of the word, and consequently he had been seeing the English word in reverse, that is to say, although his eyes saw LAHORE, they did not see LAHORE because they had been looking at EROHAL. Now he would have to start again if he wanted to work out how the English letters could add to the word Lahore. He must shut his eyes, forget that he had ever observed the English word for Lahore in reverse, open them and examine the letters with a new interest. He shut his eyes. He had not heard what he ought to have been hearing, what he would have heard if he had not been so preoccupied with one word, which had been a useless preoccupation because he already knew the meaning of the word, that it was the name of the city he had come to and which he was leaving, and what else mattered about a word apart from the thing which it named, he had not heard that the sparrows were chirping, twittering, squeaking, tweeting, as though the station were an old spring mattress on which he lay and he was turning restlessly and the rusted old springs were chirping, twittering, squeaking, tweeting like sparrows waking up. He had not been deceived about the crows. He was positive that he had heard crows cawing earlier, for now the sparrows were raising a din, he could see them fluttering about the station, making long journeys within the station, travelling the great distance of the platform, flying down and landing on the platform, turning their heads to the right and to the left in order to look straight, picking up bits of paper, bits of straw, flying up, stopping in mid-flight and alighting upon posts, sign-boards, any object which had a protuberance wide enough for their claws to grip, and cleaning their beaks like a barber sharpening a razor on the palm of his hand, now one side and now the other, their little heads saying no to the thing on which they were wiping or polishing or sharpening their beaks. There were other noises now, people, porters, coolies, coming and going on the platforms, carrying buckets, brooms, brushes; soon taps were turned on, there was water flowing on the platforms, the brooms were sweeping, the brushes were scrubbing. It was dawn. It was still dark enough for the lights to be on and yet there was enough day-light for the lights to be purposeless, like the eyes and the limbs of a body which was certain to die in a moment or two, another breath and perhaps another, and then the breath would be exhausted, the body would be useless and if the eyes remained open, someone would remember to draw down the eyelids. Sooner or later, someone would remember to switch off the lights. Had the night passed, was the waiting over? He rose from the bench and walked to the public lavatory. Sweepers were busy there, the smell was like a fist which hit you in the face as soon as you entered. He withdrew as hurriedly as he could and found a tap on the platform which had been turned on to wash the platform. He cupped his hands under it and washed his face. He went to the refreshment room and saw that there was a crowd of people there. It was six o'clock. And now that he entered the lit room, he saw that outside the daylight had increased. The sun must have risen somewhere. He sat drinking tea. He drank two cups. He did not eat anything. He returned to the platform and again sat down on the bench. The station began to be crowded. Boys were selling newspapers; other boys were going from person to person, offering to shine their shoes, their cry of *boot-polish* condensed into a drawn-out *pleeesh*.

Again he could not find a seat and had to sit on the floor and, when the train moved, again he had no way of telling which way he was going. He dozed off, his body shaking to the movement of the train. He woke up and could not tell for a moment whether he was going to Lahore or coming from it, whether his journey of two days ago was over or whether it was still the same journey and he had not as yet reached Lahore. The people around him could be different or they could be the same; if different, he could not tell how different for he had not closely observed the former people from whom these people must be different. He concentrated. He thought of the three police officers, of the judge, of the woman in the witness box with her jewellery and heavy make-up, her air of being perfumed for the visual seduction of passers-by. He thought of the men he had passed in the streets, the suited ones. The chained dog of a sentry outside the high court. What could he tell Rafiq and Javed when he reached home? He had forgotten to take a gift for Zakia. They do not want you, my sons, they do not want you. Harvest time was approaching, there would be work to do. His head nodded, the train spoke, they do not want you, his head nodded, the train spoke, they do not want you, then faster, they do not, they do not, they do not, his head nodded, his head nodded, his head nodded, the whistle, his head jerked, his ears listened, the whistle again, the darkness, the train was shouting, the whistle again and then the bursting into light, and then the same rhythm, the same, steady reproachful voice, they do not want you, they do not want you, they do not want you, his head nodded, his head nodded. Will this journey never end?

At Kalapur he had to stand still on the platform for a moment in order to stop the train which was still running under his feet. He decided he would take a *tonga* and ride home in peace, let the slow trotting of a horse accustom him to a gentler pace. But when he put his hand in his pocket to take out his ticket while he was a few paces from the exit, he found that his purse was missing. He searched in the other pocket. It was not there. His pocket had been picked, he had lost all the money that he had.

He began to walk home. It was no great distance, he told himself, he had walked it many times. He walked slowly. He was in no haste. In the bazaar, people watched him walk past. He saw their eyes, he saw them stop talking when they saw him. He saw them whisper a word to others who had not yet seen him and the others turned round to show him their eyes. No one came to talk to him. He walked steadily on. There were faces he recognised, voices, which, had they spoken, would have been familiar. But while there was talking and noise at the far end of the bazaar and also in the part of the bazaar which he had left behind, the immediate area in front and behind him was a pocket of silence. It followed him and preceded him. He walked on and was soon passing among the mills. The stone wall of the mills seemed to be throwing out the heat of the sun, and he crossed the road to be away from the wall. When he passed the gate, he saw the sentries notice him and one sentry speak to another and one of them going away, inside to where he could not have seen had he stood to look. He walked on and turned towards his land where the road forked. He noticed that the stone road seemed slightly unfamiliar. He looked at the fields around him. It was the right road, he knew the trees. Then he realised what was unfamiliar; the stones had been disturbed as though there had been a lot of traffic on the road, as though heavy lorries had been driving there. He walked on, thinking Rafiq or Javed would be able to tell him what had been going on. It had been a long night, a long journey, and perhaps he was seeing things. He noticed activity in the distance, movement where his land ought to be. He quickened his pace, feeling the heat in his throat. He saw more as he approached and what he saw he thought he should not be seeing, for that was not what his land looked like. He saw wooden posts from a distance, some six or seven feet high. Occasionally, something would reflect, catch his eye. As he walked on, he saw that there were lines of light connecting one post to the next. It was wire, he realised, barbed-wire. He reached the fence and stood holding the wire, pressing his hands to the wire's claws. The posts went right round his land. It was not his land. The withered plantations were not there. Three bulldozers were going up and down the sloping land, tearing up from the roots whatever grew there. He walked on along the fence. The heat was like a fishbone which had got stuck in his gullet and would not go down, although he swallowed more and more air. Two men stood by an opening in the fence, guarding the drive to the house. They had been watching him and stood erect now to reassure themselves of their strength. Aziz Khan stood a few yards from them and looked at them. He did not care to see what weapons they carried. He looked past them towards his house. There was no one he could see outside the house. Perhaps there was someone inside, he could not tell. The bulldozers were going up and down, up and down. He looked away and began to walk again along the fence. He walked as far as the stream which ran under the road where his land came to an end. The fence turned a corner there and proceeded parallel to the stream, a foot away from the stream's bank. It was a narrow path, but he continued to walk slowly along the fence, his eyes turned to the land. He walked on, he walked on. There was no other opening in the fence. Even at the farthest end of his land, he could hear the bulldozers going up and down, up and down. He walked on and on, never taking his eyes off the land. The heat was pressing a piston down his gullet. The sun that late summer afternoon seemed to be made of steel, the air of concrete.